THE COMPLETE SYMPHONIES OF ADOLF HITLER

& Other Strange Stories

Reggie Oliver

Tartarus Press

*The Complete Symphonies of Adolf Hitler
& Other Strange Stories*
by Reggie Oliver
First published 2005
This new edition published 2013 at
Coverley House, Carlton-in-Coverdale, Leyburn,
North Yorkshire, DL8 4AY, UK

All stories © Reggie Oliver, 2013
All artwork © Reggie Oliver, 2013

ISBN 978-1-905784-51-6

The publishers would like to thank
Jim Rockhill and Richard Dalby

Printed and bound by CPI Group (UK) Ltd, Croydon, CR0 4YY

THE COMPLETE SYMPHONIES
OF ADOLF HITLER
AND OTHER STRANGE STORIES

By the same author

Plays
Imaginary Lines
Put Some Clothes on, Clarisse!
The Music Lovers
Winner Takes All
Once Bitten

Biography
Out of the Woodshed, the Life of Stella Gibbons

Story Collections
The Dreams of Cardinal Vittorini
Masques of Satan
Madder Mysteries
Dramas from the Depths
Mrs Midnight and Other Stories
Shadow Plays

Novel
The Dracula Papers

CONTENTS

Introduction by Glen Cavaliero	v
The Complete Symphonies of Adolf Hitler	1
Lapland Nights	13
The Garden of Strangers	37
Among the Tombs	56
The Skins	81
The Sermons of Dr Hodnet	97
Magus Zoroaster	110
The Time of Blood	129
Parma Violets	155
Difficult People	169
The Constant Rake	190
The Blue Room	212
A Nightmare Sang	225
The Babe of the Abyss	264
Bloody Bill	296
A Christmas Card	317

INTRODUCTION
Glen Cavaliero

The phrase 'Something nasty in the woodshed' has become proverbial, a form of shorthand denoting psychic trauma. Whatever that something was, it was seen in her youth by Great-Aunt Ada Doom in Stella Gibbons' satirical parody of rustic fiction, *Cold Comfort Farm*, a book whose popularity threatened to discredit rural novels altogether—but not, be it noted, supernaturalist ones. Although it may seem appropriate that Reggie Oliver should be Stella Gibbons' nephew (he paid tribute to her in a biography called *Out of the Woodshed*), his gifts for parody and pastiche being akin to hers, in his macabre tales he none the less leads us firmly back into that woodshed, and does so with a detached aplomb worthy of his aunt's heroine Flora Poste (although displaying a good deal more empathy with his material than she did).

The Complete Symphonies of Adolf Hitler

Oliver's handling of his chosen subject matter is always level-headed, inventive and humane. Such an approach may well reflect his experience as a playwright; but he is in any case a born storyteller. Some of his tales, 'The Blue Room', for example, or 'The Skins', begin with a confident kick-start; other openings are more elaborately informative, but in each one we embark upon a narrative that propels us unerringly toward an inexorable and enigmatic close. Such stories tread the borderline between the recognisable and the seemingly impossible, between plausibility and the jolt of the unexpected; and in doing so they question the simplistic outlook that regards external appearances as wholly objective and reliable.

All writers who work in the supernaturalist tradition subvert the idea of such a norm, employing a wide diversity of methodologies in order to do so, methodologies which in turn reflect the author's temperament and sensibility. It is accordingly understandable that they should attract the investigative attentions of psychoanalytic biographers and critics: by its very nature their work invites deconstruction and decoding. Even so, it generally eludes such attempts at exegesis, elusiveness no less than illusion being integral to this particular art. A writer like Robert Aickman, for instance, can legitimately obstruct every effort towards precise interpretation, for his narratorial technique embodies an awareness of a mystery that by its very nature must remain unplumbed.

Reggie Oliver is not a writer of this kind. In his case we are less interested in the teller than the tale. His style is direct, unmanipulative: it aims at persuasion rather than enchantment, is the essence of 'cool'. His work is full of literary stylistic echoes and cross-references, exploring familiar supernaturalist themes from a twenty-first century standpoint. Lacking the open-endedness of an Aickman story, Oliver's are not so much evocations of the dormant terrors of the mind as records of events that indicate the presence of an abyss that lurks beneath

Introduction

the surface of material reality and draws its victims down helplessly into indifferent, mysterious depths.

Some of these stories have a strong and most convincing 'period' flavor (the world of the 1890s, of eighteenth century France, of seventeenth century London, for example); others evoke the worlds of provincial theatre, of religious communities, of English public schools: all are the product of a cultivated and well-informed intelligence steeped in a feeling for the past, but in touch also with computer technology and present day social pressures and concerns. Oliver's various narrators are correspondingly diverse. They include actors, a clergyman, a playwright, an academic, even a giddy social debutante: he is a master of capturing the inflexions of the individual human voice. So too he provides variants on werewolf, vampire and doppelgänger themes, and on the Dickensian fable; there are glimpses of the workings of the commercial art world; nightmare fantasies in the manner of Franz Kafka; and a scathingly grotesque account of a witches' coven. No one story is like another.

The last-referenced tale ('A Nightmare Sang') highlights another element in Oliver's work distinguishing him from most practitioners in the genre: he is both morally and critically engaged with the phenomena he describes. For instance, one story calls into question the wisdom of an aspect of the spiritual teaching of the poet-novelist Charles Williams; in another, the self-serving exploitation of a haunted room comedically recoils upon the manipulator. (There are times when Oliver's work reminds one of the jocular outrages perpetrated in Matthew Lewis's notorious Gothick shocker, *The Monk*.) Indeed, there is a good deal of tart humour in these tales, and with it at times a sardonic detachment which, along with frequent references to contemporary preoccupations and to currently famous public personalities, render their impact as bracing as it is disconcerting. However, when he wishes to, Oliver can arouse not only powerful sensations of dread but unpleasantly convincing causes for it—as he does in 'The Time of Blood' or, more palpably, in 'The Babe of the Abyss', the ending of which contains a minatory twist that drives the story's point discomfitingly home. In another tale the terrors attendant on old age are treated with a certain relish, in which horror and laughter are so closely combined as to invite a hysteria that is only partially cathartic.

Through their diversity of theme and setting, of type and mood, Oliver's stories amount to a comprehensive portrayal of how easily the imagination can trespass onto dangerous ground. What exposes some of his characters to forces hostile to their well-being is their moral weakness; in others it is their curiosity or vanity or greed that sets the destructive tide in motion. But if Oliver's world is as rigorously moral as that of Ruth Rendell, it avoids the logical foreclosures of the well-crafted crime novel, being full of uncontrollable energies, of entrapments and eruptive nightmares. Moreover it exists within a metaphysical context. In the Foreword to his previous collection, *The Dreams of Cardinal Vittorini* Oliver writes that 'What I do believe is that every act and every thought in the world has a metaphysical resonance. . . . Each of these stories is in some way an exploration of these spiritual reverberations.' It is a sobering concept and one that governs the present book as well.

But we remain in daylight: Oliver eschews the shadowy perceptual uncertainties that distinguishes the narratives of Walter de la Mare and Phyllis Paul, though he achieves something of their poetic quality in what is one of his finest stories, 'Bloody Bill'. His stories convey a quality of freshness. Their crisp and lucid style enables both author and reader to retain a hold upon a stable world even while that world's reality is invaded or outraged by an apparently irrefutable contradiction of its laws. One is not so much lured into participation in the characters' experiences as presented with hypothetical evidence of the continuing strangeness of the material world that we

Introduction

inhabit and are required to take for granted. If one purpose of supernaturalist fiction be to produce cautionary reminders that 'It ain't necessarily so' (to quote the salutary words of Ira Gershwin), in tales as skillful and accessible as those of Reggie Oliver the proviso is brought, quite literally and most pertinently, to book. His stories convey a sense of relevance and linger in the mind. In such competent hands the supernaturalist tradition flourishes to good effect, retaining its power to disturb its readers as well as entertain them.

THE COMPLETE SYMPHONIES
OF ADOLF HITLER

Quite absurd how it began, especially when you consider how it seems to be ending. I have to go back to yesterday afternoon—dear God, is it only yesterday? I am walking along Piccadilly, on my way to the London Library to pick up some books on Henry Vaughan (I am giving a seminar on the Metaphysicals to a group of mature students at the North London College), when suddenly the sky turns black and it begins to rain heavily.

The nearest shop is the new Magnum Music Store, just opened, so I turn in there. Not that I need much inducement. Apart from English Literature my great passion is classical

The Complete Symphonies of Adolf Hitler

music, especially the late Romantics, Sibelius, Bruckner, Mahler and the like. You don't share my interest? Never mind. You'll find out why this matters soon enough. But I do collect more widely: in fact my collection of CDs is vast. My wife (herself a music teacher) says that it is ridiculous, because I will never have time to listen seriously to every recording I possess. She is right, of course, yet still I collect. It is a kind of disease, an addiction, a lust for the artistic experience. I am particularly interested in out-of-the-way composers, those who for some reason have fallen from favour. They may not be as good as the famous ones, but that doesn't matter; in fact their very mediocrity has a kind of secret charm for me. For that reason I had, for instance, a complete set of the symphonies of Joachim Raff before I owned all of Dvorak's or Brahms's efforts. I am also a great bargain hunter. I object strongly to paying more than £7 for a disc. On the other hand if I see anything that I haven't heard on sale for less than £4 I will snap it up. I tell myself that one of these days a recording of seventeenth century sacred motets, or a set of piano variations by Sigismond Thalberg on a theme from Meyerbeer's *Robert le Diable*, might be just the thing I want to listen to.

So that is how I find myself in Magnum Music, sheltering from the rain. There don't seem to be all that many people about and the light, perhaps in consonance with the dark rain outside, is dim. Never mind that, though. I am bounding up the stairs, past the Rock and Pop and the Easy Listening—I shudder at the phrase!—and I am into the Classical Department. I tell myself that I have half-an-hour's leisure to spend here before I must move on to the London Library and that I can spend £20 at the most on my passion.

My first search yields little of interest. There are few bargain labels on the covers of discs. Anything new or interesting is at full price which means over £15, and that I am not prepared to pay. Besides, I find the atmosphere slightly oppressive. Apart

The Complete Symphonies of Adolf Hitler

from one shabby old browser in a heavy overcoat, looking through the section devoted to Early Music (not one of my passions), I am the only customer there. This always makes me nervous, as I feel I am being watched by the staff, in this case a shaven-headed young man, abnormally tall and thin, in a black t-shirt who is leaning over the cash desk and who actually *is* watching me.

I decide that this is not the moment to be browsing, that I should collect my books from the London Library and go back to work, so I make for the door of the Classical Department. As I do so, my eye is caught by a pile of boxed sets on a display table. Now I don't normally go for boxed sets, because it usually means I will be duplicating at least some piece of music that I already possess, but this display has some very tempting-looking bargain labels on show. And there is one boxed set whose title I have to read once, twice, three times before I can believe my eyes, and even then I can't. I pick it up and scrutinise it minutely, and, no, it's not an illusion, nor a misreading due to my mild dyslexia. The words are there in thin white lettering on a sepia ground, and I can't be mistaken:

THE COMPLETE SYMPHONIES OF ADOLF HITLER

The background on which the white lettering has been printed is a faithful depiction of the man himself, with his familiar brooding expression like that of a disgruntled Alsatian, the flat sweep of damp dark hair over his forehead, and the absurd little slug of a moustache. Yes, it is he, and not another of the same name.

Obviously this is some sort of spoof, a curious concept album, so I look on the back of the box, and there the hoax appears to go on. Under the name Adolf Hitler (1889-1945) is a solemn list of nine symphonies with their respective movements and durations in minutes and seconds. I look for some sort of joke, but no. Here, for example, is Symphony Number 1 in E Major: '1st Movement, *Allegro Vivace*, 2nd Movement *Adagio Maestoso, Sehr Langsam*,' and so on. The only joke that I can see is that the 7th symphony, unlike the others, has a name; it is called 'The Polish'. And all these works, I notice, are played by 'the Berchtesgaden Symphony Orchestra, Conducted by Anton Heydrich'. I stare and stare, and don't know what to make of it.

The price on the round bargain sticker is £19.95, just within the price limit I have set myself, and that clinches it. I take it over to the counter and pay with cash. The tall, shaven-headed man barely looks at me as he takes my £20 note.

I remark that the item I am buying is an unusual one, or something like that. I want a reaction; I want him to share my wonder, amusement even, but he looks at me without a flicker of interest in his eyes. He simply puts the box into a Magnum Music plastic bag and hands it to me together with my five pence change. He says not a word.

I descend the stairs of Magnum Music which now seems to be utterly deserted, except for someone who is walking down the steps behind me. I do not look round, but it must be the old man in the heavy overcoat who was looking through Early Music. I go out into the street. It has stopped raining: the sky is now paper white, like the ceiling of a sanatorium. I start to walk towards the London Library, still in something of a daze.

The trouble is, I am so obsessed by my extraordinary purchase that I have no recollection of what I do next. I must have fetched the books from the library and got myself back to my home in Camden Town, because the next thing I remember is taking one of the discs out of the box, that for the first and second symphonies (there are four discs altogether), and putting it on my CD player. I am still expecting some sort of hoax, but I don't know what. My wife is out and there is a note from her to say she will be late in, something about a choir rehearsal at the school. She gives private piano lessons at home, but she also teaches once or twice a week at the local comprehensive. She likes her job and she likes children. We want children and we're still hoping; we've also talked of adopting, but no luck so far. That's beside the point. I put on the disc.

Well, it's not a hoax, at least not an obvious one: no 'Variations on *The Teddy Bear's Picnic* in the style of Bach' or any of that. I hate musical jokes anyway. The music that I hear is curiously, you might say surprisingly, unsurprising. Given what one knows of Hitler's musical tastes, it *is* the sort of thing he might have written. Wagner is the main influence, of course, but also Bruckner, Hitler's other favourite composer. Perhaps there is a hint of Richard Strauss in the orchestration, but his lightness of touch is absent. The opening movement of the first symphony begins with a long wailing trumpet call, rather like the opening to Wagner's *Rienzi* overture. Then there are some portentous chords on the brass, followed by a restless and rather incoherent allegro theme. I take out the booklet which has come with the boxed set. Perhaps this will help.

The booklet, written by someone called Isolde Hoess, is quite useless, as far as I am concerned. It is written in the dullest musical programme note style. As so often with this kind of literature, the obscurity has been compounded by the fact that it has been translated from the German by someone with an unidiomatic grasp of the English language. 'After the first twenty-four measures, the main theme group is continued by a section expounding a new theme in E minor then going on to be transposed into G minor which leads to a motif of unrestrained violence modulating in steps with a Wagnerian turn, interventions of horn and tuba forming the main element of the movement's entire concept. . . .' and so on.

I have been reading the notes about the first symphony itself, and it is only when I turn to the general introduction that I notice the strangest thing of all. It makes absolutely no mention at all of Hitler's political career, of his persecution of the Jews,

The Complete Symphonies of Adolf Hitler

or even of the Second World War. The only reference to any historical event is to be found in the statement that 'the second and third symphonies were written shortly after his return from the war of 1914—1918 while he was recovering from injuries, both mental and physical, in a sanatorium'.

I try to concentrate on the music, but it eludes me. The general musical style is one to which I respond—as I say, I am one of those people who is not bored by Bruckner—but this music is full of gestures rather than ideas. Even the moods of the piece shift and do not settle; fragments of melody appear and then are swallowed up in storm and stress before they can be grasped. Nevertheless I listen intently because I believe I have gained access to a mind which, after all, shaped our world. There comes a moment when an insistent motif on the woodwind is just about to reveal something to me when the door bell rings. I curse, I switch off the player, I go to the front door.

It is four in the afternoon of a late September day. There is no blue sky, and on the doorstep a man in a heavy, old-fashioned overcoat is standing. His head is hairless, his skin is grey; he looks old but I cannot tell his age. He stares at me with brooding, poached egg eyes. I ask him what he wants and he says he would like to come inside to talk to me about something. The voice is indistinct, monotonous, slightly scratchy, as if it were coming from an ancient gramophone recording. Taking him for a religious nut, I refuse to let him in but he does not move. He stands there, a blot on the darkening landscape of our road. Again I ask him what he wants. He clears his throat, a curious breathy, crackling sound as if he were trying to vacuum the dust of ages out of his throat.

He understands that I bought some music at the Magnum Music Store this afternoon. I nod. He tells me that it was sold to me in error and that it should be returned. I ask him to explain, but he simply repeats what he has just said and insists that I give it to him. I ask him to name the music to which he is referring.

The Complete Symphonies of Adolf Hitler

He says that it is the music that I bought at Magnum. I ask him what he means when he says it was sold to me in error. He will not explain but demands that I return it. The conversation continues in this way for some minutes, going round in circles, getting nowhere. The man is relentless: he does not tire, but I do. I shut the door in his face.

I am half expecting him to ring the doorbell again, but he does not. I go back to the living room where the CD player is and I draw the curtains. As I do so, I notice that the man is still there, not outside my front door, but in the street facing me as I stand at the living room window. I block him out with the curtains and return to my music. I am tired of the storms of the first movement so I switch to the second: '2nd Movement *Adagio Maestoso, Sehr Langsam.*' It is indeed *sehr langsam*, very slow, an orgy of sorrow, with wailing strings and heavy brass plodding along to an insistent pulse on the timpani. I sit down to listen. It is compelling in its monotonous way. The stifling warmth of self-pity engulfs me. I mourn my lost aspirations, to travel, to be a 'writer', rather than a mere academic. I mourn the sterile tedium that has overtaken my marriage. There is a self-indulgent tear or two on my cheek as I drift into a doze.

The doorbell arouses me. I turn off the music, then go to the window and look through the curtains to see if it is the man in the overcoat, but he has gone. Instead, in the dimness, I can make out two men in uniform. I go to the door and when I open it to them they ask to come in. They are policemen and I am suddenly afraid.

It is my wife they have come to see me about: she has had an accident in the car. They offer to take me to the hospital and on the way they tell me she is dead. Her car was hit sideways on by a lorry at a crossing. They say she had gone through a red light. How unlike her. I see her at the hospital, barely recognisable. I return home where the hours are full of dullness and weeping. Once, during some unslept moment of the night, I look out of

The Complete Symphonies of Adolf Hitler

my window and think I see the man in the overcoat in the street below.

In the morning the police are here again. They want to question me, purely routine you understand, because our car has been examined and there is a possibility that the brakes have been tampered with. This makes no sense at all. Who would want to kill me or my wife? We are utterly harmless and unimportant people. Even my theories about the Metaphysical Poets have aroused no controversy, not even very much interest to be honest. They ask me, purely routine you understand, where I was yesterday afternoon between two and five. I tell them about the London Library and about being in Magnum Music, though I don't tell them what I bought there. They seem satisfied. When they have gone I have nothing better to do, so I play the third movement of the first symphony. It is not the usual *Scherzo*. After all *Scherzo* means a joke and one cannot imagine Hitler making many of those. It is designated: *Marsch—Tempo*, and that is what it is, a march. It is stirring, defiant and rather relentless. The tune, and there is an identifiable one this time, reminds me of something I have heard before. Is it the third movement of Raff's *Lenore* symphony? Well, it takes me out of myself and I start to march up and down in the sitting room in time with the music. Then I stop. Good God, my wife has just been killed and I am marching up and down my sitting room to a piece of music written by Adolf Hitler. I must get out of the house.

It is early afternoon, and I have not eaten, so I go and have something at The Engineer in Gloucester Avenue. From there you can walk across the road, down some steps and on to the towpath beside the Regent's Canal. I call it 'the dull canal' after that line in Eliot's *The Waste Land*, but it suits my mood, as does the sky which is grey and threatening rain once more. I walk for miles along the canal. Sometimes I find myself humming that wretched march and walking in step to it, but when I do I stop and try to shove the thing out of my mind.

Towards evening, after miles of wandering along the towpath, I am about to pass under yet another cast iron footbridge when I can just see that something strange and black is wriggling under it, dangling over the water. Whatever it is, it is on the other side of the bridge to me, so I go under it, turn round and look back.

What I have seen from the other side of the bridge are two feet encased in black boots. Their struggle belongs to a man with a hairless head and a long black overcoat who is hanging on to the balustrade of the bridge. No sound comes from him, but it is clear that he needs help, or he will fall into the oily waters below. It looks too as if he is attached to the bridge by a rope and that the rope may be round his neck.

There are steps up from the tow path which give access to the bridge, so I climb them. I look around, but there is no-one about to help me. I reach the point where the man is hanging from the bridge. One bone-white hand is gripping the balustrade. I take hold of his arm and the hand relinquishes the balustrade to grip my arm in turn. It is a strong grip and almost pulls me over the bridge. I look down and see the top of the man's grey, hairless head. Then the head tilts upward so that now I can see the face. A pair of remorseless eyes lock on to mine, their hold as fierce as the grip of his hand on my arm. He has a noose around his neck, but the rope has slipped so that the end of it now trails in the water. I try to pull him up, the effort nearly wrenching my arm out of its socket. His mouth opens and he grins, revealing a set of irregular teeth, green and yellow, like the lichen covered menhirs of a primitive stone circle. His breath, smelling of rotted vegetation, comes in irregular, rasping gulps and exhalations, but he says nothing.

A wordless wrestle with the man's dead weight continues for several minutes until at last he is hauled over the side of the bridge and we sit there panting together for the same length of time that it took me to rescue him. At my suggestion we find a café and sit down over two cups of sweet, watery tea. We talk.

Or rather he talks and I listen. He does not answer my questions, but he has much to say about himself, though in many ways it is curiously vague. He says he is an artist, a musician of sorts, I think, but also a painter, and his enormous gifts have been unrecognised. An idiot world has failed to acknowledge his genius. He seems to blame and hate everyone for this, and I find myself compelled to take on some of the responsibility for his misery. He talks much about the soul of an artist and how a work of art may embody it. It is all very high-flown and pretentious; a little old-fashioned too, I think. I begin to be tired and horribly bored.

Then he starts to talk about how something has been taken from him and that he will be lost until it is returned. He says that every artist is like Faust. Faust sold his soul to the Devil for wisdom, for money, for a woman; but the artist, he sells his soul to his own Art for the sake of fame and glory, and if that fame and glory is not granted to him then his soul has been given away for nothing. As far as I can understand his drift, I think this is rubbish, but I do not say so. By this time I am so bored and exhausted that I am close to falling asleep where I sit. I am just about to do so when he grips my arm and begins to talk urgently about wanting something back, something apparently that I have.

Then I notice—how could I have failed to notice before?—that I know this man; his eyes are familiar, those bloated, poached egg eyes, the grey, hairless face, the heavy, damp overcoat. I wrench my arm away. I tell him to go to hell. I run out of the café. Some time later I find a taxi and go home. I want to sleep. I must now sleep.

But sleep is denied me, because the police are waiting for me when I get home. They want to question me further. It is about the death of my wife. Apparently someone was seen yesterday afternoon tampering with her car, and they want to check again, purely routine you understand, on my movements that day. I tell them once more about the London Library and Magnum Music. Well, they haven't fully checked with the London Library, but there is a slight problem with Magnum Music. You see, the official opening of Magnum Music was today, and yesterday it was not open to the public, so I could not have been in Magnum Music at the time that I said I was. I ask if I am being charged with anything, but the police say no, they are just pursuing their inquiries. They suggest that I keep in touch with them, keep them informed of my movements.

I cannot stay here. They cannot keep me. Events have been too much for me, so I must move. I cannot sleep here tonight in case the man in the heavy overcoat returns and rings the bell, and drives me mad with his rubbish about Art and the Soul.

As soon as I know the police are out of the way I set off. I put a few things in a plastic bag, not much, but for some reason I have to take the boxed set of symphonies with me. I carry it like a talisman, and because I have paid for it dearly I will not let it go. I am not quite sure where I am going, but I need to see other people, some sort of life, so I head south towards the heart of London. I have been walking for little over half an hour when it begins to rain.

The wet pavements reflect the pinchbeck gold of the street lamps. There is a sick feeling at the back of my neck. I must sleep. I must find somewhere dry where I can hide for a while because I cannot return to my house. Now I am near King's Cross. The rain falls on. I find a hotel, one of those wretched hotels that are to be found near King's Cross, frequented by pushers and prostitutes, whose foyers look like entrances to the Underworld. Two letters from the orange neon sign over the door do not light up, so that in the dark it reads H EL. Nevertheless I go in. The only room available is at the front, over-

The Complete Symphonies of Adolf Hitler

looking a main road. The grinding sound of traffic penetrates through the window, the yellow street lights shine through the thin curtains. The candlewick bedspread is lemon yellow. The walls are the colour of nicotine stains. I switch on an electric heater. I undress and attempt to dry myself.

On the dressing table I lay my one significant possession, the boxed set of THE COMPLETE SYMPHONIES OF ADOLF HITLER.

And now, just now, the telephone in my room is ringing. I pick up the phone: it is Reception. There is a gentleman downstairs who wishes to come up and speak to me: something about wanting his music back.

I can't let him up because I know what he will do. In that heavy old overcoat of his, he will sit down in my room, and fill it with the smell of damp streets. He will fix me with those gloomy poached egg eyes, and, in that voice like scratched fog, he will talk and talk and talk. He will ply me with self-pity, with his shallow, pretentious views on Art and Music.

He will bore me to death.

LAPLAND NIGHTS

As almost everyone knows the acronym OPEN stands for Old People's Exchange Network; and, as everyone—or almost everyone—agrees, it is a brilliant idea. Jane Capel certainly thought so when she first paid a visit to the OPEN offices in Panton Street one July afternoon.

The increasing longevity of the population means that many elderly people are living in the care of their offspring who are themselves approaching old age. When money is scarce and the old people in question require much looking after, this can put a great strain on their carers. Help from Social Services is also stretched. Carers have to find a cheap way of obtaining respite from their onerous and often dispiriting duties.

The idea of OPEN is a simple one, and operates on the same principle as that of exchange students. An old person would come to stay with a carer and their old person for two or three weeks and then that carer would send their old person to stay with their guest's carer for the same amount of time. In that way each carer would be granted a time of respite. OPEN, being a registered charity, and receiving some funding from the Government and the Lottery, only charged a nominal registration fee for its work as an agency. Jane Capel saw an article about it in her *Daily Telegraph* and decided to try out the enterprise.

Jane was sixty-three and lived on a street of semi-detached houses in an outer London suburb called Westwood. She was a widow, her husband, an art teacher and would-be painter, having died of drink and disappointment some years back. Her eighty-nine year old mother had been living with her for three years. She had been independent until visited by dementia and Parkinson's disease which rendered her frightened and lonely. A Home was out of the question: Jane could not afford it; her mother, with every fibre of her fading faculties, would not contemplate it.

Jane had a younger brother, Tony, but he was unwilling—or, as he liked to put it, 'unable'—to shoulder much of the responsibility. Tony, an investment banker, was married with two children, and the idea of Mother living with them was unfortunately out of the question. As he explained to Jane over the phone, his wife Fiona had 'never got on with Mother'. ('Did anyone?' thought Jane, but she said nothing.) Even when Jane suggested that they take on Mother for a couple of weeks while she went on holiday, this proved too difficult. Melissa, the daughter, was just coming up to her GCSEs, and their son Charles was about to take his Common Entrance Exam for Eton. As Tony explained: 'the children have to come first.' Was there an implication that Jane, whose marriage had been childless, did not fully understand the priorities of family life? The possibility of Eton was also a reason why Tony could not offer Jane any financial assistance at that moment, but he was always very generous with his advice.

Tony said: 'What you ought to do'—a favourite phrase of his—'is get on to Social Services and tell them . . .' At that point Jane stopped listening. It was no use telling Tony, who knew just about everything anyway, that she had spent the last three years 'getting on' to Social Services with very meagre results: a wheelchair, a Zimmer frame, and a bossy woman who helped bathe her mother once a week.

This might have been the point at which she gave way to self-pity, but Jane hated self-pity in herself as much as in others. She had experienced its ugly consequences with her husband Jack, so she would not give in. She looked around for other ways of alleviating her condition and found OPEN.

ಬ

The offices of OPEN in Panton Street were discreetly grand, as befitted its well-connected founder, Martha Wentworth-Farrow. Apparently Mrs Wentworth-Farrow liked to interview all her clients herself, so Jane was feeling nervous as she waited in the outer office. She cursed herself for not having brought anything to read and tried to find interest in her surroundings. On the wall of the outer office, above the receptionist's desk, was a framed and illuminated text elaborately inscribed on vellum. It read:

An Old Age serene and bright
And lovely as a Lapland night

The Complete Symphonies of Adolf Hitler

Jane recognised the quotation from Wordsworth and wondered whether the poet had ever had to cope with elderly parents, or indeed whether he had visited Lapland. She doubted it. One day though, she thought, 'when it is all over' (her pleasant euphemism for the death of her mother), she would spend time reading Wordsworth. She might even visit Lapland.

'Mrs Wentworth-Farrow will see you now,' said the receptionist.

The room Jane entered was panelled except for an end wall which was lined with books. It had the look of an old-fashioned solicitor's office and was evidently calculated to impress. Behind a fine old mahogany desk sat the founder of OPEN who graciously invited Jane to sit opposite her.

Mrs Wentworth-Farrow, a tall, smartly dressed woman with well-ordered features, exuded the slightly condescending sympathy of a privileged do-gooder. Jane tried not to waste time hating her because, she reasoned, it was after all better to do good with your privilege, however condescendingly, than to do bad. She was certainly a clever and forceful woman because, by the end of the interview, Jane had told Mrs Wentworth-Farrow far more than she had expected to about her marriage, her exasperating younger brother, relations with her mother. For some moments after their conversation had finished Mrs Wentworth-Farrow wrote in a ledger; then she laid down her pen, looked up and smiled at Jane as she leaned back in her chair.

'Well, Mrs Capel—may I call you Jane?' Jane nodded. 'Oh, and you must call me Martha, of course. You are just the sort of person we want to help.' It was an ambiguous sentence, but Jane smiled hopefully. 'Your mother does sound quite a handful, so we're going to find it rather difficult to get hold of someone to "team you up with", as we say.' Jane had had a feeling that teams would come into the conversation at some point. Martha had the look of a former hockey captain and head girl. 'I wonder...' Martha tapped her teeth with her fountain pen, then typed something into her computer, after which she frowned at the screen for a few seconds and turned to Jane. 'Would you be prepared to take on a couple?'

'Well . . .'

'There's a Mrs von Hohenheim. Lives down in Wiltshire. Widow like you; interesting woman. She has two parents, in their early nineties, believe it or not, but still quite hale, I understand. A Major and Mrs Strellbrigg. I realise that it's something of a challenge, but—'

'No. No,' said Jane who wanted to cut Martha off before she said something to the effect that beggars could not be choosers.

So it was agreed. Letters were exchanged and within a month, Jane was driving her mother down to Wiltshire to stay with Mrs von Hohenheim and the Strellbriggs for three weeks.

മ

They lived in a large bungalow at a place called Lockington Magna on the outskirts of Savernake Forest. Mrs von Hohenheim was a big bony woman who wore a tartan skirt and bright red lipstick. Jane was slightly disconcerted by her because she could not quite shake off the impression that she was a man dressed up as a woman, but Mrs von Hohenheim was effusively welcoming. Jane watched closely to see how her mother reacted because, though her mental faculties were impaired, her capacity for registering complaint was as sound as ever. Her mother seemed fascinated by her new hostess, but not afraid. Mrs von Hohenheim was voluble without being in any way informative about herself or her situation. She had a slight accent—German or Netherlandish at a guess—and a hooting falsetto voice. She ushered them into the sitting room to meet her parents.

Major and Mrs Strellbrigg sat either side of the fireplace in identical chairs. They looked frail but their expressions were alert. The Major was a big man with a blunt, military cast of countenance and a short moustache which stuck out under his nose like a hog's bristle. His wife, Daphne, was a slender, delicate creature with thick, creamy white hair in a page boy cut. She wore a black velvet ribbon around her temples.

Though old couples are reputed to grow like each other this was not the case with the Strellbriggs, except for one curious feature: they both had a small black mole above the left eyebrow. They greeted Jane politely, he with bluff, soldierly courtesy, she with simpering charm. They also spoke to her mother in a friendly way to which she responded with a few broken sentences and a smile. She had accepted them.

Jane left soon afterwards not so much because she was confident that all would go well, as because she was beginning to feel that Mrs von Hohenheim wanted her to go. And, after all, her mother had come with all the necessary instructions, medication, equipment. There really was nothing more Jane could do to ensure the success of the venture.

All the same, as she drove back from Wiltshire to begin her three week break, Jane felt anxious. Something about the menage she had just left made her uneasy. Mrs von Hohenheim for example must have been the daughter of the Strellbriggs: were she a daughter-in-law, she would be Mrs Strellbrigg. Yet she had a foreign accent while her parents were so very English. Then there was her mannish appearance, her big clumsy hands, her strange voice. It was not exactly sinister, but it was odd.

When she got home Jane telephoned Martha Wentworth-Farrow at OPEN to express her misgivings. Martha was soothing. 'You mustn't worry,' she said. 'It's like your child's first term at boarding school. You have to cut the cord. Now go and enjoy yourself. You deserve it.'

Jane did enjoy herself. She went with a friend to the Lake District. Perhaps the best time of all was when it rained and Jane spent a whole day in their rented cottage reading a novel. She had not indulged herself in this way since adolescence.

Lapland Nights

༶

During the three weeks of her break she did not ring up to find out how her mother was doing. This was one of the rules that Mrs Wentworth-Farrow had laid down, that carers were to be contacted in dire emergencies, but otherwise they should take a complete holiday from their concerns. Jane had obeyed, but she became nervous again when she drove down to Wiltshire to collect her mother whom nevertheless she found in excellent order. The Strellbriggs, seeming rather less frail than they had appeared to be when Jane had first met them, were very pleasant but Mrs von Hohenheim, without any overt rudeness, made it clear that Jane should not delay, but take her mother and go. The visit of the Strellbriggs to Jane Capel's house was to take place in a week's time.

On the way back Jane tried to interrogate her mother about her stay, and received the barest monosyllables in reply. Had she had a nice time? 'Yes.' What was the food like? (This was an abiding concern with her mother.) 'Not bad.' Had they gone anywhere? Seen anything? Done anything special? 'Oh . . .' This was a new development for her mother who hitherto had always been talkative, if incoherent; but Jane was not too concerned. Her mother seemed quite placid and Jane, with an occasional pang of guilt, had stopped wanting anything from her other than placidity.

༶

As the day approached for the Strellbriggs' arrival Jane began to feel nervous again, though without much rational cause. The instructions she received through the post from Mrs von Hohenheim were of the barest kind. The Strellbriggs, much to Jane's surprise, took no medication beyond a few vitamin supplements with which they travelled. Their dietary requirements were simplicity itself. The Major liked his daily paper and his whisky before the evening meal: that was it. They were capable of getting up, dressing themselves and putting themselves to bed at night. Jane, a natural worrier, found herself concerned about the apparent absence of difficulties. Was there something which she had not been told?

The Strellbriggs arrived promptly at the time appointed, driven by their daughter. Once their bags were in their room, Jane received the distinct impression that Mrs von Hohenheim did not want to stay. She did not even look in to greet Jane's mother who was in the sitting room.

Over the next few days Jane got to know something about the Strellbriggs, for they were fond of reminiscence. He had been a Major in the King's African Rifles, which he always referred to as 'the old K.A.R.', and they had spent much of his working life in Kenya which they pronounced 'Keenya' in the old-fashioned way. Their views on race startled Jane. While the Major was forthright, his wife, whose name was Daphne, was simperingly apologetic, but no less virulent.

'I'm afraid Arthur and I are very against black people.' she said at dinner on their first day. 'We always have been. We saw what they did in the Mau Mau, you see.'

'The thing about blacks,' said the Major, 'is that they're not a fully developed species. They're like little children. You have to treat them accordingly. Horses for courses, that sort of thing. Give them a bit of stick now and then and they'll tow the line. My Sergeant in the old K.A.R. was a chap called Pigby. Terrific bloke. Know what he used to do to them?'

Jane did not want to know, but the Major was going to tell her, whether she liked it or not.

'Whipped the soles of their feet with a bamboo whangee! And you know, they were grateful to him. Taught them discipline, you see. That's what they ought to do here, you know, to keep them in line.'

Lapland Nights

'Oh, Arthur, you are terrible!' said Daphne indulgently.

'I mean it! That's why the Mau Mau happened. We got too soft. No. Whip the soles of their feet: that's the ticket. They called it the *bastinado* in medieval Spain. It's a time honoured form of torture.' The Major's conversation often ran on such lines. Whenever he began Jane tried to find an excuse to leave the room, which could be difficult at meal times. He often talked of his Sergeant Pigby who was with him 'out in Africa'.

'My Sergeant, Pigby. Terrific chap. He came from the gutter —Bermondsey, I believe—but salt of the earth. He'd do anything for you if you won his trust. Give you his right arm, his eye teeth. Find anything for you; God knows how. I'd say to him: "Pigby, I'm after a boot jack", or a rhino hide whip, or whatever. And blow me, in a day or two the thing would be in my bungalow. How he got hold of it, damned if I know. No questions asked. Mum's the word. That's the sort of chap he was.'

Once, Jane, who did not quite believe in this amazing factotum, asked what had happened to Pigby and whether he were still alive. The Major sighed.

'The Mau Mau got him. Strung him up on a tree by his feet and disembowelled him, damn their black hides. And after all he'd done for them! There's no gratitude.' But he spoke philosophically without any great emotion.

There was something about 'The Major', as he liked to refer to himself, which worried Jane. He did not seem quite real: he was like a caricature, a minor character out of a novel or play, crudely sketched in for knockabout purposes.

Daphne Strellbrigg had a similar effect on Jane, but not to the same degree. She gave the impression of living in another era. Her clothes vaguely suggested the 1920s and, at dinner, she often wore an ostrich feather attached by a brooch to the black velvet fillet she wore round her head. It gave her the look of a flapper at a society dance. She would often talk about the many admirers she had as a young woman. This did not seem to bother her husband, who listened to her recitals with the utmost complacency. On their second night there they were all watching an old film on television when Daphne suddenly pointed at one of the actors on the screen, a minor Hollywood star.

'I had him once, you know.' she said.

Jane who was not quite sure she had heard correctly asked what exactly she meant.

Daphne said: 'It was when we were in Kenya. He'd come out to do some sort of filming. We met at the Muthaiga Club. I went to bed with him. Not up to much, I'm afraid. Frankly, a great disappointment.'

The Major roared with laughter; Daphne simpered.

They had information and opinions, often of the oddest kind, to impart on most subjects, but about one they were reticent. Whenever Jane tried to ask about their daughter Mrs von Hohenheim they became vague and steered the conversation towards other topics.

In some ways they were untroublesome guests. They did not ask to be entertained, or to go anywhere. The Major went for a short 'constitutional' in the afternoon; Daphne spent long hours crocheting a strangely amorphous grey blanket. More importantly, they had no objection to her mother's presence. She often sat with them in the living room, quite silent, often watching them with that mesmerised look so common to Parkinson's sufferers. Occasionally Daphne or the Major would address some remark at her to which she would respond with a slow nod of the head.

'All right, mother?' the Major would ask. 'Everything hunky dory?' He always called her 'mother' which irritated Jane.

The Strellbriggs ate a surprising amount and, after a day or two, began to be particular about their food. It was that annoying kind of particularity which masquerades as unfussiness.

Lapland Nights

'Really,' said Daphne, 'just the plainest of food for me. Just the simplest piece of beef or chicken cooked just so. No frills.'

'That's right,' chimed in the Major, 'None of your fancy muck for me either.'

There was one occasion when Jane had taken particular care to give the Strellbriggs what they wanted for lunch, a home-made steak-and-kidney pie. After much of it had been consumed in silence, Jane, hoping for some compliment, asked the Major if he was enjoying his meal.

'Don't think much of this grub, to be frank with you,' he said.

Jane restrained herself and said in her mildest voice: 'Oh dear, and I cooked it specially for you. What do you think, Daphne?'

'Well,' said Daphne with a tepid smile, 'I'm rather afraid I have to agree with my husband.'

'There you are! Told you!' said the Major. Then, turning to Jane's mother who was, as usual, toying dreamily with the food on her plate, he said: 'What's your view of the rations, mother?'

Jane's mother looked up and said clearly: 'I think it's absolutely disgusting!'

The Major roared his approval and banged the table with a fork. Jane was astonished as it had been weeks since her mother had come out with a coherent sentence.

'You mustn't encourage her,' she told the Major.

'Why not?' he said belligerently. 'Somebody has to encourage her. I don't see you doing a hell of a lot.'

This was true, and Jane knew it: the Major had landed a shrewd blow. The rest of the meal was eaten in silence, and thereafter Jane fed everyone exclusively on ready-made meals from the supermarket, about which there were no complaints.

Small concerns and annoyances began to build up. The strangest of these concerned their daily paper. Jane had the *Daily Telegraph* (approved by the Major) delivered every morning by the paper boy from Patel's the local newsagent. One morning it did not arrive, so Jane rang Mr Patel to ask him why the paper had not been delivered. Mr Patel answered her enquiry with his usual precise courtesy.

'I am sorry, Mrs Capel, but you will have to come and collect it from the shop.'

'Why? Is your paper boy off sick?'

'Not exactly, Mrs Capel.' She could detect hesitancy and embarrassment in Mr Patel's tone.

'Well, what is it?'

'I understand you have guests staying with you at the moment, Mrs Capel?' He pronounced her surname with a stress on the last syllable, like his own.

'The Strellbriggs, yes?'

'One of them being, excuse me, an elderly gent with a moustache?'

'Go on.'

'He frightened my boy.'

'Good God! How?'

'Well, it sounds stupid speaking about it, but my boy, he said he was terrified. He is coming along the pavement, like as usual, up to your house. And you know there's a hedge along your front garden?'

'Privet hedge, yes.'

'Well, my boy is walking along past your house. This is seven in the morning, you see. Hardly anyone about. And your guest, he suddenly put his head up above your hedge and sort of growls, forgive me, like a wild animal of some kind. That's what my boy says. He was so scared he ran all the way back to the shop and he won't go near your house again. I've spoken to him, but I am sorry, Mrs Capel, he won't, and that is all there is to it.'

Lapland Nights

Jane put down the telephone in a rage. She went into the sitting room where the Strellbriggs were sitting with her mother. She gave them a précis of her conversation with the newsagent.

'Good grief, what a palaver!' said the Major. 'I was just having a bit of fun with the lad!'

'Apparently you frightened the life out of him.'

'Young people today . . . ! Soft! Mollycoddled! You know what my Sergeant Pigby used to do with the young recruits out in Africa—'

'Please! Major, I do *not* want to know what your Sergeant Pigby used to do. I am asking you please, while you are in my house not to do such a thing again.'

'Okey dokey, ma'am!' said Strellbrigg. He seemed quite indifferent to the whole affair.

This was the first incident which caused Jane real concern but she did not think of worrying Mrs Wentworth-Farrow with it, let alone Mrs von Hohenheim, whom distance had converted into a fearsome, almost mythical figure. By the beginning of the second week, however, Jane was becoming seriously agitated.

She had begun to sleep badly. Strange, repetitive dreams turned her hours of rest into unsettled fragments of fitful dozing. She would wake up suddenly as if alerted by some disturbance and lie in the dark straining to hear a noise. One night she did hear something. It was a low, human voice which she could not identify. She tiptoed to her bedroom door and opened it a fraction.

Now she recognised the voice: it was the Major's, breathy, low, urgent, barely above a whisper. He was saying: 'Come here, Pigby! Come here, sir! Come here, I say!'

There was a silence, then again, even more urgently this time: 'Pigby! Come here, I say!'

After a long silence Jane thought she heard a snuffling, grunting sound somewhere in the house, like the noise made by a wild animal. Courage deserted her. She shut and locked her bedroom door, and scrambled back into bed. There she lay for the rest of the night frozen, guilty, wide awake, waiting for the recurrence of a noise which never came.

At breakfast the following morning Jane mentioned casually that she had thought she had heard an animal in the house during the night. The Major, intent on his second piece of toast, barely looked up.

'Not a dog or a cat, I hope.' he said.

Jane was surprised by his reaction. She said she didn't think it was.

'Arthur and I don't care for dogs and cats,' said Daphne.

'Not proper animals,' said the Major. 'Not like lions and jackals, leopards and hyenas. You can respect *them*. You shoot 'em but you respect 'em. Know what I mean? I've bagged my fair share of big game in my time. Pigby and I used to go out into the Masai Mara and do it. Once got a brace of bull elephants with two successive rifle shots. Gave one of the heads to Pigby as a memento.'

The mention of Pigby made Jane scrutinise the Major closely. He did not look mad; in fact he looked extraordinarily healthy. Recalling his frail appearance when she first met him, she could not help congratulating herself on the beneficial effects of her hospitality. He looked ten years younger, and so did Daphne.

The following night Jane listened out for noises but heard nothing except for a faint pattering of feet at three o'clock in the morning. It sounded neither human nor elderly, but its indistinctness allowed Jane to put it down to illusion.

The next day Mrs Chicopera from two doors up came round to ask if Jane had seen her missing cat, Buzz. Jane had not. They talked on the doorstep and Jane did not invite her in for coffee as she usually did because she did not want the Strellbriggs to meet Mrs Chicopera, who was from Zimbabwe.

When Jane came into the sitting room after this interview she was puzzled not to see her mother. The Major was reading the

Lapland Nights

paper and Daphne was examining her crocheted blanket which she had draped over an armchair. Its grey colour, irregular stitching and indeterminate shape made it resemble the web of a giant spider. It took a few seconds before Jane realised that Daphne had draped the blanket over her mother's chair and that her mother was under it.

Jane removed the blanket to reveal her mother who looked bewildered, but not greatly agitated. 'Oh!' she said. 'Are we having lunch?'

'Poor mother!' said Jane, as lightly as she could without removing a hint of reproof. Daphne took the blanket from Jane with a smile but said nothing.

The Major said: 'Having a bit of a lark, weren't we, mother? Having a bit of a game.'

'What sort of game?' Jane asked.

'Pigby,' said her mother.

Jane looked at the three of them and they stared blandly back. It was as if they were all in a conspiracy against her. She left the room. There was another week to go and Jane was not quite sure whether she could stand it.

ജ

The nights began to exhaust her. They were full of small movements and noises beyond Jane's bedroom door which, to her shame, she was now too frightened to open. Once or twice she thought she heard the Major calling: 'Come here, Pigby! Come here, sir! Come here, I say!' But she did not try to verify her supposition.

On the Tuesday of the Strellbriggs' last week Mrs Chicopera called to say that their cat Buzz had been found. It was dead and looked as if it had been attacked savagely by a wild creature. One leg had been chewed at and half torn off. Jane commiserated.

'Oh, how awful. A fox?' she ventured.

'Maybe,' said Mrs Chicopera. They were standing at the little wrought-iron gate of Jane's front garden. She noticed that Mrs Chicopera was looking past her at her house. Jane turned round and saw the Major staring at them through the front window. He was moving his mouth in an odd way so that the hog's bristles of his moustache wagged up and down.

'When are your guests leaving, Mrs Capel?' asked Mrs Chicopera. Jane was surprised. The Strellbriggs were not a secret, but she had not bothered to tell anyone in particular about them.

'This Sunday,' said Jane.

'Okay,' said Mrs Chicopera, apparently satisfied, and moved on.

෨

It was a relief when Sunday came. Mrs von Hohenheim was due at midday and the Strellbriggs were packed and ready to go by ten o'clock. They waited in the sitting room with her mother, looking subdued. Jane smiled on them benevolently. Now that they were going she felt indulgent towards them. The unspecified, unspoken fear had lifted.

When it was twelve o'clock Mrs von Hohenheim did not arrive. At half past Jane irritably rang her house in Wiltshire, but there was no reply.

'Your daughter hasn't shown up,' said Jane to the Strellbriggs.

'Oh dear!' said Daphne mildly.

One o'clock came. Jane had rung the Wiltshire house several times, but with no results. Now deeply angry, she served a makeshift meal to her guests. After lunch Mrs von Hohenheim had still not arrived, so Jane tried ringing the offices of OPEN but, needless to say, it being a Sunday, she got only an answering machine. By three o'clock Jane had decided that the only course of action was to drive the Strellbriggs down to Wiltshire. The problem was that she could not leave her mother on her own for that length of time, and it would be impossible to get someone in to look after her at such short notice. She rang her brother Tony and got the answering machine. She had forgotten that they were away on holiday that week. By four o'clock rage had been superseded by an icy, despairing calm: she had put her mother and the Strellbriggs into the car and was driving down towards Lockington Magna.

The Strellbriggs' attitude surprised Jane; they seemed indifferent to the anguish that they and their daughter were causing. Jane tried to interrogate them about their daughter's possible whereabouts and what might have happened to her, but they were quite unhelpful. The Major at one point said that it was 'a rum go', and Daphne remarked that it was 'most odd', but that was the extent of their reaction. When they arrived towards evening at Lockington Magna, Jane found Mrs von Hohenheim's bungalow locked and dark. She fetched a torch from the car and shone it through the windows. The house was not only deserted, it was empty: not a single item of furniture could be seen.

Jane wanted to scream loud and long, but she did not because she knew it would upset her mother. She steadied herself, returned to the car, got in and explained the situation to the Strellbriggs. The Major once again said that it was 'a rum go' at which Jane felt a strong desire to get the Strellbriggs out of the car with the luggage and leave them there stranded. Restrained by fifty or so years of self-sacrifice, she drove them back to her home. Repeatedly she asked them about their daughter, but the Strellbriggs' ignorance or reluctance to communicate was phenomenal. The only fact that they were able to vouchsafe was that her husband Mr von Hohenheim had died many years ago.

The Complete Symphonies of Adolf Hitler

In exasperation Jane asked if Mrs von Hohenheim really was their daughter.

'Oh, yes!' said the Major. 'Daphne had her out in Africa. Funny little thing she was: looked like a monkey. Do you remember, Daphne, we used to call her "little monkey"?'

'Little Monkey,' said Daphne fondly.

'And good old Pigby stood godfather at the christening in Kampala Cathedral. Gave her a mug made out of rhino horn.'

'What is her Christian name?' asked Jane who felt that these reminiscences had got out of hand.

'Molly. No! Magda,' said the Major.

'No, Molly,' said Daphne.

'Well, she'd answer to "hi!" or any loud cry, as they say,' said the Major with an ugly catarrhal chuckle. After that, the Strellbriggs lapsed into silence and would only respond to Jane's questionings with the briefest of monosyllables. So she gave up.

ဢ

It was a sleepless night, but fortunately one undisturbed by mysterious noises. The following morning, as soon as she could, Jane began to ring the offices of OPEN, demanding to speak to Martha Wentworth-Farrow. Mrs Wentworth-Farrow heard her out and expressed the deepest sympathy.

'What are you going to do about it?' demanded Jane.

'Well, of course, we'll do all we can. We'll make enquiries immediately.'

'Don't you think that the time for enquiries was before you put Mrs von Hohenheim on your books?'

'We don't use references, as you know,' said Mrs Wentworth-Farrow. 'We operate on the principle of trust.'

'A principle which in this instance has served you very ill,' said Jane who liked the occasional literary turn of phrase. Even in these appalling circumstances she derived some satisfaction from scoring over Mrs Wentworth-Farrow.

'Please do not take that attitude, Jane. It is very unhelpful.' This attempt to regain the high ground failed. Jane simply rang off.

In the afternoon Jane rang the police. A pleasant policewoman came round to interview the Strellbriggs who were, as usual, genial but unhelpful. The policewoman recommended that Jane should 'get on to the Social Services'. Jane did as she was told but was informed that a social worker was not available at the moment, and because this was not an emergency, she was not likely to receive a visit for another couple of days. Then Mrs Wentworth-Farrow rang to say that she had 'done what she could', which was to find out that the house in Wiltshire had been rented on a six month's tenancy by a Mr Villach, that no references had been given as the rent had been paid in advance to the agent, and that no forwarding address had been given. Moreover, there seemed to be no records of anyone of the name of either Villach or von Hohenheim or Strellbrigg existing in this country. Jane asked Mrs Wentworth-Farrow what she was going to do about this mess, to which Mrs Wentworth-Farrow replied that while she was doing all she could, the responsibility of her organisation did not extend beyond the periods during which the exchange of old people took place. Jane once more put the phone down. It immediately rang again, the caller this time being her brother Tony making his regular monthly enquiry after his mother. Taken off guard, Jane told him about her difficulties to which Tony responded by saying that if only she had consulted him before embarking on the venture, he 'personally' (a favourite word of his) would have advised against it. He also recommended that she should 'get on to a solicitor and sue Mrs Wentworth-Farrow'.

Meanwhile the Strellbriggs were in her living room calmly consuming large quantities of tea and Bourbon biscuits. Their equanimity in Jane's eyes amounted to a kind of madness, or pathological callousness at the very least.

That night the house was once more full of noises until about three in the morning when it suddenly became quiet. In the silence that followed, Jane's ears, attuned by rage and anxiety to an abnormally high degree of sensitivity, caught the faint creak of a window being opened in the sitting room which was below her bedroom. She went to her own window and looked out.

In the yellow glare of street lamps she saw a large, crouched shape in striped pyjamas climb out of her sitting room window. It was bent low so that its hands almost touched the ground. She could not see the face, only the back of its head on which wayward, uncombed grey hairs stuck out in all directions. It shambled across the front lawn, moving crookedly yet with some fluidity; then, instead of passing through the front gate, it scrambled awkwardly onto the low garden wall and wriggled through a gap in the privet hedge. Once behind the privet hedge Jane could no longer see it, but it must have passed along the other side of the wall, still crouched low, until it was out of sight from the house.

Jane felt her heart beating fast. A detached part of her worried that what she had seen would give her a heart attack; and then what would become of mother? What had she seen? It must have been the Major, except that it did not quite look like him, and certainly the creature's movements were not those of a ninety-year-old man.

The thumping of Jane's heart made her so breathless that she had to sit down on the bed. At some point after that she fainted. When she came to there was a hint of early morning in the sky. Jane listened for noise, but there was none. She went downstairs and into the sitting room. All windows were closed and bolted on the inside. She told herself that she had had a peculiarly vivid dream, but she lied.

Lapland Nights

The following day a social worker called Lorna came. She asked a great many questions and wrote down the answers on a notepad attached to a clipboard. Jane thought that she had been interrogated rather aggressively, as if she was to be held responsible for the situation. After this Lorna insisted on interviewing the Strellbriggs alone.

When Lorna came out of that meeting Jane saw confusion and shock on her face.

'Did you get anything out of them?' she asked.

Lorna took her notes off the clipboard and placed them in a large straw bag. 'Mrs Capel,' she said. 'I will have to go back and discuss the case with my colleagues. We'll get back to you as soon as possible.'

'When?'

'Our guidelines are to respond to these situations as soon as possible, Mrs Capel.'

'In the meanwhile what do we do about them? I have two strange, unwanted old people cluttering up my house. I'm perfectly within my rights to turn them out onto the street.'

'I'm sure you don't want to do anything like that, Mrs Capel.'

'But what are you going to do about it?'

'Now, Mrs Capel. We will be prioritising your dilemma here, but I have to review the situation, discuss the case with my colleagues. I do assure you, I will be getting back to you as soon as possible.'

At that moment Jane hated Lorna, with her complacent professionalism, her fat, bespectacled face, her dreadful taste in jewellery, more than she had hated anyone since her schooldays. More than the Strellbriggs? Certainly. Jane found that she could no more hate them than she could the wind and the rain, or her poor crazed old mother. The white heat of her rage stifled all speech. She saw Lorna to the door in silence. Just before she left

Lorna turned to Jane and, pointing to the sitting room where she had just interviewed the Strellbriggs, she said:

'Mrs Capel, I have just been called a black bitch in there by that man. Now I don't have to put up with that sort of thing. You won't understand how much that hurts; but I tell you, I will do the best for you and your case, but I am not coming back into this house ever again.' And with that, she left.

Jane rang up her solicitor and arranged to see him the following morning.

༄

Normally Jane would not have left her mother in the care of the Strellbriggs for more than an hour at most, but she was past caring. She had to go into central London to see Mr Blundell, whose firm had dealt with her family's affairs for years. Mr Blundell listened to Jane's story with enormous professional sympathy. Could she sue Mrs Wentworth-Farrow? Possibly, but the expense might be prohibitive. Did she have the right simply to evict the Strellbriggs? Possibly, but then again. . . . He would have to do some research into that.

Jane came away from her meeting unsatisfied, but oddly soothed. She felt that Mr Blundell, however ineffectually, had been wholly on her side. She returned to Westwood rather late and found her guests the Strellbriggs waiting expectantly for lunch. For some minutes she was so preoccupied that she failed to notice that her mother was not with them.

'Where's mother?' she asked eventually.

'Oh,' said Daphne. 'Has she gone?'

'Of course she's gone. She was here in the sitting room with you. Did you put her back to bed or something?'

'Why would we want to do that?' said Daphne.

Jane looked all over the house. Everything that belonged to her mother was there but not her mother. When Jane returned to the sitting room she asked the Strellbriggs again where her mother was.

'Haven't an earthly,' said the Major from behind his *Telegraph*.

'Neither have I,' said Daphne. 'Awfully sorry.'

Jane stared at them. It was extraordinary how well and placid they looked. Their flesh had filled out; it was pink and unwrinkled.

'Look. She was here with you when I left this morning. She can't have just gone out without you noticing. Dammit, she can barely walk.'

'Aha!' said the Major. 'The great disappearing mother mystery!'

'It is *not* funny!' replied Jane, stamping her foot, the tears starting from her eyes.

She went out into the street and looked up and down. Her mother could not have gone far. She searched the street, knocked on doors and asked neighbours. No-one had seen her, and Jane was getting suspicious looks. Someone asked: 'Are those friends still with you, then?'

'They are NOT friends!' said Jane with a violence which startled even herself. More suspicious looks followed.

After two useless hours, she returned to her home to find that the Strellbriggs, together with all their bags and property, had also gone. She telephoned the Police. The Police responded surprisingly quickly to Jane's call and sent two men round, a Sergeant and a young Constable. As the Sergeant sat very patiently listening to the whole story, the Constable began a rather desultory search of the house and garden. Suddenly Jane and the Sergeant heard him cry out from the back yard.

They found him leaning against a wall, pale and in a state of shock. He pointed to something lying beside one of the dustbins. It appeared at first sight to be a withered and desiccated chipolata sausage. One end, a tangle of dark brown sinews and gristle, looked as if it had been chewed; at the other end were the chalky remnants of a finger nail. The object was still loosely encircled by Jane's mother's engagement ring.

The Sergeant lifted the lid of the dustbin, looked inside, and then replaced the lid very rapidly. Before Jane fainted, the last thing she remembered was the sensation of seeing stars explode in front of her eyes.

THE GARDEN OF STRANGERS

I was ambitious; that is why I wanted to meet him. I cannot honestly say that I felt compassion for the man, though now, fifty years after, I have come to believe that he deserved it.

It was in the summer of 1900, the year of his death, that I sought him out. I knew he was in Paris and, armed with that information alone, I made my way there. For a man so universally shunned he was surprisingly easy to find. It was all quite deliberate and coldly calculated on my part. I would offer to buy him dinner; he would accept out of necessity; I would then write the article for the *New York Sun* (with which I had some connections), and it was to make my name as a journalist. I even had a title fixed up; it was to be called: 'I had dinner with Oscar Wilde'. I thought that was neat.

But somehow I never got to write the article, though I did have dinner with him. I'd like to say it was some kind of delicacy that prevented me, but I don't think so. I funked it, I guess, and it's only now that I can look at my efficient shorthand notes—made, it seems, by a stranger—and set down my account. Maybe it's because Death is looking me in the eye, just as, fifty years ago, He was looking at poor Oscar.

Oscar used to say that when good Americans die they go to Paris. I don't know about that—not just yet—but I do know that way back in 1900, there was quite a set of live Americans there who stuck together and prided themselves upon their cosmopolitan sophistication. They knew all about Oscar, though most of them kept their distance, as in those days he was still looked on as some kind of contagious disease. But someone put me in touch with the writer Vincent O'Sullivan who was American born, and he knew Wilde pretty well. He gave me some searching looks, but I told him I was an admirer who wanted to meet his hero. He just nodded: 'You can usually find him every morning between eleven and one at the Café des Deux Magots on the Left Bank.' So I thanked him and the next morning I headed off to that café.

He was not hard to recognise, even though the figure I saw was very unlike the photographs of him in his gorgeous heyday. There was something about the way he sat at the table outside the café that alerted me to a presence before I could even make out his features, that 'curious Babylonian sort of face', as someone once described it to me. He was sitting very upright, a glass of greenish liquid—chartreuse or absinthe?—on the table in front of him, and he seemed to be looking intensely at the crowd. As I discovered later this was not the case: his eyes were turned inwards on his own unhappy dreams. His right arm was stretched out horizontally, his large, clumsy hand resting on the gold head of a stout malacca cane. The pose was regal. He was kind of portly and, but for his subtle air of distinction, one might have taken him for a banker, or a financier taking a morning off from the Bourse.

I had expected someone shabby and down at heel, but he wasn't. He was very tidily dressed, though not exactly smart. Only when you looked close did you see that his cuffs were frayed and there were one or two tiny patches in his frock coat. I approached him and introduced myself as Jonah P. Ellwood, a friend of Vincent O'Sullivan (not strictly true), and a fervent admirer of Oscar Wilde (not strictly true either).

'Any admirer of Oscar Wilde is a friend of mine,' he said.

I duly laughed and I could tell he was pleased, but did not flatter myself that it was anything to do with me personally. I was company, that was all.

'Mr Wilde, I would like to invite you to have dinner with me,' I said.

'My dear Mr Ellwood, you look far too young and indigent to be taking Oscar Wilde out to dinner at an expensive restaurant. I will take *you* out to dinner.'

Just imagine my delight!

'However,' he went on. 'In order for me to do so, I shall require a small loan from you of a thousand francs.'

I hesitated for a moment. A thousand francs was a lot of dough, but I knew I could get a good return on my investment, so I arranged to meet him at the café that evening with the thousand francs. I may have been a greenhorn, but I wasn't such a greenhorn as to expect that I would ever get the loan back. As Oscar said when we took our temporary leave: 'Your reward will be in heaven, my boy.' Then he added, characteristically: 'Where mine will be is rather more problematic.'

That evening we met at the Café des Deux Magots where I handed him the one thousand francs. As soon as I had done so he became anxious that we should be on our way.

The Complete Symphonies of Adolf Hitler

'We will not go to Maxim's or anywhere like that,' said Oscar. 'I know a place that is quite exquisite and even more costly: Bignon's. We shall have a private room. They know me well there: in fact they know me so well that, out of courtesy, they always fail to recognise me. I who was once a votary of fame now worship anonymity. My reputation no longer precedes me; it dogs me like a shadow. Take my advice, my boy, and never become notorious: it is so horribly expensive.'

With an imperious gesture he summoned a fiacre which he ordered to take us to Bignon's. When we were in the carriage he said: 'After we have dined, I shall tell you all the dreadful secrets of my hideous life. That is what you want me to do, isn't it?'

I tried to offer up some protest, but he waved it aside.

'No, no. I could tell at once that you were a perfectly normal healthy young man and therefore eager to learn every sordid detail. It is quite natural. We love to contemplate the vices to which we have never been tempted. I, for instance, am always anxious to learn everything I can about the selling of insurance. It seems to me a most romantic and dangerous profession.'

At Bignon's we were given a private room and Oscar ordered a sumptuous meal with all the best wines, making substantial inroads into that one thousand francs. During dinner, he asked me about myself and my life and seemed genuinely interested in the most minute and mundane details of my existence. I noticed that, though he plied me with food, he ate sparingly, and there were times when he appeared to be in pain, yet he said nothing of it. He consumed a great deal of alcohol by which he seemed quite unaffected, as the elegant flow of his conversation was unstemmed.

It was when the meal was almost over that Oscar began to talk about himself. He was obviously reluctant to discuss certain incidents in his career—in his present state both his triumphs and tragedies must have been equally painful to recall—so he confined himself to observations about life, art and his approach

The Garden of Strangers

to them both. With many of these I was familiar, and I waited for an opportunity to probe beneath this urbane, epigrammatic surface. I knew I must do so subtly, because he would immediately shield himself against any crude attempt to crack the carapace. However, a moment came when I saw my chance.

'I am one of those people,' Oscar was saying, 'like Théophile Gautier, "*pour qui le monde visible existe*". For whom the visible world exists. As for the invisible world . . . ah, that is a more troublesome issue! I acknowledge its existence, I admire its advantages, but I have no experience of its attractions. One reads Dante, of course, but his charm for me lies in the certainty that he is reporting inaccurately. His *Divine Comedy* is like the best journalism, full of the most fascinating gossip that one may choose to believe or disbelieve according to taste.'

'But there must have been times,' I said, 'when you would have been tempted to pierce the veil and find out for yourself.'

There was a pause during which Oscar stared at me, then he drained his glass of burgundy and said quite casually:

'Suicide, you mean? I was never really tempted to kill myself. Even when a part of me died in Reading Gaol, I never thought seriously of that as a way out. What I felt was that I must drain the chalice of my passion to the dregs.'

'You have written that "each man kills the thing he loves".'

'My dear Ellwood, what on earth makes you think that I love myself? Self admiration and self love are quite different things. To love oneself is the beginning of folly, to admire oneself is the beginning of an exquisite career, and perhaps the end of it too. Besides, to commit suicide is not to kill oneself. On the contrary, it is to destroy everything but oneself. Don't you see? We can escape all things but ourselves. That is man's glory and his tragedy; at least it is mine, and that amounts to the same thing.'

'But there must have been times, nevertheless . . . ?'

Another long pause followed, and I thought he was not going to rise to my challenge, but eventually he said: 'You are quite right, and there was one occasion when I thought of ending my life. There is at Naples a garden where those who have determined to kill themselves go. It is called, I believe, *il Giardino dei Stranieri*, the Garden of Strangers. I do not know if the name has some sinister import or if it was called that long before it began to be put to such deadly use. Well, some two years ago, after Bosie had gone away, I was so cast down by the boredom of leaving the villa at Posilipo, and by the annoyance that some absurd friends in England were giving me, that I felt I could bear no more. Really, I came to wish that I was back in my prisoner's cell picking oakum. I thought of suicide. Yes! Oscar Wilde, the passionate worshipper at the shrine of life, once contemplated such a thing.'

'Did you go to this garden with the means of performing the act? What did you take with you? A gun? Prussic acid?'

'Oh, my dear Ellwood, nothing so vulgarly practical.' He laughed. 'I suppose I had a vague notion that someone would be there to sell me the means, just as in pleasure gardens there may be sellers of balloons or ice cream. Incidentally, dear boy, talking of ice cream, they do a *Bombe* here which is a work of art. It is the *Mona Lisa* of ices. Shall we indulge, before our cognac?'

We ordered our ices and he continued.

'It was too far to walk from my hotel in Naples so I determined to take a carriage. I tried any number of drivers, but they refused, even for ready money. They seemed to look upon the act of driving me to my grave as ill-omened. Eventually I secured the services of a villainous old fellow who was prepared to take me there in his dreadful old *carrozza* for a perfectly ridiculous sum of money.

'The Garden of Strangers is situated on a little hill overlooking the bay of Naples. I had occasion to reflect that the rather absurd injunction to "see Naples and die" had an ironic appropriateness for me. At any rate the view was, I suppose, as views go, a good one. Personally, I have very little time for views.

The Garden of Strangers

Views are like women of a certain age: the vaster they are, the less they have to offer. Give me a simple silver-crowned olive tree to contemplate, or a dew drop upon a rose. It is the small things which enlarge the soul.

'As for the garden itself, I understand that it had once been attached to the villa of a Neapolitan nobleman who, in a fit of misguided philanthropism, had left it upon his death to the Municipality. He had evidently disregarded the universal truth that what belongs to everyone, belongs to nobody; but perhaps his bequest was a subtle act of revenge on the world, for the Marchese di Catalani del Dongo—yes, that was his extravagant name—died by his own hand. It was the old story: unrequited hatred. He could not bear the fact that the friend whose wife he had so callously seduced was still very fond of him. Can you imagine a more cutting insult to an Italian lover? In England and France they do things differently, of course. In France they are realists and know that it is always the lover and not the cuckolded husband who is the true injured party, so they shrug their shoulders. In England respectability is everything: in private you threaten to horsewhip your wife's lover; in public you take him out onto the golf course and offer him an insulting three stroke advantage. The Italians know nothing of golf: that is the secret of their charm, and the origin of their misfortunes.

'Well the garden is not a very exciting affair. A few dusty paths wind between overgrown and uncared-for shrubberies. Tall sentinels of cypress—that most melancholy of trees—pierce the sky. There are a number of terraces where one may sit down upon a stone bench to contemplate the view, and, presumably, commit the awful act. So I went and sat down upon one of these.

'It was a dull evening, thick and oppressive, and I knew that the coming night would be unblessed by stars. I was relieved to see that there was nobody about, nobody living, that is; but I immediately became aware that I was, nevertheless, *not alone*. I felt, as one sometimes feels when walking along a busy street in a great city, oppressed by the massed crowd of strangers whose lives are unknown to you, who pass by uncaring, who mean nothing to you and to whom you mean nothing. I thought then that the garden was well named.

'Actual physical impressions were slight. I heard a rustling noise which might only have been the fluster of a bird in the shrubberies, and a sighing which could have been the breeze. Cloud-like things seemed to cluster round me, but that could merely have been the evening mist. But there was life there, of a sort, I was sure of it: the very stillness was like a live thing, and no bird sang.

'I sat on my bench, now not daring to move, feeling the presence of many beings very near. They seemed to come close to me for warmth and for the little life that I had within me. I sensed that some wished to communicate with me, but either they could not or did not know how; yet there were three presences, less insubstantial than the rest, who appeared to have that ability. Why these three and no others I cannot say; it is a mystery to me. They clustered round me so close that I could vaguely discern their shape. I could just feel their cold breath upon my cheek and hair; and I could hear their voices, at least with my inward ear.

'The first spirit to address me was, I think, the youngest and female. A vision was impressed upon my imagination of a beautiful raven-haired girl. Her origins were humble, she told me, for she was one of seven, the daughter of a small shopkeeper in Porto Ercole. She could not have known English and my Italian was somewhat more classical than hers, but when our minds met we understood one another perfectly. Her name was Simonetta.

' "My father wanted me to marry some man just because he had a shop that was much bigger than our own," said Simonetta. "Everyone said it was a good match, even though he was old and fat. But I could not have married him because I was already

The Garden of Strangers

in love. Carlo was a fisherman working on the boats out of Porto Ercole. He was dark like me, and tall, and his eyelashes were long. I had seen him first on the beach walking with bare feet down to his boat and I knew then that he must be mine. He walked so easily; it was the walk of a man who knew what he was doing, where he was going, and he had beautiful feet. So I found a way in which we should meet and we fell in love. We did not say much to one another—there are some things which are beyond words—but he told me he was alone in the world, his mother and father having both died. Carlo and I exchanged tokens. I gave him an old ring which I had found in a drawer of my father's house and he gave me a little sea shell on a silver chain. Then one night, on the beach, beneath a crowd of stars and a crescent moon, we became man and wife. The next day at dawn he and his boat sailed out into the bay to catch tuna. The weather changed: there was wind and rain, and the sea turned black, but he did not return. I became half mad with grief. I begged some of the other fishermen to go out and look, but they would not for fear of losing their own lives. On the fifth day after he had gone Carlo's body was washed up on the shore. His face was half eaten away with fishes and gashed by the cruel rocks but the other half I knew to be his. He appeared to be asleep, looking as I had last seen him when I had left him on the beach in the green dawn, and my ring was still on his finger. You think that was what made me come here to cut my throat with a knife? No, it was not that; it was what happened at the funeral. Few went, but there was one there whom I had not seen before. She was a young woman like myself, but painted and dressed in cheap finery. I had seen such women parading up and down on the Strada della Marina and I knew what sort she was. I wondered what she was doing there, and my heart became full of terror. When the coffin was lowered into the grave this woman took something from around her neck and cast it into the grave, and I saw that this thing was a little seashell on a silver chain, like mine. At that moment, I believe I lost my soul. I became distracted. I was a mad thing, and there was no-one who could do anything for me. At last I found myself in the Giardino dei Stranieri because there seemed to be nowhere else that I could go. It is a hard thing to make oneself die, but what followed was still harder. At the moment of my death Carlo, my beloved Carlo came to me in a vision, weeping.

' " 'Why have you done this thing, carissima?' he cried. 'We might have been together for all eternity, but now a gulf is fixed between you and me because of your terrible act.'

' " 'Do not speak to me, Carlo,' I shouted at him. 'I have no desire to spend all eternity with a faithless lover.'

' " 'Faithless? How faithless?' said Carlo. 'I was never faithless to you, Simonetta.'

' "I told him not to lie to me, but Carlo said that the dead cannot lie, only the living can do that. So I asked him what that woman was doing at the funeral and why she was wearing the same love token that he had given me.

' "Carlo said: 'It was my sister. Fool that I was, I never spoke of her to you out of shame for what she had become. I did not want even the thought of her to soil the purity of your innocence.' And so my true lover Carlo left me, and I remain in this place."

'With that the shade of Simonetta drifted away, leaving me filled with an immortal sadness. By this time night had descended over the Garden of Strangers and I could see little save the lights of Naples glimmering fitfully in the distance. As I rose to go, shivering, another presence held me, this time a man. He pleaded to be heard and I could not deny him.

' "Signor," he said, "I know you to be a great artist, and because of this you will understand and sympathise."

'So you see, my boy, my reputation extends even beyond the grave. It is quite wonderful what publicity will do these days. Well, this person, or shade, who insisted on calling himself

The Garden of Strangers

Maestro Martini, was a curious fellow. I sensed rather than saw that he was a small nervous person, forever restless, and he told his story, accompanied by a whole repertoire of little groans, grunts and squeaks, as if the air around him was infected by his turbulence.

' "Signor," said Martini, "I was born in the city of Nola, the son of the town choirmaster and music teacher, and early I showed an aptitude and a diligence for the art of music. My talent was for the violin and very soon I exceeded what my father could teach me, so I was sent to Naples where I had lessons with Maestro Tardini. I made good progress and was accepted among the second violins at the San Carlo Theatre. But my ambition was to be a great virtuoso, like the great Paganini, travelling the world and exhibiting my art to the admiration of all. I longed above all else to show everyone what an artist I was, so I practised, gave lessons on the instrument to unruly boys, and saved from my meagre salary, because I had decided to prove myself by giving a concert in this city. Eventually I imagined that I saw my opportunity, having discovered from my teacher, Maestro Tardini that the great virtuoso and composer Sivori was about to visit the city. I would persuade Tardini, a friend of Sivori's, to invite the Maestro to my concert after which he would praise my great gift, endorse my genius and initiate my career as a virtuoso. What I could do in the way of assiduous practice, the hiring of a concert hall, the engagement of musicians and their rehearsing, I did. When the great day arrived I was as ready as I would ever be.

' "For the first half I had prepared some Paganini caprices, then after the interval I would play the great E Minor Concerto of Mendelssohn which was just then beginning to be all the rage. Ah, signor! I know what you are thinking! You are thinking that the whole concert was a fiasco and that is why I am here! You are wrong, signor. The concert went superbly and I played as well, if not better than I had ever played with the result that the reception I received was most gratifying. Afterwards I awaited a visit from Maestro Tardini and the great Sivori, but imagine my disappointment when it was only Signor Tardini who called on me after the concert. He said that Sivori had sent his profuse apologies, but that he could not come to thank me in person for he had some pressing business. I asked Tardini what his friend had thought and then I saw my teacher hesitate. Sivori, he said, had thought my playing most correct and accurate, that I would always be a most valuable member of an orchestra, and, no doubt, in time an admirable teacher of the instrument, but I would never be a virtuoso. I lacked the fire, he said, the inner spirit of the true maestro. It was nothing to be ashamed of, he said: some had the spark and some had not. Maestro Tardini laid a kind hand on my shoulder and said that this too was his opinion, but that I was not to be downhearted for such gifts were given to very few.

' "When he had left me, I went out and wandered the streets weeping, because I too knew that he was right. I possessed everything in the way of diligence and knowledge, but I lacked the one thing that I needed and wanted. After I had wept I felt a great rage inside me against God who had denied me the only thing that I had ever desired. The prize that I would have toiled through wind and rain to achieve had been capriciously snatched from me. I had done so much; I had achieved so little. I thought that God was a cheat and this world was a sham, so I thought I would cheat both of them. I bought some spirits of aconite and some drops of laudanum at an apothecary's. I mixed them together in a small glass bottle and set off for the Garden of Strangers.

' "It was on an evening just like this," said the little violinist, "I do not know how long ago, for time has ceased to have a meaning for me, that I came here to die. I have drained my little bottle of laudanum mixed with spirits of aconite, and, as I wait for the poison to work, a terrible thing happens: a nightingale begins to sing his song in a nearby brake. You might ask, signor, what is so terrible about the song of a nightingale. Well, in itself nothing. What I hear is a passionate trill of pure untrammelled beauty: the great maestro Paganini himself could not have produced such ecstasy. It ravishes me, but its beauty scorches my soul, for it makes me see the truth of what I have done. God made this little brown bird to give us a night song more exquisite than anything made by the mind and skill of man, and yet—and yet!—that little brown bird would never be aware of what he was doing. It would be his song, no more than that to him. Its loveliness would quite escape him, and I who perceived it could never tell him. The supreme gift that God gives to man, is not the gift of making beauty, like this nightingale, but the gift of appreciating it, and I have thrown it away. I could have lived out my entire life among the second violins of the San Carlo, and still triumphed because I could in my humble way have lived in beauty and for it. I have cast my life into the shadows, not for the sake of art, but for the sake of vanity. I thought I had taken revenge upon God but I have only taken revenge upon myself. And you, signor, have you lived for beauty?"

'I told the wretch that I had, that I had drifted with every passion till my soul was a stringed lute on which all winds could play. I told him many wonderful things, but I doubt if he listened: the dead never do. I could have told him that I had lost everything for beauty, except for my life and perhaps my soul, but by that time the little cloud which was all that was left of Maestro Martini had gone. I myself was getting cold and weary and was about to rise when something huge and monstrous sat down beside me.

'I wanted to leave but I felt transfixed by this cold and malignant presence: something told me that he was the one last vision to which I would be subjected. It was a man who had quitted his life in his sixties: I was in the company of a being bloated by experience.

The Complete Symphonies of Adolf Hitler

' "Allow me to introduce myself, Signor," he said. "I am the Count of San Gimigniano. My family is the ancient one of Contarini. When I was young I had wealth and position; more importantly I had the assurance to know what I wished to do with my powers. I determined to use them to experience everything, to drain, as you might say, the cup of pleasure to the dregs. I was a fine looking young man, made many conquests, and married well. Yet I was never satisfied. Was it Augustine who declared himself restless until he found rest in God? I too was restless until I could rest in the perfect enjoyment of pleasure. I counted myself a saint of sensuality, a mystic of the flesh.

' "My search took me to strange places, earning me the hatred and disapproval of many small-minded moralisers. My wife eventually refused to speak to me and I was shunned by my own people, but this did not matter to me. I was a seeker who was still wealthy, so I moved to Naples. There, as I grew old, my body was scarred by the scourges and diseases of my quest, but my appetite remained undiminished.

' "It is a fact that the older one becomes the more one seeks out youth, perhaps because it has properties that can revive the old. It is also a fact—a most regrettable one—that the young so seldom appreciate what the old can give to them in the way of wisdom and experience. All too often one is forced to pay heavily for what might previously have come to one joyously, freely given and freely taken.

' "I became in my latter years fascinated by the concept of purity; so I made it my mission to seek it out and capture it. There may be some foolish and mean-spirited people who would see this as a corrupt and corrupting thing, but I did not. I took to going to church—a practice which I took less than seriously in my youth—and found myself especially beguiled by the sacramental rite of the first communion in which young boys and girls dressed in virginal white come to taste of the body and the blood of Jesus for the first time.

The Garden of Strangers

' "I was in the Duomo one Sunday watching this adorable ceremony when I saw her. She was no more than twelve years old and her face was like a flower. I was captivated. To me she was the beatific vision to which the saints of old laid claim. Oh, she was pure and sweet, and I felt that I could be pure and sweet with her! I paid my old friend the sacristan a few scudi to discover the name of the blessed infant and where she lived.

' "I found to my joy that she was an orphan, a foundling, that her name was Maria and that she was cared for in a convent by the Sisters of San Pancrazio. This was the most infernal good luck, because I happened to know one of the Sisters, a certain Sister Marta. Our past association was such that, by means of bribery and threats of disclosure, she was persuaded to obtain access for me to this Maria. I was in Paradise, but the girl was to be my crucifixion and downfall.

' "I presented myself to the Convent of San Pancrazio as a benevolent elderly gentleman of means who wished to do something good for the girl, to aid her prospects in life. And so I would have done, had fate given me the chance. I visited her several times in the convent and managed to gain her trust, even, I think, her love. I then initiated legal proceedings to adopt her as my daughter, but the Mother Superior, a cursed, meddling old woman must have made enquiries as to my reputation, and she suddenly denied me all access to my Maria. By this time, you must understand, Maria had driven me half mad with passion. I swear she had encouraged my feelings, but it was then—I freely admit it—that I made a tragic mistake. Instead of biding my time and slowly regaining the trust of all, on a reckless impulse I hired a pair of ruffians to seize the girl on her way to confession and bring her to me.

' "They succeeded, but Maria had been put into such a state of shock by their clumsy violence that she resisted all my efforts to calm her. Perhaps I tried too hard to pacify her, but she was overwhelmed by it all. In short—I will not burden you with the details, signor—she perished in my arms. I had crushed the flower which I longed to nurture. Then, of all the outrageous acts of hypocrisy, those guttersnipes I had hired to capture the girl suddenly became full of remorse, and unknown to me, they went to the authorities.

' "The morning after Maria had died—I had spent a virtually sleepless night on her account—I woke to the sound of a hammering on my door. I looked out of my bedroom window to see the Carabinieri at the head of a rabble howling for my blood. Fortunately I was still fully dressed and I had a way of leaving my house secretly through a passage in my cellar which let me in to the next door house. I had not a moment to lose though, so seizing a loaded pistol from a drawer—I always kept one by me for such eventualities—I made for the cellar and the secret passage. Barely had I bolted the cellar door behind me when that stinking rout of rogues and Pharisees burst into my house.

' "In the event I was only a few minutes ahead of them. I knew by this time that there was only one means of escape, so I climbed the hill towards the Garden of Strangers. I heard their baying behind me and knew fear, but also a strange kind of exhilaration. At least my death would not be a slow descent into neglect and debility. I was past sixty, with all the ills that attend such an age, but for a while the chase put blood and fire into my old limbs. I gained the gate of the Garden with the rabble still a few hundred paces behind me.

' "Even in death I won a victory. I cheated them. I reached this very bench with the mob hard on my heels. My old legs had begun to give way so that my pursuers had all but caught up with me. I showed them my gun, which held the cowards at bay, but my time had run out, and I prepared to die. I placed the muzzle of my pistol behind my left ear, slightly pointing upwards into the cranium. It was how an old Austrian General had once told me I should perform the act. That had been in my youth

The Garden of Strangers

after the first of my disgraces, and I had repaid the General for his kind advice by using my pistol on him rather than myself. Then, as my persecutors closed in, I pulled the trigger. There was a momentary flash of agony, then I was dead and laughing at my persecutors with their shirt fronts and faces filthied by my blood and brains. So I remain, beyond them all, for ever.

' "I am not like the others here in this Garden of Strangers. I am one of the elect. I am not miserable like them; I am in ecstasy! I have an eternity to myself in which I can remember every twitch of pleasure, every gradation of the exquisite corruption of the flesh, every touch of my wrinkled finger on soft skin, every convulsion of pain, every scarlet scratch on the smooth white surface of youth, every hot tear that scalded the innocence of heaven. My soul still runs like fire through the lilies of God and scorches them with my everlasting lust!"

'What else that monster shrieked in my ear—vile things that I will carry with me to my grave—I dare not repeat. I, Oscar Wilde—I, who thought he had plumbed the depths of sin!—could take no more of this. I knew that I must leave that garden at once; because, whereas my first two visitors had been sad creatures drifting through limbo, this last thing was a soul in Hell. I knew that I must escape him or risk eternal damnation.

'The Count went on whispering his carnal litany in my ear as I tried to rise, but something physical was holding me there. I looked behind me and saw what looked like the black web of a great spider which had been woven onto the back of my coat, binding me to the seat of the bench. I tried to detach myself from it but my hand became ensnared. It stuck to me, this black and viscous horror.

'Ah, you will say, it was merely pitch or black paint which I had inadvertently sat down upon. You Americans are irreconcilably prosaic, but that is because you are young. Youth is the oldest tradition of your nation, and the young are always prosaic. The young believe that poetry is only a beautiful way of telling lies; whereas the old know it to be the sole medium of bitter truth. Where was I?'

'Still in the Garden of Strangers.'

'Ah, yes. Well, I believe that I might have been caught forever in that dreadful web, but just then the sun broke from behind the hills overlooking the bay of Naples, and it was at last a new day. With the dawn all my spirits fled from me, their mist burned up by the sun's morning rays. So I wrenched my coat off the seat, quitted the Garden of Strangers and never returned. My coat was ruined which saddened me because we had become attached to one another. After all, I owed my tailor a great deal of money for it.'

He broke off wistfully and stared into space for a moment. 'The really precious things in life are those for which one cannot pay. Would you care for another brandy, or does your soul revolt against such excess?'

I shook my head.

'I should not have asked. One should never try to lead others astray: it is the one unpardonable sin and a privilege one must reserve for one's self. I was once very nearly tempted into playing a game of football. Fortunately I was able to plead successfully that I had a feverish intellect, so they let me off. But had I succumbed, only think what dreadful consequences would have ensued. I might have become respectable.'

'What is so wrong with that?' I asked, hoping, I guess, to provoke him once more, but I got more than I bargained for.

'My dear Ellwood,' said Oscar, now without a trace of melancholy or languor in his voice, 'respectability is the only crime because it is the betrayal of the self. Respectability is the taking up of moral attitudes and the denial of morality. It condemns the sinner in public, but in secret condones the sin. How could I, its most notorious victim, defend respectability? It prefers the simple lie to the bewildering truth. It is the comfort of cruel men, the ice on the mirror, the cloak that hides the dagger. It

The Garden of Strangers

was the crucifier of Christ; it is the suicide of the soul. If I had murdered myself that day in the Garden of Strangers I would have become respectable because, in the eyes of my fellow countrymen, I would have "done the decent thing". And there is no more indecent act in this world than to do the decent thing for the sake of respectability.'

When Oscar had finished there was a silence while the fire slowly departed from his eyes. He sighed as if suddenly exhausted by his own conversation; then summoned the waiter to order another cognac for himself. I asked him if, since his adventures in the Garden of Strangers, he had ever been tempted again to take his own life.

'No. I was cured of that. You see, I knew that all three of those shades had killed themselves in vain. And when I thought that such would be the fate of my soul too, the temptation to kill myself left me and has not come back.'

'And after all, how could you have imagined spending all your after-life in Naples?' I said.

Oscar laughed: 'No, the cooking is really too bad. At least I shall be dying in Paris where the cuisine approaches that which one can expect from the after-life at its best. When one is about to feast with the dead, it is as well to know what is on the menu.'

'And who pays for that particular feast?' I asked, as the waiter entered the room. Oscar settled the bill with an extravagant tip. As he struggled to rise from the table, he grimaced with pain, so I helped him to his feet. He acknowledged my assistance with a smile and a movement of the hand that was like the blessing of a dying pontiff.

'My dear Ellwood,' said Oscar, 'a gentleman knows but never tells.' Absently he patted the waistcoat pocket in which reposed the sad remnants of my one thousand francs.

AMONG THE TOMBS

'I don't think the Church of England will ever take kindly to the idea of sainthood,' said the Archdeacon. 'No. It won't do. It's not in our nature.' The Archdeacon is one of those people who has decided views about absolutely everything, a useful if exhausting quality.

It was the first night of our annual Diocesan Clergy Retreat at St Catherine's House. Most of the participants had gone to bed early after supper and Compline, but a few of us had accepted Canon Carey's kind offer of a glass of malt whisky in the library. It was a cold November evening and a fire had been lit. Low lighting, drawn damask curtains, and a room whose walls were lined from floor to ceiling with faded theology and devotion contributed to an intense, subdued atmosphere.

I suppose whenever fellow professionals get together there will tend to be a mood of conspiracy and competition, and clerics are no exception to the rule. Serious topics are proposed so that individuals can demonstrate their prowess and allegiances. The Archdeacon, in any case, does not do small talk.

'But there are people in our tradition whom we do revere as saints,' said Bob Mercer, the Vicar of Stickley.

'Name them!' said the Archdeacon belligerently.

'George Herbert, Edward King of Lincoln. . . . What about the martyrs Latimer and Ridley? And Tyndale?'

'Yes, yes. But these are figures from the past. Anyway, ask the average man or woman in the pew what they know about Edward King. I mean that we have no living and popular tradition, no equivalent to Mother Teresa or Padre Pio.'

'What about Meriel Deane who started the Philippians?' said Canon Carey.

A young curate who had just crept in confessed he had never heard of Meriel Deane. I would have said so myself had I been less timid about showing my ignorance. Rather condescendingly the Archdeacon enlightened us. Meriel Deane, he said, had founded the Philippian Movement to help the rehabilitation of long term, recidivist prisoners who had just left gaol. They could spend their first six months of freedom at a Philippian House, usually in a remote country spot, supervised by one or two wardens. The regime pursued there was at once austere and easy-going. Inmates could come and go as they liked, and had no work to do apart from minor household chores, but there were regular meals and periods of silence and meditation. People were given space to reflect on their lives. The charity was named after the town of Philippi where St Paul had been imprisoned. The Philippians were still in existence and doing good work though their founder was now dead.

The Complete Symphonies of Adolf Hitler

The Archdeacon concluded his lecture by saying 'I met Meriel Deane on several occasions. The woman was nuts. No doubt a good person in her way, but completely off her head, so not in my view a candidate for sanctification.'

'Oh, yes, she was rather disturbed at the end, but she wasn't always like that,' said a voice none of us recognised.

The speaker was an elderly priest whom I noticed had been placidly silent all through supper. He wore a cassock rather like a soutane which put him on the Anglo-Catholic wing of the church, an impression which was confirmed when I heard him being addressed as 'Father Humphreys'. He must have been past retiring age, a small, stooped man with a wrinkled head, like a not very prepossessing walnut; but, as he spoke, his face gradually assumed character, even a certain charm.

'So you knew her, Father?'

'Very well, for a time. One of her first 'Philippian' houses was in my parish, Saxford in Norfolk.'

'And she wasn't potty?'

'She was not potty *then*.'

'So when and how did she go potty?' asked the Curate. The Archdeacon was frowning. He obviously felt that repeated use of the word 'potty' was lowering the tone.

'Well,' said Father Humphreys, who had sensed the Archdeacon's unease and seemed amused by it. 'That's not the adjective I would use, but something definitely went wrong. As things do. One wonders why, but there is no real answer. Not this side of the grave at any rate.' The last sentence was spoken faintly, as if he had forgotten the presence of others and was talking to himself.

'Do you know what exactly "went wrong", as you put it?' asked Canon Carey.

'No. Not exactly. But I'll tell you what I know if you like. It would be quite a relief. I've never told anyone before, and it might be good to unbosom.'

Among the Tombs

The rest of us began to settle into armchairs and sofas. A bedtime story! What a treat! That word 'unbosom' had marked him out in my mind as an unusual and interesting person. And yet—and I don't think this is merely hindsight—I am sure I felt uneasy, even a little fearful about what Father Humphreys was going to reveal. Despite offers of a more comfortable seat he established himself on a low footstool in front of the fire. In that pose, crouched with his knees almost up to his chin, there was something in his appearance which made one think of a little old goblin out of a book of fairy tales. As he spoke he barely looked at us, but addressed most of his story to the pattern on the threadbare rug at his feet.

༄

Was Meriel Deane a saint? She had saintly qualities certainly, but I tend to think that true saints are less self-conscious about their sanctity, and less disposed to remind you of it. Let us just say that in her eccentric way Meriel was on the side of the angels and leave it at that.

I had been the Rector of Saxford for about five years when she came to our village and I remember clearly the first time I met her. One's first and last images of a person are often the most vivid. With Meriel, it was the same one: the back of her head. Which was appropriate, I suppose, because she was as distinctive in appearance from the back as from the front.

Every morning I would open the church at seven, say prayers and then go to the Rectory for breakfast. In those days—I am talking about 1964—we were less careful about keeping the church under lock and key. I don't know whether any of you know St Winifred's, Saxford? Not very special, but some nice Norman corbels in the porch and a painted rood screen which somehow managed to survive both the Reformation and Cromwell's iconoclasts. One of the panels has a rather lively depiction of St George and the Dragon on it.

I mention that because one morning in March 1964 when I returned to the church after breakfast I found it to be occupied. A woman was kneeling, very upright, in one of the front pews, directly opposite that painting of St George and the Dragon. She did not move an inch as I entered. She was wearing a coat and skirt of some loosely knit woollen fabric, rather indeterminate in colour, but it was her head which attracted my attention. It was small and neatly shaped; her iron grey hair, obviously long, had been coiled up into an elaborate bun on the back of her head. It reminded me of a sleeping snake.

I don't know what you think is the correct etiquette when you find someone praying in your own church. I tend to sit down quietly in a pew and wait for them to finish. I read a prayer book and tried not to look at her too much, but she did rather fascinate me. She was formidably motionless: evidence of a disciplined, perhaps rather rigid, piety.

After about five minutes she got up, turned round and smiled directly at me.

'You must be Father Humphreys, the Rector,' she said. 'I am most frightfully sorry. I should have come to introduce myself before, but we've just moved in to the Old Tannery in the village and chaos has been reigning supreme. This is positively the first instant I've had to myself. I'm Meriel Deane.' She came forward and shook me firmly by the hand.

I rather liked her. I suppose she must have been in her late fifties. She had a handsome, apple cheeked, sexless face and strangely bright eyes. Her body was tall, spare and without shape; she moved in long, determined strides. She seemed completely unselfconscious, oblivious of the effect she was having on people, like a schoolgirl before her first erotic awakening, but not at all gauche or ungainly. Her voice was an upper class, intellectual bleat, like a Girton professor, easily parodied

Among the Tombs

and in itself unattractive, but not offensive in her because she spoke without affectation.

I had vaguely heard of Meriel Deane and the Philippians, but she filled me in on her work. The Old Tannery was her third Philippian House, and she was going to stay to run the place herself for at least a year. By the end of our first meeting I had offered to take Compline for them at the Old Tannery on Friday evenings and had given her a spare key to the church so that she could go in any time she liked and, as she put it, 'have a little pray'.

I was soon a regular visitor at the Old Tannery. It was a pleasant atmosphere. The furnishing was rather Spartan—very few easy chairs, rush mats on the floors—but it was always warm and clean.

You might think that the village would have objected to an invasion by this strange woman and her gang of ex-convicts but reaction was very muted. The men who stayed with her were all middle-aged to elderly. One would occasionally see them lumbering about the village, usually in small groups of twos and threes, rarely alone. They bought sweets and tobacco at the local post-office-cum-general-store, but otherwise kept themselves to themselves. They did not go into the pub, having been forbidden it by one of Meriel's few House Rules. Otherwise, they had little impact on the community.

I do not remember Meriel's men as individuals. In my memory they all seem to merge into a single generalised portrait. They were big people with simple, troubled faces, and plain, monosyllabic names like Bill and John and Pete. Meriel behaved towards them like a kindly schoolmistress in charge of a class of not particularly bright infants, a treatment to which they responded surprisingly well.

'They are Life's Walking Wounded,' Meriel used to say to me. There was something about that phrase, or perhaps the way she said it, that I did not particularly like. It was just a little

The Complete Symphonies of Adolf Hitler

smug, I thought. That was the one aspect of her which I found mildly objectionable. She could appear rather pleased with herself; but then she had good reason to be.

I say that all these Johns and Bills and Petes were indistinguishable in my mind, but there was one very notable exception. This was a man whom I shall call Harry Mason, and he was distinctive in every way.

He arrived in the summer of that first year, round about July when the air was heavy and hot and green with growth. I noticed him at once because he was one of the few men who always walked alone around our village.

He was maybe a fraction younger than the average run of Meriel's inmates, early forties I should say. He was of average height, but thin with spindly arms and legs. He had a very prominent lower jaw and lip, a near deformity which made him look as if he were permanently and joylessly grinning. This Hapsburg trait, combined with a neat moustache and beard, gave him a striking resemblance to the Emperor Charles V, as portrayed by Titian. Had he cultivated the likeness? It is possible, because, unlike the others at the Old Tannery, he was clearly an educated man.

I never knew what he had been 'in for'; I never asked and I doubt if Meriel knew herself. She had a habit of acting as if her charges had no past and that only the present mattered.

One Friday evening soon after he had arrived I conducted Compline as usual at the Old Tannery. These occasions were not in any way solemn or pompous. We all gathered in the main room and seated ourselves in a rough circle. There was no kneeling or anything like that. The men would often follow the service with a prayer book in one hand and a mug of tea in the other, sometimes slurping it noisily during the pauses. But nobody minded and there was a good deal of chatter and laughter when it was all over. Compline is in any case the most simple and beautiful of services.

Among the Tombs

The Gospel reading for that evening was from Mark Chapter 5: the possessed man called Legion who dwelt among the tombs and whose Devils Jesus cast out into the Gadarene Swine. It had been in the lectionary for that day, but I remember wishing I had taken thought before and chosen a rather less sinister passage. Meriel read it for us in her clear, high bleat, and it was heard in an unusually intense silence. The customary shuffles and sippings of tea for once were banished.

After it was over normality returned. I was pressed to stay for cocoa and a ginger biscuit, and there was general chat of a not very interesting kind. Meriel was trying to recruit some of the men to go with her in a week's time to an organ recital at a neighbouring church. There were few takers, and she was being mildly teased about her enthusiasm for such things. While this was going on I had an opportunity to observe Harry Mason, the new resident to whom Meriel had briefly introduced me before the service.

He was standing by the window, apart from the others, looking on but not participating. I saw one of the other men pass him carrying a tray laden with mugs of cocoa. It seemed to me that the man made studious efforts to keep as far from Mason as he could. When it was Mason's turn to be provided with a cup of cocoa the man did not hand it to him directly but put it on an adjacent table where Mason could pick it up.

Mason noticed that I had observed his tiny humiliation. He picked up his mug and saluted me with it before drinking. I returned the compliment.

A little later in the evening I was aware of him threading his way across the room towards me. Again I saw how the others drew away from him as he passed and wondered if it was because they knew what his offence had been.

' 'Evening, Vicar,' he said. 'Enjoying your cocoa?' There was a touch of mockery in his voice which took me aback. The other men treated me with a respect that bordered on reverence. I tried not to bridle; there was no reason why he should be deferential, so I smiled and nodded.

Mason paused. He appeared to be searching for something to say to me, then a thought came to him. He put his head on one side and said: 'That story we read from the gospels about the man in the cemetery and the pigs.' His voice was clear and well produced, in the tenor range, with a slight South London twang.

For a moment I did not know what he meant. It was such an odd way of talking about the story of Legion and the Gadarene Swine.

'What about it?'

'Well, let me make it clear, I am personally an atheist, so I have a rather different perspective on these things.' He paused again, perhaps to study my reaction to his words. 'But if you want my opinion,' he went on, 'I would say that whoever wrote down that story—'

'St Mark.'

'—whoever—had got it all wrong.'

'In what way?'

'Well, for a start, everybody seems to have assumed that this man Legion needed to be healed somehow, *wanted* to be healed. But that was their assumption, wasn't it? I mean, suppose he just liked living that way. Among the tombs and that.'

'Cutting himself with stones?'

'Yes. All right. Similar to what some holy men do in your church. Don't they call it mortification? That was his choice.'

'It's an interesting point of view,' I said, turning away from him. I had had enough of this conversation, but Mason hadn't. He moved uncomfortably close to me.

'You know why everyone wanted him dealt with?' he said.

'No. Why?'

'It says why in the story. It says they had chained him up several times, and he always broke the chains. So he had strength. He had power. And he wouldn't fit in. That's why they

Among the Tombs

wanted to get him. They wanted to destroy his power.' By this time, though his voice was not raised, there was something nakedly aggressive about his tone. One of the men close by must have become aware of this because he turned round and said:

'Is this man bothering you, Reverend?'

'No. No,' I said. 'But I really must be going.'

Meriel escorted me to the door. When we were out of earshot of the others, she said: 'You've been talking to Harry.'

'Yes.'

'You mustn't let him bother you.'

To anyone else I might have said 'he doesn't', but you didn't lie to Meriel. I was silent.

'He's a rather more difficult customer than my average, but we'll soon have him "clothed and in his right mind", as they say.' It was an odd choice of phrase, though it would have seemed even odder if it had not occurred in the gospel reading for that night. I wondered if Meriel was trying to tell me something about Mason which she had guessed at but was not quite prepared to admit openly.

My walk back to the Rectory that night was dominated by thoughts of Harry Mason and Meriel. She had exuded confidence in her work, complacency even. I wondered for the first time whether her confidence was well placed.

The following morning I was on my way to the church when I was waylaid by Mason. It was a disconcerting experience because he suddenly emerged from behind a tombstone in the graveyard. I make no claim to psychic gifts, but I have a strong sense of the presence of other people. Like most of us, for example, I usually know when I am being watched. What shocked me about Mason's appearance was that I had no intimation of his presence until he was there. One moment the churchyard was empty—I was sure of it—the next he was about ten feet away from me standing quite still behind a tombstone and looking at me.

'I apologise if I startled you,' he said.

I said: 'Not at all,' or something equally foolish.

He then embarked on a long and rather rambling apology for what he had said the night before. I am not quite sure what he thought he was apologising for; except that he seemed to feel that I had been shocked by his unorthodox views. As a matter of fact, I had not. One phrase he used I can remember. He said: 'I had no intention of offending the sensibilities of a man of the cloth.' It struck me as oddly ponderous, pompous even, and besides, I don't know about you, but I have a peculiar aversion to that phrase 'a man of the cloth'. Whenever it is used I always feel that there is some sort of sneer behind it.

He talked at great length and I found it extremely difficult to disengage myself from him politely. At one point I thought he was going to follow me into the church, but when I opened the church door he backed away. The next minute he was gone.

It seems rather shaming to have to admit it, but when I came out of the church again after about an hour, I felt deeply apprehensive—afraid even—that Mason might be waiting for me among the gravestones. Fortunately he wasn't.

From that day onwards I was plagued by Mason's attentions. He never called on me in the Rectory or the Church, but I am sure that he often contrived apparently accidental meetings: in the village, sometimes when I was walking in the fields, but most often among the tombs in the churchyard. Then he would engage me in conversation. I can't really remember what he said; perhaps I have deliberately blocked it from my mind. Details escape me but I do have a clear impression of always coming away from those meetings the worse for the encounter: distracted, uneasy, drained. But it was not that his talk was wild or evil in any obvious way. Do you know that expressive word 'witter'? Well, that describes exactly what he did. He wittered at me. He launched on me a barrage of inconsequential chat about nothing in particular, and, what was worse, he constantly invited my reaction to what he said, so I could never switch off.

I once asked him directly why he needed to talk to me so much. I remember his reply distinctly because it was odd, and, for once, concise.

He said: 'I talk to you, Vicar, because I'd rather not talk to myself.'

When I saw him walking in the village or in the fields I am ashamed to say I would often hide myself so he wouldn't see me. As a result I was occasionally caught out by my parishioners in undignified positions because I felt a curious compulsion to observe his movements unseen. There was something peculiar about him which struck not only me but others as well.

'There goes that Mr Mason,' the villagers would remark, usually with a slight frown, and their eyes would follow him until he disappeared from view. It was as if, one of them observed to me, it was necessary to 'keep an eye' on him.

His walk was odd. He moved quickly, taking long strides with his stick legs, his body bent forward, shoulders slightly hunched. It was as if he were hurrying somewhere with a heavy but invisible weight on his back. Occasionally he would take a quick glance to his left or right, but he never seemed to notice his surroundings much, let alone enjoy them.

I felt I needed to speak to Meriel about him, but what was I to say? That he talked too much? That he had a strange walk? Fortunately, I was relieved of this responsibility by Meriel herself who came to see me at the Rectory. We discussed various churchy affairs. She even canvassed my opinion about a religious controversy which was then raging, but I could tell that something else was on her mind. Her usual stillness—a unique blend of rigidity and serenity—was absent. At last she blurted it out.

'I've never done this before, but I'm going to have to ask him to leave.' I asked who she meant, but my question was redundant because I knew she would say it was Mason. 'He's upsetting the other men,' she said.

'In what way?'

'Nothing violent or insulting. He walks into a room and the atmosphere becomes unsettled. You know me, Rector. I don't judge. It's a necessary principle with me: I have to take people as they are. But there is something wicked about poor Harry.'

'You think he's wicked?'

'No. No. I didn't say that. I said there was something wicked *about* him.'

She then started talking about Tibbles, the ginger Tom who kept down the mouse population at the Old Tannery. Apparently Tibbles would rush headlong out of a room whenever Mason entered it, very unaccustomed behaviour for this dignified old bruiser. I thought this was fanciful nonsense, but, all the same, I was very relieved to hear that Mason was going. I felt ashamed at my relief, so I tried to enjoy our conversations when he waylaid me. But he didn't go. And so the summer passed.

One other thing happened that summer which may be of no relevance at all. We had a Summer Fête and Flower show. It was in its way rather well run—not by me, you understand—and used to attract people from miles around. They were very welcome, but it was an invasion, and some of the visitors could be less than considerate, particularly where parking was concerned. There were, of course, fields set aside as car parks, but some found it easier to park in the village with little regard for the convenience of the locals. On this occasion some particularly inconsiderate persons had put their car directly across the little drive which went up one side of the Old Tannery, and it so happened that Meriel had chosen that day to visit a sick friend thirty miles away. For this she needed to use her battered old Morris Oxford which was in the drive.

The first I knew of it was a furious Meriel bearing down on me as I was judging vegetable marrows in the main marquee. I had never seen Meriel in a temper before. Every aspect of her seemed out of joint. Words poured from her in an incoherent stream; her movements were jerky and uncoordinated. Under other circumstances it might have been comical. She demanded that I make an immediate and stern request over the public address system that the offenders should immediately remove their car. This I did. I escorted Meriel back to the Old Tannery where we discovered that the car had been moved, but evidently not by its owners.

It was a medium-sized saloon car—I cannot remember the make, a Rover perhaps—quite a bulky and heavy thing, but it had been tipped over on its side into a ditch. Two strong men could not have done it, three possibly.

There was a terrible to-do about it. The owners of the car transformed themselves in an instant from offenders into irate injured parties and became particularly indignant when they discovered who the inhabitants of the Old Tannery were. The police were called in and the men interviewed, but the mystery was never resolved. Most of the men had excellent alibis for the time when the deed could have been done. Meriel happened to remark to me much later that the only one who didn't was Mason, and he was the only one she knew had witnessed her rage about the car. But, of course, everyone agreed it would have been quite impossible for one man singlehandedly to have overturned a medium sized saloon car. What made it all the more mysterious was that there had apparently been no witnesses to the incident.

At the end of the Summer, I began to wonder why Meriel had not let Mason go, if not altogether, at least to another of her Philippian houses. He had committed no offence, of course, but the atmosphere at the Old Tannery had noticeably deteriorated. There was none of the relaxed warmth that there had been before. My weekly Compline Services were held in a stiff reverential silence. Mason was always present, but always apart and aloof. Usually he sat in the window which faced West so that his shadow blocked out the rays of the declining sun.

Eventually I tackled Meriel about it. We were taking a walk together after an early weekday communion at which she had been the only person present. When I pressed her she smiled, as I thought, in an irritatingly superior way.

She said: 'You have heard, Rector, of the Doctrine of Substitution?'

I knew about it theoretically. Certain advanced Anglicans of a mystical persuasion were very keen on it at one time, I remember. The idea is that, like Christ, albeit in a very minor way, you can take on the sins and afflictions of others. In other words, you can not only be the beneficiary of the Passion of Christ, you can also, in a small way, participate in it.

Meriel told me that Mason was suffering from some kind of deep-seated spiritual trauma and that she had been having sessions with him, and also engaging in severe personal mortifications in order to take on some of his burden. When I pressed her for details she became vague and evasive.

Well, I don't know about you, but I have always been somewhat wary of this Doctrine of Substitution. I think you have to be a very saintly person indeed—or a very arrogant one—to undertake such a task. So which was Meriel? You may think I have prejudged her, but I haven't. I have no way of telling whether she was acting out of vanity and spiritual pride, or a kind of divine and humble recklessness. Or was it a strange mixture of the two?

All I was sure of then—as I am now—was that she was attempting something very dangerous and of dubious practical benefit. I told her so and she disregarded me, as she had every right to do, of course. I was not her spiritual director; that office was filled by the Abbot of a local Friary of Anglican Franciscans.

For several days after my meeting with Meriel, I did not see Mason. It was the end of summer and the earth was warm.

Among the Tombs

Leaves gave off their last dusty glitter before turning yellow. I wondered whether my unaccustomed feelings of goodwill had anything to do with Mason's absence. As each day passed I began to lose my dread of his sudden appearance in the churchyard. I wondered if he had left altogether as he did not put in an appearance at Compline for two weeks running, but Meriel assured me that he was 'still with us'.

Then one morning he was there again. This time I knew it the moment I had stepped out of the Rectory at six forty-five. It was a pleasant morning as I remember, sunny, but moist with a slight chill in the air.

Though the Rectory is adjacent to the church you cannot see it from there. It is hidden by a belt of magnificent and ancient oaks. You walk down the Rectory drive past these trees and then, as one comes out of the drive, the church is there, embedded in its green graveyard, with its tower of knapped flint tall against the sky. That first sight of St Winifred's used always to take me by surprise, and often filled me with joy.

On this occasion the joyous expectation was missing. When I reached the end of the drive I looked towards the church. It was the prelude to a hot day. A slight mist was rising from the dew on the grass between the tombs. Behind one of them, and slightly obscured by the haze, stood the figure of a man, rigidly still. Had I not known my own churchyard I might have taken it to be part of some funerary monument. As it was, I knew who was there, and I felt sick.

Of course, I told myself, it was only Mason, and yet the dread of having to pass him on the way into church was very great. I could not understand it. I had never quite felt fear in his presence before: annoyance certainly, and unease, but nothing worse. As I came towards him he did not move, but he was staring at me with that mirthless Hapsburg grin on his face.

He was a few feet away from the church path behind a gravestone which leaned at a slight angle away from it. One hand of

Mason's was resting on the stone. I noticed how the fingers were reddish pink but the prominent joints and knuckles were white. I felt that I must say something, because to let him speak first would be to show weakness.

I said: 'Hello, Harry. How long have you been here?'

He did not seem to notice my question at all, but continued to stare and grin. After a pause, he said: 'Do you believe in angels?'

I asked him what he meant by angels. He said: 'I mean spirits of the air who fly in and out of you.' I said nothing and he seemed to be enjoying my discomfort. When he spoke again it was in a different tone of voice, higher in pitch, and full of that intense yet understated menace which I had experienced the first time I met him. He said: 'Tell Meriel to lay off me. It won't work.' Having said this he rolled up his left sleeve. His bare forearm, thin and sinuous, was covered with wiry black hairs through which I could see the livid scars of some half dozen diagonal cuts. They were very evenly spaced; it was a hideously controlled piece of mutilation.

I ran inside the church. I could not help myself. When I came out again after an hour's prayer—I call it prayer, but it was really only a period of agonised mental confusion—he was gone. Later that morning I rang the Old Tannery and asked Meriel to come over to see me.

Once the formalities were dispensed with and she had refused refreshment—a little brusquely, I thought—she dropped into an armchair in my study and anticipated my preamble by saying: 'It's about Harry, isn't it?'

When I told her what had happened I could see that the account of my flight inside the church had not raised me in her estimation. Her manner towards me changed so that she began to treat me with benign condescension, almost as if I was one of her men at the Old Tannery.

Among the Tombs

'Oh, I know all about the self-mutilation,' she said. 'That's been going on for some time now. We've got it down to a reasonable level. The fact that Harry told you to warn me off him is actually a hopeful sign, you know. It means I'm getting through to him.'

'But what's wrong with him?' I asked.

'He's possessed, of course!'

It was a shockingly simple answer, but it begged a whole series of further questions. How was he possessed? And by what? I asked them and received the vaguest of answers. I think she was not quite prepared to admit her ignorance. 'What matters is how we heal him,' she said. I asked her if she was considering exorcism, but she dismissed the option almost contemptuously. She said: 'I have been involved in cases where exorcism was used. The effects are very uncertain. I believe there are other means.' Then she looked at me with that sudden intuitive gleam which was so characteristic of her. 'Now, I know you think I'm being very vain and full of spiritual pride, presuming that I can manage it all by myself, but I'm not, you know. I'm fully aware of the dangers involved and I know I need as much help as I can get. I've got the Franciscans over at the Friary all praying away for me like billy-o!'

I smiled, she laughed, the tension eased. 'And I want you to pray too!' she said, patting me on the knee, then, for a second, almost caressing it. In that brief space of time I was aware of another Meriel, not the pious, enthusiastic God Lover, but a rather lonely, slightly immature woman with sexual and emotional needs like the rest of us. I felt touched, honoured even, that she had allowed me to see this side of her. Not that the saintly Meriel which was what most of us saw most of the time, wasn't perfectly real; but she was Legion like the rest of us.

So there was nothing more I could do, except pray and await developments. This is where the story becomes unsatisfactory, because I have very little idea what passed between Meriel and

Harry Mason during the following days. I cannot even speculate. I can only tell you what I saw.

For three days after the events I have described I saw neither Meriel nor Mason, then on the Thursday I saw something which I hesitate to tell you. There are certain images which stay fixed in one's mind as memories, but their vividness is no guarantee of veracity. So when I say I saw it, it would be more accurate to say that I have a strong impression of having seen it.

It was late September. I was taking a favourite walk through a little coppice of ash and hazel which bordered some fields which had been harvested a day or two previously. Clouds were high and there was a brisk little wind busying the branches. I happened to glance through the trees and into the field where I saw something moving. It was hard to tell what through the screen of twigs, but I could see that it was a four footed creature of sorts, and larger than a fox. I could not tell what colour it was—darkish brown I think—because I was looking into the sun.

My first thought was that it was one of the Muntjac deer, escaped from some country estate or other, which had just begun to become a pest to the farmers in our neighbourhood. But there was something about the posture and the shape of the legs which contradicted this theory. I pushed my way through the thicket to the edge of the field so that I could get an unimpeded view.

Then I saw that it was not an animal of any kind but a man on all fours, his legs slightly bent, his long arms serving as forelegs, so that his whole body was arched and leaning forward. I thought the man would soon stand up and assume a natural posture, but he did not. He bounded forward in an ungainly way, but with surprising speed and agility, using all four of his limbs. Moreover the man was naked. The limbs were hairy and scored with red marks and blotches. Something attracted its attention to me and it turned its head in my direction. The face was that of Harry Mason, but the eyes did not have a human expression in them. There was an instant of feral recognition before the creature started to bound away from me at extraordinary speed.

It is hard to describe the horror that filled me. That is perhaps why a part of me is still trying to insist that what I saw was some kind of hallucination.

I ran back to the Rectory to ring Meriel and found her equally agitated because Mason had disappeared the night before. When I told her what I had seen—or thought I had seem—she said nothing for a moment, then, with sudden decision, she announced that she would ring the police. Ten minutes later the police rang me to confirm the sighting. I told them that Mason was naked but not that he was on all fours, knowing that this would invite scepticism. ('Are you sure it wasn't an animal you saw, Reverend?') I do not know how assiduously the search was conducted but it was fruitless. The following morning, however, on my way to the church I saw something I did not want to see.

Most of the graves in our churchyard are marked by an upright tombstone, but a few are of the flat-topped sarcophagus type, like a rectangular stone box. There was one in particular, of a pale yellow stone, which stood next to the east end of the church and housed members of a long extinguished county family called the Orlebars. It had first been erected in about 1710 and was notable for having carved in low relief on its top a cartouche of the family arms surmounted by a skull and crossed bones, as if predicting the demise of the family. The carving was much worn, but its quality still showed. That is by the by. The point is that though I could barely see it from the church path through the forest of tombstones, it was a notable feature of the place. That morning I noticed that something was different about the Orlebar tomb. Someone was lying down on it.

My heart started to bang inside me. I went to look. The figure that lay there was long and thin, so tall that the head and feet hung over either end at a slight angle. It was the body of a naked man, horribly emaciated and scarred, the limbs and chest covered in coarse dark hairs, sparse but unnaturally long. The open eyes were completely black without whites or irises, and the half open mouth was prognathous, insensately grinning. It was Mason and he was dead.

One evening a few days later, I found myself sitting in Meriel's little study at the Old Tannery. It had been a troublesome time for all of us, so Meriel had decided to sell the Tannery and plant another Philippian House elsewhere. I asked her precisely what had brought about Mason's terrible last journey to the tomb. Meriel was evasive. She was highly strung and in no mood to look at the events clearly or dispassionately. Her conversation kept hopping from subject to subject: the move, the future of the Philippians, the trouble she was having with her teeth. But she did let out a few hints.

The day before I saw Mason in the field she had had what she called 'a long session' with him. When she had asked him to unburden and 'share' his troubles with her he had been more forthcoming than on previous occasions and at one point had completely broken down. They had prayed together and it was while they were doing this that something had happened. She would not say what, either because she was afraid to, or because no words could describe the experience, or because it had been wiped from her memory. I do not know.

Towards the end of our talk she suddenly said: 'The one thing I failed to realise was that after the thing had come out of him, there was very little of poor Harry left. I think he died because there was nothing left of him to live, if you see what I mean. I'm probably burbling, so you must shut me up.'

I asked Meriel if she knew anything about Mason's past.

'Virtually nothing. I never ask, as you know. He was an educated man. He told me he'd once been a teacher; and he implied that he could never go back to teaching. That's all. Something had obviously gone wrong.'

Just then we both became aware of a sound. It came from over our heads, and must have emanated from the room above, but in a curious way it seemed to be in the room with us.

It was a creaking noise. Something up there was moving rapidly to and fro, not quite running but travelling fast. The feet were not heavy, they did not thump the old elm boards above our heads but they made them creak and groan as if oppressed by the weight which bore down on them. It is a strange thing to talk about a mere pressure on an old piece of wood like this, but it felt clammy and vile, conscious malice was in every footfall.

Meriel pointed upwards and said: 'That was Harry Mason's old room.' I crossed myself. Meriel said: 'Go in peace' and the sound diminished then ceased altogether.

'It will be back, I'm afraid' said Meriel quite calmly. Then she leaned forward and said to me: 'But it's not Harry, you know.' Her usually bright eyes were dull; it was as if the hope had gone out of them.

A week later Meriel was gone and the Old Tannery was up for sale. In case you were going to ask, the next occupants experienced nothing unpleasant about the house, though I had, I must admit, thoroughly blessed the place before their arrival.

I made no effort to keep in touch with Meriel. I'm not quite sure why. It was not a conscious decision, but I have a feeling that some kind of self-protective instinct held me back. However, I did see her one last time and it was quite by chance about twelve years later. I had been asked to address a group of Anglican nuns about something or other—pastoral theology I think it was—because that was what I was teaching at the time at Cuddesdon. Well, this convent was a small establishment in Buckinghamshire, part of the Community of the Resurrection. On my arrival I was shown round the place—one always is—and made to admire its polished floors and orderliness. All was going well until we entered the chapel, when the nun who was showing me round muttered a half-suppressed, 'Oh!' It was an 'Oh!' I recognised; it said, 'if I'd known this was going to happen, I wouldn't have brought you here.'

The chapel was lit only by a pair of candles on the altar and a sanctuary lamp. It was one of those gloomy, over-decorated places, built around 1900 at the height of the vogue for mystical Anglo-Catholicism. The architecture, by an uninspired follower of Butterfield, was a neo-Byzantine riot of liver-coloured marble columns, alabaster screens, variegated courses of brick and mosaic panels of biblical scenes: a joyless exuberance. At the ornate brass altar rail knelt a figure that I recognised instantly.

It was the same rigidly upright posture, the same small, neatly shaped head. Her hair, now white, was coiled up into the familiar bun on the back of her head like a sleeping snake. It was Meriel. I felt the nun tugging at my sleeve and urging me to come away. But I resisted, held against her will and mine.

She was the same and yet different. The stillness had gone. The head twitched slightly, as if she were constantly looking from side to side. I wondered if she had Parkinson's disease. I explained to the nun, now very bothered and eager to get away, that I had once known Meriel well. She relaxed a little, explaining that Meriel was having 'one of her bad days'.

'She harms herself sometimes,' she said.

I dismissed the nun, saying that I would like to pray for a while in the chapel. She went reluctantly. I did not go far into the chapel, but knelt in a stall some distance from Meriel.

Something else was wrong. It was as if the air around Meriel was disturbed. There were tiny sounds—whispers, grunts, creaks —all of which emanated from her direction. At the same time the light near her was somehow being broken into little irrational sparks and shadows. It is hard to describe, but it was as if her head were surrounded by a swarm of invisible insects, buzzing, whining, fluttering; the occasional flash of an iridescent

Among the Tombs

wing coruscating weakly in the gloom. I wondered if she would turn and see me, as she had done all those years ago when we first met. She did not, so I said a prayer for her and left the chapel.

That was the last time I saw her, except possibly for the following morning. I had risen early and was taking a walk in the convent's Calvary garden before morning prayer. The garden, as is customary, adjoins a small burial ground for the nuns. It was one of those damp November mornings when the earth seems entombed in a white fog. There is a special quality to their silences which can be conducive to meditation. I could hear nothing except the faint crackle of my feet along the gravel path, and when I stopped before the stone Calvary in the centre of the garden there was perfect stillness. So it could not have been a noise which made me suddenly turn and look in the direction of the cemetery. There, through the mist, I thought I caught a glimpse of a thin white figure standing very upright by one of the nuns' gravestones. It appeared to be naked. I cannot be absolutely certain if it was Meriel, but I think it was, and I think she saw me. When I tried to approach the figure it moved off rapidly into the mist.

Meriel died at the convent a few months later.

ஐ

There was a pause after Father Humphreys had finished, then Canon Carey asked: 'Do you mean she had taken on his—demon, burden—whatever it was?'

'I really couldn't say. That is a possible explanation.'

'No, no!' said the Archdeacon. 'This contradicts the entire doctrine of the Gospels. If you must allow this notion of demons, they can be cast out. Our Lord cast out demons. Why didn't she let herself be exorcised by a properly trained member of the priesthood licensed by the bishop?'

'Perhaps because everyone just thought she was nuts, like you, Archdeacon. Or perhaps she thought she ought to let the entity die with her in case when it was thrown out of her it entered someone else and carried on with its work there. Like the Gadarene Swine.'

I suddenly noticed that the lights in the room were very dim. Father Humphreys looked at us and smiled, not altogether encouragingly.

'We all carry our own shadows. They run by our side when we are young; they creep behind us when we are old; they sleep with us in the grave. We must learn to live and die with them. We should not try to cut them off, and we should not try to take on anyone else's shadows. Perhaps a real saint could do it, but I'm not sure. A good deed like that never goes unpunished in this world.'

THE SKINS

I first met Syd and Peggy Brinton in August 1977 on the Sunday after Elvis Presley died.

It was a sultry evening at the Pier Pavilion Theatre, Scarmouth, and an argument was simmering before the show in No 5 dressing room which Victor Bright and I occupied. We had come in early that day to gorge ourselves on images of the doomed star in our shared Sunday papers. Details about hamburgers and drugs, the distended, tawdry glamour of Graceland, were pored over with sickened fascination. Thinking of that mountain of flesh, now cold and corrupting, I felt a strange, guilty satisfaction: I would never know such stardom; but I would equally never know the futility of success, or its ignominious end.

To purge myself of these unworthy thoughts, I gave way to pious platitudes. 'What a waste!' I said. 'That fantastic talent. It's just such a waste . . .'

Victor, who loved to pick a fight, took the opposite view. Of course it wasn't a waste. It was the inevitable end. Elvis was finished, had been finished for years. He had done what he was meant to do: changed the face of modern music. He had nowhere else to go, nothing to do except give increasingly pathetic displays of his spent talent. Dying was the best thing he could have done. He ought to have died sooner.

I rose to the bait and was beginning to challenge Victor when there was a knock at the door. It opened a fraction and two smiling heads popped round it simultaneously, a male and a female.

'Hello,' they said, almost in unison. 'We're Syd and Peggy. We're the new Spesh!' The next instant they were gone.

It had all been done with such precision, such show-business flair, it had come as if on cue at such a critical moment, that the tension was immediately relieved and both of us burst out laughing. So they were Syd and Peggy Brinton, the new Spesh.

The 'Spesh', or Speciality Act, was a feature of our Sunday nights at the Pier Pavilion, Scarmouth. During the week we performed in a couple of plays, a comedy and a thriller, changing midweek, but on Sunday, the night when we regularly filled the theatre, there was 'Old Tyme Music Hall with Special Guest Stars', two of whom were Syd and Peggy.

They came to us nearly at the end of the season because the management, 'Bunny G. Enterprises', had a violent disagreement with the previous 'Spesh', an Ultra Violet Puppet act called Fantastique! We were not sorry to see it go because the two men who were Fantastique! gave themselves airs. They thought they were better than us lowly actors; they called themselves artists

The Skins

rather than 'artistes'. Entertainment, not art, was what Bunny G. Enterprises was about and Syd and Peggy Brinton had similar priorities.

Their bill material was 'Syd and Peggy Brinton, Comedy Tap Sensation'. Their act, always a precise and theatrically correct twenty minutes, began with 'Happy Feet' and ended with 'Me and My Shadow'. Between these two numbers, the tap dancing elements of their performance, they executed a harmless and fairly ordinary magic act involving balloons and mild comic banter. Their routine never varied and was always well if not enthusiastically received.

I had watched them from the side that night and enjoyed their performance. Syd had winked at me once through his sweat as they clicked and shuffled round the stage to 'Happy Feet'. Peggy had barmaid blonde looks, a good figure and excellent legs. At five foot five, Syd was no more than an inch taller, lithe and slightly wizened. They seemed to my young eyes pretty ancient but they were only in their mid forties. He wore a dinner jacket, she a gold lamé leotard and fishnet tights; both carried straw boaters and canes for their numbers.

I saw them in the theatre bar after the performance. Syd stood at the bar with the boss, Mr 'Bunny' Warren Goldman, who had come down specially to see them into the show. Syd was laughing uproariously at Bunny's jokes, as one had to, but I noticed that Peggy was sitting alone at a distant table sipping from a schooner of sweet sherry. The rest of the company were ignoring her for some reason. When our eyes met I felt compelled to go over and keep her company and I saw relief in her smile as I joined her. Close to, her face, still carrying a heavy stage make-up, looked quite deeply lined. She fished in her bag, took out a packet of cigarettes and offered me one. I declined and she lit up with a quick, almost convulsive movement.

'I enjoyed the act,' I said.

'Yes. We spotted you in the wings there. Did you really like it?'

I made further noises of assent, surprised by the plaintive note in her question. I had thought Peggy too consummate a professional to need reassurance because I had not yet learned that everything in show-business is an act, including, and indeed especially, complete self-confidence.

'Isn't it terrible about Elvis?' she said after a slight pause. I nodded. She went on: 'It's terrible the things they're saying about him in the papers now he's dead. I'm sure none of them are true. He had a lovely act. Syd used to do an Elvis impersonation in the routine. We couldn't do it now of course.'

I was intrigued. As a young actor in 'legit' theatre I had very little understanding of the Variety side of things and was curious to know more about it.

'Mostly we do the clubs and guest appearances, like this,' she told me. 'We have done summer season variety, but we like the clubs. We always go down well in the clubs. It's a clean act: I think they like that for a change. There's a lot of blue material in the clubs these days. Yes, it's a good act. But there's always room for improvement, isn't there? That's what I say. I keep telling Syd. We ought to change now and then. Put in more gags. We've got to move with the times. But he's happy as it is. He won't budge. Typical man. We could be a top flight supporting act. We've done it before. Once we closed the first half for Frankie Lane at the Empire, Hartlepool, you know. We're very big in Hartlepool.'

I looked impressed and asked her if they worked the clubs all the year round.

'Oh, no! We're always in Panto at Christmas. We do the skins, you see.'

I must have looked blank, so she explained. 'We're in the skins. Like Pantomime Horse. And Daisy the Cow, you know. They call it the skins. People don't understand, but it's a very

The Skins

specialised field. Not just anyone can do it. Our feature is a tap routine in the skins. It's famous. We're one of the top skins double acts in the country. Of course, you know, the great skins role in panto is a single. It's *Mother Goose*. You've got a real character there in Priscilla the Goose. You have to do pathos and everything. She's central to the subject, you see; lays the golden eggs. I could do that. I haven't yet because of Syd. He wouldn't have a role, you see. So it's Daisy and Dobbin for us.' She sighed resentfully and pulled hard on her cigarette.

Over the course of the next few Sundays I had several talks with Peggy. She and Syd always seemed on amicable terms but, as if by some unspoken ritual, they never drank together in the bar after the show. Peggy liked to talk but she did not have Syd's natural gregariousness. 'Syd's a man's man, you see,' she said to me once when we heard his loud laugh above the others at the bar. I gathered that she and Syd had teamed up and married early. They had one son, Mick, who was grown up and in work 'stage managing at the London Palladium'. Peggy was inordinately proud of this. 'He's doing really well there,' she would say. When I asked what position he occupied in the stage management hierarchy she was vague, but she said that he got on really well with everyone and 'they all love Mick'.

I found that few people in the company cared to spend time with Peggy. I couldn't quite see why. Victor in particular took against her: he objected to her smoking. 'That's bad enough,' he said. 'One has to look after one's voice. But she will wave the bloody cigarette around in that twitchy way.' Admittedly too, her conversational range was limited. She really only had two subjects: their son Mick and their professional status. She would often tell me how they were one of the top skins acts in the country and that her great ambition was to play Priscilla in *Mother Goose*.

On the last Sunday of the season there was a party in the bar afterwards; the drinks were on Bunny Goodman and everyone

The Complete Symphonies of Adolf Hitler

got a little drunk. I remember once again finding myself with Peggy who had abandoned her strict rule of one schooner of sherry per night and was on her fourth or fifth. She told me twice about how they had closed the first half for Frankie Lane in Hartlepool, then suddenly and quite unexpectedly she seized my knee under the table in a strong nervous grip.

With little relevance to what had gone before she fixed me with a stare and said: 'Don't get me wrong. Syd's all right. I'm not complaining. But he doesn't satisfy me. You know what I mean? I need to be satisfied.' I saw her hazel eyes begin to flood with tears. Those eyes were the only real thing about her face: the rest was green eye shadow, false lashes, lip gloss, Max Factor pancake and powder. It was like a mask, or another skin.

Then, just as suddenly, she released my knee and began to apologise abjectly. I found this as embarrassing as what had gone before, so I made excuses and left her as soon as I could.

၈

At Christmas a couple of years later, having nothing better to go to, I accepted an offer from Bunny to play Will Scarlett, one of the Merry Men in *Babes in the Wood* at the Alhambra, Brightsea. Victor Bright was playing the Sheriff of Nottingham and since we had last worked together he had become a 'name'. He had landed the role of one of those ruthless yet virile businessmen, so beloved of TV soaps, in a thing called *Seaways*. So he was near the top of the bill as 'Victor Bright, TV's Mr Nasty'. Also in the cast were Syd and Peggy Brinton who, in addition to being 'Merry Men', were in the skins as 'Dobbin, the Wonderhorse'. At the first rehearsal Peggy greeted me pleasantly but quite distantly. I wondered whether she remembered our intimate conversations at Scarmouth, or whether she had chosen to forget them. Victor Bright was similarly aloof, but for different

The Skins

reasons. Success had clad him in a hard, shiny carapace of invulnerability.

We opened on Boxing Day. It was a good show and there was talk of 'breaking all box office records', something which is done more frequently than you might imagine. To me everyone seemed happy, but I was wrong: I do not have the kind of sensitivities which detect what is going on in a company.

About a week into the run I happened to be in the wings watching Syd and Peggy as Dobbin the horse doing their tap dance. I regularly watched it from the side as it was a most expert performance. Peggy took the front half of the horse and Syd the rear. Suddenly I became aware of Freddie Dring, our Dame, gigantic in a white frock covered in huge red polka dots, standing beside me. He was waiting to make his entrance.

'That's a very Biblical Horse you've got there, my friend,' he said, nudging me in the groin with a vast purple handbag. On and off stage Freddie Dring spoke almost entirely in gags, so I knew what was expected of me.

'Oh, and why is that a Biblical Horse?' I said, feeding him the punch line.

'Because the back legs knoweth not what the front legs doeth.'

'Oh, I don't know,' I said. 'I think they're amazingly co-ordinated. And that dance—'

But Freddie cut me off. 'Don't be green, son. Don't be green,' he said and made his entrance.

It often happens that when you get wind of trouble from one source it is almost immediately confirmed from another. During the interval I happened to overhear a conversation between the two actresses playing Principal Girl and Principal Boy. They had gone for a smoke just outside the stage door.

'Bastard!' said Robin Hood. 'He thinks he's God's gift. I told him when he tried to put a hand up my tunic, "My boyfriend's a black belt and he's taught me a move or two".'

'Is he?' asked Maid Marian. 'A black belt?'

'No. He's a chartered surveyor. But he was in the Territorials. You know who Mr Wonderful's trying it on with now?'

'No! Who?'

'Dobbin.'

'No! Front or back?'

Robin Hood let out a snort of laughter. 'Oh, Please! One thing he's *not* is a wrong ender.'

'Be a lot less trouble if he were, if you ask me,' said Maid Marian, who was newly married and had a philosophical approach to life. 'But that is *so* disgusting! Peggy! I mean she's . . . Just because he's been in some poxy soap he thinks he's God's gift. What's Peggy doing about it?'

Robin Hood said: 'You won't believe this—' But just then she saw me and drew Maid Marian away to share further secrets, unspied on.

I had heard enough, and next day a fresh piece of news was all over the company. Syd had caught Peggy and Victor 'at it' in Peggy and Syd's camper van in the theatre car park. 'I tell you, he wouldn't have minded only they were doing terrible things to the suspension,' said Freddie Dring.

That evening we saw Peggy and Syd enter the theatre, silent, tight-lipped. An equally taciturn Victor played the Sheriff of Nottingham with such venom that several terrified young members of the audience had to be removed from the auditorium. When it was time for Dobbin to do its tap dance most of the company was gathered on the side of the stage to watch the spectacle.

It seemed a monstrous thing that clattered and stamped its way about the stage that night. Syd and Peggy, consummate professionals, were giving their usual well-drilled performance, but perhaps their steps were more percussive than usual, their taps more brutally metallic. Every ripple of the shabby cloth skin, every nod of the clumsy beast's head seemed a sign of the

The Skins

terrible, claustrophobic conflict that must be raging within. Freddie, who might have been expected to come up with something humorous, was in a gloomy mood. 'I tell you,' he said. 'There's worse to come. I've never liked *Babes in the Wood* as a subject. It's always been a jinxed panto. It's a well known fact.'

§

The following morning I was summoned to the theatre. Syd had had an accident after the previous night's performance; he had injured his leg badly and was in hospital. The cause of the accident was not vouchsafed to me: I was there because Peggy had selected me to take over the back legs of Dobbin while Syd was out of action. I knew that any protest on my part would not be tolerated because Bunny Goldman had driven down from London and was sitting stony faced in the auditorium.

Peggy seemed unnaturally calm. She said that 'everyone' had thought it would be a shame to remove Dobbin altogether from the pantomime, but that I would not be expected to do anything too difficult like the tap dance. From now until the first show at 2.30 Peggy was to give me a crash course in 'working the skins'.

It was a strange, uncomfortable time which Peggy handled better than I. Perhaps the concentration required in giving instructions to a novice purged her mind of other, more troublesome thoughts. And I was in the acutely embarrassing position of having to enter Syd's skin.

Nothing quite prepares you for the experience of being 'in the skins'. You are not entirely in the dark because gauzes set into the cloth give you glimpses of the stage, but the sense of entrapment and enclosure is astonishingly intense. The feeling was enhanced for me because I was acutely conscious of occupying another's space. The smell inside was not particularly offensive but it was somehow personal to the body which had once occupied it and the body of the former occupant's partner

The Complete Symphonies of Adolf Hitler

which still did. I felt an acute and irrational terror of touching Peggy in the skins.

Before I made my first entrance in this new role Freddie Dring winked at me and said: 'Sooner you than me mate. Talk about dancing cheek to cheek, eh? Eh?'

'We're not doing the dance,' I said solemnly.

'Don't be green, son. Don't be green,' said Freddie.

I thought that, all things considered, the matinee performance did not go badly. I performed as instructed by Peggy and was hoping for some word of commendation at the end of it. Instead, when we had taken off the skins for the last time I was met with a set face and an angry stare.

'When you're in the skins, you keep your hands to yourself. That's one of the golden rules. I thought every professional knew that. Don't you ever do that again.'

I was astonished. I had avoided any physical contact with her whatsoever. The last thing I had wanted to do was touch her. My protests and denials were cut short.

'Don't insult me by lying, young man!' she said as she stalked off to her dressing room carrying the empty horse.

∽

Between the matinee and the evening show I visited Syd in hospital. I had learned that the night before, after the show, Syd had wandered off and got drunk. On his way back to the camper van late at night he had lurched out into the road and was run over by a car. His right leg was badly damaged; how badly I did not yet know. There had been conflicting opinions among the company, some saying that he would be out of hospital and dancing in a matter of days, others offering less hopeful prognostics.

Syd occupied a private room in the hospital. I found him sitting up in bed surrounded by flowers, fruit and get well cards.

The Skins

His right leg was under a frame which formed a long barrow in the blanketed surface of the bed. As I entered the room he gave his cheerful grin and wink, but I was immediately aware that a change had taken place in him. What first prompted this feeling were his teeth. I had never noticed them before but they seemed more prominent than usual: his grin was wolfish. His face, never in any way chubby, had sharpened; flesh had collapsed onto the bones.

'Hello, son,' he said. 'What do you want?' The bonhomie was now no more than a façade, and I could smell something confused and resentful beneath. I did my dutiful best to wish him well and express the hope that he would be out of hospital and performing within a few days. As I did so his face remained blank, and he nodded sharply at each clumsy expression of good will. He seemed impatient. His hands fumbled with a piece of dark cloth. I asked him about the leg.

'It'll be fine,' he said. 'Just give us a few days. It'll mend. They're operating tonight. Don't you worry. That's a good leg. I'm not having it off in a hurry.' I was puzzled: the possibility of amputation had not occurred to me. Syd's hands continued to work at the piece of cloth: he seemed to have taken on some of his wife's restlessness. When I told him that I now occupied his position in the skins he became animated.

'You don't want to do that, son,' he said frowning.

I told him that I didn't want to do it, but that I was doing it under Bunny Goldman's orders. Syd did not take this in.

'Listen to me, lad,' he said, drawing me closer to him with a beckoning finger. 'She'll never work those skins without me. I tell you she's nothing without me. Nothing's going to change that. She can talk all she likes about Priscilla and *Mother Goose*. Oh, I know. It's Priscilla this, sodding Priscilla that. Well, she won't do no Priscilla. Understand? I'm seeing to that. Peggy and I do the skins together or we don't do it at all. All right, son?'

The Complete Symphonies of Adolf Hitler

He bared his teeth again. The lustreless eyes were no longer on me but had concentrated themselves on a distant object. The skin was pale, tautly folded and shining. Something convulsed under his sheet and I left quickly.

ೂ

I felt still more nervous about the evening performance. The atmosphere in the theatre had not improved. I gathered that Victor was not speaking to anyone, least of all Peggy. Quite why he had pursued an affair with her in the first place was beyond me. Maid Marian and Robin Hood's speculation was that it was wounded vanity: the star's *droit de seigneur* had been denied him in other quarters, so he had settled for the only available opportunity. Peggy alone was hurt by his aloofness because the rest of the company, in one of those periodic fits of self-righteousness that sometimes grip theatrical people, had decided to shun him as coldly as he shunned them.

Peggy herself had absorbed some of this mood of indignation and the object of her censure was still me and my alleged offence inside the skins that afternoon. I had stopped protesting my innocence. In her dressing room, I allowed her to give me a talking to and to heal her guilt with the balm of moral superiority.

'Whatever happens,' she concluded. 'I'm going solo in the skins after this. I'm going to ask Bunny to give me Priscilla next year, but I'll settle for Puss in Boots.'

She was sitting at her dressing table as she said this and Dobbin's skins were lying at her feet, looking like the desiccated corpse of a farm animal. As she spoke the last words she must have kicked the skin accidentally; at least, I saw one of the cloth legs give a strange twitch like the last convulsion of a dying beast. Peggy noticed this too and seemed shocked. She put one

The Skins

of her stockinged feet carefully on Dobbin's head, then looked at me defiantly.

Long before the thing happened I was determined that this would be my last night in the skins. The stage lights beat down upon my mobile prison and made its darkness noisome and oppressive. I felt beads of sweat crawling off my bent back. The other occupant, so near yet so distant, was also in a state of agitation. How it was I don't know—perhaps it was my eyes—but the gauzes in the skin out of which I could see onto the stage had become more opaque. The events outside seemed dim and remote, and among the unpleasant odours which surrounded my captivity was a faint scent which oppressed me most of all, that of another person, not Peggy, but another.

It was our last entrance before the 'Walk Down', the curtain call of the Pantomime. In this scene the Sheriff of Nottingham's villainy was finally exposed and Dobbin had to come on to nudge him off to prison. We were waiting for our entrance in the wings when I felt something pass across my face, something yielding, cold and damp, like a cloth. It filled me with terror because it had no explanation and it left behind an intense version of that alien smell which so revolted me.

I heard Peggy's muffled voice urging me to 'Get a move on! We're missing our entrance'. So we trundled on, I now in a state of incommunicable panic. Then it happened again, just as Peggy had given the Sheriff of Nottingham the first butt with her head, rather more violently than usual as I remember. It was at that moment that I felt as if someone or something was trying to suffocate me. The cloth—if that was what it was—was being forced over my mouth and nose. I tried to bring my hands up to pull it off, but I was paralysed and somehow I dreaded touching the thing. Its odour was intense: it was yielding, a little slimy and somehow soft. It felt like someone's skin.

The Complete Symphonies of Adolf Hitler

I was told later that having been violently sick inside the pantomime horse, I collapsed on stage. And the audience, seeing all this from the outside, roared with laughter.

That was my last night in the skins. I learned later that Syd had died in the early hours of the following morning. Gangrene had set in and he stubbornly refused amputation. I had the impression from the nurse I spoke to that a loss of the will to live had played its part.

※

In the summer of 1981 Bunny G had nothing for me in the way of theatrical work because he had closed down the Repertory side of his enterprise—it had never made much of a profit—and was concentrating on Variety. But I was desperately hard up and out of work, so he took me on as a kind of office boy at their London headquarters. I also became a roving trouble-shooter if there were stage management problems at any of his theatres. Bunny Goldman was one of those hard-faced businessmen who liked to think of themselves as having 'a heart of gold' underneath it all. Everyone at the office repeated this mantra about Bunny's heart of gold, but I never saw enough of his heart to say what metal it was made of. Unless you count that blazingly hot August day when he came in and leaned over his secretary's desk.

'Millie, my love, I wonder if you can find a nice bouquet of flowers for me.' There was something in his tone of voice which announced to the world that he was about to make a gesture. 'I've just heard some very sad news about Peggy Brinton.'

He turned to me. 'You remember Peggy, don't you?'

I nodded.

'Lovely lady. Real Pro. One of the old school. A trouper. Salt of the Earth.' Moved by his own eloquence, he wiped something from his eye, then mopped his huge sweating head. He sighed.

The Skins

By this time he had commanded the attention of the whole office.

'I fear she is not long for this world.' A pause, then he announced solemnly: 'The big C.' After which he nodded several times in a thoughtful way, as if he had personally given the diagnosis. Everyone in the office began to make aggrieved and sympathetic noises.

'I want a nice bouquet of flowers,' he said, handing me a £10 note. 'Nothing fancy. Just a nice bouquet of flowers. And I would like you, my friend—' putting his hand on my shoulder— 'to take it round to Peggy, personally, from me and all of us here. I have a card here which we can all sign.' He produced a large specimen decorated with yellow roses. He had already signed the card with an enormous flourish and our little messages were to adorn the empty spaces around this central signature. After we had put our names to the gesture, he told me where to go. Peggy had recently come out of hospital and rather than returning to her house in Southend she was being looked after by her son Mick at his flat near the Elephant and Castle.

That day London rippled in white, airless heat. Having bought the flowers—and even in 1981 a decent bouquet cost more than £10—I made my way to Mick's flat. It was on the fifth floor of a huge block on the Old Kent Road. The lift had failed and the walk up a baking concrete stairwell was an exhausting, despairing journey. I think the heat blacked out some of my conscious memory because I remember suddenly and unexpectedly finding myself in front of a red door, one of many which opened onto a narrow balconied walkway. Down below traffic roared, houses hazed and shivered in the heat. I had a chance to recover my senses because a long time elapsed between my ringing the bell and the door being opened.

Standing in the doorway was a very large man in his thirties with a great senseless slab of a face. His huge bulk was clad in shorts and a black sweatshirt with LONDON PALLADIUM emblazoned on it in white.

'Hello,' I said proffering a hand. 'You must be Mick.'

Mick looked at the hand, but did not move. He said: 'Have you come to see Mum?' He pronounced the last word 'Moom' which, in his cavernous, colourless voice had a suggestion of threat to it.

I nodded, showed him the flowers and explained their origin. Mick stared blankly at them and retreated an inch or two inside the doorway. I could see a narrow passage beyond and an open door to the right through which I could just discern a small, sweltering sitting room. There was a smell of unemptied kitchen bins and fried food.

'Moom don't like company no more.' he said eventually.

'Will you give her these, then?' I said handing him the flowers. He hesitated warily before accepting them and withdrew a little further into the hot darkness of the passage.

Mick's great bulk made it impossible for me to pass him, but I could now see a little more of the sitting room. It was lit by the sun made pallid and bland by the yellow muslin curtains through which it filtered. The room was crammed with photographs and ornaments. Someone had decided to collect gaudy little china figurines of animals. In the midst of this in an armchair sat Peggy, her face white and shrivelled, the air and blood sucked out of her. She was smoking hard. From time to time she gave a convulsive twitch as if she were trying to shake off the loose robe of flesh which still clung to her bones. It was hot, horribly hot and stuffy, but she seemed to be wearing a sort of white woolly jump suit. I noticed that where she ought to have had shoes there were great orange webbed feet.

She saw me and opened her mouth, but no sound came out.

'Moom won't move out of the skins now,' said Mick.

THE SERMONS OF DR HODNET

I first became acquainted with my friend Professor Price in connection with a short article which I was preparing for the *Cambridge Review* on the windows of some of our college chapels. He at once showed himself sympathetic by sharing with me a distaste for the gaudier products of the last century, and proved to be a fount of information on the windows in the chapel of his own college, St James's. They had been designed in the 1630s by the brothers Abraham and Bernard Van Linge who are perhaps better known to the general reader for their work at Oxford during the same period. In 1650, not long after they had been installed, the Provost, a Dr Young, had shown great foresight and no little courage by having the windows taken out of the chapel and hidden in his own lodgings to save them from Puritan depredation. When King Charles was restored, so were the windows. Though mainly armorial, the glass is in the Van Linges' best manner and is worthy of more attention than it has yet received.

While showing me the documents connected with these matters in his College Library, Professor Price also drew my attention to a number of papers concerning a slightly later period in the history of the College. The Professor said that, knowing my 'interest in such matters', he would value my opinions on certain MSS and printed materials relating to the Provostship, of Dr Young's successor, the Reverend Dr Elias Hodnet, in the years 1678 and 1679.

Dr Hodnet, according to that invaluable volume *Parnassus Cantabrigiensis* (1685), was 'a most learned and ingeniose divine' and 'an ornament to the Church'. He was a fellow of St James's and a celebrated preacher whose sermons regularly attracted much appreciative attention. The taste for pulpit oratory, and perhaps its practice, has been in decline since the beginning of the last century, so it would be hard for me to pass judgement on the quality of his effusions, even if sufficient examples remained for me to do so. Unfortunately, apart from some fragments which I shall come to later, no sample of his style has survived. Suffice it to say that contemporaries compared him with the great Jeremy Taylor who had died just over a decade before the events which concern us. Indeed the *Parnassus* informs us that 'by some he was dubbed *Taylor Redivivus*'.

The first documents which should help us to piece together our narrative are a series of letters written by Dr Hodnet to a friend of his, the Reverend Mr Beard, the Rector of Grantchester. The first is dated the 5th of October 1678. I have, for the convenience of the reader, corrected some of the vagaries of seventeenth-century spelling in the foregoing MSS.

The Sermons of Dr Hodnet

News may already have reach'd you of the demise of our worthy Provost, Dr Young. It was an ague, they say, that carried him off, but, truth to tell, he had been like to die these many months, being infirm both in body and mind. He hath seen his three-score-and-ten years, so we may not weep over an untimely death. He was buried with much pomp and at the service in the chapel I pronounced the oration which many declared to be a very fine thing. Knowing me well, you must understand that I speak not out of vanity, but from a desire to acquaint you with all particulars. *Non nobis Gloria!*

Now there is much ado about the election of a new Provost. Two names are mentioned, my own being one of them. The other, being that of the Revd Mr Sammons, I find hard to account for. He is reckoned a fair scholar and a loyal fellow of the college, yet beyond that I have heard little that would lend weight to his cause. Some of the younger fellows find him convivial for he gives them good Canary Wine in his rooms. I have no doubt he is a very pleasant fellow, for all say he is, but what of that? Mr Catton, an undergraduate, tells me that he hath Popish Leanings. I would ask of you whether you have heard the same.

The next letter to Mr Beard must have been sent over a month later, though Dr Hodnet has not dated it. The University Annals record that Dr Hodnet was elected Provost 'by his fellows and by the Grace of Our Sovereign Lord the King, on the 7th day of November, 1678'. Hodnet writes:

I am preferred, and have already taken my place in the Provost's Lodgings which I find in a sorry state and much in need of repair. The circumstances which have attended my elevation were surrounded by such idle and malicious talk that I beseech you, in the name of our friendship, and of Christ's Mercy, to quell any disposition that you find among your acquaintance to talk of such things. It is all mere whim-wham.

The Complete Symphonies of Adolf Hitler

I did tell you in my last letter that Mr Sammons was thought Popish in his leanings. This I had of Mr Catton, and from others of whom I made enquiries. You well know that there is much agitation among the common people against papists since the late Sir Edmund Berry Godfrey was found murder'd. [I would remind the reader that we are in the time of the Popish Plot, and the brief heyday of Titus Oates.] It was said even—with what truth I know not—that Mr Sammons was in league with the Jesuits. These rumours reached the ears of the townsfolk, certain of whom, inflamed by wine and zeal, waylaid Mr Sammons and threw him from Queens' Bridge into the Cam, whereupon, being in himself distempered by over much eating and drinking, the putrid humours of his body and the weight of his belly did cause him to sink and perish in the waters by drowning. Now this unfortunate accident was about the time of the election and there are certain giddy-heads who say in consequence that it was I who incited the town against Mr Sammons so as to secure my preferment. That this is a most pernicious calumny, I would have you at all times and in all places declare. Certain of my acquaintance such as Mr Catton who now bids fair for a fellowship at this college also stand accused of aiding my cause by spreading news abroad against Mr Sammons and provoking the rabble to violence. It is most injurious to the dignity of my office which I hold dearer than myself. Besides who knows but that these tales of Mr Sammons were not true? This Sunday I did preach a sermon to condemn those murmurings against me, taking as my text the words of Zecheriah: 'This is the curse that shall go forth upon the face of the earth for falsehood, false swearing and perjury; and this curse shall enter into the house of the false man and into the house of the perjur'd man, and it shall remain in the midst of his house and consume him.'

The next letter, like its predecessor, is undated, but I should guess it to come from the early part of December 1678.

The Sermons of Dr Hodnet

If I seemed distracted at my last visit to you, which I greatly fear I was, then I must own to you that I have been much vexed in spirit. You have heard from me how my Provost's Lodging stood much in need of repair. Indeed, at the time, I only knew the half of it. The whole house is most prodigiously infected with damps, unwholesome airs, noisome stenches, cold blasts coming from under doors and through ill-made casements; moreover with every form of vermin and pestilent insect such as spiders, beetles, bats, mice and rats who are forever skittering and scuttering behind the panels and wainscots and most especially at night when the very walls of my bedchamber seem alive with their gnawings and scrapings. It is, in truth, a *Pandaemonium* and I sleep but fitfully. I have had poisons set down and have put cats and terriers to the hunting of my tormentors, but to no avail. Last night I was in my bed and having sunk into a fitful doze, I felt something fall upon my bed. Putting out my hand I touched a *thing*, I know not what, it must surely have been a rat, but heavier and more monstrous than any I have known [the word 'thing' was heavily underlined by Hodnet]. Its hairs were sparse and more like the bristles of an old hogg to touch. I leaped up and the thing made off. The curtains of my bed being drawn, and it being dark, I saw nothing of it and I thank my Saviour that I did not. Truly, it may have been a dream, and I pray it was, but yet it was like no dream that I ever had or hope to have.

You may well suppose that much of my life has fallen into disarray as a consequence, but, by God's Grace, I have held my mind together to do the business of the college with the zeal and dispatch for which I was elected Provost. I show no outward signs of dismay, except to such as you who are my intimates, and I thank God daily for this fortitude of Spirit.

One matter, I must confess to you, vexes my soul more even than my nightly torment. You would know that the small skills and reputation I possess have put me much in request as a preacher and that this is a Holy Work I love to do. Last week, being called upon to deliver the University Sermon at Great St

The Complete Symphonies of Adolf Hitler

Mary's you can conceive with what diligence I composed it. Indeed, being more than ever reluctant to go to my bed, I spent the best part of the two nights preceding my delivery of it in the writing. To tell truth, I felt myself much soothed and satisfied by my efforts. It was a Divine Consolation to me that, in the midst of tribulation, I could yet abundantly fulfill a duty so pleasing to my Lord and Saviour.

Imagine then my consternation when, upon mounting the pulpit to deliver what I had set down, I found my writing in parts so badly crabbed that I was at pains to read it out. My natural fluency was stemmed, though I thank my God that I made good without undue stumblings, until I came upon this passage which should have read as follows:

'It was with great courtesy and most sweet humility that our Saviour did act as intercessor for us and did establish that Mystic Union between God and His Church which endureth for Ever More.'

Yet this was not what I had written down, and what I had written is what I here set down:

'It was with great courtesy and most sweet humility that our Saviour did act as intercessor for us and did establish that *Mistaken* Union between God and His Church which endureth for *Never* More.'

How I could have brought forth such a grave and blasphemous error I know not, for I had read and read again these words to my complete satisfaction but a few hours before. And yet, there it was, writ down in my own hand. I confess it made me halt and for some moments in that pulpit I was robbed of all composure. At length I gathered together my distracted wits and did continue, but without that winning fervour and fluidity as I had formerly evinced. My congregation fell to coughing and did

The Sermons of Dr Hodnet

not enjoy that grace of the Spirit through me as I would have wished to have granted them.

The next letter to Mr Beard comes from the early part of 1679.

> My griefs come upon me thick and fast. I did tell you that my friend Mr Catton was like to be elected to a fellowship and indeed all fell out as I desired. But on the night of his preferment and much against my admonishments he went a carousing with certain of his fellows in a low ale house not far from the river. A short while after midnight he was seen by his companions to start up from the table and to address words unto the empty air. They, thinking that this was some idle jape brought on by strong ale, bade him sit down again. But he paid them no heed and continued to discourse with vacancy, his eyes fixed upon the open ale-house door. Presently he leaves his companions and goes out into the night. They did not follow him and, being craven-hearts and empty-skulled fellows, gave as their reason that they were suddenly struck with much fear. What befell Mr Catton then, God, He knows, but I do not. Yet, when I was walking early on the morrow in the Fellow's Garden—my nights being restless, I did often walk abroad early in the cool of the morning to soothe my spirits—I spied what I first thought to be a great mass of clothes and clouts all wet upon the grass. First wondering if this were some knavery of the serving men or the students I approached and beheld that it was the figure of a man but so swelled and distended in the face and belly that it scarce resembled a human creature. Summoning Courage to my aid I did approach still closer to see the face and there—I shudder even now to recall it—I saw the features of my poor friend Mr Catton all pumpled and bloated as if by the plague, and his skin as gray as an old shroud. Yet, by some foul circumstance, he still lived, and was taking in great gasps of breath like a trout landed upon the river bank by an angler. Then of a sudden, in one great convulsion, his whole body seemed to burste open and great

gouts and floods of water did pour out from him as though he were a leaking flagon or a torn wine skin, and all the water was noisome and stinking and full of corruption. There was such a vast outpouring that it seemed that all the jakes and privies of the city were disbouched from my poor friend's body. And at the end he lay there a dead corpse, emptied of those foul waters which now lapped about my feet like the very waters of Acheron and Styx. Aye, and would it had been Lethe! Long may I live, but however long, Time will never take from me the fearful horror of that hour. See how the strokes of my pen are all of a tremble as I write!

I have sought consolation in prayer and holy meditation, yet nothing will assuage my amaz'd despair. I seek to do the Lord's work in preaching the word, yet even in this my endeavours turn to ashes. I find that when I turn to the writing of them my thoughts are confounded and corrupted and know nothing of their former fecundity. By a great endeavour of body and soul I fashion my discourse, yet when I rise to deliver it in the House of God, I see nothing but confusion on the page before me. And lo! like the apostle Paul, what I would that I did not, and what I would not that I have done. I see things that I cannot have written and yet I have. In my homily and exhortation against the fear of death which I was to deliver in the college chapel I read: 'Remember, o man, that thou must die. Ere summer thou shalt be no more.' Whence comes this? And here I see: 'I await thee. Water shall cover us both.' What manner of thing is this that I write not what I would? Do my enemies go about to bewitch me? Am I plagued by the spirit of one I have wronged? Yet, before God, I have wronged none and none should be mine enemy.

The last letter written to the Revd Mr Beard again has no date but it must come from some time in March 1679. It is an angry document, in parts barely coherent, and would appear to indicate an irrevocable rift between the two friends. It seems that Dr Hodnet had been invited to the Revd Mr Beard's parish

The Sermons of Dr Hodnet

at Grantchester to deliver a Lenten sermon, and that this sermon had not gone well. Mr Beard had evidently objected strongly to some of the matter in Dr Hodnet's discourse and he in turn had taken exception to these objections. His letter concludes thus:

> You tell me that I said of our Lord that for forty days and forty nights he feasted in the desert when I had meant fasted, I protest before God that I did not. I protest. How could such a thing have passed my lips? What calumny is this, sir? Do you seek to drive me mad? And when you say that I had told your congregation: 'he that hath fears to fear, let him fear,' I did not. Do not try me with your foolishness, sir, and let all communication between us be at an end.

The final document I would have you consider is a pamphlet of a kind produced in thousands throughout the sixteenth and seventeenth centuries but which are now accounted rarities. This one is particularly rare. Indeed, the only one extant that I know of is in the possession of the St James's College library. It is dated 1679 and is entitled: *A True and Faithfull Relation of the Most Lamentable and Mysterious Death of the Rev'd Elias Hodnet D.D., sometime Provost of St James's College in the City of Cambridge.* The front of it carries a woodcut in a black border, crudely drawn but not without a certain power. It depicts a man standing in a pulpit in church, dressed in the usual lawn-sleeved surplice and black stole of an Anglican divine of that period. As no portrait survives of Dr Hodnet we do not know how true a likeness it is, but the figure is tall and lean with long lugubrious features. He is in the act of preaching but on his right shoulder crouches a curious black, misshapen creature with little stumpy wings. This demon holds up his hand to his mouth and whispers privily into Dr Hodnet's ear. To the right and pointing downwards is a huge hand emerging from a cloud, such as you will see often in this kind of print and depicting the hand of God. The scroll along the top of the woodcut bears a quotation from Genesis 11 verse 7. 'Go to, let us go downe and there confounde their language.' I will spare you the pious moralising with which this 'Relation' (like so many others of its kind) is larded and confine myself to the significant facts.

The pamphlet begins with a generally laudatory account of Dr Hodnet's career, but then it states, rather vaguely, that ''twas thought that in his latter years he became known of the Devill and reaped many rewards and benefits by that hellish association.' It tells how, having once been a noted preacher, his sermons began to decline in popularity because he 'began to wander in his wits, and dwelt overmuch upon the tortures of the damned.' Then came the fatal day in the April of 1679 when he preached his last sermon in the church of St Bene't's in Cambridge.

The pamphlet reports:

> He was to preach on that text from the Revelation of John: 'Behold, I stand at the door and knock.' And yet, in the course of his sermon, he was heard to travesty the words of this most sacred text as: 'Behold, I stand at the bridge and wait.' And each time he in error spoke these words—by what devilish prompting we dare not say—he did pause and look aghast and the most deadly pallor overspread his cheeks. Yet he continued to speak until his final peroration which we now set down just as he wrote it without alteration. Thus:—

> 'It is certain that the Kingdom of Hell is of a truth within us, but also upon this earth. Surius saith that there be certain mouths of hell, and places appointed for the punishment of men's souls, as at Hecla in Iceland, where the ghosts of dead men are familiarly seen, and sometimes talk with the living, and where lamentable screeches and howlings are continually heard, which strike a terror to the auditors; moreover, fiery chariots are commonly seen to bring in the souls of men in the likeness

The Sermons of Dr Hodnet

of crows, and devils ordinarily go in and out. For God would have such visible places, that mortal men might be certainly informed that there be such punishments after death, and learn hence to fear God. Thus we may glimpse, but through a glass darkly, what torments the Lord of this World hath prepared for they who serve him. In the vaults of his darknesse, beyond the wall of Death, are many cries, but all unheard there, for every appeal to mercy, every supplication for pardon is swallowed up in the maw of Him whose mouth is that of a Raging Lion, whose stare, like the Basilisk's, turns all to stone, whose breath, like the Dragon, consumes with a raging fire, and whose body, like the Serpent's, returns upon itself and choketh all within it. Very truly hath Isaiah spoken: "There is no peace, saith the Lord unto the Wicked." For hath not the Lord of Heaven put those wicked persons into the hands of the Lord of this World? And hath not the Devil, for it is He, confounded their sleep with a thousand creeping things that wander unceasingly through the mazings of their house and minde, with many curious whisperings and scrapings? And hath not his servant Death put up his raw and bony head against my head and shrieked aloud words which I dare not speak? And are not the very waters of Baptism turned into a foul and stinking puddle? For when the soul is corrupted, then all is corrupt and there is no joy any more, and all the world is become a painted show. And behold he stands not at the door to knock, for the door is barred and bolted everlastingly. Behold there is another, by which I mean Satan, Lord of Hell, and he stands at the Bridge and waits, but he will not wait for long, for he is ravening to take us unto himself eternally.'

As he spoke these words all the congregation did sit in great amazement, and many, beholding his grasping of the air and the rolling of his eyes as he spoke, thought his wits distracted; and some said he was bewitched and thought to lay hold of him. But he of a sudden did run from the pulpit and out of the church

The Complete Symphonies of Adolf Hitler

door, and though some followed him few saw what happened next for he did run with great speed like a wild horse affrighted.

But there was a certain undergraduate, a Mr Kimball, who in an idle hour was standing fishing by the Queens' Bridge over the Cam and we have it of him what happened next. As he was fishing by the bridge he noticed all of a sudden a figure upon the bridge that was dressed all in black with a black hat on his head. His features Mr Kimball could not see for they were all in shadow which he said was a curious thing for it was a fine morning. And another thing he did observe of the man which struck him with much amazement and that was that the man in black who had a large and corpulent body seemed to glister all over with water and that an odour was wafted from him which smelled much of the corrupt mud at the bottom of an old mill pond or of graveyard mould. Then, as he looked, Mr Kimball did see another man come running towards the bridge from the city, and this man was in his middle years, he said, narrow-looking and thin as a rush-light, and he ran, said Mr Kimball, as if seven devils were after him. Then, when this running man, who was Dr Hodnet, came to the bridge he halted as he saw the man in black. Then the man in black did stretch his arms towards Dr Hodnet, whether in greeting or for some other reason, Mr Kimball cannot say. Then Dr Hodnet uttered a great cry and ran at the man in black as if to strike him down, but the man in black folded his arms around Dr Hodnet and held him fast. Anon began a struggle which, sayth Mr Kimball, was most terrible to see for the man in black did grip Dr Hodnet with big splayed hands which, Mr Kimball reports, must have been gloved for they were as black as the rest of him, and the fingers being long were like the talons of a great eagle around the mean and frail body of the Reverend Dr Hodnet. And all the while Dr Hodnet did utter the most piteous cries, such as 'Christ have mercy!' and 'Lord defend me, though I am but a sinner!' Mr Kimball says that he dared not bring aid to this distracted man for, he said, he was held fast by mortal terror for his life and soul. Then Mr Kimball saw that with one great heave, the man

The Sermons of Dr Hodnet

in black did heave Dr Hodnet over the bridge and that he went with him into the flood. And they were swept down beneath the waters and in a moment had vanished from sight.

Such was the most lamentable and tragicall fate of the Reverend Dr Hodnet. Some days later his corpse was discovered some two miles down the river from where last he was seen, at Horningsea. His features being much blackened by corruption and eaten away of vermin, it was only by the aid of the Revd Mr Beard, who knew him from the rings on his fingers, that the body was shown to be the mortall remaines of the Provost of St James's College. Of the Man in Black no trace or sign was ever found.

The reader may imagine for himself the kind of vapid moralising with which the pamphleteer concludes his sensational account. As to Hodnet's sermons, whose beauties were said to rival those of Taylor himself, they were never to be published, as the Doctor dearly wished them to be. Moreover, the manuscripts have been lost to posterity, though I yet live in hopes of unearthing an example among the archives of St James's College.

MAGUS ZOROASTER

Only the day before it happened I had been telling my agent how much I resembled Clive MacIver. And now he is dead; MacIver, that is; not—alas—my agent.

I was always being mistaken for him. This led to some embarrassing moments, such as when I was asked my opinion of the latest novel by Martin Amis in a book shop, or when I was attacked in an art gallery for not approving of Balthus. (And *I* like Balthus.) Sometimes I told them I was not Clive MacIver, but I wasn't believed; so I found it easier just to give some drivelling reply and clear off.

Magus Zoroaster

I should explain. I am Alec Soames, a mere actor; Clive MacIver is—sorry, *was*—a television personality, an arts presenter, a regular participant in those programmes which review the week's cultural highlights. He projected a personality of amused contempt, knowledgeable, not to say knowing, but detached. This appealed greatly to the British public, an essentially Philistine lot, which prefers expertise to enthusiasm. His languid voice had a slight Scottish accent which prevented him from appearing too snobbishly superior. I learned to do the voice very well, and amused my friends with a pastiche of his style:

'I don't understand why the English can't play Brecht. What is Mother Courage after all but a lower class Lady Bracknell?' And so on.

Well, I can't do all that now because he is dead. Murdered in fact.

It all happened on a slightly sultry June night in London. At the time I was appearing at Wyndhams Theatre in a revival of *The Clandestine Marriage*, the eighteenth century comedy by Garrick and Colman. I was playing the not very large part of Traverse, a lawyer who appears at the start of the third act and then again in the last scene. It was a pleasant enough job, but I was not as busy as I would have liked or deserved to be. The production had received lukewarm reviews and was coming to the end of its shortish run.

The known facts about MacIver's death, as far as I could gather from the newspapers, were these. On the night in question he was heard and seen leaving his flat in Ebury Street a little after seven. His movements after that were uncertain until he turned up at Harpo's, a fashionable club in Dean Street, Soho at 9.05. He had some conversation with the barman, but seemed restless, had one drink and left. He must have gone straight back to his flat because at 9.40 the police received a frantic call from him on his mobile that he was being attacked in his home. When the police arrived they broke in to find him in his bedroom, stabbed. There were obvious signs of a struggle, but the knife which killed him had disappeared, as had the mobile phone with which he warned the police.

The obituaries and tributes spoke fulsomely of MacIver's intellectual and presentational gifts. He was 'a true populist and yet a brilliant academic who maintained his scholarly integrity in bringing culture to the masses.' At the same time I detected a certain lack of personal warmth in these eulogies. One colleague described him as 'a lively and entertaining companion', but that was as far as it went. I gathered that there was a wife and child from whom he had been living apart, but that there had been no-one in particular in his life when he died. A rather irregular sexual lifestyle was hinted at.

A week after MacIver's murder the notice went up at the theatre: we were to close in a fortnight. I was not looking forward to being out of work. When I rang up my agent she told me that things were 'very quiet just at the moment'. It is a phrase which her profession uses all too often. The life of a theatrical agent, it seems, compares favourably with that of a Trappist monk for quietness.

Then I had a bit of luck; and it was all thanks to Clive MacIver, I suppose. A day before the last night at Wyndhams, Betty, my agent, rang me up to say that she had something for me. There is a television programme called *Criminal Records* on the BBC which is about real life crimes and which claims to help the police by performing reconstructions of these events. They had been desperately searching for a MacIver look-alike to appear in a programme on his murder. Could I see Jean Box tomorrow morning? Jean Box was one of the most successful of the new independent television producers, and one of her shows was *Criminal Records*.

It was quite funny really. Jean Box could hardly contain her excitement that she had found someone who was not only a dead ringer for MacIver, but was also an established actor. At the same time, she had to be terribly solemn about it all. A respected colleague, a TV presenter no less, had been murdered. It was the most appalling tragedy. The programme, which was to be entirely devoted to MacIver, would, she hoped, not only help to catch his killer, but also be a tribute to him. I went along with this and said that anything I could do to help I would. I gave Jean Box a little taster of my impression of MacIver's voice and she was in raptures. As soon as I was out of the building I rang Betty and told her that we had Jean Box by the short hairs and we were to ask for silly money. An offer came through, we rejected it and finally we settled for a very respectable sum indeed. Filming was to begin the following Monday evening.

The most interesting thing about the filming for me was meeting the police. Detective Inspector Bentley was in charge of the case, and on the Monday afternoon I met him for what he called a 'briefing' at the local police station. He showed me the murder room, introduced me to the other officers on the case, then ushered me into his office. I liked him immediately, and I think he liked me. He is one of what the newspapers are always calling 'the new breed of policemen', neat, efficient, thorough, with a nice line in dry humour. Like Jean Box, he was amazed by the resemblance.

'This actually could be very useful,' he said. I told him that I would like to know as much as possible about MacIver, so that I could get inside him, so to speak. He looked at me curiously for a moment, then nodded. It was a gesture of respect, the acknowledgement of one professional by another.

'Our real problem is the missing two hours,' he said. 'Between his leaving Ebury Street at about 7.05 and his turning up at Harpo's just after nine we have no record of where he was and what he was doing. He seems to have vanished into thin air. I gather that he made some loose arrangement to meet some friends in a restaurant at eight. Yet he misses them, but turns up at this club, has one drink and then goes straight back to his flat where he is attacked, apparently by someone he knows because there's no sign of a break-in. If we can solve the mystery of those two hours, we've cracked it. That's where you come in; you just might be able to jog someone's memory.' I said I'd be only too glad to help.

'Those two hours are the main difficulty,' said Bentley, 'but it isn't the only one. In a real murder case, as opposed to a fictional one, there are plenty of loose ends, but usually they don't add up to anything; they're just odd coincidences, but this one is different. I'm sure they all mean something but we can't think what. You understand this is all background for you and goes no further?' I nodded.

'First thing: MacIver was seen leaving the flat wearing a light fawn overcoat, known to be his. Odd to be wearing it on a warm night. He has it on at Harpo's too, then it disappears. We can't find this overcoat anywhere in the flat. Has the attacker or attackers taken it? If so, why? Second: MacIver is found stabbed, lying across his bed. It was a warm night, as I said, but the bedroom central heating had been full on and so was the electric blanket on which he was lying. All that's made it very difficult to establish the time of death.'

'But surely you know the time of death? Some time between when he made the call on his mobile and when the police found him.'

'Yes. But there's this other odd thing, the mobile. There's a telephone in the bedroom; why didn't he use that?'

'Easier to use if he had it in his hand and was trying to fend off his attacker.'

'Possibly, but then his mobile was missing from the flat. We found it in the street not far from the flat the next morning. It had been thrown under a car, presumably by his attacker the night before.'

'The attacker stole it, then realised it could incriminate him, so he got rid of it. Any fingerprints?'

'None. Then there's the oddest thing of all. MacIver lets in his assailant, so presumably he knows something about them. Then the attacker or attackers get nasty, so he flees the room and rings the police on the mobile from his bedroom. He gives his name, part of the address, says he is being attacked, but—crucially—he doesn't reveal who's assaulting him.'

'Panic. Runs out of time. Just wants to warn his attacker off.'

'Or attackers. Maybe. Anyway, food for thought. We'd better get to the location, as I believe you call it. I think they're going to start with a shot of you leaving the flat.'

The rest of the evening was less interesting. I was dressed up in a replica of the famous fawn overcoat and filmed repeatedly from various angles leaving the Ebury Street flat and walking along the road.

The following morning was more interesting as we were shooting at Harpo's and I had lines to say, and it was then that the full weirdness of my position hit me. It was particularly odd because the other people I was filming with were not actors but the actual people who were there on the night of MacIver's death.

MacIver had entered the club, flashed his membership card nonchalantly at the receptionist and entered the bar. There he had ordered a large neat scotch and talked briefly to the barman. On seeing an acquaintance he had waved at him, drained his scotch, and left muttering to the barman that he 'had to get back', presumably to meet his killer.

It was while I was enacting all this that an event occurred which seems, especially in the light of what followed, rather uncanny. The barman and I had reconstructed what he considered to be a fairly accurate version of the conversation he had with MacIver the night he was killed. The first time we rehearsed the scene, I took the glass of scotch from the barman and happened, for some reason, to tap the rim of the glass twice with the fingernail of my left index finger. The barman looked at me in blank amazement.

'My God!' he said. 'That's a habit of his. He did that with his glass that night!'

Everyone was silent. Cold sweat ran down my back. For the first time, I am ashamed to say, I became fully aware of the horror of what had happened. Until that moment the job of impersonating MacIver had been nothing more to me than a bizarrely interesting assignment. Now I felt an obligation to the victim, and an inexplicable identification with him. After a pause the Director said: 'Right, Alec. Keep it in.' It was a pity they had not been recording that rehearsal. We did several fairly successful takes of my little scene with the barman, but none had the spontaneous electricity of our first run-through.

We broke at midday and I had nothing to do until that night when I was filmed going in and out of Harpo's. Jean Box came up to me after we had wrapped to say that she was terribly pleased with what I had done that morning. She wanted to retain me to do various other scenes of me as MacIver which she and the director proposed to blend in cunningly with actual footage of the man, thus making the programme a uniquely seamless drama documentary. She was going to make this edition of *Criminal Records* a specially extended one. It could be remarkable, she said; it could win BAFTA awards. She didn't say that it could catch MacIver's killer, but I am sure she meant to.

The experiences of the day had disturbed me. My identification with the dead man had been more complete than I had wanted it to be, and though this had probably enhanced my performance, it left me emotionally battered. When I want to unwind I have found that walking soothes me as nothing else can. People are funny about walking about London late at night, but I like it and, if you avoid the pockets of poverty, you are safe. Those leafy streets of modest Victorian terraced houses are the ones I enjoy walking the most. Their inhabitants are neither very rich nor very poor, and, because they often fail to draw blinds or curtains at night, one can often catch a glimpse through their front windows of the lives they lead. They are all very different, all subtly imperfect, like me. They fill me with a sense of the richness of life, and the need to struggle and succeed in a way that neither the squalor of poverty nor the airless perfection of wealth can.

It was a long walk to Willesden Green where my flat is, but I was in the mood for it. The first part of my walk, from Soho, via Oxford Street and up the Edgware Road, I enjoyed. It was when I got into Kilburn and Queens Park, those areas I usually like best, that I began to feel uneasy. I suppose I could attribute it all to strain and exhaustion, but it was more than that. I have been exhausted before and not felt the same. At first it was no more than a vague sense of not being free. Usually these walks are liberating experiences which detach me from my own life and put me in touch with the lives of others. This time it was as if I was carrying myself with me, like a snail with its shell. I could not shake off my own environment as I usually could. However fast I walked something always kept pace with me.

By the time I was past Queens Park and into Brondesbury the feeling was no longer so vague, but had acquired some sensory manifestations. I thought I heard footsteps which were almost in step with mine, but they stopped a beat or two after me when I paused to listen to them. If I turned to look behind me there always seemed to be part of the street where the shadows seemed unnaturally thick. Imagination? It is possible, but if these things were its product, then a part of me was observing them with extraordinary coolness and rationality. I was not afraid, you see, only intensely annoyed that my walk had not done its usual healing trick.

When I finally reached my flat, I was so worn out that I simply undressed and got into bed before immediately falling into a heavy, dreamless sleep.

The Complete Symphonies of Adolf Hitler

In the course of the next week I did some more filming. I also became increasingly aware of being followed, not only at night, but during the day too. I was happily released from the idea that it was my own aberrant brain playing tricks on me when I actually saw my stalker, a man wearing an overcoat. He was too quick for me to see him for long, but I did get quite a good look on two occasions when I happened to glance out of the window of my flat. It was dark and I saw only his shape, but it was more than a shadow. He was standing under a plane tree talking into a mobile phone. In my experience imaginary beings do not carry mobile phones.

On my last day of filming for *Criminal Records* I was at the BBC. They wanted some shots of MacIver at a planning meeting and walking on and off the set of a discussion programme. By this time my performance as MacIver had become alarmingly accurate, and I had the pleasure of giving Germaine Greer a nasty shock. She and MacIver had recently crossed swords over Sylvia Plath.

I was surprised to see that Detective Inspector Bentley had turned up for my final outing. I was glad to see him, because I needed to satisfy myself that it was not the police who were following me for some mysterious reason. Bentley seemed genuinely surprised to hear what I told him. He said vaguely that he would look into it, but it was obvious he didn't believe me. He even asked me directly if I was quite sure it wasn't my imagination.

When the programme came out a week later it was highly praised, and my performance was commended. My agent became excited by the prospect of offers pouring in, but I pointed out to her that there was a limited market for impersonators of dead media personalities. My stalker was becoming increasingly assiduous, and occasionally I had the impression that there was more than one of them. Once I rang up Bentley, but he was dismissive, almost rude.

Magus Zoroaster

Then one morning the bell of my flat rang. It was the police. They wanted to take me in for questioning about the murder of Clive MacIver.

They took me to the Belgravia police station where the murder room for MacIver had been set up and I was made to wait for something like four hours. At last I was shown into an interview room. There was Bentley and a sergeant. The sergeant seemed familiar to me: had he been one of my stalkers?

Bentley sat down opposite me and introduced his assistant as Detective Sergeant Weyman. They asked if I wanted a solicitor present, but I declined the offer, so there were the usual formalities connected with switching on the tape machines, then the interrogation began.

'Mr Soames, why did you never tell us you had recently met MacIver?'

'Have I?'

'While you have been waiting here at the station we had your flat searched. We found this on your shelves. It's inscribed.' Bentley threw down a book onto the table. It was a copy of MacIver's last work: *Goya's Dream: The Origins of Contemporary Culture*, based on his television series of that name. The cover featured a reproduction of Goya's etching: *The Sleep of Reason Brings Forth Monsters*.

I was not rattled. I said: 'I hardly call a few seconds in a crowded book shop a meeting. I happened to be in Waterstones when he was signing, that's all.'

'More than a few seconds. Look at the inscription: "For Alec, '. . . ere Babylon was dust . . .' Astonished good wishes, Clive MacIver." "... ere Babylon was dust..." What does that mean?'

'Some sort of quotation. I can't remember the significance.'

'Rather incurious of you, Mr Soames. Well, Sergeant Weyman tracked it down for me. The internet's a marvellous source of information. Apparently it's from Percy Shelley's poem *Prometheus Unbound:*

> "... ere Babylon was dust,
> The Magus Zoroaster, my dead child,
> Met his own image walking in the garden.
> That apparition sole of men he saw."

'MacIver had seen his double in other words, and was remarking on it in a rather cryptic way in his inscription.'

'Ah.'

'A little more than just "Ah", I think, don't you? Did you talk at all with Mr MacIver?'

'No. I told you. It was a brief encounter in a book shop. There were crowds waiting for his signature. There wasn't time.'

'He didn't ask you to have a drink with him or anything at his flat?'

'No. Why should he? What are you getting at?'

'Mr Soames, I believe you murdered MacIver.'

I was half expecting something like this after all the bluster. As a result, I didn't explode with indignation or do anything that innocent people are supposed to do. I remained terribly calm; I almost frightened myself with my own calmness. The only physical reaction to the shock was that the extremities of my fingers went cold.

'How d'you make that out?' I asked. 'In the first place I was in the theatre on the night in question. Hundreds of people saw me.'

'I enquired about your role in *The Clandestine Marriage*. Not a very big one, was it?'

'Traverse the lawyer. It's an important part. And I was understudying Melvil.'

'The performance began at 7:45, you're on stage at around 8:30 and off at 8:40. Then you go on again at about 9:50 and the curtain comes down at about 10:10.'

'What are you suggesting? That I went all the way to Ebury Street, killed MacIver and came back between 8:40 and 9:50?'

'No.'

'Then how? And why?'

'I'm not concerned with the motive at the moment; but I do know how you did it.'

'I didn't. And anyway it's impossible,' I said, but Bentley was quite sincerely convinced I had done it. He and his sergeant did a lot of 'Why don't you make it easy on yourself and confess now?' stuff, to which I responded with the contempt it deserved. I pointed out to them that I had an unshakeable alibi for the time between 9.40 when MacIver phoned the police and 9.53 which was when the police finally broke into MacIver's flat.

'Only if he was killed then, which he almost certainly wasn't.'

'He can't have been killed *before* he rang the police.'

'*If* it was MacIver who rang the police.'

'Even if someone faked his voice—and I suppose you think it was me—he can't have got back to his flat much before 9.40 if he left Harpo's at 9.10.'

'If he ever did go to Harpo's.'

I told Bentley that he wasn't making any sense at all. He leaned back in his chair and contemplated me. It was not a look of hostility; in fact I don't think I'm flattering myself if I say that he was looking at me with admiration. Misplaced, of course.

'I told you that I thought that all the little inconsistencies and oddities of this case had a single solution. The trick was to make some sort of leap of the imagination and find it. I began to suspect you very soon after we had first met. You were so eager to oblige. There is a type of psychopathic criminal who loves to help the police with their investigations, especially investigations of their own crimes. It somehow confirms their cleverness. At that stage the suspicion was only a vague uneasiness, but one learns to pay attention to these intuitions. Then there was your performance at Harpo's, again almost too good to be true, even down to imitating MacIver's little mannerism of tapping his glass with his fingernail. Of course, it could all have been an uncanny coincidence. It occurred to me then that you might have known more about MacIver than you were letting on, and that out of some actor's bravado or vanity you were incorporating that knowledge into your performance. This led me on to the even more radical possibility that the mannerism was not, after all MacIver's, but yours.'

I could do nothing but shake my head in bewilderment. He went on: 'The barman recognised that little mannerism as MacIver's because he had seen MacIver do it in the bar on the night he was murdered. But what if that *wasn't* MacIver in Harpo's bar. Mightn't it have been you?'

'Impossible. I was at the theatre all night.'

'Harpo's is in Dean Street, about five minutes very brisk walk from Wyndhams. You came off stage at 8.40 which gives you a good twenty-five minutes to change out of your costume and into MacIver, slip past the stage doorman—elderly and not very attentive, as I discovered—and go to the club. You had stolen MacIver's wallet when you killed him, so you had his membership card, not that you needed it. You have one drink, establish your presence there and leave. Plenty of time to change back and make your final appearance on stage in the last act at 9.50.'

'You're forgetting the phone call from MacIver's flat at 9.40.'

'It might not have been from his flat. It was from his mobile which could have been anywhere. I suspect that you took the mobile to some remote corner of the theatre's backstage area and made the call using your excellent impersonation of his voice. Then after the theatre you went to Ebury Street and threw the mobile under a car expecting that it would probably be found in the morning after the car had driven away. Anyway, we're liaising with the phone company now: they may be able to pinpoint the specific location where the call was made. We should have the results back very soon'

Magus Zoroaster

I had to concede that his conjectures appeared possible but hardly likely. Perhaps the phone company would come up with something. But it was intolerable to be accused in this way, so I felt it my duty to find some flaw in his argument. I pointed out that he was forgetting that MacIver had been heard and seen leaving his flat at 7.05.

'That was you again. The fact that the man seen leaving the flat did so rather noisily suggested that he might have been drawing attention to his departure. As soon as I realised it was you all the little problems seemed to resolve themselves. The fact that it was a hot night and yet MacIver was found dead on a warm electric blanket in an overheated room always suggested that someone was trying to confuse us about the time of death which must actually have occurred at about seven. The fact that the man seen leaving was wearing a fawn overcoat on a sultry night was also suggestive. That overcoat was a characteristic garment of his and would provide an effective yet simple disguise for you. Once it was off, you could become yourself. You wore it again at Harpo's and then you got rid of it. Everything is explained, you see from the missing overcoat to the apparent missing two hours of MacIver's life between seven and nine.'

'It's a theory,' I said. 'That's all it is, and there's no way you can prove it.'

'Until we hear back from the phone company, that is,' he replied carefully.

'If they can give you the information you require. Which I doubt.'

After this there was a long pause and then Bentley said: 'I'm aware of that. I just wanted to tell you that I know *how*. But I'd also very much like to know *why*.'

So would I, as it happens.

The Complete Symphonies of Adolf Hitler

He was standing in my way. That's the clearest explanation I can give, though I know it's hopelessly inadequate. Like Magus Zoroaster who met his own image in the garden, he blocked my path. I am an actor, a good one. I need success. I didn't realise it at first when I began to see him on television. It irritated me, that was all. There was this impostor with my face, mouthing pseudo-intellectual rubbish, favouring a reluctant public with his ingenious, inane opinions. I would watch him fascinated, regardless of whether his wretched programmes were interesting or not.

Then I noticed something. I leave you to draw your own conclusions. Whoever 'you' are, because I don't want anyone to read this, naturally. I have to pretend that there is a 'you' to share my thoughts.

Where was I? Yes. Those television programmes with MacIver in them. I began to realise that after I had been watching them, I felt mentally and physically drained. I was exhausted; I couldn't think straight. Sometimes the feeling lasted into the next day and I could barely get up in the morning. I tried to stop myself from watching him, but it was hard. And whenever I saw him on television it was as if he was sucking out my brain cells through the screen. At last I understood. He owed his success to the fact that he had found some way of drawing on my energies, because I was his double. Somehow he had found out about me and now he was living off two bodies, two brains, his and mine. No wonder he was a success. No wonder my career was on the slide. I had to confront him and tell him that I knew what he was doing and demand that he give me my life back. The problem—I was fully aware of this—was that he could just laugh in my face, tell me I was mad. Because that's what it must seem like to the outside world, just a mad delusion, though I happen to know it's true. So, reluctantly—

Magus Zoroaster

That quotation from Shelley which the pretentious git wrote in my book; remember what it went on to say? 'Magus Zoroaster, my *dead* child . . .' (My italics.)

He was dead. Why? *Because he met his own image, and because there was only life enough for one.* The Doppelgänger legend states that if you meet yourself, you will die soon. MacIver was slowly killing me, so it was kill or be killed. Self defence really; though I doubt that would stand up in court as an excuse. I'm not stupid enough to think that.

I followed him around a bit, got to know his habits. I laid my plans slowly, though I knew I had to do it during the run of the play. Small part, you see, not enough energy for a big one. Then, I only had to meet him. How? Well, at last this force, this energy which had been running against me for so long started to favour me. MacIver had just brought out a book and, as I was passing Waterstones in Piccadilly, I saw a poster announcing that he would be signing copies there the following week. So I went at the appointed time, bought a copy of his book and joined the queue in front of his desk to have it signed.

I could see the fear in his eyes when he saw me. He knew that I had found him out, but he made a very adequate pretence of seeming unconcerned. After he had signed my book he handed me a card.

'Here's my number. Give me a call some time. Let's have a drink.'

I have to admit, I had no idea what his game was. Perhaps he saw this as an opportunity to finish me off, drain the last ounce of energy and success out of me. How, I was not sure. That I discovered later. As far as I was concerned he had issued a challenge, and I must take it up. What he didn't know, and what gave me the edge, was that I had been laying my plans for this meeting for weeks before. I rang him up the following day, said I would be passing Ebury Street on my way to the theatre round about a quarter to seven and could I take him up on his kind invitation?

Bentley was correct, of course, about all the superficial details, the mechanics if you like, of the killing. I respect Bentley as a professional; and I believe he respects me too, as a professional. But what he couldn't know—or understand—was what happened between MacIver and me.

I arrived there at twenty to seven and he let me in. He was in a buoyant mood. He gave me a drink and started to ask me about my family. He seemed obsessed by the idea that our resemblance had some sort of genetic origin, but I knew this was just a blind. Well, we drew a blank on the ancestral front. We were not related, and we both knew that the explanation lay far deeper than that anyway. MacIver paused and smiled: the first skirmish was over.

'I'm doing a Sunday Arts programme on self portraits,' he said at last. 'Perhaps we could use you. I can't think how at the moment, but it's an interesting idea.' He led me towards the huge mirror he had over the fireplace. We stood side by side looking into it. I was marginally taller, I suppose, with perhaps a little more hair, but otherwise it was uncanny. Once or twice I found myself looking into my eyes and then realising that they were not my eyes but MacIver's. That must have been a trick of his, to make me do that. He smiled, then he said: 'Have you ever fantasised about having sex with yourself?'

I stayed calm, but it was a horrible moment. MacIver had planned to take the last drop of energy and spirit from me by means of the sexual act. My last vital fluids would be absorbed into him and he would be filled with my life. It was something finally to know his game. Swallowing my revulsion, I smiled at him.

'It's an intriguing idea,' I said.

'The charm of novelty,' he replied. Our eyes locked in the mirror and again I had the odd sensation of looking at myself and then finding that it was him. He put his hand on my shoulder and with a friendly compelling movement pushed me through into the bedroom. When he took his jacket off I knew the moment which comes only once had arrived, so I took the knife out of my pocket and stabbed him to death.

Now they suspect me of murder. I don't mind that because after all it's true. Bentley is a smart man and I would have been disappointed if he hadn't guessed. We both know that a jury cannot convict on an ingenious theory alone. I had been very careful not to leave fingerprints or other traces. I even took precautions at Harpo's, though I must admit that that little trick of tapping the glass with my fingernail (which is my mannerism) was a mistake. The tricky thing will be the phone records. I still don't know what the results of their enquiry have been. But if they're bluffing, as I suspect, my position is still very strong, which means there will be a stalemate.

All the same, I am annoyed that they won't believe me when I say I am being stalked. I *am* being stalked; it happens more and more; I can barely stir outside my flat without hearing the footsteps behind me, but they won't believe me. I also know *who* is following me. I caught a glimpse of him in a shop window; and they *certainly* wouldn't believe me if I told them who it is. I'm not afraid, though. He's not a threat to me now that he's dead, just a damned nuisance. The police should believe me and do something about it; that's what they're there for: to help the living, not the dead.

Aristotle said that one of the advantages of being thought a liar is that no-one believes you when you tell the truth. Of course, he was being ironic. (How the hell did I know that about Aristotle?)

The Complete Symphonies of Adolf Hitler

Note by D.I. Bentley:

The above document was found on an encrypted computer file after a second, more extensive search of Soames's flat. It was this which finally secured his conviction for the murder of MacIver. He received a life sentence because he refused to plead diminished responsibility. Oddly enough, though at the time I didn't believe the story about his being followed, it did turn out to be true. I had put Soames under surveillance and D.S. Weyman, who is not given to imaginative flights, swears that he saw a man shadowing him on a number of occasions. What Weyman also swears is that Soames's pursuer looked uncannily like Soames; and uncannily like MacIver for that matter. Weyman tried several times to apprehend the stalker, but failed. I leave readers of this file to draw their own conclusions.

During the trial some facts emerged about the origins of Soames and MacIver which could be of significance. They were twins and had been secretly adopted by two sets of parents. This had never been disclosed to them because the birth mother and father, as well as the surrogate parents, had all been members of a strange cultish commune called the House of the Moon which had broken up amid considerable scandal in the late 1960s. The true parents of Soames and MacIver could not be traced because they were only ever known by their cult names of Baphomet and Selene. Rumour had it that they were brother and sister.

The last word should go to Shelley's *Prometheus Unbound* which was, in a way, what had turned my vague suspicion of Soames into a conviction, so to speak:

> For know that there are two worlds of life and death:
> One which thou beholdest; but the other
> Is underneath the grave, where do inhabit
> The shadows of all forms that think and live
> Till death unite them and they part no more . . .

THE TIME OF BLOOD

The dream came again last night with greater intensity.

It was a warm night and so in my dream I got out of bed to open the window, but the view that met me was not the familiar one of the town square and the *mairie*. Instead, under the moonlight, a great sea stretched from a distant horizon right up my hotel's façade against which it slapped and lapped. It was not a rough sea, but something stirred beneath its surface like a restless sleeper under a blanket. Then from the far distance a speck of white began to move towards me. The speck resolved itself into a young woman in a white shift streaked and splashed with blood and she was running over the sea towards me. I could see now that, as her bare feet struck the surface of the sea, it sent up little splashes onto the bottom of her shift, and the splashes were not of water but red blood. So, as she ran towards me over the sea of blood, she became bloodier and bloodier from the splashes. I could see that her eyes were bright and fixed on me with a dreadful purpose. By this time I had become aware that I was dreaming, and I knew that it was absolutely necessary that I should wake before she reached me. I began to struggle in the straitjacket of sleep which held me sluggish and half paralysed. At last I snapped the bonds and broke the surface into wakefulness, sweating and struggling for breath. The room was stifling, so I walked to the window, opened it and looked out. The *mairie* and the town square stood still under the moonlight. Far away on a road below the town, a solitary motorbike roared its way to an unknown destination, an oddly reassuring sound.

෨

Montjouarre in Burgundy is one of those French provincial towns you pass through on the way to somewhere else. You might even have broken your journey there for a coffee or a beer, because it is a pleasant looking if unspectacular place. It is situated on the Petit Morin, a tributary of the Marne, in fertile arable land. It has a fine Romanesque church on its highest point and near to the war memorial in the municipal gardens can be seen the ruins of an Ursuline convent built in the sixteenth century, but they are neither extensive, nor particularly interesting. The former convent had been the headquarters of the local Gestapo and was razed to the ground when the Germans withdrew in 1944.

Two days ago I arrived there on a soft grey September afternoon when the whole town seemed to be so fast asleep that I wondered if it would ever wake up. I booked into the Hotel du Commerce in the main square, then walked across it to the *mairie* which stood opposite. There I managed to rouse a somnolent concièrge to make an appointment to see M. Le Maire the following morning.

It was three o'clock in the afternoon, and there was nothing else to do. I looked at the church and then walked into the municipal gardens. In a dusty open space flanked by two rows of heavily pollarded plane trees stood the war memorial. It was carved from a mottled grey stone and showed a stolid, bucolic looking *poilu*, in an aggressive pose, rifle clutched in his big, clumsy stone hands. Underneath the words MORT POUR LA PATRIE was a long list of those from Montjouarre who had been killed in the First World War. A shorter list of names from the 1939-1945 conflict were carved on the reverse of the monument. The stone *poilu*, turning his head, stared fixedly, and, as I thought, rather fearfully at the ruins of the convent which were situated in the shade of a grove of plane trees to his left. I walked in the direction of the *poilu's* gaze towards the ruins, because, after all, it was they which had brought me to the little town of Montjouarre.

For the most part I could barely see the outline of the foundations. Here or there a wall was standing which showed an architectural feature of some sort, an arched entrance, or a traceried window. Where there had once been flagstones there was grass, criss-crossed by yellow trackways where countless feet and bicycle wheels had worn through the sward to the sandy clay beneath. I sat down on a stone bench, and stared at a bare archway at the base of which had been put a small notice.

ABBAYE DU SAINT ESPRIT, XVIième SIÈCLE

A sudden little wind whipped up a few newly fallen leaves and sent them eddying across the grass before they flattened themselves against one of the convent walls. I felt cold and damp. I would rather spend my time reading in my dreary hotel room than sitting here where the air seemed loaded with unspecified threat.

⚜

For some years I had been researching a book about Fénelon, Bossuet and the controversy over that extraordinary mystic Madame Guyon in late seventeenth century France. Researches led me first to the Bibliothèque Nationale, then to the cathedral archives at Meaux where Bossuet had been bishop for the last twenty-three years of his life. Much of his correspondence is easily accessible. The French revere this great preacher, theologian and controversialist so that almost everything he wrote has been published. But, like most scholars, I dream of finding that little cache of enormously significant documents which have somehow escaped the defiling hands of time and scholarship.

In the cathedral archives at Meaux are a number of documents relating to Bossuet's time as bishop there. They are mostly routine stuff: charter renewals, ecclesiastical licenses, reports of legal disputes over church lands. Perhaps the most interesting papers—and even they are not that interesting—are those relating to the annual visitations which Bossuet made to the convents, abbeys and monasteries in his diocese. Being a strict and upright churchman he was capable of making very trenchant remarks wherever he found that discipline was lax, or the finances disordered. I was skimming through these, looking for any letters, indeed anything in Bossuet's own hand when, among the papers relating to a foundation of Ursuline nuns at the Abbey of Montjouarre, some twelve miles southwest of Meaux, I discovered a note—not, however, in Bossuet's own hand—which intrigued me. It was written in sepia ink, possibly by Bossuet's secretary, Ledieu, on a single sheet of paper, and was dated May 5th 1704, a little under a month after the Bishop's death. It read: 'All papers relating to Madeleine Lapige, née

The Time of Blood

Chanal (Sister Angélique) returned to Montjouarre at the request of the Lady Abbess, Mme de Lonchat.'

Though I looked everywhere I could find only the most cursory reference to the Abbey of Montjouarre and none whatsoever to Sister Angélique. I might have stopped there except that on my return to the Bibliothèque Nationale in Paris I decided to look up Montjouarre in the indexes and see what books they had on the subject. A rather dull-looking local history written in the 1950s yielded the information that the Abbey of Montjouarre had been almost completely destroyed in the Second World War. It had however not been an abbey for some time, the nuns having been expelled and the building turned into a military academy by Napoleon. A footnote informed me that at the time of the Abbey's conversion from a spiritual to a warlike function all the papers relating to the Abbey on the command of the Emperor had been moved to the *mairie*. It was somehow a typically Napoleonic act: the attention to detail, the respect for the past combined with ruthless secularism. Now that I knew there was a possibility of these papers still existing I felt obliged to pursue my researches into them, even though they probably had only a marginal connection with my chosen subject. As it happened, I felt the need for a break, so the following day I left Paris for Montjouarre.

ଔ

The next morning I was at the *mairie* sitting opposite a neat, bright-eyed, plump little man in a large, sombre office. My experience of French mayors is slight but on the whole very favourable. Their attitude is serious but relaxed and affable and they are often men of culture with a high regard for the arts. M. Georges Hubertin, Mayor of Montjouarre, was no exception. After a brief interview he told me that there was indeed a box of papers relating to the Abbey and invited me to dinner at his home that night to discuss the matter further.

The dinner was excellent: Cepes à la Bordelaise, followed by Chateaubriand; the wine was a superb Chambertin; Madame Hubertin and their two teenage daughters were charming. The French have a natural reverence for scholarship and intellect and I was an object of particular interest in being an English intellectual with an interest in French culture. After dinner Hubertin and I were left to discuss matters over coffee and cognac.

'I have only heard of the Abbey papers mentioned once before,' said M. Hubertin. 'In about 1890, the local priest, a man with some intellectual pretensions, asked to see the papers, and, having done so, requested that he might take them away and destroy them, claiming the right as a priest of the Church to have jurisdiction over ecclesiastical documents. The then mayor, who happened to be my great-grandfather, also a proud bearer of the name of Hubertin, was most indignant that such ancient documents should be consigned to the flames. Besides, he was a good freethinker and had no great love for M. Le Curé. However, he was a politician and therefore always ready to compromise for the sake of peace, so he promised that these papers should be placed in a box and locked up. He assured M. Le Curé that the box would not be opened for a hundred years and that the key to the box should be passed from Mayor to Mayor with this explicit instruction. M. Le Curé was not happy with the arrangement, but he had to content himself in the face of my great-grandfather's inflexible will. He was heard to mutter that he wished he had destroyed them while he had the chance. Not long after he died in what I believe were bizarre circumstances. I cannot remember what they were: I will try to find out for you. And now the one hundred years is up, Monsieur. More cognac?'

It was that night—the night before last—that I had the dream for the first time. The first time it merely puzzled me.

The Time of Blood

The following morning M. Hubertin and I met at the *mairie* and went down into the cellars where the papers were kept. He told me with great pride how for nearly six months towards the end of the war two Jewish families had been hidden by his father and uncle in these cellars, 'right under the very noses of the Gestapo!'

After some rummaging around we discovered a very large japanned tin box with a label on it announcing that it contained papers relating to the Abbaye du Saint Esprit. As he did not want them to be moved from the *mairie*, Hubertin arranged that a small room in the building be allocated to me for their inspection. I could have access to it in normal office hours, and it would be locked at night. If, at the end of my examination, I required any copying to be done, this could be negotiated. It seems a very fair arrangement, though the prospect of spending a week or so in Montjouarre at the Hotel du Commerce is not altogether agreeable to me.

The papers relate to every part of the Abbey's history from the foundation in 1583 until its dissolution. I soon discovered that the papers concerning Sister Angélique mentioned in the archives at Meaux consist mainly of a correspondence between Jacques-Benigne Bossuet, Bishop of Meaux, and Madame de Lonchat, Abbess of Montjouarre.

At this point let me insert a brief note about Madame de Lonchat. She had been the wife of the Viscomte de Lonchat and, like most of the aristocracy, had spent much of her life in the suffocating splendour of Versailles at the Court of the Sun King, Louis XIV. There she had enjoyed an unusual reputation for virtue and piety. On the death of her husband in 1692 she determined to leave the court immediately in order to lead a life of contemplative prayer. Within a very few years, thanks to the influence of her friend Madame de Maintenon (by then Louis' morganatic wife), she had became Abbess of the Ursuline

Convent of Montjouarre. Aristocratic Abbesses were a feature of seventeenth century France, and, while some were lax and dissolute, many, like Madame de Lonchat, were conscientious, even if they had obtained their positions through birth and influence.

The letters begin in February 1702 when Bossuet was seventy-five, two years away from his death. At that time he was a revered figure, but no longer the power in the land that he had once been. Only three years before the famous controversy with Fénelon had ended with an apparent victory for Bossuet, but many believed that his reputation had been tarnished by the scandal it had caused.

ೞ

From Mme de Lonchat, Abbess of Montjouarre to M. de Meaux 16th February 1702.

Your grace's last visitation was a precious encouragement to us all. My Sisters have well heeded your counsel regarding over-scrupulousness and excessive mortification. But I write to you because I have a concern regarding one of my charges, Sister Angélique, not long consecrated in our Sisterhood. You may remember this girl. The daughter of a prosperous grain merchant, M. Chanal, she came to our Abbey to be educated with her sisters at the age of nine. She proved herself most apt and obedient, not only in her schooling but in her devotions, and she endeared herself to all here by her sweetness and natural piety. When the time came for her to be removed from our care at the age of sixteen, she begged to be allowed to stay and become a postulant of our order. M. Chanal objected strongly for he had plans to marry her off advantageously as she was a girl of great beauty. Madeleine, as she was then called before she took the name of Sister Angélique at her clothing, resisted his wishes

The Time of Blood

most vehemently and ran away from home several times to find refuge with us. At last we appealed to you on her behalf to arbitrate in this matter and you yourself were gracious enough to speak to the father and persuade him that God had indeed called his daughter to a life of prayer and renunciation.

That was three years ago and Sister Angélique is now a full member of our order. Until recently I can report nothing but good things of her. She has increased in grace and favour with our Lord Jesus in every way. She has been dutiful, but never over anxious. Only in one respect had she troubled us and this was not her fault. I hesitate to mention such matters before you, Monseigneur, but I believe it to have some bearing upon what follows. From the age of fourteen when these things began, somewhat later than is customary, she had very grievous periods [*Elle avait des règles tres douloureuses*]. The effluxes of blood were great, and she herself—until reassured by myself and Sister Jeanne, the Mistress of Novices—was convinced that they were the consequence of some mortal sin. These events coincided almost invariably with the appearance of the full moon, a fact which added to her distress. Indeed, while she was still a postulant it was the occasion of some teasing among the other Novices, but Sister Jeanne and I put a stop to that.

Of late the fluxes of blood have become even more grievous, so much so that I called in M. Filerin the apothecary who prescribed an infusion of Bay and Camomile, but this has had no effect.

These afflictions which cause Sister Angélique much pain and distress may occasion much sympathy in your Grace's munificent heart, but this is not the reason why I have called them to your attention. They appear of late to have affected her mind.

As you know, we allow a short hour of recreation for the sisters between Vespers and Compline. During this time the sisters generally congregate in the garden in summer or, when it is cold, in the parlour where a fire is always kept burning for visitors. On a number of occasions I have noticed that Sister Angélique was not present. Though I am not, as your grace is aware, well disposed to idle gossip in the parlour, it worried me that Sister Angélique was keeping herself from the society of others. Such a habit, as you have often so wisely pointed out, leads to the errors of singularity and spiritual pride. Last Friday, which was, as it happens, a time of the full moon, Sister Angélique being absent from the parlour as usual, I sent Sister Jeanne to fetch her from her cell. Jeanne returned without Sister Angélique and apparently much troubled, so I accompanied her to Sister Angélique's cell where I found the girl in a distracted state, her robe dabbled with blood and the floor awash with it.

But there was something which troubled me more than this. Upon the white wall of her cell some words had been written it would appear in blood. That they had been traced in her own menstrual blood and with her own finger was evident. The words were as follows.

> *Ictibus flos Galliae quattuor verberabitur belli*
> *Incipiet quarto, sanguinis aevum, anno.*

It is, as you, Monseigneur, will know better than I, a Latin elegiac couplet, but its meaning is to me quite obscure. Though it is no doubt of little merit as verse, and full of false quantities, it is strange to me that this young girl to whom only the rudiments of the Latin language have been taught, should have written such a thing. When asked why she had done it Sister Angélique replied, in great distress, that she could not remember how it came to pass. I am disposed to believe her, for she is not in herself wicked or malicious.

[Mme de Lonchat is correct: the verse is an Elegiac Couplet of sorts. Translated it means:

> *The flower of Gaul shall be struck by four strokes of war*
> *The Time of Blood shall begin in the fourth year.*]

The Time of Blood

I am informed by Sister Jeanne that at her time of trouble Sister Angélique is prone to strange utterances, and that she is regarded by some of the more credulous among our community to be gifted with prophesy. Whether her words are of God or the Devil is beyond my competence to say. Though I would be very disinclined to dismiss any manifestations which may be true fruits of the Spirit, I am concerned that she may be having an undue influence over her fellows. This would have an unfortunate effect on them, but chiefly on her, giving the girl an exaggerated sense of her own importance. Sister Angélique's family is perfectly respectable, but she is a bourgeoise and cannot hope to obtain any great position of eminence within our order except by corrupt and illegitimate means.

I would be most obliged if your grace would offer us the benefit of your sacred guidance on this matter.

From M. de Meaux to Mme de Lonchat, Abbess of Montjouarre 19th February 1702.

The ways of Divine Providence, my dear and reverend Mother, are very great, and we should not hasten to pass judgement on strange events and happenings. A study of the scriptures reveals a wealth of utterances which astound those who boast of worldly wisdom. However you are right to be concerned that a young untried soul such as Sister Angélique should be the vessel of such mysterious sufferings. But I would ask you respectfully Madame to reflect carefully on the words you wrote about Sister Angélique's station and ancestry. The honours of your own rank and family are a blessing if well used, but God's dispensation extends to all. I would remind you that the situation into which God called me to be born was not exalted. God in his wisdom calls monarchs and nobles to a special privilege and office, but he does not neglect his little ones. Though in the eyes of the world we are called to our appointed places, in the eyes of a Merciful God we are as one. As Christ called his disciples from the humble fisher folk of Galilee, so he called me from a line of Burgundian drapers to drape myself in the mantle of priesthood and perhaps Sister Angélique from the family of a seed merchant to cast the seed of the word of God among men. It is not for us to question His ways.

It is, however, our duty before God, at all times to show wisdom and moderation, and here I must commend you highly, firstly in showing restraint towards Sister Angélique, and secondly in seeking my counsel which is ever, my dear Madame, at your disposal.

I have read and pondered over your letter with much prayer but I have not yet a complete answer for you. The direction of souls is a mystery: I strive to be faithful in passing on what is given to me; when I seem to have received nothing I yield the whole to God and beseech Him to compensate for my deficiencies.

In the meantime, my counsel is this: when Sister Angélique's time of trouble—which you say is at the full moon—comes upon her, let her be separated from her companions and watched by a Sister upon whom you can rely for the utmost discretion. Let all her words and utterances at this time be noted down and sent to me, but let them be shown to no-one else. In all other respects you are to treat Sister Angélique as quite ordinary. She is neither to be despised for her curious conduct, nor exalted for it. Let her be encouraged to associate freely with her fellow sisters and not hold herself in any way apart. Let her be seen at all times whenever possible as one like all the others.

I commend this counsel to you, Madame, as the best that my human and fallible intellect can devise. I pray for the guidance of the Holy Spirit when I am better informed, and beseech you therefore to hold this humbly-born servant of God in your prayers, ever willing, however falteringly, to walk in His ways and dwell in the Light of his Mercy.

From Mme de Lonchat, Abbess of Montjouarre to M. de Meaux 18th March 1702.

Taking your grace's excellent counsel to heart, I did as you requested, and, at the last full moon, when Sister Angélique's affliction came upon her, I set her apart in an unused quarter of the Abbey in the charge of Sister Jeanne, our Mistress of Novices. I enclose the report that she compiled of her observations. You may rely on her account both for its veracity and its discernment. She is a Montmorency and a niece of the Duchesse de Chevreuil.

Account of Sister Jeanne's observations regarding Sister Angélique over a period of three days. For the eyes of Madame, the Abbess and M. de Meaux alone.

On the day commanded by the Lady Abbess, I brought Sister Angélique to a room in the East Wing of the Abbey which is no longer inhabited. Sister Angélique at first complained at being brought into such unfamiliar surroundings, which were, moreover, both incommodious and cold; for this wing has fallen somewhat into disrepair: there are birds nesting among the broken roof tiles and the wind moans along the corridors at night. But I told her that she was not to object for it was the will of God that she should be kept apart. And, moreover, that it was the will of Her Lady Abbess and His Grace of Meaux. I further told Sister Angélique that if I could suffer discomfort to fulfil my vow of obedience to the Lady Abbess and M. de Meaux then surely she could, as she was the cause of it all. At this Sister

Angélique consented with a reasonable grace, and showed some humility.

I had contrived to make our accommodation as pleasant as possible without in any way submitting to the temptation of illicit comforts or self indulgence. Towards the evening of the first day Sister Angélique began to bleed. I ministered to her as best I could. The efflux of blood was very great, but she did not seem much weakened by it, though she had become very pale.

She called for pen and paper which, following my instructions, I supplied to her, and yet she did not use them. I urged her to write her thoughts, but she remained abstracted, her eyes rolling in her head, never fixing themselves on any object. Then I saw that she was in pain and once more afflicted with a great outpouring of blood. I became more troubled when it began to appear to me that she was attempting to harm herself with the pen which I had given to her. But then I saw that she had merely intended to dip the pen in her own blood which she contrived to do, and then wrote the following:

> For the Ludovici one more and then a time of blood shall come for the Kings of the earth.

When I encouraged her to use the ink which I had supplied for her she hurled both ink pot and pen into the corner of the room and sat at her table sulking, rapping the table with her fingers, making a sound like a drum. When I tried to remonstrate with her she shouted 'Silence!' at me in a most terrible voice.

She then began to speak very rapidly in an unnatural and rasping voice. So I, recovering the pen and the pot of ink (which, fortunately, was not all spilt), took down her words as best I could. In obedience to my instructions I place before M. de Meaux a record of what she said:

The Time of Blood

'It is the ninety-third year. My years are thirty-eight. I climb a wooden stair towards the sky. Slowly. My feat are heavy, but now I stand upon the stage. Below me heads, nothing but heads, as far as the eye can see, an ocean of them agape and chattering. They come to tie me and throw me down. Do not resist: the Saviour, in whom we trust, submitted to be bound. The sky holds a heavy knife above me. Frenchmen, I die innocent . . . I desire that France—'

At this she resumed the drumming of her fingers on the table which I could not in any way prevent. Then, suddenly, she stopped and resumed her speech :

'Six men of blood seize me: do not bind me to the plank. Son of Saint Louis, ascend to Heaven. I lie down and wait. An eternity awaiting the fall. A sharp pain. I am a tumbling helpless head, sickened, held on to life by a string. A hand lifts me and shows me to the heads. My lips gasp. A raw rush of air drowns me in agony. I am your . . .

'See the Head. Hear the shout. Caps upon spears, hats waving in the air. The licking of the blood. Let the King beware.'

All the time that she was speaking these words the blood leaked from her, and when she had done speaking she collapsed in a swoon and I ministered to her as best I could.

                                    Sister Jeanne of the Holy Child.

Note by Mme de Lonchat, Abbess of Montjouarre.

Soon after this, the effluxes of blood ceased in Sister Angélique. I have since questioned her and she says that she can recall nothing of what she said before Sister Jeanne. It is clear to me that in these states she is the unwilling instrument of some power, but whether this power is celestial or infernal I have no way of knowing. Your own discernment, Monseigneur, would shine a precious beacon of light into this troublesome business, and I would beg you therefore to speak to Sister Angélique herself and then give us guidance with regard to her condition.

From M. de Meaux to Mme de Lonchat, Abbess of Montjouarre 5th April 1702.

Madame, I have little to add to what I said to you when I came to interview Sister Angélique at the Abbey. She seems in many ways a docile and obedient creature. I am convinced that her utterances are involuntary, but as they appear not to be conducive to the safety of the Sacred Person of His Majesty, I require that you should continue to confine her during her periods of affliction with one other Sister for companion. I furthermore request that you should make no further record of her utterances and that any writing of hers should be destroyed.

From Mme de Lonchat, Abbess of Montjouarre to M. de Meaux 23rd May 1702.

I must beg your indulgence, Monseigneur, but since we last corresponded a calamity has occurred, the magnitude of which it is hard to calculate and for which we must bear some responsibility. With regard to Sister Angélique, I naturally followed your instructions most diligently and saw that, whenever she appeared to be afflicted, she was strictly confined. I put Sister Jeanne, my Mistress of Novices, in charge of her as before, and all appeared to go well. I did notice, however, that Sister Jeanne was in Sister Angélique's company perhaps more than was necessary and that she had a great influence over her. I spoke to

The Time of Blood

Sister Jeanne, advising her to moderate this familiarity, and she appeared to listen to my admonitions. However a few days after Sister Angélique and Sister Jeanne had been confined together at the time of the Full Moon, Sister Jeanne disappeared. Sister Angélique was bereft and had no idea where she had gone. In a few days, however, news came that Sister Jeanne was in Paris with her brother Jacques. This Jacques de Montmorency is considerably older than Sister Jeanne and a man of most evil reputation. It was said he was an associate of Catherine Montvoisin who was at the heart of the Affair of the Poisons. I was at court at the time and remember the dreadful scandal that it caused, as it reached up to the very person of His Majesty himself. Of course, I had no knowledge of this, but it would appear that Sister Jeanne had been communicating the utterances of Sister Angélique to this Jacques who saw in them much profit in publishing them as prophesies. (Your Grace knows well how much such things delight the vulgar populace, especially when they concern the fate of those set over them by God.) I have since ensured that Sister Angélique is confined where she can do no further damage and is in the hands of trustworthy custodians. I beg, your Grace, to consult further with me in this matter and give us the benefit of your Holy guidance.

From Etienne Planteloup, Lieutenant General of Police to M. de Meaux 26th May 1702.

I am authorised to inform Monseigneur that the brother and sister Jacques and Solange de Montmorencey, formerly Sister Jeanne of the Ursuline convent at Montjouarre in your Diocese, have been imprisoned in the Castle of Valenciennes by sealed letters [*lettres de cachet*] of His Majesty for attempting to publish sedition. They are to be kept separate from all other prisoners, for an indefinite period on a diet of bread and water.

The Complete Symphonies of Adolf Hitler

No one, unless authorised, to speak to them on pain of death. You are required by His Majesty to say nothing of what you know of the said Sister Jeanne and to silence all rumours concerning the matter of the alleged prophesies which she sought to disseminate.

From M. de Meaux to Mme de Lonchat, Abbess of Montjouarre 29th May 1702.

Madame, since your last communication, I have suffered much anguish and trouble as a result of your carelessness in the matter of Sister Jeanne and Sister Angélique. You were so kind as to suggest that I bore some responsibility for the calamity that has occurred, but, I assure you, this is a burden of guilt you must bear alone. Had you followed my counsel and kept Sister Angélique well confined in the hands of some responsible person instead of this Sister Jeanne in whom your trust was most lamentably ill-placed, none of this would have occurred. I am now convinced that Sister Angélique is no longer safe in your keeping and that she has mistaken her vocation as a nun, a fact which greater attention and humility on your part should have recognised long since. I have spoken with her father, Monsieur Chanal, and we have agreed that she should receive a dispensation from her vows and be married as soon as convenient. There is a widower of M. Chanal's acquaintance, a M. Lapige, who is prepared to waive the matter of a dowry on account of certain debts that he owes M. Chanal. He is some twenty years older than Sister Angélique, it is true, but in good health and, M. Chanal informs me, a worthy man. He owns several hectares of land and a farmhouse where he lives with his elderly mother. The house, though furnished in adequate comfort, is remote from populous habitation and there a life may be lived secluded from prying eyes and ears. In these surroundings Sister

The Time of Blood

Angélique, or Mme Lapige as she soon will be, will find her time fully occupied with useful duties and cares, and, if M. Lapige does his duty, her monthly afflictions will cease when she finds herself with child. I will ensure that all these matters are expedited so that you will be relieved as soon as possible from a responsibility which, it would appear, you have found yourself ill-equipped to undertake.

[Evidently Sister Angélique sent Bossuet a letter some time in the July of 1702. Of this there is no trace, but we do have a copy of his reply.]

From M. de Meaux to Madeleine Chanal, formerly Sister Angélique July 14th 1702.

My child, I am by no means insensible to the pleas which you have laid before me with a sincerity and respect that does you credit. However, I must ask you in your turn to be assured that at all times I have been guided by your best interests in the sight of God. Do I presume too much on my sacred office? I assure you that I do not. Dear child let me make myself clear: though it is I who speaks to you; it is I who admonishes you; it is I who claims your attention; yet in secret the voice of Truth is speaking in my inmost being and equally to you. If this were not so all my words would be but a vain beating of the air. Outwardly I speak and you listen, but inwardly in the secret of our hearts you and I alike should be listening to the Truth which is speaking to us and teaching us. Follow then that Divine Truth to which I direct you and do not listen to the vanity of your heart. All will be made plain in due course; for Divine Providence, which speaks through me its humblest vessel, will always reveal itself to those who follow its sacred paths. You say that you have wept tears every day since your good father told you that you were to be taken from the Abbey and married; but let me, as your Father in Christ, assure you that in time that those tears that you shed out of wounded pride will be turned to tears of joy when you have abandoned all thought of self and given yourself to the path which wiser heads and Divine Guidance have laid down for you to tread.

[The final letter in this correspondence comes from the Abbess over nine months later, in 1703. By this time, Bossuet, a sick man, was no longer living in his diocese, but was being cared for in Paris.]

From Mme de Lonchat, Abbess of Montjouarre to M. de Meaux April 17th 1703.

Since your Grace has been so much in Paris of late, you doubtless will not have heard the news concerning Madeleine Lapige, formerly Sister Angélique. She was duly married according to your instructions to the man Lapige, quietly, soon after the dispensation from her vows was obtained, and went to live with him at his house which is situated some distance from the village of Bois-Oudry. No more than ten days after the marriage one of the sisters brought to me a poor girl who had been begging at our door for comfort and sanctuary. Her clothes were torn, her legs were caked with dried blood and she had been severely bruised about the face. She was quite incoherent, and it was some time before I recognised this poor wretch as Sister Angélique. From the very first, it would appear, this Lapige (who, we now discover, has a most evil name in the neighbourhood) had ill-treated her terribly. I will not shock you, Monseigneur, with a catalogue of the cruelties that this vile beast had inflicted upon her. Let it be sufficient to say that had I not been under the strictest instructions from your Grace, I would have had compassion on her and let her stay at the Abbey. Indeed she begged to stay, saying that she would have been happy to become the most menial of lay servants in the Abbey, to scrub floors and wash clothes, rather than return to Lapige and his devil of a mother who, if anything, appears to be more cruel than her son. It was with a heavy heart that I obeyed your Grace and sent for her father who took her back, weeping and protesting most piteously, to this Lapige. For some months no news of her reached me and I tried to put the poor girl out of my mind, having committed her to the Eternal Mercy of God. Then a few days ago the girl's father came to see me, a wretched, weeping and most penitent man. He accused himself of having killed my poor Sister Angélique, but this was not the case. When she returned to Lapige and his mother she was treated worse than before, but in the course of time she became with child. Rather than softening the hearts of these two monsters, it hardened both Lapige and his mother, who would not have her sleep in the house, but made her sleep among the animals in the barn. When the time came for her to be delivered of the child they secured the services of an old wise woman from the village of Bois-Oudry. She came most reluctantly, being under some obligation to Lapige and his mother. And so, Madeleine Lapige, once Sister Angélique, was brought to birth of a child in a barn among the animals; but such was her loss of blood during the birth, and such was the ill-treatment which she had suffered through no fault of her own, that she expired soon after that birth. There were also rumours about the nature of the child, that it was an abomination of deformity. Some even said that it had been born with a tail and was the Antichrist, but this is the gossip of foolish and ignorant people. It is true that the old woman who had been charged with delivering the child and who, the child having been born dead—this much is almost certain—disposed of its remains, was seemingly much distressed by the events. It is true that shortly after the death of Madeleine

The Complete Symphonies of Adolf Hitler

Lapige and her child this same old crone hanged herself, but that means nothing. She was a woman of the lowest sort and any number of explanations may be found for her untimely death.

Such was the dreadful end of a child of God who least deserved such afflictions. Her father, M. Chanal, a man for whom I never had much regard, did, at least show a decent regret that, under your instructions, Monseigneur, he had chosen such an unworthy husband for her. He presented me with some papers which, he told me, Madeleine had written in the last months of her life and these I send to your Grace. I do not know what they contain, and have no desire to know. The matter is at an end, and what remains of it is now in your hands.

I understand that your grace has of late not been enjoying your customary good health. May I assure you that I and my small community are earnestly praying for your speedy and complete recovery.

༄

Of the papers mentioned only one sheet appears to remain. It is written on very coarse paper and in writing that varies in size and legibility. Nothing is written in a straight line. It looks like examples I have seen of automatic writing in books on psychic phenomena. At the top of the page the following had been written in capitals:

NOVA APOCALYPSIS SORORIS ANGELICAE
[The New Apocalypse of Sister Angélique]

Of the storm-tossed sentences that followed this is what I could decipher:

Woe to the makers of war though they be princes.
The first blow shall be on Ister.

The Time of Blood

In the Time of Blood heads of kings and princes shall fall into the gutter. A king by his own falling knife felled. Woe to the mind that invented but did not see.

Gaul shall perish in the snows and her false king, alone, upon an island.

Then shall the nephew of the false king rise up and bring blood upon the nation from Rhenish Lords of War.

A black hand shall strike down a Prince and the whole world will shudder. Men will sink into mud to die and the Empire of Muscovy shall perish in a cellar.

Behold I saw beneath the storm clouds of a grey sky a new sea and that sea was a sea of blood. I walked between walls of wood and high hedges of sharp steel and my footfalls were in blood. Woe to you O Zion. Your people shall suffer and die in the years when the crooked cross [*la croix crochue*] shall reign.

Blood in the sky over a land of the rising sun. The sky blood will darken the whole world.

[There was then a space, and at the bottom of the paper in minute script was written:]

After the two towers have fallen the eagle and the lion shall capture Babylon and the wicked one shall be drawn from the tomb. Not long shall last their triumph, for weeping shall come upon them. Then comes the night time of our world when God shall sleep.

These last sentences have haunted me. When last night I dreamed again that a bloodstained woman came to me over the sea, I heard her speak for the first time, and those were the words she spoke.

∽

This morning M. Hubertin called on me in my little room in the *mairie*. He seemed particularly cheerful and asked if I would like to hear what he had found out about the priest who had handled the documents before me. I did not want to know, but I could not prevent him from talking. There was something about Hubertin's self-satisfied, almost exultant manner that I did not like. 'I found the information in my grandfather's memoirs,' said Hubertin. 'He wrote it purely for consumption by the family, but I must say it is a most fascinating document. Perhaps I shall have it published with an introduction by myself. Then I shall be a writer like you, Monsieur.'

'You were going to tell me what happened to the priest.'

'Ah, yes! To be sure. Poor M. le Curé! His housekeeper found him one morning lying at the foot of his bed. He looked as if he had had some sort of seizure; at any rate, he was dead. Two curious things were noted. Firstly, though it was a cold November, the windows of his chamber were wide open. The second was that his face and night-shirt appeared to be covered with curious brown stains. They were analysed by the pharmacist who pronounced them to be dried human blood; but no further investigations were made as there was little evidence that he had been attacked. It was curious, since he had not been cut or wounded in any way, and the blood did not appear to be his.'

M. Hubertin seemed delighted by his researches, but he did not leave me a very happy man.

I have with me a copy of Ledieu's Journals which record, in journal form, the last years of Bossuet's life and I have been searching them thoroughly for any mention of Sister Angélique or the Abbey of Montjouarre, but can find nothing. The only possible reference comes from almost the last entry in his journals. Bossuet was dying in the Rue St Anne in Paris in April 1704, almost a year after the Abbess's last letter to him. He was attended by Ledieu, his faithful secretary, and the Abbé St André, one of the most trusted of the clergy in his diocese. By the evening of April 13th he was sinking fast. Ledieu writes:

The Time of Blood

Then the Abbé St André asked if he should pray with him, to which Monseigneur [i.e. Bossuet] replied: 'Pray often, but only shortly, for I am in pain. Say the Lord's Prayer with me.' This the Abbé did, Monseigneur following him faintly, but when they came to the words *'adveniat voluntas tua'* ['Thy kingdom come'], I noticed that Monseigneur faltered and did not say those words, but spoke others of which I could not divine the meaning. Those words were: *'adveniet sanguinis aevum'*. Not 'May thy kingdom come' but 'The Time of Blood shall come'. The good Abbé tried to correct Monseigneur gently, but Monseigneur continued to repeat the phrase *'adveniet sanguinis aevum'*. When the Abbé once more remonstrated, Monseigneur looked at him with great sorrow in his eyes and said: *'Quod dixi, dixi.'* ('I have said what I have said.') Then my good master spoke no more.

Jacques-Benigne Bossuet, the great Bishop of Meaux, died in the early hours of April 14th 1704. In August of that year Marlborough inflicted the first of his four crushing defeats on the French at Blenheim. That is why some may interpret Sister Angelique's Latin couplet as a prophesy of these events.

> *Ictibus flos Galliae quattuor verberabitur belli*
> *Incipiet quarto, sanguinis aevum, anno.*

> The flower of Gaul shall be struck by four strokes of war
> The Time of Blood shall begin in the fourth year.

I wish to remain sceptical, though in fairness I must add that in her document NOVA APOCALYPSIS SORORIS ANGELICAE she wrote 'The first blow shall be on Ister'. Ister is the Danube and the Battle of Blenheim took place not far from the Danube.

As for the rest of her prophesies . . .

The Complete Symphonies of Adolf Hitler

It is two in the morning as I write this. I am seated at a table in my hotel room. I will leave tomorrow. Certainly I will leave tomorrow, if I can stay awake. I fight sleep in this lonely, quiet place. I must not fall asleep in case I dream and she comes to me again over the sea of blood. This time she will reach me, I am sure. Last night she had run to the bottom of the hotel wall and was beginning to climb up it to my window. She climbs well. Her fingers penetrate the walls as if they were made of soft cheese, and the blood from her torn fingers runs down the walls in streams.

When she reaches me I shall be told what is to come, and the hateful gift must pass to me.

PARMA VIOLETS

'She's been here for over fifty years,' said Dr Maddox, the Senior Consultant Psychiatrist at the Morsby. 'There's nothing much wrong with her really, except that she's completely institutionalised. Care to ask her something? She's quite harmless. Won't attack you or anything.'

Smith peered through the little window in the door onto which had been screwed a small rectangular label bearing the single word, CANTEMERE. He had come to the Morsby Hospital to be interviewed for a post as a Junior Psychiatric Consultant and was conscious of being under scrutiny himself.

The Complete Symphonies of Adolf Hitler

The room was like the private room of any hospital, perfectly comfortable and well appointed, but bland. The colours were mushroom, pink and pale blue, and there were no pictures on the walls. Nothing there seemed to be the private property of its occupant, an elderly woman who sat very upright in a chair by the window, quite still, doing nothing. She must have been in her seventies at least, possibly much older. Her hair was white and her face still carried traces of great beauty. Her lips smiled but the large blue eyes, remarkably clear and bright for one of her age, told a different story, one of fathomless grief.

'Go in and talk to her,' said Dr Maddox.

Smith entered the room and introduced himself. The woman nodded, shook his hand then waved him to a seat opposite her. Smith was conscious, even before she spoke, that he was in the presence of 'a lady'.

'My name is Cantemere,' she said. 'Mrs or Miss Cantemere, whichever you prefer.' The accent was clipped and upper class, of the kind Smith had rarely heard except in old films of the 1940s and 50s. Having spoken these words the lady smiled sweetly, but when Smith tried to engage her in further conversation she remained silent. It was not that she was ignoring his presence: she looked him straight in the eyes and nodded from time to time quite equably. It was as if she had set herself a vow of silence and was determined to keep it. After a while Smith said goodbye to her politely and left the room.

As they were walking down the corridor Dr Maddox said: 'It's a rather odd story, would you like to hear it?' Smith nodded eagerly. This was turning into a very odd job interview.

Once they were in his consulting room, Dr Maddox went to a set of shelves containing rows of cassette tapes, all neatly labelled. He extracted one and put it in the cassette player on his desk. Smith had the feeling that everything had been prepared beforehand and that from the first Dr Maddox had intended him to hear the story of 'Mrs or Miss' Cantemere.

Parma Violets

'This is her speaking, about ten years ago now,' he said. 'The tape's been edited to cut out pauses, repetitions, extraneous material, but every word of it is hers, unprompted.'

He switched on the cassette player.

ಬ

My name is Cantemere. Mrs or Miss Cantemere, whichever you prefer. Julia Cantemere, actually. It's an unusual name. The legend has it that we are descended from the Cantemir family who were Princes of Moldavia. There is supposed to be a direct ancestor called Prince Dmitri Cantemir who was Imperial Chancellor to Peter the Great and all that. I don't know if this is true, or, if it is, how our branch of the family came to England. So there it is.

Well, my grandfather was a rich man, owned a couple of coal mines in Derbyshire, don't you know. He had two sons and my father was the younger. Of course the elder son got most of it, but my father was quite well provided for. He was a parson and when he moved to a London parish, I was able to do the Season. This was 1937. Just before the War, you know.

I had the best time. Absolutely killing. I was presented at Court as a *debutante*, then there was Queen Charlotte's Ball and after that there were dances every night, or so it seemed. Even my Pa gave one. Pretty smartly I palled up with two other girls that I'd been at school with: Bunty Hetherington and Ida Hart-Hemsley. We called ourselves the Three Musketeers and, my dear, we just *shrieked* with laughter the whole time. Bunty was our leader. She was an absolute hoot, got us into all sorts of hot water, but fun, don't you know. Nothing nasty.

Well, one evening, fairly late in the Season, we'd been to the Huntercombe's dance and it had been pretty drear, for some reason, so Bunty said 'Let's go somewhere else'. I said 'Where?' and she said 'Oh, anywhere, darling, let's just go out and explore.' So we left, there and then. We had a couple of boys in tow as I remember, Roddy Samford and Billy Millington, but they don't matter. I believe they died in the war.

The Huntercombes lived just off Belgrave Square, so we—or rather Bunty—thought it would be a lark just to wander about till we saw a house with lights and a bit of noise coming from it and simply invite ourselves in. Well, nothing looked terribly promising till we came to Chester Square. There was a house—I don't exactly remember now, but it was down the end where the church is, on the right hand side. We could see that the drawing room on the ground floor was lit up and there were people dancing to jazz on the gramophone, so Bunty said 'That looks like fun,' and just marched up to the front door and rang the bell.

Well, the door was opened by this positively svelte looking butler, and Bunty said: 'We've come to the party,' and the butler just let us in! So we went in to the drawing room where there were about a dozen people, men and women, like us in white tie and evening dresses, some dancing to the gramophone, some just sitting about and talking. They were a bit older than us, but I must say, they were awfully decent, and welcomed us in positively with open arms.

I felt a bit embarrassed about crashing like this, so I asked who our host or hostess were. I had this vague idea of apologising to them or something. But they said that the host wouldn't mind. He wasn't there at the moment, but he would be shortly. His name was Diels, apparently, and he was something frightfully high up in the German Embassy.

It was good fun; there was some top-class champagne, and the other people were fearfully interesting. Artists, you know, and that kind of thing. There was a painter and a poet and, my dear, this world-famous violinist whose name I've quite forgotten, but you'd know at once who it was if I could remember it. All the same, I still had a nagging feeling of guilt about our host,

Parma Violets

so I got it into my head—I don't know why, it must have been the champagne—that I must go and look for the host and personally thank him.

I went out into the hall, intending to ask that glamorous butler, but there was no-one about. Everything was terribly gleaming and polished, you know. There were these black and white marble flagstones on the floor and this great mahogany staircase with a red carpet on it. So I started to climb the stairs.

When I got to the top of the stairs, I saw all these doors on the landing, and only one was open. It was the one that opened on to a room directly above the one where the party was going on. So, greatly daring, I went in.

It was a library: my dear, simply floor to ceiling with books. There were a couple of electric table lamps alight and a fire burning in the grate. I was quite overawed, you know, but hold on! There's something I should say here that's frightfully important. The door I'd come in by was the only door to this library. I couldn't see any other. You must remember that.

Well, I suppose I should have got out at once, but I just loved that room. I had this thing about books and libraries, you know: must have got it from my Pa because he was a frightful old bookworm, bless him. So I started to look at the books. It was the most marvellous collection and all bound in leather and vellum and that sort of thing. Most of the titles meant nothing to me, but I do remember there was an edition of Suetonius's *Lives of the Caesars* bound in purple leather. Too sumptuous! And this made a great impression on me because, you see, my Pa used to teach me Latin and Roman History. That was his favourite, and he let me read all sorts of things, but the one thing he wouldn't let me read was old Suetonius. Apparently it has all this terribly shocking scandal in it about the emperors of Rome. So you see when I saw that Suetonius in purple leather I thought it was the most fearsomely decadent thing I'd ever seen. After all, I was only twenty, you know.

The Complete Symphonies of Adolf Hitler

I pulled one of the volumes out, and I remember thinking I'll just have the tiniest peep when I heard a voice say 'Hello!' It was the most tremendous shock and I dropped the book and turned round. And there at the far end of the room was standing this young man in white tie and tails.

It was too odd, you know, because I had been standing looking at the books just by the door and he would have had to come in and cross all the way to the far side of the room without my hearing him before he spoke. I wish I could describe him to you properly, but somehow I can't. Isn't that the most awful thing? I know he was dark and slim, about my age and a little taller than me. I do remember that he had the most beautiful hands. And I can't tell you what his voice sounded like either, except to say that it was a very nice voice. Nicest in the world, don't you know.

As you can imagine, I was simply covered with embarrassment, but he didn't seem at all bothered. I asked him if he was our host, Mr Diels. No, he said, Herr Diels was his uncle and he was staying in the house with him. He told me he was studying music. I asked him what his name was and it was then that I got the second shock of the night.

He told me his name was Julius Cantemere. The surname was spelt exactly like mine. And I'm Julia Cantemere. It was terribly odd, because I'd never heard of any other Cantemeres outside my immediate family. Julius told me that both his parents were dead, but that his father had been English. As far as we could tell we were no relation or anything. His mother, Hannah Diels, sister of Herr Diels, had been born in Hanover.

I'm not sure what people mean when they talk about 'love at first sight'. You hear someone saying how they saw this other person across a crowded room, their eyes met and they just immediately know. Well, that wasn't me. Not bang, like that. For me it was rather like when you go to stay in a house in the country where you've never been before. You arrive in the dark,

Parma Violets

and the next morning you wake up in your bedroom to find the sun is shining through the curtains, and for a moment you don't quite know where you are. Then, slowly, very slowly, you come to your senses, and you begin to realise that you're just in the most lovely place in the world. Well, that was how it was with me and Julius. After a few minutes we simply knew we were made for each other; can't explain it: we used to finish each other's sentences, that sort of thing.

I can't remember how the evening ended, but I know Julius and I arranged to meet somewhere the next day. The other thing I do remember is that I left without having met Julius's uncle. I never knew whether he was somewhere else or had been in the house the whole time and just didn't appear.

After that Julius and I were meeting the whole time. Suddenly I found that he was at all the dances I went to. Bunty and the rest just accepted him as one of us and we went round together. They thought he was wonderful, of course, but they knew he belonged to me. Naturally we were known as the Cantemeres from the off, and it was just taken for granted that we would marry. I took him to see my parents and they loved him too. He wasn't earning any money really, though he was already a wonderful pianist, but he had a generous allowance from his uncle who was childless, apparently.

Well, we wanted to get married straight away, and my parents just didn't have the heart to object. They could see how blissfully happy we were. Of course we needed to ask Julius's uncle too, because, though Julius was over twenty-one—just—he had, as they say, 'expectations' of his uncle. Everything was so perfect then, I barely noticed how reluctant Julius seemed for me to meet his uncle, but eventually a day was arranged and I went to see him at the house in Chester Square.

I met Julius in the hall and he told me that Uncle Joachim, as he called him, was waiting for me in the library. Of course, I had expected us to go and meet him together, but for some frightful

Germanic reason, Uncle Joachim had insisted apparently that he interview me alone. Well, I can't deny I was frightened, but at the same time, you know, I was so deliriously in love, I think I could have walked through fire for Julius.

So I climbed the stairs and found the library door which was shut and knocked on it. After a while I heard a voice say: 'Come!' (It sounded more like 'Kom!') I went in.

It was a dull, overcast sort of day—fearfully drear—and what light there was in the room came from the two great sash windows that looked out on Chester Square, so it was pretty gloomy as you can imagine. At the far end of the library stood a man. Half of him was in shadow but I could see enough to make out that this was the biggest man I'd ever seen in my life. Simply too enormous, my dear. He must have been at least six foot six and broadly built with it. He was pretty fat too, but he carried his weight well, so I got the impression that a lot of it was muscle rather than flab. His head was a matching size and what hair he had was cut 'en brosse'. I don't want to give the impression that he was some sort of comic book Teuton: there was nothing at all ridiculous about him. I don't remember too much about the face: heavy features, sort of brutal in a sophisticated kind of way, if you know what I mean.

He told me to sit down, which I did, as far away from him as possible, but then he approached. He had a heavy tread and his vast thighs chafed together as he walked so there was a great rustle of cloth on cloth. Then he was standing over me. It was like being at the bottom of a huge rock or something. Too frightful. But what I remember most was a smell, because it was so unexpected. It was a perfume, quite feminine, very strong. I couldn't place it at first, then I remembered. It was Parma Violets, a scent you could buy from Floris in Jermyn Street, you know. My mama was specially fond of it and I'd bought some for her that last Christmas.

Parma Violets

When Uncle Joachim spoke it was in a low, throaty voice—almost a whisper—with a heavy German accent. He said: 'So! You like the books.' You see, I'd been looking round at them: anything rather than look at him. He said: 'I have many books, concerning all kinds of things. All knowledge is good, no? None should be forbidden. This is how we become strong. Do you not think so, Miss Julia Cantemere?'

I nodded. I was simply petrified by this time. Then he walked over to the bookcase and pulled out one of the purple volumes of Suetonius and he started to read a bit from it about the Emperor Tiberius on Capri. Oh, it was utterly frightful, my dear, too disgusting—I can't tell you! All about these young boys and girls he got to—well, enough said. And every few sentences he would look at me and study how I was taking it all. It was awful. It was somehow like being watched while you're undressing, only worse, because it was as if he were seeing right inside me. It's terribly hard to describe. It was like a rape.

Well, in the end, he finished and put the book back. He came over to me and put his hand—horrible great paw—on my head. And he said: 'But soon you will be married, no?' I looked up at him and he was laughing at me. 'You must not look so shocked, little Miss Julia. Here! I will give you another book. A charming one, and you must read it. It will not hurt you.'

He walked over to a shelf and pulled out the most beautiful calf-bound volume with wonderful gilded stamping on it. The book had been bound in the eighteenth century but the printing was sixteenth or early seventeenth. It was William Adlington's translation of *The Golden Asse*—Apuleius, you know. I never read it till long after: wish I had read it sooner!

He pressed the book on me and said: 'Here! I give you. It has the most beautiful love story of the young lovers Cupid and Psyche. It is my present for your engagement. My blessing on your union!'

The Complete Symphonies of Adolf Hitler

Well, of course, I suppose it was very kind of him, but there was something about the way he said it that was really rather beastly—I don't know—as if he were picturing in his mind Julius and me—together, if you know what I mean. So I took the book, thanked him and literally fled downstairs. And that was the first and last time I ever saw Uncle Joachim.

I had to wait for a while in the hall for Julius because he wasn't there. After a bit he came out of the drawing room, and I showed him the book and told him that Uncle Joachim had given us his blessing. So then we went off and had the most huge tea at a Lyons Corner House and everything was bliss again.

We were married the following Spring and I'm relieved to say that Uncle Joachim could not come to the wedding. Apparently he was away on some terribly top-secret German Embassy business. This is 1938, I'm talking about, Munich and all that, so you can imagine. But he did give us wedding presents. To Julius he gave a simply vast cheque. I was not quite so delighted by my present, though. It was that awful purple leather bound edition of Suetonius and a huge bottle of perfume from Floris. The fragrance was Parma Violets.

You can't describe happiness. For the first six months Julius and I were in heaven; that's all I can say. We found this dear little flat on the top floor of a house in Fitzroy Square, and we just lived. Julius went on with his studies, but he was already beginning to make a name for himself as a pianist. He could play anything, you see, from Mozart to Gershwin at the drop of a hat, so he was always in demand at parties, and I went with him.

I think it was towards the end of the year that things began to change ever so slightly. Oh, it wasn't Julius's fault. He was still the same loving, darling Julius that he ever was, but, you know, he was beginning to be really rather successful, and he couldn't take me everywhere to all his concerts. And they used to take a lot out of him. He would come back simply drained and just sleep the clock round. I got terribly bored when he wasn't there,

Parma Violets

and just a little frightened. Suppose he had an accident, you know, on the way home, that sort of thing. Add to that, I somehow thought I'd be pregnant by then but I wasn't.

Don't get me wrong: by any normal standards we were still pretty blissful. I was a young chump, I suppose. I expected the heaven to last for ever and I wanted to bring it back to what it was. Anyway, that was why when our wedding anniversary was coming up, I got this simply wild idea into my head. Or it may have been Bunty's idea, I don't remember. I used to confide in Bunty, and she was bored as well because she'd just married this fearfully rich man, in ball bearings or potted meat, or something too mundane like that. Anyhow, the idea was that Julius and I would go to Uncle Joachim's house and go into his library and, my dear, we would re-create that moment when we first met. And we would do it on the anniversary of our wedding. Too romantic, or so I thought.

Julius didn't seem awfully keen on the idea. In fact, I think he secretly hated it, but because he was a darling and loved me to distraction, he agreed to go along with it. So we arranged to go to the house in Chester Square on our anniversary. Uncle Joachim was away on business, as usual, but the place was still fully staffed, apparently.

It was a lovely April evening when we got to the house in Chester Square. The butler let us in and we went upstairs together. Before we went in to the library Julius turned and looked at me, and he just said: 'Are you sure?' I can't describe how he looked at me, but it was as if I were a sort of stranger. I said yes and we went in.

There were two lights on in the library, one at a desk, the other a standard lamp by a wing chair. I had the strange feeling that the room had only just been occupied, but by whom? Uncle Joachim was away and I didn't think the servants would be great readers. I told Julius to stand exactly where I had first seen him that night, at the far end of the room. I took up my position by the books where I had been. Then for some reason I shut my eyes for a couple of seconds and turned round to see Julius. But he had gone. He wasn't there! Oh, God—!

[There was an obvious break here in the recording which, when it resumed, was in a slightly different acoustic.]

I called for him. I yelled. I ran all over the house looking for him. I shouted and rang for the servants, but they had all gone for some reason. Perhaps they were only hired by the day, I don't know. I tried the library for secret doors in the bookcases, all that lark, but nothing. I screamed the place down. I remember running into the library for the umpteenth time and just completely collapsing onto a sofa in utter floods. It was then that I became aware of this smell. I could smell that scent of Parma Violets that Uncle Joachim wore. It was so strong it was like a handkerchief drenched in the stuff being put over my face. It suffocated me. I think—I'm sure—I must have fainted.

I don't know quite what happened after that; I can't really tell you anything except that I was in sheer Hell, my dear, and have been ever since.

ಸಿ

'I won't play any more, of the tape,' said Dr Maddox. 'After that she becomes incoherent. But, from bits and pieces she's said since, I gather that she went on frantically searching for Julius, but he had simply vanished, leaving behind not a single clue to his whereabouts. She got the police to search the house in Chester Square, but by the time they had a search warrant to go in, they found the place deserted. Everything—servants, books, furniture, the lot—had gone, and no trace of Uncle Joachim. It appears he was merely renting the place. We're talking about only five months away from war by this time. Well Julia just

Parma Violets

went on looking—hired private detectives, the lot—and became more and more desperate. The war came, and then the Blitz. The house in Chester Square took a direct hit one night and the following morning they found Julia Cantemere wandering about in its ruins and refusing to leave. That's when her parents decided to have her committed to an asylum; they died soon after in another air raid, and she's been in institutions ever since. She came here about six or seven years after the war was over.'

Smith asked: 'What else do you know about her? I mean beyond what she's told you.'

'Well, not much. Her name really is Cantemere. She was a debutante and a parson's daughter and all that. And she did marry a Julius Cantemere in 1938. We have her marriage certificate. And we know he disappeared in April 1939, but beyond that, nothing.'

'What about Uncle Joachim?'

'The German Embassy has no records of such a person having been on their staff, but that proves nothing. So,' said Dr Maddox. 'Do you believe her story?' Smith hesitated. He had a feeling that he was being tested in some way, and that the job he had applied for might depend upon the answer he gave.

At last he said: 'Does that matter? Surely the important thing is that *she* believes it.'

Dr Maddox nodded approvingly and got up. 'There is one further piece of evidence I'd like you to look at,' he said.

He went to a glass fronted bookcase behind his desk and opened it. 'Mrs Cantemere came to us with very little personal property, but there were these.' Smith saw that among the medical texts and psychiatric journals were three books sumptuously bound in purple calf with gilded lettering. Dr Maddox took the first volume out of the bookcase and handed it to Smith.

'Suetonius?'

The Complete Symphonies of Adolf Hitler

Maddox nodded. 'But read the inscription on the fly leaf,' he said.

Smith opened the book. There were some fine marbled endpapers, innocent of a bookplate, and then two blank pages, one of which was inscribed in slightly faded blue-black ink:

To my darling Julia, with unfailing love, Julius.

Smith looked up at Maddox, baffled. 'It's from Julius, not Uncle Joachim,' he said. Dr Maddox merely nodded. Smith again examined the fly leaf which he now noticed had been very faintly stained by the drops of some liquid. Tears perhaps?

Wafted from the gentle upward blow of air as he closed the book, Smith caught the scent, faint but heady, of Parma Violets.

DIFFICULT PEOPLE

One Saturday in the Summer of 1968 a young man walked into my father's art gallery in Jermyn Street with a large portfolio under his arm. I was seventeen at the time and happened to be present when this occurred. During the school holidays it was my treat every Saturday morning to help out my father at the gallery, then we would go to lunch at the Traveller's Club.

The young man seemed an unlikely customer. He looked barely twenty and he wore ultra-fashionable Carnaby Street clothes, a turquoise shirt with a floral pattern and skin tight vermilion corduroys.

'Can I help you?' said my father, an unfailingly polite man.

The Complete Symphonies of Adolf Hitler

'Old Master Drawings,' said the young man. His face interested me. It was not exactly good looking—the mouth too wide, the brow too prominent—but his features were distinctive. He was of medium height, broad shouldered and stocky; a powerful physique lurked under the floral shirt. His deep set blue eyes looked at you with unhurried intensity.

'We do have a number of Old Master Drawings,' said my father. 'Which period interests you in particular?'

'I don't want to buy. I want to sell,' said the young man, holding up his portfolio. I knew even then that this was not the way my father usually did business.

'I see,' said my father, allowing an uncertain note to creep into his voice. 'May I have a look, Mr—?'

'Paul Xavier,' said the young man.

My father indicated a table upon which Xavier could lay his portfolio. 'I'll be happy to have a look,' said my father. 'Give you my opinion, but naturally I can't promise . . .'

'Yes. I understand,' said Xavier. There was something about the way he said these words which appealed to my father. It was neither truculent, nor obsequious: he spoke as if he were making a simple statement of fact.

My father opened the portfolio. In it were about thirty drawings mostly on tinted paper, in pen-and-ink, silverpoint, sanguine, chalk and other media. There were drapery studies, nudes, portrait heads, and one or two exquisite botanical drawings in conté highlighted with white chalk. They were beautifully done, but something about them made me uneasy, and I knew that my father felt the same.

'I'm afraid I don't deal in Modern work,' he said. 'These are not by Old Masters.'

I could see now that they weren't. They were highly accomplished pastiches of Old Master drawings in the style of Leonardo, Dürer, Raphael, Mantegna and others of the High Renaissance.

Difficult People

'They're not fakes or anything. I'm not saying they're actually old,' said Xavier.

'Who did them?' my father asked.

'I did,' said Xavier.

My father complimented him on his remarkable accomplishment and asked him where he had studied.

'I didn't,' said Xavier. 'I started by copying out of books. Then I used to go and copy at the National Gallery. But I'm not self-taught. The Old Masters taught me.'

Again my father complimented him and said that regretfully he could not sell any of his drawings. In his gallery he dealt exclusively in Italian and Flemish work of the High Renaissance and Baroque period. There were people, he was sure, who would be delighted to sell his work: he would be happy to give him some names and introductions.

Xavier nodded, shut the portfolio, said 'Okay!' and started to walk out of the shop. My father stopped him. He said he genuinely would like to help, and he would like to buy some drawings, not to sell, but for himself.

That morning my father bought two drapery studies and secured a promise from Xavier that he would come and discuss his career with him. This was something I had never known my father do before, but I think it was because of the guilt he felt about dealing in dead art while doing nothing to advance its living cause. His profound lack of sympathy with Modernism—indeed with almost anything produced after the Impressionists—inhibited him. Perhaps he saw Xavier, who seemed to have the skills and ideals of his favourite Old Masters, as a way of salving his conscience.

So my father became Paul Xavier's mentor and Paul, in many ways, became mine. I was an only child and he was the ideal older brother. Though only four or five years older than me he was a decade ahead of me in experience. He had come from a broken and impoverished home in Stepney, and almost everything he knew he had taught himself. His extraordinary gifts as a draughtsman had been recognised early on: there had been a flurry of interest in the papers and then he had been forgotten, but he persisted. At the time I first knew him he was living with his girlfriend Christine in a flat in Hammersmith. They survived on Christine's income as a travel agent and by his doing occasional labouring jobs himself. His views on life were sometimes crude, but forged by his own experience, not someone else's. However, as with all autodidacts there were gaps in his expertise. To some extent, we complemented each other because I, cautiously brought up and well-educated, had acquired a little learning in just those areas where he was weakest.

One of his lacunae was in the field of professional relationships. Like many artists, particularly at the beginning of their careers, Paul believed that talent would carry all before it; that as soon as his astonishing gifts were recognised, art lovers would flock to buy his work. The concept of cultivating clients and patrons was alien to him, whereas I, from an early age, had watched my father at work and absorbed some of his diplomatic skills. This is how I came to be involved in the whole affair of Victor Lyons and the portrait.

Before I knew Paul I had met Victor on several occasions at my father's gallery. The name Victor Lyons means nothing today, but at that time he was quite famous. He had a habit of appearing in the gossip columns and society pages, his name always prefixed by the words 'Property Tycoon'. He was one of the first and most successful of the developers who emerged in the late 1960s, men who took unfashionable and run down areas of London like Islington, Fulham, or Clapham, and turned them into nesting places for the up-and-coming. I have no idea whether Victor was typical of their breed, as I never met another like him, but, as a person, he gave the impression of being a type rather than a complete individual. He was in his early forties, on the small side, but well built, with a square head and decisive regular features. He dressed smartly but somehow not very elegantly. Even in casual clothes there was a sense that he was wearing what was expected rather than what suited him.

The feeling that he had no real taste of his own was confirmed by my father to whom Victor had gone to find out what sort of Old Master paintings he ought to have hanging in his home. Victor had said to him: 'Always go to the top man, whatever you want, whether it's bricks, ball bearings or great art.' He was full of such materialistic maxims, culled probably from one of those self-help business manuals with catchy titles that still regularly make the best-seller lists.

My father found him something of an embarrassment because Victor seemed almost to take pride in his philistinism. 'I just want the best, and you know what the best is,' he would say to my father who reluctantly obliged by producing for him some well-provenanced and solid artistic property.

When Victor decided that he wanted a portrait made of his new young wife—there had been a previous model, discarded for unknown reasons—he consulted my father who decided to take the risk of recommending Paul Xavier. He told Victor that Paul was comparatively unknown, but that he was destined for great things. This delighted Victor who saw an investment opportunity in his romantic gesture.

My father negotiated a good price for Paul but was too tied up with other affairs to tackle the business of introducing client to artist. This fell to me, as I had the leisure, the inclination and an opportunity to make use of my very recently acquired driving licence. So, one Saturday morning in May, I drove Paul out to Victor's house at Gerrards Cross in the white Mini I had been given on passing my test. I was an indulged young man.

I am not sure that I had any idea of the responsibility with which I was being entrusted, even though my father tried to impress its seriousness upon me.

'I want you to be careful,' he said. 'See that Paul doesn't put his foot in it too much. You've met Victor, and you'll meet Carmen his wife. They're what I call "difficult people".'

I had heard him use the phrase before and I asked him what he meant exactly.

'Observe and find out for yourself,' he said.

We had been invited to lunch. For Paul and I the expedition was pure adventure; it was a crystal bright early Summer's day, and our spirits were high. As we drove there we talked incessantly, so much so that twice we got lost and I had to stop to consult a map. (Paul, for all his visual sense, was quite hopeless with directions.) Paul did most of the talking: speculating on his future fame as a portraitist, telling anecdotes about his vagabond boyhood in Stepney and his trips across London to art galleries where he would sit down and copy the paintings for hours on end.

'You know I told you that the Old Masters taught me? Well, it's true. Quite literally. I don't want you to tell your father this. I have a great respect for him, but he wouldn't understand. They talk to me. I sit in front of Caravaggio's *Supper at Emmaus* in the National Gallery trying to capture that amazing foreshortening of Christ's arm, and he talks to me. He wasn't a queer by the way. He told me so. All the critics are saying he is, but it's rubbish. I know.'

I made no comment. In quite a short while I had acquired an understanding of how Paul was to be dealt with. You could laugh with or at him about everything except his opinions and his art. These were to be beyond ridicule or criticism. For someone as essentially tough as he was he could be morbidly sensitive. When discussing Paul's character with my father, I asked him if this is what he meant by 'difficult'.

'Oh, no. Paul's a mighty ego, but ultimately not difficult at all. He has bottom, you see.'

Difficult People

This was another of my father's enigmatic phrases which I could never persuade him to explain. He seemed to regard it as part of my education to find out for myself what he meant.

∽

Both Paul and I had somehow expected Victor Lyons to live in a grander house, but Gerrards Cross goes in for substantial comfort rather than grandeur. His home was one of those detached mock Tudor mansions set in its own grounds along a leafy avenue of similar mansions. The wheels of my Mini crunched into deep gravel as we came to rest beside Victor's Bentley. Paul stared at the spacious but unexciting proportions of the house, an apotheosis of suburban living.

'I'd pay good money not to live in a place like this,' he said defiantly. 'It's so dead.'

The door was opened by a swarthy Hispanic butler and we were ushered into a large mock baronial hall. The place was bigger than it had appeared to be from the outside. Everything, including the suit of armour which guarded one of the wooden pillars of the stairwell, was new. The place had the feel of a luxury hotel rather than a home.

We were ushered through to a large conservatory where, beyond the lush tropical vegetation, great sliding glass doors opened onto an emerald lawn, smooth as a billiard table; beyond that, a belt of poplars; beyond that, a white wicket gate leading onto a golf course. Now I realised why Victor Lyons had chosen the house. An exquisite Persian Blue cat reposing on a white wrought iron table stared at us in a nakedly hostile manner. We were allowed what I suspect was a precisely calculated minute to take in these splendours before Victor made his appearance. A chrome plated trolley laden with glasses and a huge jug of iced and fruited Pimms was wheeled in.

'Carmen will be with us in a minute. She's just upstairs . . . doing things.' I thought I could detect a trace of nervousness in his manner. He wore an immaculate pair of fawn slacks and a canary yellow cashmere cardigan over a check shirt, his Saturday uniform.

Embarrassing preliminaries were glossed over by the distribution and sampling of Pimms, a drink Paul had never tasted before. During a pause I complimented Victor on his proximity to the golf course. It should have been the right thing to say.

'They tried to blackball me, you know,' he said resentfully.

'What's—?' began Paul, but I restrained him with a warning glance.

'Luckily,' Victor went on. 'I already had a stake in the place. I was able to point out a number of legal difficulties which they might be getting into if they refused me. Anyway, water under the bridge. I'm on the committee now.'

'But why—?' began Paul again. Fortunately, at this moment, Victor's wife Carmen made her entrance.

Her feet were bare and she would have looked as if she had just got out of bed had she not been so carefully made up. She was dark and a great sweep of deep chestnut-coloured hair half covered one eye. Her figure was superbly voluptuous, her legs perfectly shaped. Her face was heart shaped and dominated by large, sleepy brown eyes. She wore a simple dress of dark red shot silk. Something about her confused me. The physical impression that she exuded was immensely sophisticated. She had the sexual allure of a thirty year old, and yet it would have been quite obvious, even if I had not been told, that she was actually not much older than I was.

She walked slowly over to Victor and kissed him on the mouth. I saw that they were almost exactly the same height. Then we were introduced. Having shaken my hand Carmen took no further interest in me, but she paid great attention to Paul, who was equally enthralled. This mutual fascination, I

Difficult People

think, had little to do with mere sexual allure; but they were both acutely conscious of the curious, dispassionate intimacy of their forthcoming relationship as artist and model. I do not remember what was said during these opening gambits; I only remember Victor's behaviour. From the time when Carmen had entered the room and went over to kiss her husband on the lips I do not think there was a moment when some part of him was not touching her. He did not paw her; his contact was light but it was constant. And yet they barely looked, let alone smiled at one another. Once I saw him touch her hand; instinctively, her fingers curled round his and squeezed them, but that was the extent of her response. My inexperienced, adolescent mind registered these details greedily but had no means of analysing them.

Before lunch Victor took us into the lounge, a large, lavishly furnished room which looked as if it had never been used. Above a Carrara marble fireplace of Rococo design—elegant in itself, but quite unsuited to the room's low-ceilinged mock Tudor proportions—Victor indicated a large area of wall covered in nothing but sea-green watered silk wallpaper.

'That's where I want Carmen to be,' he said.

'Her portrait, you mean?' asked Paul with seeming innocence. I glanced at Carmen who started a choking fit. Victor slapped her back quite smartly and looked at us all severely. He was acute enough to recognise that there was a joke at his expense, but he could not unbend enough to share it. The three of us could have been his children. Happily his butler José entered at that moment to announce lunch.

Over the meal it was decided that when Victor and Carmen were up in London—they had a service flat in Dolphin Square—she would come to Paul's studio to be painted for a couple of hours each day. It was agreed that half Paul's fee was to be paid at once, half on the painting's satisfactory completion and delivery. It was all very tidy and businesslike, and I believe I had a hand in its smooth negotiation. I can only recall one snatch of conversation which came after a pause towards the end of the meal. Suddenly Victor, who had Carmen seated on his immediate right, grasped one of her smooth white arms and said:

'My wife is a very beautiful woman, you know.' When he said this Victor looked straight at Paul, as if issuing a challenge.

I looked at Carmen to see how she had taken his remark, but her expression was quite inscrutable. I saw neither pleasure nor irritation, nor embarrassment on her face, and yet she must have felt something. That amount of concealment in one so young was impressive, perhaps even a little frightening.

'How did you two meet?' asked Paul.

'She was a model,' said Victor, as if this explained everything.

'A fashion model,' added Carmen. I had been trying to guess her origins from her accent, but could get nowhere, especially as she talked so little. She spoke in the socially neutral tones of what is called 'received pronunciation', acquired perhaps at a modelling school. At any rate, after that little exchange, no further information on Carmen's life before Victor was made available. As we drove back to London after lunch, Paul was unusually taciturn and thoughtful.

۞

During the following week Paul started on the portrait. I did not see or speak to him for a fortnight, until, quite unexpectedly, he invited me out to dinner at a restaurant with his girlfriend, Christine. When he was in funds Paul, who had an innately generous nature, liked to indulge his passion for sensual enjoyment with friends, and would refuse all offers to share the expense. We met at Paul's flat and walked to the restaurant. It was the first time that I had been with Paul and Christine outside their home where Christine kept herself in the background.

Difficult People

They had been together for some years when I knew them and had been, as they put it, 'childhood sweethearts' before that. Christine was a quiet, intelligent beauty who showed no signs of being overawed by Paul's personality.

During dinner Paul was the principal conversationalist. In particular he talked with enthusiasm about the sexual revolution and about the 'open relationship' he enjoyed with Christine who listened to him impassively.

'We believe that we have the right to explore the limits of sensual experience with others, but we remain totally faithful in terms of our commitment to each other as lifetime partners. That's something sacred to us. We believe that freedom and fidelity are compatible. I'm happy if Christine experiments with other relationships, and she's happy if I do, because we both know that there is something between us that can't be broken, that's just . . . eternal. You agree with that, don't you, Christine?'

'Yes. Right. No, I'm very happy with that,' said Christine, firmly but without enthusiasm.

Paul was in an exuberant mood, but more restless than I had ever seen him before. He ate and drank prodigiously, but without the alcohol seeming to have any effect. I asked him about the portrait but he brushed my enquiries aside with the words: 'Wait and see.'

One afternoon about a fortnight later Paul summoned me over to his flat with the simple words: 'It's finished.' When I arrived there was in the middle of his sitting room a five foot by four canvas on an easel draped rather dramatically in a black silk sheet.

'Apart from Christine, you're the first to see this,' said Paul. Without any flourish, but hesitantly, I thought, for him, he slowly removed the sheet. It slid down the canvas and lay shimmering on the floor like a dark pool. I saw the portrait of Carmen Lyons for the first time.

'My God!' I said involuntarily. Usually I had better control over my reactions, but this defeated me. Paul, whose mixture of arrogance and vulnerability was uncommonly explosive, even for an artist, looked dismayed.

'But don't you think it's a great picture?'

'Of course! It's incredible.'

'So? What's wrong?'

I was going to find it difficult to explain without offending him. Rather feebly, I said: 'But do you think they'll like it?'

'That's funny,' said Paul. 'It's exactly what Christine said.'

Against a deep black background Carmen in a short, tight black dress was seated in a plum coloured wing chair, her legs, shoeless as when we had first met her, crossed seductively. The left hand rested on an arm of the chair, her right arm curled upwards around one of the wings. She faced forward directly at the viewer with an intense, menacing stare. You could not define that look as one of malevolence exactly because malevolence is a human feeling and this look was not quite human. I have seen similar looks on predatory animals. It was unfathomably dark and dangerous.

When I had collected my thoughts I asked Paul if he didn't think that the picture was a little 'overpowering'. Paul did not appear to understand.

'No. That's just how I saw her, that's all.'

'Is she really like that?' I asked.

'Like what?' said Paul who was being unusually obtuse, I thought. On an instinct I asked him if he had had an affair with her.

'Yes. Briefly,' he said. 'Just a physical thing. I wasn't that interested to be honest. Funny thing. She wanted it a lot, but she didn't seem to enjoy it. It was all a bit of a grind.' I could not tell if this coldness and casualness was a pose or not, but it upset me. I did not stay long after that and we parted less than warmly.

Difficult People

I should add one more thing about the picture. Paul had included the Persian Blue cat in the portrait though it was little more than a slip of furry tail around Carmen's ankles and a glitter of two eyes under the chair. It was an effective piece of trickery, if slightly unsettling. It was as if this secret presence, once noticed, made it a different picture altogether: no longer a portrait, but a picture about a girl and her cat.

The trouble that followed the presentation of the portrait to Victor fell mostly on the head of my poor father who, characteristically, shouldered the blame without reproaching either Paul or myself. Victor hated the picture. My father who tried to take a detached interest in Victor's reaction attempted to make him explain himself. Did he think it was badly painted? No. Victor had to concede that it was 'quite well done'. Then what was wrong? Was it a bad likeness? At this Victor hesitated because he was discerning enough to understand that from a purely physical point of view it was an extremely good likeness, but. . . . But what? The most coherent answer that Victor could give to my father's probings was that the picture was 'not right' and not what he had wanted. The upshot of it was that Victor refused to pay the second half of his fee for the picture, and even demanded the return of his first instalment.

A week or so of argument and negotiation followed. Paul was desperate and distressed, but chiefly, I think, because he had already spent the money he had been given and had incurred debts on the expectation of the second tranche.

Eventually it was decided, to nobody's satisfaction, that Paul was to keep his commission fee, but that the painting was to be returned to him without any further payment. I was appointed to drive to Gerrard's Cross in my father's estate car and fetch back the offending item. My father, unsurprisingly, wanted nothing more to do with the whole wretched business. It was not a job I relished, but, like my father, I felt in some way responsible.

The Complete Symphonies of Adolf Hitler

I arrived at Victor's house at exactly the hour agreed and rang the bell. After a minute or so it was answered not by José, but Carmen. She wore no shoes as usual and seemed paler than when I had last seen her. I said I had come for the picture and she laughed. It was a perfectly pleasant-sounding laugh, but it disturbed me because it made no sense.

She said: 'He's in his study. Top of the stairs, first door on the right.'

'Can't I just take the picture?' I asked.

'The picture's up there with him,' she said. She made a disdainful little pushing gesture with her hands, as if shooing me up to see him. As I mounted the stairs I was conscious of her standing at the bottom of the staircase and watching me.

I had to knock twice on the study door before I heard an indistinct human sound which I took to be a summons to enter. It was a large room lined with shelves full of impressive leather bound volumes which I suspected that Victor had bought by the yard, just as he had bought his Old Masters. Victor was seated with his back to me in a high-backed leather swivel chair. All I could see of him was his right hand which cradled a monstrous balloon glass half full of brandy. I could tell, however, what he was looking at. Facing both of us was the portrait on its easel, a third living presence in the room.

I coughed and announced that I had come to take the picture. The chair swivelled round rapidly and revealed Victor sitting there naked, his face contorted with fury.

'How dare you come in without knocking!' he shouted.

I said I had knocked. In my embarrassment I chose to stare past him at the only object worth looking at in the room, the picture. Since I had last seen it Paul had altered it slightly so that the Persian cat was a little more in evidence. Not simply two eyes, but a whole head was peering out very close to her legs from under the chair. Keeping my eyes on the painting I told Victor that I had come, as arranged, to take it back.

Difficult People

'Well, you can't have it!' he said aggressively and swivelled his chair back to look at the picture. Spared now the embarrassment of talking to a naked man, I recovered my courage and told him that I was not going to leave without either the picture or a cheque for the remainder of Paul's fee. There was a silence. I coughed again, just to remind Victor that I was still there.

'What do you think of it?' asked Victor.

Choosing my words carefully I said that I thought it was very powerful.

'Yes, yes!' he said. 'But is it *her*?'

I said I didn't know.

'I think it is,' he said. 'I think it is her.' I saw his left arm stretch out and point directly at the canvas. 'I think THAT . . . IS . . . HER!'

After a pause I said in what I hoped was a firm voice that if he was keeping the picture I would need a cheque from him now. With a sudden convulsive movement Victor bounded out of the chair, went over to a desk by the window, pulled a cheque book out of a drawer, wrote the cheque, blotted it and held it out to me with a trembling hand. My mind, overwhelmed by what had gone before, took in the absurd scene with detachment. He is handed a cheque by a naked man in a book-lined room, I thought to myself, as if composing a scenario for a film in my head.

He said: 'If that really *is* her, I'll have to keep it, won't I?' I nodded my agreement with this strange statement and left the room. When I reached the top of the stairs I paused for breath. On looking down I saw Carmen at the bottom of the stairs looking up at me with those great dark eyes of hers. She was not standing but crouching in an odd position, a little like an athlete, poised for a sprint. She rose from this position slowly and seemingly without embarrassment.

'He's keeping the picture,' I said and for the second time that afternoon she laughed.

The Complete Symphonies of Adolf Hitler

༄

Paul was delighted with the cheque, but did not seem to be particularly interested in the story of my adventures with Carmen and Victor in Gerrard's Cross. It was only when I mentioned the alteration he had made to the painting with regard to the cat that he became animated. 'No!' he said. 'You must be mistaken. I absolutely did not alter it by a brushstroke after I showed it to you.' This was odd, but I did not press the point, sensing that Paul would be irritated. When I told my father about it all he simply commented in his characteristically enigmatic way that 'humankind cannot bear very much reality'.

A year passed and I was at Bond Street Station one evening when I noticed the headlines on the late edition of the *Evening Standard*. They read: TYCOON FOUND DEAD and there was a photograph of Victor Lyons. His death would have made a headline in any case, but its bizarre circumstances had propelled it onto the front page. He had been found dead, having blown out his brains with a shotgun while seated in front of the portrait of his wife Carmen.

Not long after this event, Paul broke up with Christine and went to America. He enjoyed great success in the States where I believe he settled, but I never saw him again. I retained an interest in art which took a less commercial turn than my father's. I became an academic and lectured in Art History at the Courtauld. My father lived to see the appearance of my book on Adam Elsheimer, the great German Mannerist, which I think pleased him.

I kept my contacts with my father's world and was occasionally consulted by dealers. One of those who regularly called on my services, and an old friend of the family, was Adrian Martock. A bachelor of the most refined sensibilities and tastes, he operated out of a tiny but exquisite flat in Kensington Church

Difficult People

Street. How he worked was something of a mystery, but he was someone who knew everyone and everything in the art world, and, unusually, he was liked by all.

One morning, thirty-four years after the suicide of Victor Lyons, I received a telephone call from Adrian: 'My dear,' he said, 'are you, in any sense of the word, available?' This was a familiar opening gambit. I replied that that depended. After chiding me for my defensiveness he went on to explain that he had a client who wanted to sell an Elsheimer and that I was the very person to come with him to verify its authenticity and provenance. I was intrigued of course, but I knew that his real reason for asking me along was rather more mundane. One of Adrian's oddities was that he had never learned to drive, so that if he needed to visit a place that was not reasonably accessible by train or taxi, he would call upon one of his many friends to act as chauffeur. It is testimony to his charm that if ever I was 'available' I never refused him.

'It is, my dear, in the wilds of Lincolnshire,' he explained to me as we began our journey. 'We are visiting a Mrs Foxley, the owner of the alleged Elsheimer. Knowing you to be a respectable married man and easily shocked, I think I should warn you in advance about her menage. She is a mature lady who lives with a great many cats and a charming young West Indian gentleman called Sheridan who acts as her companion, shall we say, though liberal shepherds might give it a grosser name. I have an idea that her finances are in decline, hence the need to sell the Elsheimer.'

All the way up to Lincolnshire Adrian kept up a flow of elegant conversation punctuated by the occasional direction. ('Now, my dear, if you could take a right turn at this forthcoming cross-roads, that would make me very happy.') I am not quite sure why I did not find him unbearably irritating, but I didn't. The drive, however, was long and, though Lincolnshire has its advocates, I am not one of them.

The Complete Symphonies of Adolf Hitler

Mrs Foxley's house was to be found up a long, rutted track, amid flat arable land. It was large, rambling and parts of it were in disrepair. ('I know, my dear, just too *Cold Comfort Farm*,' said Adrian apologetically.) It seemed a bleak, lonely sort of place for a middle aged woman to live with her young black lover.

Sheridan, who opened the door to us, was tall, spectacularly handsome and very courteous. He seemed calm, but I detected an undercurrent of unease. He welcomed us in assuring us that Mrs Foxley would be with us shortly but was 'busy just at this moment'.

As we entered I was aware of a familiar atmosphere. There is a kind of squalor peculiar to each of the social classes; and this I recognised as Upper Class squalor. The rooms were modestly sized and dimly lit, not notably clean: little attention if any had been paid to decor. There was fine furniture scratched and neglected, claret stains on chintz, waste bins belching gin and champagne bottles, copies of *Vogue* and *Tatler* lying about, a backgammon board in disarray, a general sense of undedicated idleness. Then there were the cats, roughly a dozen of them, who roamed about, or slept, most of the time oblivious of their fellow felines or any humans who intruded. As we entered the sitting room I noticed one casually eating some leftover curry off a plate perched on the arm of a sofa. Sheridan apologised and removed the plate to a battered Regency side-table.

'You wanted to see the Elsheimer, I guess,' he said. We nodded. He pointed to a smallish painting in a gilded frame above the fireplace.

It was indeed by Adam Elsheimer, in his usual medium of oil on copper, the subject being *Judith in the Tent of Holofernes*, a late, mature work of 1608 or thereabouts. The painting, like many of Elsheimer's, full of atmosphere and Mannerist chiaroscuro, depicts the moment just before the Jewish heroine murders the Assyrian warlord. It is midnight and the scene is lit

Difficult People

by a single oil lamp which Judith holds with her left hand over the sleeping Holofernes. In her right hand is the scimitar with which she will behead her enemy. The full glare of the lamp is on Judith's face and it is her expression, the central focus of the painting, which fascinates. She looks down at her victim with detached curiosity mingled perhaps with faint disgust. Holofernes is sprawled over a couch in a drunken stupor, a great bearded brute, his mouth half open. He is probably snoring. And Judith seems to be saying to herself, quite coolly: so this is what a man looks like a few seconds before his death. She feels no pity; only perhaps, a faint, apprehensive excitement in that strange still moment before she enters the annals of Biblical heroism. Her face is the face of a destroyer, and, like many such faces, it has a kind of vacancy, innocence even.

I knew the painting at once, because it was one which, long ago, my father had sold to Victor Lyons. In that moment of recognition I sensed that someone else had entered the room unseen by me, and yet I knew who it must be. I turned round and saw Carmen.

She was dressed very much as when I had first met her. Her feet were bare as before and her dark hair, now streaked with grey hung lustrously down over one eye. Her figure, coarsened by time, was still voluptuous, but it was to her face that the thirty-four years had done the most damage. Something, hidden before, had been uncovered: rage and insatiable hunger. She noticed my stare.

'Do I know you?' she said.

'We met long ago.'

'You weren't a friend of Victor's were you?'

'No,' I said.

'Well, thank God for that!' she said and turned her attention to Adrian, who explained that I was here to verify the painting's authenticity and provenance. She asked how much she could expect to get for it and when Adrian mentioned an impressive but not unjustified sum she merely nodded.

'I'll be sorry to let it go. It's the only one of Victor's bloody paintings I really liked.'

I told Carmen that my father had sold it to him and suddenly her dark eyes were on me again. This time they were full of animation, but what feeling lay behind I could not fathom.

'I know you now,' she said. 'You were the young man who came down for the portrait.' I nodded.

'I've still got it, you know,' she said. 'Like to see it?' I did not reply. I did not want to see it, but she seized my wrist and almost dragged me out of the room.

At the back of the house was a conservatory of sorts. All the plants in it had withered from lack of water and the panes of glass were greened with mildew. It contained little except a few threadbare wicker chairs and some piles of newspapers and magazines, but the portrait was there. At some stage it had been taken off its stretcher; so, to be displayed, it had been pinned up on a wall where it hung, flapping slightly in the draught that filtered through a cracked pane of glass. It was as I remembered it, strangely, horribly animate.

Carmen still held my wrist as if she were forcing me to look at it. Her grip was tight and astonishingly strong. Ten long seconds went by as we stared together at Paul's portrait of Carmen, then I noticed something which made my stomach turn over. The Persian Blue cat had come out from under the chair and was crouching at Carmen's feet. It stared at me out of the picture as if daring me to expose its secret.

By this time Adrian and Sheridan were also in the conservatory. Carmen let go of my arm and said: 'Now, you three go away and make the arrangements about the picture. I'll stay here for a while. Go on! Off you go!' And she made that shooing gesture with which she had impelled me upstairs to see Victor.

Difficult People

When we were in the sitting room again Sheridan said: 'She spends hours sitting in there with that picture. I don't like it. It's not good.'

I am afraid we showed very little sympathy for Sheridan who seemed genuinely concerned for Carmen. I think he wanted us to stay and talk, but Adrian and I were both anxious to get away as quickly as possible. We concluded our business briskly.

As we were getting into the car to return to London, I turned to look back at the house and saw the tall, dark, princely figure of Sheridan framed in the doorway. I told myself that he looked poised and in command, but he also looked horribly alone. Adrian and I said nothing to each other until we were at least a mile from Carmen's house, then Adrian sighed: 'Oh, dear,' he said. 'I can see that we are going to have problems with this one. Carmen is clearly what your father used to call "difficult".'

'What did father mean by "difficult"?' I asked. 'I never got a straight answer.'

'Nor did I. But I don't think he just meant being an awkward customer. He never called me difficult, despite my being a fearful old nuisance, as you well know. I think he meant people without a centre to them. People without a beginning or an end. People who are empty and so perpetually hungry.'

'Hungry for what?'

'They don't know. That is why they are empty.'

It was only a week later that I heard from Adrian that Carmen had died suddenly. 'Heart failure due to alcoholic poisoning', was the official verdict, but the manner of her passing was odd. She had been found dead sitting in front of her portrait, through which she had blasted a hole with a shotgun.

'Difficult to the last!' was Adrian's only comment.

THE CONSTANT RAKE

*The 1st Act, Scene the 1st,
St James's Park. Enter Lady* LAVISH
attended by TOWNLEY *and* CARELESS.

Lady LAVISH.
Oh, Townley, Townley, as you love me do not mention that word 'country' to me. I truly think it is the most odious, provoking sound in all the world unless it be surpassed by the lowing of an ox or the crying of a sheep. Ah, Townley, I never knew till now that the sound of mutton was so mean and unmannerly. I shall never again taste a ragout with composure.

The Constant Rake

TOWNLEY.

Come, Lady Lavish, I have heard the country commended by some of quality. They say it is a healthy place.

Lady LAVISH.

Healthy! Well, I dare say it is. Indeed there is nothing in it but health. A person may die of health there and not notice she hath done it.

CARELESS.

And I have heard it is a solitary place, not much noted for company.

Lady LAVISH.

Company! Oh, pish, there is company of a sort, and a deal too much of it. For you must know, Careless, that the country is full of neighbours. There is Parson Dull and my Lady Dreary and Mistress Prattle and Squire Oldsaw. And they must be always calling on one another to tell how the weather is and if there will be rain and how the corn grows.

CARELESS.

But did you not have some amorous swain there to attend you and compliment you? Did you not find a good fellow to be Shepherd Corydon to your Phyllis?

Lady LAVISH.

Oh, never doubt it, Careless. I found such a man, for I went into the country of a purpose to find him. Since my Lavish died, leaving me little but his bad debts, I found myself in want of a husband of five thousand pound a year and no vices. For there is no man in town, having such a competency, but is not thoroughly debauched. And I would not have such a thing as a debauched husband. They live without consideration and die without warning.

The Complete Symphonies of Adolf Hitler

TOWNLEY.
And who is your gallant of five thousand pound a year?

Lady LAVISH.
Why have you not heard? It is Sir Prosperous Fairacres.

TOWNLEY.
Fairacres. They tell me he is a very worthy man.

Lady LAVISH.
Indeed, Townley, I never knew such a man for being worthy. But he is a very proper man, truly, though unpolish'd in his manners. Yet that is of small account, for, when we are married, he shall be little in town.

CARELESS.
What: And are you to stay with him in the country?

Lady LAVISH.
Lord no, sir. I shall keep my town house and servants. I am not to be locked up in a field. It shall suit us very well. I shall hold to the town and he to the country and we will visit one another on occasion like good friends. A husband and wife should not be too often together: it confounds their felicity to be mewed up in the same place.

TOWNLEY.
And so your old acquaintance is not to be forsaken.

Lady LAVISH.
No, indeed, I shall be seen as often in my box at the Playhouse and my acquaintance shall be as liberal as formerly. But, in deference to my husband, I will not allow any particular friendship among men. Nor will I permit familiarity from any man of low reputation, however polished his wit.

The Constant Rake

CARELESS.
Then we must all be chary.

TOWNLEY.
And what of that old beau who ever pursues you, Sir Lascivious Overspend?

Lady LAVISH.
Pish, Townley, pray do not speak to me of Sir Lascivious. I have forsworn him.

TOWNLEY.
He will not be denied.

Lady LAVISH.
I abominate the man. He is obscenity all over. For there is nothing so unpleasing to me as an old rake: they have neither the freshness of youth nor the wisdom of age. Their eagerness will constantly bring them to a pitch which their parts cannot match. Faith, I never gave old Sir Lascivious encouragement, but he was ever drawn on by his own folly which, even in the very springtime of his wits, can have been no small thing.

TOWNLEY .
Well, my lady, this same sapless shrub told me but yesterday that he was very eager to see you, and to render you a signal service.

Lady LAVISH.
A service? To me? My gorge rises at it. Faith, I almost wish I were among my good neighbours Dull and Dreary in the country again.

CARELESS.
They say that nature there does not allow the branch to wither much with age but that ancient trees have a robustness you do not see in town. And so with the people.

The Complete Symphonies of Adolf Hitler

Lady LAVISH.
Oh, talk not to me of Nature. It is a very ill thing, I think, unless temper'd with a little civility. For who can view Nature without accusing herself that she wants much of it? And to accuse oneself is an indiscreet pastime, for it leads one on to praise others and then one might lose one's inclination for the only theme of well-bred conversation: I mean, the disparagement of others and the exaltation of folly.

TOWNLEY, *aside*
How just she is, and with how little benefit to herself!

As I read this opening scene I began to wonder if, for once, Montague Summers had been right.

In his monumental work *The Playhouse of Pepys*, he heaps praises on Henry Ovenstone's comedy of 1683 *The Constant Rake, or Sir Lascivious Overspend*. I had made a note of it but held out no great hopes of finding it. Neither the British Library nor the Bodleian had this work in their catalogues, which is unusual, but not unknown. Published plays at that time enjoyed a status little higher than pamphlets and other ephemera. Having established that it was the single dramatic work of a very obscure writer, I was not really expecting it to be any good if I did happen to find it. Summers' enthusiasm for even the feeblest Restoration comedy had led me astray before. Works trumpeted as neglected masterpieces often turn out to be quite justly neglected. This is something I do not readily admit, as an academic, for whom all ancient documents should be equally valuable, but I am incorrigibly susceptible to literary judgements. It is partly my business, after all. In addition to being Congreve Professor of Theatre History at London University, I act occasionally as dramaturg to the Rose Tree Theatre in Richmond, which is dedicated to the revival of little-known but meritorious plays.

I found *The Constant Rake* one day as I was browsing in Parsons', the theatrical antiquarian bookseller in Cecil Court off St Martin's Lane. It had been bound together with Lee's *The Rival Queens* and Ravenscroft's *The London Cuckolds* at some time in the nineteenth century and the pages cropped so that their sizes matched. It was a villainous edition and the price old Parsons had pencilled on the flyleaf was absurd, but I had to have it.

THE
Conſtant Rake
OR
Sʳ Laſcivious Overſpend

A
COMEDY.

Acted at His
HIGHNESSE the DUKE of YORK'S
THEATRE.

Written by
HENRY OVENSTONE Eſq;

LONDON,

Printed for *D. Longhorne*, at the Sign of the *Sunne & Dragon* at the Corner of *Chancery Lane* in *Fleet-ſtreet*, 1683

The Complete Symphonies of Adolf Hitler

Parsons was an elderly man with a searching look and dirt under his fingernails. I had discovered that he knew a great deal about the theatrical books in which he dealt, but that he guarded his knowledge like a miser. What little he did disclose was nearly always calculated to tease rather than inform.

'Ah!' he said, when I tried to ask him as casually as possible what his best price for the book would be. 'I notice it's *The Constant Rake* you're after.'

I murmured that it was quite an interesting group of plays, but he was not deceived.

'Summers once thought of bringing out a scholarly edition of *The Rake*, you know, and putting it on. In the 1930s, as I am sure you are aware, he ran the Phoenix Players which revived little known Restoration work. Wisely, he thought better of it.'

'Why? Is the play obscene?'

Parsons smirked. 'No. Not exactly. No more than others of a similar period and provenance. You'll see what I mean. There was quite a story behind the first production. Mrs Barry scored one of her greatest successes as Lady Lavish but she never repeated the role.'

'Why not?'

'Peculiar woman, Mrs Barry. A *femme fatale* if ever there was one. Think of Rochester and poor Otway. . . .' He checked himself, as if reining in garrulous enthusiasm. There was a silence while he studied me with detached interest, as if I were a rare insect on a window pane. Finally he said: 'Do you intend to buy my book or do you merely want to grope it lovingly?' Parsons had a gentlemanly way of staying just this side of rudeness by maintaining a bantering tone. Ignoring him I turned to the title page opposite which was an engraving of the author Mr Ovenstone. Beneath a luxuriant periwig could be seen one of those characteristic late seventeenth-century faces: slightly puffy with a pouting lower lip and heavy-lidded, protuberant eyes that brooded over you from beyond the grave.

The Constant Rake

'Who was Henry Ovenstone?'

'Illegitimate son of a nobleman, or so they said. Made a brilliant start. Wrote superb Latin verses at Cambridge, that sort of thing. When he came to London he found a patron in Lord Selgrave. Ovenstone wrote this play. He and Selgrave fell out, then Ovenstone died.'

'How did Ovenstone die? And why did they fall out?'

'All this information I'm giving you, I ought to be charging you extra.'

'I thought you already were.'

I am no good at haggling, so I gave Parsons what he asked, and left him to his hoard of literature and information.

To be brief, *The Constant Rake* lived up to its opening scene. As a Restoration comedy it belonged to the boisterous, farcical end of the spectrum. It had none of the refinement of Congreve, or the elegance of Dryden, let alone the sentiment of Addison or Steele, but it was not without wit. It reminded me most of Shadwell, Ravenscroft and Aphra Behn. One scene in particular seems to prefigure one in Aphra Behn's *The Lucky Chance* of 1686. In it Sir Lascivious has been tricked into a false marriage to Lady Lavish with Townley acting as the bogus parson. The ancient Sir Lascivious is eager to bed his bride but is being constantly put off by Lady Lavish with ever more elaborate and absurd excuses. Meanwhile, she is dallying with her lover Bellcourt on the other side of the bedroom door. Eventually Lady Lavish agrees to submit to the old rake's embraces but only if he is fully fit for the ordeal. To this end he must enter the Rejuvenating Cabinet invented by a Dr Crankum. Dr Crankum is, of course, her friend Careless in disguise, and he, like Townley has been promised, but hitherto denied, her favours. Sir Lascivious is inveigled into the cabinet which is then heaved into the Thames. This incident is, of course reminiscent of *The Merry Wives of Windsor* but has a much crueller edge. Sir Lascivious emerges half dead from his immersion, though how he manages to escape from the cabinet under water is not explained. The play ends with the arrival of a *deus ex machina* in the form of Sir Prosperous Fairacres who claims the penitent Lady Lavish as his bride and carries her off to the country.

Apart from this slightly tame ending—and one feels that Ovenstone's heart was not in it—the play is vicious amoral fun, fast-moving, full of a kind of ebullient rage at the follies of high society. Ovenstone spares none of his characters: even the one unequivocally upright person in the play, Sir Prosperous Fairacres, is obviously a booby. But the author's fury is particularly reserved for the Rake, Sir Lascivious. By the end of the play his humiliation is complete and abject, and no shred of dignity remains to him as he is dragged off to prison for debt, having spent the last of his fortune on the appalling Lady Lavish.

I laughed a good deal at the play, but my laughter was tinged with guilt. It was like watching the school bully cleverly humiliate an unpopular victim. Of course Ovenstone tries to dress it all up with a high moral tone at the end. The concluding couplet of the Epilogue ('spoken by Mrs Barry') reads—

> Take heed, ye Gallants, learn from this our Rake
> For we have drubbed him solely for your Sake!

—but I doubt if anyone was fooled.

The printed play was supplied with an 'Epistle Dedicatory to the Right Honourable James, Earl of Selgrave' and also some dedicatory verses to the same:

> Selgrave! Thou monarch's Counsellor and Friend;
> Now to thy Servant design to condescend.
> Let Muses congregate to swell thy Fame
> And add fresh Lustre to a Noble Name . . .

The Constant Rake

—and so on: engine-turned verse in the usual flowery, vapid style.

I scanned and transcribed *The Constant Rake* onto disc which allowed me to adjust some spellings and obscurities as well as to suggest cuts. Restoration dramatists (like Shaw) always need cutting, but, unlike Shaw, they have an excuse. Lights were on during the performances, intrigues were being conducted, oranges and other even more tangible commodities were being sold. Intelligent padding was required to compensate for the wayward attention of the audience. Having prepared the text, I sent it to Tom Travers at the Rose Tree.

The night on which I completed my work for Tom I dreamed I was standing on the edge of a stretch of water, still, silent, illimitable. Not the faintest shadow of land could be seen on the horizon. The sky above was an unyielding monochromatic white, the water below it the colour of slate. The shore on which I stood was of grey grit against which the water lapped in infinitesimally small waves. The quality of the dream was unusual in that it presented to my half conscious state a steady and almost motionless image accompanied, as so often in dreams, by a powerful mood. That mood is not easily defined except by the image which represented in it, but I felt isolation, heaviness, despair. As I looked at the water I began to notice that in parts something lurked beneath the surface, almost at times emerging above it. It looked like a weed, slightly variegated in tone from iron to steel grey, and it stretched beneath the water in long, curling tendrils. Then one of these heavy corkscrew curls began to extend itself and rise above the water. It waved slightly as if groping blindly for somewhere to attach itself. Then it seemed to sense my presence and move in my direction. I woke, damp and cold from chilled sweat.

☙

The Complete Symphonies of Adolf Hitler

Anyone familiar with the academic world will know about the importance of publication. I had produced nothing since my seminal work *The Colonial Experience in 19th Century Drama*, and that was five years ago. Admittedly events, such as my wife leaving me for a fellow academic, had intervened; but who cares about that? In this world one must publish or be damned. So it seemed to me that a study of Ovenstone, obviously an interesting figure if not a significant one, would be just the thing to restore my reputation and I began my research.

Secondary sources quickly gave me 'the shilling life'. The salient facts are these. Ovenstone acquired the patronage of the Earl of Selgrave, wrote complimentary odes, dedicated a verse translation of Statius to him and so on. He then decided to try his luck in the theatre at a time when relations with his patron appeared to be cooling. He wrote *The Constant Rake* and in doing so came into contact with Mrs Barry, one of the leading actresses of the day. She proved to be his nemesis, as she had for so many others. He fell hopelessly in love and, in the course of his affair with Mrs Barry—perhaps to impress her—he introduced her to his patron Selgrave. She, ever on the lookout for a more lucrative and influential lover, very rapidly became Selgrave's mistress, and abandoned Ovenstone. At this, by all accounts, Ovenstone became quite unhinged. He began abusing Selgrave all over town, writing lampoons, openly declaring—though ''twas known already'—that Selgrave was the model for Sir Lascivious Overspend in his play. Poverty, disgrace and death were the inevitable outcome of this and they came in 1685. The diarist, the Rev. Robert Higgs, vicar of St Mary Axe, a city church, wrote in his entry for September 14th of that year: 'It was in the Dogge and Bitch by London Bridge that Mr Ovenstone met his unhappy end. Some say that overcome by much wine he fell into the water from a window of the Inne, others that he had hurled himself thence in a most damnable and ungodly fit of despaire, others still that My Lord's [presum-

The Constant Rake

ably Selgrave's] men came, for he had offended His Lordship grievously, and made away with him. His body was discover'd next day on the strand. 'Twas curious, but his periwig was still on him, yet all dabbled with blood and filthe.'

Further research led me to the library of Clare College, Cambridge where Ovenstone had been a Commoner. What papers he left on his death in 1685, had been bequeathed to the college. When I asked to see them the librarian had expressed mild surprise because someone else had only recently made the same request. It seems strange to me now that I did not question him further about it.

The papers were in considerable disorder, which led me to believe that whoever had asked to see them had not yet done so. I won't list them all, except to say that there was a manuscript poem of inordinate length in rhyming couplets entitled *A Satiricall Epistle Upon Patronage*. It is unnecessary to quote from it as the title is an adequate indication of its contents, which are full of bile and pall very quickly, as bile does. A proper name, represented by a capital S followed by a long dash, occurs frequently in the text. Reference to the meter shows it to be a two-syllable name, which together with the abuse heaped upon it would confirm that Selgrave is intended.

Two documents will suffice to portray Ovenstone towards the end of his life. The first is a letter. It is undated but someone, not Ovenstone, has written on its reverse: 'To Mrs Barry. Sent back unopen'd.' The contents in Ovenstone's own hand read as follows:

Three o'clock in the morning

Madam,

Anger, spleen, revenge and shame are not yet so powerful with me as to make me disown this great truth, that I love you above all things in the world. 'Tis impossible for me to curse you, but give me leave to pity myself, which is more than ever you will do for me. That you have bestowed your heart on that [something heavily crossed out here] person is more disgusting to me than to believe that you have no heart at all. Which, if this is so, and I have good reason to credit it, yet still in my folly and to my own destruction I would humbly beg leave to subscribe myself

 Ever your most loving and obedient servant unto Death

H.O.

The other was the manuscript of a play, a tragedy in heroic verse entitled *Zelmira, or the Empress of the Indies*. It was unrevised and clearly had never been produced. Even by the standard of the time it is a confused affair, set in a fantastical kingdom, supposedly in what we now call South America. It looks like a last mad attempt by Ovenstone to re-establish himself on the stage. The action is full of poisonings, stabbing, cannibalism, intrigue of all sorts, at the centre of which is the ambitious, cruel and rapacious Zelmira. It seems probable that the actress for whom this leading role was undoubtedly intended was also its model and inspiration: Elizabeth Barry.

Her death scene would have called for more than even the considerable resources of stage machinery at the time could have coped with. Having set out with her entire fleet to invade the neighbouring nation of Bell-Imperia, Zelmira finds herself caught in a storm. The final scene takes place on the deck of a sinking ship. Her dying speech is crazed and far too long, but its last lines—and the accompanying stage direction—are worth recording:

> My braine is burst, I see the storm has won!
> Shatter the stars and put out ev'ry Sunne!
> We'll walk a darkling pathway to the grave
> Where fishes glide beneath the glassy wave.
> Neptune, our Monarch now, with Coral crowned,
> Shall guide to Pluto legions of the drowned.

The Constant Rake

> Lethe awaits, with drafts of liquid Peace;
> Though Joyes may falter, all our Sorrowes cease!
> —*stabs herself, then casts herself into the waves.*

The insistent images of drowning throughout the play were disturbing and made me incline towards the suicide theory of his death. But Selgrave's last years were troubled too, perhaps by his conscience. He certainly never shook off the whispers about his involvement in Ovenstone's end. Mrs Barry outlived all her lovers and died in 1713, appropriately enough from the bite of a rabid lapdog.

My work on Ovenstone had gone on for some months when I suddenly had a call from Tom Travers at the Rose Tree. Tom is like that. You may hear nothing from him for months, even years, then suddenly, when you least expect it, he rings up, full of enthusiasm for a play you once sent him. Tom was fascinated by *The Constant Rake* and was seriously interested in a production at the Rose Tree. As we discussed the play I could tell that Tom was both intrigued and a little disturbed by the harsher aspects of the play.

Tom said: 'He's quite vicious about old Selgrave, isn't he?'

'In the play you mean?'

'No. In the dedicatory verses. You sent them to me with the prologue and the epilogue.'

I was baffled. 'I don't remember them being particularly offensive. Respectful to the point of obsequiousness, I would have said.'

'Good God, no! Go back and have a look at them.'

I didn't argue, but I was very puzzled. There must have been some mistake because I remember the opening lines of the dedicatory verses very well:

> Selgrave! Thou Monarch's Counsellor and Friend
> Now to thy Servant deign to condescend . . . and so on.

The Complete Symphonies of Adolf Hitler

As soon as Tom had rung off I went to look in the printed text. There under the familiar superscription, *Verses Dedicated to the Right Honourable James, Earl of Selgrave* was the following:

> Selgrave! Thou Monarch's Pandar and False Friend
> Let all the Plagues of Hell on thee descend.
> Let Rumour hasten to defile thy fame
> And add fresh ordure to a Cursed Name
> With ev'ry day your morbid Vices swell:
> Defiling Heav'n, you merit worse than Hell.
> When you are rudely and untimely slain
> May Demons taunt thee with perpetual Pain
> May your unhappy corse rot in a Tomb
> Base as thy Mother's prostituted Womb
> And may your Shade blown by the viewless wind
> No tranquil Haven and no solace find,
> Wander distracted, vainly search for rest,
> Spewed out by sea, by land cast from her breast.

Had I misremembered the bland lines I first read, or invented them? It is a strange thing to be frightened by a few rather undistinguished verses, but I was. It was not the words themselves but my mind that terrified me. I had tricked myself. How? Why? I pored over the pages again and again in case I had simply overlooked those verses, or the pages had previously been stuck together. But no, there was no mistake except what my head had made.

One other thing troubled me. The engraving of Henry Ovenstone seemed to have changed slightly. Its execution appeared more lively and one of the curls of his capacious periwig was trailing over the side of the oval frame in which his portrait had been set. It was a spirited little touch of originality, but it troubled me that I had not noted it before.

The Constant Rake

These disturbances, aberrations, call them what you will, together with the beginning of a new university term, held up my researches. I did, however, manage to complete a paper on *The Constant Rake* and send it to the *Journal of Theatre Studies*.

It came as a shock when the following week my paper was returned with a polite note from the editor to the effect that the Journal was already printing a paper on the subject of Henry Ovenstone. I was astonished, but my astonishment abated slightly when I learned that the author of the paper was Dr Pring.

You will have heard of Dr Daniel Pring of Leeds University. No? But surely you know of his groundbreaking text, *Critiques of Patriarchal Hegemony in the Victorian Novel*? No again? Well, let me reassure you that whatever made Hermia leave me for him it was not the originality of his intellect, or the quality of his prose.

They say that the offender never forgives. Dan Pring has never quite forgiven me for the fact that I 'allowed' him to seduce my wife and then saw to it that he had to leave London University for the less salubrious academic groves of Leeds. It did not require an alpha mind to guess that Pring had somehow got wind of my Ovenstone project and was trying to frustrate me. It was a curiously base thing to do, even by academic standards, but then Dan Pring's academic standards had never been of the highest.

I realised that it would be quite useless to arrange an interview. I would have to confront him unexpectedly, beard him, so to speak. Oh, yes! He has a beard. Ginger. Fortunately I knew the Prings' address in Leeds, so I drove up and presented myself at their door one mild October evening. The door bell was answered by Hermia.

I wondered how I would feel on seeing Hermia again. As it happens, I felt nothing. For her part, surprise but not hostility greeted my unannounced arrival. I asked to see her husband, but unfortunately 'Dan' was out at a faculty meeting.

Hermia invited me in. I noticed that she was filling their little house, as she had mine, with imported ethnicity. Batiques and Moroccan rugs adorned the walls; the fashionable colours of the soukh—oatmeal, blood red and ochre—dominated. She still had a taste for those nasty little cushions covered in heavy gold thread with sequin mirrors sewn into the fabric. That made me smile. What finally reconciled me to Hermia's departure had been the thought that I would never have to have another badly stuffed, scintillating lump of pseudo-primitivism biting into my back as I sat on the sofa watching television.

Hermia is a big woman, not fat, but big. Her features are big too: big nose, big feet, big hair. That hair, which had once been described by a friend of mine as 'looking like dark diarrhoea' was now tinged with grey. She still wore it in a great untidy frizz around her long face, a sort of Satanic halo, or periwig. I had never liked frizzy hair, but curiously Hermia's had been one of the things that had drawn me to her, Eros having a strange habit of reversing the poles of attraction and repulsion. Besides, I had always entertained the quite irrational prejudice that frizzy-haired women were more sexually eager than their lank-locked sisters. In the case of Hermia my prejudice had been fully and rather unpleasantly confirmed.

She offered me a glass of wine which I refused. There was a strange silence in which for a moment I completely forgot what I had come for. Hermia gave me a troubled look.

'Are you all right?' she asked. 'You look awful. Poor old Henry!'

The next moment she was embracing me. Her coarse hair scoured my cheek and I smelt her familiar perfume, a peculiar musky odour. I remember that it had recommended itself to her because the manufacturers boasted that no animals had been tortured to bring it into being; only, they might have added, as a

The Constant Rake

result of its being worn. I disengaged myself gently. The wiry scrape of her hair had reminded me of what I was here for.

I told her plainly that her husband had somehow got hold of my research on Ovenstone, that he was trying to sabotage my work. I told her that I knew what his game was and that he would not get away with it. Her response was to put on an elaborate pantomime of astonishment and incredulity.

I said: 'Just tell Dan I know.'

'Henry, I have no idea what you're talking about. Would you like some herb tea?'

'No!'

'You really ought to get some help, Henry,' she said, assuming a concerned face. How typical of her. For Hermia the compassionate gesture had always been a more than adequate substitute for compassion itself. (Hence the awful musk!) I left.

The Constant Rake went into production. I travelled down for the first read-through, but it was thought better that I should not attend subsequent rehearsals in case I burdened the cast with too much academic background. I prepared some detailed programme notes and consoled myself with the thought that with the Rose Tree production at least I had stolen a march on Pring.

But even here he was plotting to bring me down. A week into rehearsals a letter arrived. The envelope had a crest (eagle with a viper in its beak) embossed on the flap and the letter itself was headed 'From the Earl of Selgrave, Selgrave House, Arundale, W. Yorks.' It read:

Dear Mr Bourne, [the proper address is Professor Bourne, but never mind, never mind!]
Will you please refrain from sending me any more notices of your play production. I cannot imagine why you should suppose

that I have any interest whatsoever in the theatre. I have never heard of Mr Ovenstone; I have no idea who he is and I do not wish to know. Your constant bombardment of me with these wretched leaflets is becoming an actionable nuisance. If you do not cease forthwith I shall put the matter in the hands of my solicitors.

Selgrave

Was this a hoax? A brief consultation of the appropriate reference books revealed that the Earldom of Selgrave did still exist and that George James Mordern Sykes Daubeny tenth Baron Arundale seventeenth Earl of Selgrave ('Recreations: Hunting, Bridge') was the sixty-five year old descendent of Ovenstone's despised patron. From Burke's Peerage I learned that he was the last of his line and that there were no descendants, direct or collateral, to inherit the Earldom. Needless to say I had never sent any leaflets to the man, so I wrote him a letter categorically denying my having done so and delicately suggesting the name of the culprit, Pring. The reply to my letter did not come from the Earl but from his solicitors. In the tersest possible language they intimated that any further letters sent by me to Selgrave were to be regarded as an actionable nuisance, and the matter would be referred to the police.

I felt helpless in the face of this malice and conspiracy and did not know where to turn. But I have a certain vague belief in Providence which is often strangely justified. The evening I received the solicitor's letter I picked up my little edition of *The Rake* (as I now affectionately called it) and began to leaf through it. Henry Ovenstone stared at me out of the engraving—his periwig a little looser than I had thought?—but the stare seemed to be companionable. I browsed my way idly through my favourite parts of the play and reread the Epilogue. Four lines from it which I had not noticed before impressed me for some reason:

> The faults of Vice are Virtue's surest shield
> Oft Villainy's by Villainy revealed
> Rogues are conjoined by knots of foul Deceit
> Unravel one, and here's another Cheat!

I felt that the lines were intended for me, but what did they mean? I only had to wait twelve hours for the answer. It arrived by the next morning's post in the shape of the *Journal of Theatre Studies*. I won't bore you with an analysis of Pring's lamentable article on Ovenstone. The quality of Pring's writing may be amply demonstrated by two details: he referred to John Dryden as 'Charles II's Spin-Doctor' and he misused the word 'disinterested'. But the revelation came at the end of the article in the following acknowledgement: 'I am greatly indebted to the generosity of the Earl of Selgrave, in allowing me to inspect the papers relating to Henry Ovenstone in his family archive.'

Ovenstone was right: there was a conspiracy.

∽

Following people is a fascinating occupation; really, it is scholarship by other means. Selgrave has a small flat in Onslow Square which he occupies intermittently throughout the year. A bald, stooping, shambling apology for a man, he carries a stick and has a slight limp from a hunting accident. Having no immediate family and apparently few friends, he spends most evenings playing cards at his club, Boodles in St James's, from which he emerges rather the worse for drink at around midnight and takes a taxi home. It is a worthless life.

You will be asking why I began to follow him. Well, a few weeks ago the production of *The Constant Rake* at the Rose Tree was cancelled. All kinds of reasons were given: sickness, tensions among the cast, artistic differences. Tom was most apologetic to me, but I could tell he was hiding something. Selgrave was at the bottom of it all, Selgrave and his lickspittle minion, Pring. So I knew what I had to do.

I bought a new suit, an Old Etonian tie and a haircut at Trumper's. I followed Selgrave to Boodles and parked the car round the corner in Jermyn Street. When Selgrave emerged from the club near midnight and started to weave around in search of a taxi, I approached him from behind, pretending to be a fellow member of Boodles who had also just left the club. He was a little offhand with me at first, but when I offered to give him a lift in my car he greedily accepted. The tie had inspired confidence. We walked round into Jermyn Street which was fortunately deserted. As the Last of the Selgraves was bending down to get into my car I hit him hard from behind with a claw hammer.

The hammer and Lord Selgrave entered the Thames at a deserted spot not far from the Millennium Dome. Grey morning was tucking its fingers over the horizon when I stood on the grey, gritty strand. The water ran past smooth and swift, tiny waves lapped at my feet.

Then I saw a disturbance in the polish'd surface of the stream. Something was rising up from it. It must have come from deep beneath the river's bed because great cloudes of black mud were discolouring the pale brown flowing water. Weeds too had sprung up from the bottom, like the weeds in my dream: steel and iron grey in long, corkscrew tendrils. They reared themselves above the surface and revealed themselves to be attached to a great grey head, scratched and lined as if marked by all the sorrowes of the Universe, but still known to me. It was my old friend Mr Ovenstone and he was coming out of the water to greet me, firstly his bewigged head, then all behind him a formless bulk of broadcloth soaked by the ages. His mouth opened and a great gush of water came from it, as

The Constant Rake

water from the grey stone conch of a Triton in a fountaine. Heavily he crawled towards me, and, as he did so the waters from his mouth abated. Dawn wind caught and waved a few strands of his perruque as my friend spoke to me, at last face to face.

> Posteritie, incline a gentle ear
> Judge if you must but judge us with a teare.
> Brand not our passions with too foul a name;
> Pity at least what you are forced to blame.
> Selgrave! thou stinking scion of an whore,
> You bray to us from sluggish Lethe's shore;
> Together bounde, in this fell mortall motion
> Let's drift as one towards the Joyless Ocean.

FINIS

THE BLUE ROOM

There can be advantages to having a snob for a brother-in-law. Occasionally I meet people whom otherwise I would never have known and see places which otherwise I would only have experienced on a guided tour. Besides, my brother-in-law Robert is the most harmless kind of snob. He is what a friend of mine calls 'a Duchess Worshipper'; he does not despise the working classes, he just loves a Lord.

For most of the week Robert is a very successful barrister in London, but at weekends he, my sister Pat and their two children go down to their cottage at Woolmington in Gloucestershire. I am frequently invited there as a guest, not so much

The Blue Room

for the charm of my company as because I can be a free child-minder to my nephew and niece. (There is an au-pair, naturally, but a spare hand is always useful.) Being an actor, I am frequently available; I am well fed and watered there; and my nephew and niece are, as children go, very easy to like.

Gloucestershire is where Robert and Pat do most of their serious socialising. I do not always accompany them on what, much to their annoyance, I call their 'climbing expeditions', but occasionally I do, which is how, about ten years ago now, I came to know Johnnie Buckland.

Johnnie lives at Swincombe, about six or seven miles from where Robert and Pat have their cottage. He is, in fact, Viscount Buckland, a courtesy title which he holds as eldest son of the Marquess of Harbourne, an elderly recluse who inhabits a vast Georgian pile up in the Derbyshire Dukeries. Swincombe, by contrast, though far from small, is not vast. It is an exquisite Jacobean mansion of honey-coloured Cotswold stone situated near the village of Swincombe on the slopes of the Cotswolds. You may have visited Swincombe House, but it is unlikely, because Johnnie only opens it up occasionally to the public, usually at the request of some earnest group of architectural or antique furniture enthusiasts. Johnnie also rents it out to film companies, and, as it happened, I had first been to Swincombe as an actor. I played Filmer Jesson in a television version of Pinero's *His House in Order,* and Swincombe had been used to stand in for 'Overbury Towers', the 'house' in question.

When, a year after this, Robert somehow got to know Johnnie, he happened to mention to him that I had filmed at his house. (My brother-in-law will make use of anyone to establish a point of contact.) Now, Johnnie loves Swincombe as a father loves his child, and he hates it when a film company does not, as he perceives it, do justice to its beauties. As luck would have it, he thought very well of the way the BBC had handled the place in *His House in Order,* on the strength of which, Pat, Robert and I were invited over to lunch one Saturday in April. I remember how Robert had put a tender hand on my shoulder and said: 'Making yourself useful at last, eh?' This, in my experience, is about the nearest Robert has ever come to a joke.

When we had filmed at Swincombe Johnnie Buckland had been away, so this was the first time I had met him. He was then in his early forties and recently divorced with a six year old son who lived mostly with his mother. In this single state he had devised what very few of us can ever afford to devise, a lifestyle which suited him and him alone. Part of the week he spent at Swincombe managing the business of the estate, as he owned half of Swincombe village, as well as a good deal of agricultural land. The rest of the time he was in London researching in a desultory way for a book he was writing on the Great War. At weekends he would be sociable at Swincombe with friends coming down to stay and locals, such as us, being entertained to lunch or supper. He had a small staff but did a good deal of the cooking himself.

He was not unattractive, being slender and dark with an aquiline, Byronic countenance. The romantic cast of his appearance was enhanced by some eccentricities of dress. He almost always wore jeans, but had a penchant for fancy waistcoats and white shirts which he liked to wear with the collars turned up. Over this he usually had on a black jacket, possibly of his own design, almost knee length, slightly flared below the waist. I got the sense of someone by no means uncomfortable with life, but, for all his luxuries and liberties, unfulfilled, drifting. He was genial but there was something about him which balked at intimacy.

We arrived at Swincombe, as requested, just before midday so that he could show us round the house before lunch. His weekend guests, he told me, were due any minute. One activity he never seemed to tire of was showing people Swincombe, so all of us enjoyed the tour.

The Blue Room

The charm of its well-mannered but idiosyncratic exterior is maintained within. The main rooms are spacious but not grandiose. The Jacobean coffered and pargetted ceilings are nicely complemented by Georgian door frames and panelling on the walls. The pictures are good, though not of the cleanest. Johnnie's family appeared to favour decent portraitists of the second rank like Dance and Devis and Hoppner. There is some very fine Georgian furniture which, as in many such houses, exists in a state which might be described as 'taken for granted', somewhere between total neglect and loving care. We only saw the ground floor reception rooms because, before he could show us the upstairs bedrooms, his house guests arrived.

These consisted of a publisher and his wife who were considering renting the gate house—an architectural gem in itself—for weekends, and a seventy-year-old spinster cousin. One of Johnnie's most attractive traits is the tenderness he feels for his many elderly relatives. The other guest was a girl in her twenties called 'Piggy' Wark-Winkworth, willowy and waif-like, with pale blonde hair that seemed perpetually to be falling into her eyes. Anyone less like a pig I never saw, but that was to be expected: aristocratic nicknames are deliberately designed to baffle the outside world. She belonged to a physical type, I subsequently discovered, that Johnnie favoured.

It was an informal gathering, so we ate in the kitchen because it was warm, spacious and convenient. It was a pleasant occasion. Both Robert and the publisher exuded the bonhomie of complacent success, and the elderly cousin, next to whom I sat, concealed beneath her placid, faded exterior a markedly original view of life. 'Piggy' said very little, but seemed content to sit and pick at her food and occasionally flick a pale tassel of hair out of her eyes. Pat and the publisher's wife talked to each other about their children.

There was one feature of the meal which alerted me to our host's deep vein of eccentricity: the table mats. They were, at first glance, of the conventional rectangular kind, made of laminated wood with green baize beneath and a pictorial upper side. However the scenes depicted on these mats were not the usual hunting or topographical prints, but erotic engravings of the most explicit nature, dating from the eighteenth and early nineteenth centuries. No one remarked on them, but when Robert noticed his he let out a sharp, involuntary bark of laughter, his customary reaction to any profound embarrassment.

After lunch Johnnie proposed a walk. Behind the house was a level lawn and an oval lake, then the ground rose steeply to a ridge of the Cotswolds. On this slope could be seen the traces of an early eighteenth-century stone cascade. At the top of the cascade was a folly in the form of a circular colonnaded structure surmounted by an obelisk. Johnnie was in the slow—very slow—process of restoring this feature and he proposed that we should inspect progress.

Johnnie likes to walk quickly, as I do, so we soon became separated from the rest of the party who were dawdling and chatting in the spring sunshine. For a while Johnnie and I climbed up towards the folly in silence. At length I felt it was necessary to say something and so, because I am interested in such things, I asked him if Swincombe was haunted.

After a pause Johnny said: 'No. Not really. But there is the Blue Room.'

'What is the Blue Room?'

'One of the bedrooms in the south wing. It has an effect on people.'

'What sort of an effect?'

'Sexual mainly.'

I pressed him for further details which he seemed at first reluctant to impart. Eventually he revealed that anyone sleeping in the Blue Room, male or female, was liable to be consumed,

The Blue Room

particularly in the early hours of the morning, with an all but overwhelming desire for sex.

'Or so they say,' he added, but I could tell that for some reason he was back-peddling. 'It's only a sort of legend. There was this ancestor of mine who lived here in the early seventeenth century. Black Jack Stanway, he was called, and he built most of Swincombe as it stands today. (Baron Stanway is one of my courtesy titles incidentally, but we never use it.) Well, according to the legend, in about 1630 Black Jack saved some shady character from being burned alive at Evesham for witchcraft. In those days a title really counted for something. So, as a return favour, they say this magician chappie put a spell on the Blue Room so that any lady sleeping in it would be so aroused between the hours of twelve and three that she would submit willingly to Black Jack's advances.'

'And did he take full advantage?'

'History alas does not record, except to say that he died in that bedroom.'

'In the arms of a wench?'

'I believe so.'

'Has the Blue Room been tested since?'

'Well,' said Johnnie. 'Here we are at the folly.' And as, by then, the rest of the party had caught up with us, discussion of the Blue Room was abandoned.

On our return from the folly Johnnie's housekeeper, Mrs Maxton, served tea in the Long Drawing Room. While the others were milling around Johnnie drew me aside and pointed to a dingy half-length portrait by Daniel Mytens dating from 1628.

'That's Black Jack Stanway,' he said.

Above a white ruff, the shape and size of a small millstone, emerged a head with lank, dirty reddish hair and a straggling beard. He had a large misshapen nose, a mean mouth and small, resentful eyes which gave him the look of a small-time criminal who has just been cheated out of his share of the loot. It was clear that if anyone required an adventitious aid to erotic success it was Black Jack.

'Something of a character,' said Johnnie complacently.

While this was happening the other house guests were asking the housekeeper, as she dispensed tea, which rooms they were to be allotted for the night. Piggy Wark-Winkworth was the last to ask.

'And where am I sleeping?' said Piggy.

Without a break in her tea pouring, Mrs Maxton said: 'You're in the Blue Room, Miss. I've already put your things there.'

As every actor knows, sometimes showing no expression at all can be as effective as making a face. When Johnnie looked at me, I looked back at him with a completely blank countenance. Our eyes met, and he understood at once that I was not going to betray him.

It was from that look that I date a certain understanding—I would not exactly call it friendship—between Johnnie Buckland and myself. When he was in London he sometimes used to invite me to have lunch with him at his club, Whites, where he would confide in me. I do not flatter myself that he found me particularly wise or sympathetic. I think it was more that he trusted my discretion, particularly because I was an outsider and, unlike Pat and Robert, had no ambitions to be part of his social milieu.

His confidences were mainly sexual in nature. He was a man of strong, almost obsessive desires. He was fascinated by all forms of sexual perversion, but not out of a wish to practice them: his own preferences were exclusively adult, consensual and heterosexual. Nevertheless he wanted, within these conventional parameters, to experience as variously as possible. Commitment to an exclusive relationship was, since the failure of his marriage, not something that interested him at all.

Once, I broached the subject of the Blue Room, and he was, after an initial reluctance, honest about it.

The Blue Room

'Oh, yes. It works, all right,' he said.

I asked whether he, as well as the 'victim', felt the room's influence. He told me that he did. I asked him what it felt like.

'It's like a vibration,' he said. 'It's as if the whole room is alive with sexual energy. Your whole mind becomes focused on one thing, and one thing alone, so that the rest of you can't think straight.'

'It sounds dangerous.'

'It is. I keep it almost permanently locked now, ever since Mrs Maxton, unknown to me, put the old Bishop of Worcester in there. He was eighty three.'

'Did he have a heart attack?'

'Oh, he survived, but Poppy didn't.'

'Poppy?'

'My favourite Labrador. She must have wandered in at the wrong time. Her grave is in the Rose Garden. I'd rather not discuss it. So I try to use the Blue Room as little as possible, but it does work as what I call "an icebreaker".'

I made no comment and later felt guilty about my silence.

One weekend when we were in Gloucestershire Johnnie came over to drinks at the cottage. I noticed at once that he was in a dejected mood, but Pat and Robert were so delighted to have him under their humble roof that they seemed oblivious to his state of mind. While they were out of the room assembling the canapés and champagne for this informal occasion, I asked him what was wrong. Johnnie slumped into a chair and dug his hands deep into his jeans pockets.

'Princess Frederica's coming the weekend after next,' he said, and groaned. (Sophisticated readers will know which late member of the Royal Family I mean by Princess Frederica; the rest will have to be content with their ignorance. It really does not matter, anyway.)

'Did you invite her?' I asked.

'You don't invite Princess Frederica. She invites herself. It's particularly bloody because Selena Selby's coming down that weekend. I'm rather keen on her actually.'

'The Blue Room?'

'She's a sweet girl. Anyway, it happened that I was at this awful bash in London a week or so ago at Clarence House. God knows why! And there was H.R.H. Frederica. Well, we've met on several occasions because she used to holiday a lot on Micky Dorset's private island off Guadaloupe and I used to go too. So she latched on to me and started going on about how she had heard so much about Swincombe, and how she would love to see it, blah, blah. You know how she goes on. . . . Well, perhaps you don't. And the next thing I know she's made me invite her down for the weekend.'

'It can't be that bad surely?'

'Good God, it's worse! Don't you know about Princess Frederica coming to stay? No, I suppose you don't.' Johnnie fished a crumpled piece of paper out of his jeans and tossed it on to the coffee table in front of him. 'That came from her office this morning.'

At this point Pat and Robert came in with the champagne, and, once the drinks were poured, we all settled down to study the document.

In it a certain Lady Florence Cardew ('Lady in Waiting to H.R.H. Princess Frederica') set down what Her Royal Highness was to expect from a visit to Swincombe. It was certainly thorough, and listed in detail not only what the Princess would like to eat and drink, but whom she would like to meet and where she would like to go. Many of the provisions were concerned with what Princess Frederica would *not* like. For example:

'Her Royal Highness will eat potatoes, but not plain boiled, and not "chips".'

The Blue Room

Evidently the proletarian word 'chips' was so offensive to her that it had to be placed within the protective barriers of inverted commas. Again:

'Her Royal Highness will drink only Glen Gowdie Single Malt [a notoriously expensive and hard to obtain brand] with Evian water (half and half) before meals. She may also drink it with meals, but will accept (though not necessarily drink) a glass of claret (Premier Cru Bordeaux only, please) with the meal. A bottle of Glen Gowdie Single Malt and a bottle of Evian water is to be placed by her bedside.'

Even Robert, a devoted royalist, had to concede that she did seem 'a little demanding'. The letter also stipulated whom she would like to be invited to have lunch and dinner with her, but conceded: 'You may invite three or four people of your own choice, provided that their names are submitted for vetting at least a week in advance.' There and then Johnnie decided that we should come to lunch on the Sunday to lend, as he put it, 'moral support'. I glanced at Robert. His expression reminded me of Bernini's celebrated statue of St Teresa at Santa Maria della Vittoria in Rome. The saint has just been pierced by an arrow of Divine Love, and a look of sanctified sensual ecstasy suffuses her entire being.

I have confused memories of the lunch with Princess Frederica. We were briefly introduced and I must reluctantly concede that she did possess an odd kind of glamour. That once legendary beauty was still somehow present, hovering like a ghost about her lined and leathery face, darting in and out of those intensely blue eyes. When told that I was in the theatre, she remarked:

'Oh, God! Not another actor!'

They were the only words she spoke to me, not notably gracious ones at that. I would like to record that I came back with a witty retort, but I did not. (One doesn't.) I retired crushed.

The lunch, which took place in the large and chilly dining room, I remember chiefly for two things. I remember my brother-in-law embarrassing me inordinately because he laughed loudly at almost everything the Princess said. Secondly, I noticed sitting next to the Princess, an exquisitely beautiful ash-blond girl in her mid-twenties with a dreamy expression. Johnnie's ideal, I thought. I asked the well-bred nonentity sitting next to me if this was Selena Selby.

'*Lady* Selena Selby, yes,' he replied with a reproachful sniff for my ignorance.

After the meal Princess Frederica, for whom some elaborate post-lunch diversion had been contrived, suddenly decided that what she wanted was a nap and marched off to her bedroom, leaving the rest of us at something of a loss. Johnny proposed a walk and a reassembly for tea at four. I saw him glance urgently in my direction: it was clear he wanted to confide.

By walking fast and climbing up narrow paths by the old cascade we managed to shake off the others. I asked him how it was going, or some similarly feeble question.

'Did you see Selena at lunch next to H.R.H?' he asked.

I nodded.

'Lovely, isn't she? I put her in the Blue Room.'

'I see.'

'Yes. Well. It was pretty agonising actually, because H.R.H. wouldn't go to bed last night at a decent hour, so of course we all had to stay up to keep her company. She would insist on chain smoking and playing this bloody game called Canasta. You know how she is. Oh, no, I was forgetting. Of course you don't. Well, it was past midnight before she eventually decided she'd had enough.'

The Blue Room

Johnnie told me that it was almost half past one before he could make his way along the draughty corridors of Swincombe towards the Blue Room and Lady Selena. He opened the door and heard a voice whisper: 'Close the door behind you.' He did so and found himself in complete darkness. He asked Selena to switch on the light, but she, whispering again, refused. By this time the atmosphere of the Blue Room was beginning to have its effect on him. His head began to pound with sexual longing. He groped his way to the bed, encouraged by her lubricious whisperings, and the next moment, it seemed to him, he was engulfed in a bout of the most torrid lovemaking he had ever experienced.

'The Blue Room was working its magic all right and in spades,' said Johnnie. 'Even I was a bit startled by it all. Either it was the room or Selena herself, but she seemed to know all the tricks. The only thing she wouldn't do was let me turn on the lights. Well, by the end of it I was too exhausted to do anything more. I just collapsed and in less than half a minute I was dead to the world.

'It must have been five when I woke. There was a crack in the curtains which threw this shaft of grey light into the room. I could see Selena's shape under the duvet. It was a surprisingly bulky shape for Selena, who's a slip of a thing, as you know. Well, that surprised me, but then I saw two things on the bedside table which made me go awfully numb. I wonder if you can guess what they were.'

'A bottle of Glen Gowdie Single Malt and a bottle of Evian water?'

'Bloody Hell. Got it in one! Selena and H.R.H. must have swapped bedrooms without my knowing. I'd had my way with an elderly Royal. I can tell you, I was out of that bedroom and into my own in double quick time. I couldn't go to sleep again, so I dressed and wandered about the house. At about half past seven I happened to come in to the Long Drawing Room, and blow me, there was H.R.H., in a dressing gown, smoking a fag on one of the Chinese Chippendale day beds.'

Conversation between Johnnie and the Princess, I gathered, was pretty sticky, but eventually he plucked up enough courage to tell her that he didn't know that she had moved to the Blue Bedroom. Princess Frederica was quite cool about it and totally unapologetic. She said:

'It was too late to tell you. Selena and I agreed to swap bedrooms. I didn't like mine very much. That shade of yellow in those damask curtains is not me at all. Blue happens to be my favourite colour. You should have known that.'

Johnnie then tried to explain that he did not want her to get the wrong impression from last night, that he had been unaware that it had been her, that. . . . He floundered.

There was a long pause before Princess Frederica said: 'You don't honestly imagine that I didn't know all about the Blue Room, did you?'

By this time, Johnnie told me, he was in a state of complete shock, or, as he put it, 'feeling like a rabbit at a stoat's tea party'. Princess Frederica rose from the day bed, ground the remains of her cigarette into the Aubusson carpet with her heel, and drifted to the window. She gazed dreamily out on to the croquet lawn where, as if by Royal Command, the sun emerged from behind a cloud and made the morning dew sparkle.

'Lady Selena is such a sweet girl. I am very fond of her,' she said. 'Did you know she is one of my goddaughters?'

Johnnie shook his head. The Princess moved away from the window and began to advance towards him rather deliberately. For a moment he thought he was going to be hit. Johnnie braced himself for the Royal clout, but it did not come. Instead she just patted his cheek. 'There was a look on her face that was almost human,' Johnnie told me. 'Humorous, even.'

'Let that be a lesson to you,' said the Princess.

A NIGHTMARE SANG

There can be few more excruciating experiences for a dramatist than to see one's play badly performed. Despite this, a mixture of vanity, curiosity and optimism always compelled Daniel Pinson, a forty year old playwright of some distinction, to go to see his work on stage whenever the opportunity arose. That was why one evening in early August he attended an amateur production of his two-act historical drama *The Poisons Affair* at the Jubilee Hall, Bidmouth. However, to save himself more embarrassment than was strictly necessary, he went incognito.

It was quite by chance that he had found himself in Bidmouth, and that the Bidmouth Players happened to be producing his play, which four years previously had enjoyed a respectable run in the West End. Pinson had been giving a course of lectures for the Department of Theatre Studies at Truro University. When the term finished, he had decided to give himself a brief holiday in the West Country before returning to London. There had been little to return to. A long-term relationship had broken up some months before, which was one of the reasons why he had gone to Truro.

Pinson had been staying with friends inland and it was they who told him that, if he wanted to spend a quiet few days on the coast, Bidmouth was the sort of place he might like. It was a picturesque old Devon fishing port, not overrun with tourists but lively enough, with one or two good seafood restaurants. His friends recommended a bed and breakfast boarding house and Pinson booked himself in for three nights.

On his first evening in Bidmouth Pinson had seen a poster for his play stuck up with sellotape in a shop window. The crude artwork, in black on pink paper, had obviously been designed by someone who had no idea what the play was about, but had made a rough guess from the title. A skull reposed under a lighted candle, corrugated with gouts of wax, next to which stood a bottle, helpfully labelled POISON. Pinson read that the last night of the show was the following evening.

When he bought a ticket at the tourist office next morning it was gratifying to find that he had secured one of the last seats available. That, and the fact that it was a fine, refreshing summer's day put him in good spirits. Pinson was someone who found solitude invigorating. He walked around the town with its narrow lanes and quaint cobbled streets, letting his mind take hold of whatever it fancied, hoping it would lead him to the subject of his next play. He had been blocked ever since Francine had left him.

Every time he saw a poster for his play he would stop and examine it with a secret smile on his lips. After a hearty fish and chip lunch at one of the little cafés on the quay he went in search of the Jubilee Hall, so that he would know exactly where to go that evening.

Outside the hall—a strange architectural mélange of neo-Classical and Byzantine—hung a board which displayed the play's poster and a number of production photos which Pinson examined with interest. The use of flash photography, customary in amateur productions, gave the scenes they depicted a coarse, two-dimensional effect, and exposed the crudities of the actors' make-up. But Pinson noted with pleasure that the costumes were authentic and well-made, in fact outstandingly good for non-professionals. In addition, from a physical point of view, the actors and actresses seemed to have been well cast for their roles.

The Poisons Affair was about the celebrated scandal at the court of Louis XIV in which various prominent members of his entourage, including his mistress Madame de Montespan, were implicated in acts of poisoning and, worse, black magic. Pinson, a writer noted for his economy and sense of form, had reduced the cast of characters to six: three men and three women. It was a play about sex and power and prejudice; it was also a kind of thriller; it had been a success.

That evening before the show, in a pub opposite the Jubilee Hall, Pinson had a light early supper of smoked salmon sandwiches and whisky. He had never been a heavy drinker, but he sometimes used alcohol in carefully calculated amounts to ease the burden of his sorrows. On this occasion he decided that two large whiskies with ginger ale would suffice to take the edge off any frustration he might feel at the performance's inadequacies.

They were enough too to make him feel a warm glow of affection for the cheerful, mostly middle-aged audience that was piling into the small foyer of the hall. Did they know that they were about to witness a rather sinister historical melodrama? They seemed wholly bent on innocent amusement. Pinson worried, but only a little and bought himself a programme which entitled him, he noticed, to 'a free interval glass of wine'. This was just as well, because the programme was otherwise not very good value. It contained little information about the play and none at all about its author beyond the bare mention of his name.

The seats were not numbered so he went into the auditorium early and found himself a place on an aisle where he could stretch his long legs. It was a traditional municipal entertainment hall with plastic stacking chairs on the flat wooden floors and a high, raised stage at one end. Pinson spent fifteen entertaining minutes watching his audience—they were always 'his' in his mind—enter, find their places, greet old friends, chatter inanely. Five minutes after the play was due to begin, when the hall was packed, the lights dimmed; a fragment of recorded Lully blared out through the loudspeakers and, with a little death rattle, the curtains were drawn apart.

One of the aspects of amateur acting which always surprises professionals is not that it is bad but that it so often lacks what one would have expected it to have in abundance: gusto, energy, enthusiasm. By and large amateurs do not go 'over the top', they go under it, often so far under as to be inaudible. These actors, at least, were not inaudible, but they were distinctly underpowered. Rage and passion came over as mild annoyance or tepid desire; anything more subtle barely registered. The moves had been carefully worked out but were executed mechanically without much reference to what was being felt. All the same, Pinson was gratified to find that the audience was listening intently to his words and laughing heartily at the wit, even when it was delivered less than convincingly.

Finding the performance itself unengrossing he began to speculate about the lives of the actors on stage. The most accomplished of them was the woman playing the leading role of Madame de Montespan, whose name, he saw from the

A Nightmare Sang

programme, was Jean Crowden. She was in her forties and though not exactly beautiful she had the big, blowsy but still voluptuous figure that Montespan herself must have had at the time of the poisons scandal. She moved awkwardly, but she had a certain panache. Pinson observed with amusement that she got all her laughs by the simple method of saying her wittiest lines slightly louder than she said the rest.

In spite of himself Pinson experienced a frisson of sexual interest. How would she react, he wondered, if he were to introduce himself as the great author of her lines? He shrugged away the thought. After all, he had just finished a protracted affair with Francine Allen, the brilliant actress who had portrayed Montespan in the original West End production.

Another performer attracted his attention for a rather different reason. This was the man who played the part of the Abbé Guibourg. Guibourg was the villainous renegade priest who was reputed to have sacrificed babies in black magic ceremonies so that Montespan might preserve her hold over King Louis. The Bastille records, unusually for them, describe his physical appearance in some detail. Guibourg had been a large, bloated, one-eyed man with a hideous face and a blotchy red complexion.

The scene in which Guibourg makes his first appearance is laid at night in the gardens of Versailles. His sinister figure, all in ecclesiastical black, suddenly emerges from the leafy shadows. It is a powerful moment and, on this occasion even Pinson, who was expecting it, received a shock. The actor playing Guibourg was so exactly as Pinson had imagined him: over six feet four, loose-bellied, with red-veined and pendulous jowls, one eye covered by a black patch, the other bloodshot. The effect was incomparably sinister, far more so even than the West End production. Pinson looked at the cast list in his programme. The name of the actor playing Guibourg was Alec Crowden, obviously related to Jean who played Montespan. But how? As husband, brother, or father even?

The Complete Symphonies of Adolf Hitler

Unfortunately, Alec Crowden's performance did not live up to the impact of his first appearance. His mind seemed to be elsewhere; he spoke his lines as if in a dream, but at least he looked the part.

For Pinson the pace of the production was unbearably slow, so, when the interval came, he decided that perhaps after all he would not stay for the second half. Seeing his work performed was a bittersweet experience at the best of times and, in this instance, bitterness had predominated. He would claim his free interval wine and then exchange the stuffiness of the Jubilee Hall for the clean sea air outside, an inviting prospect only slightly vitiated by lingering curiosity. Pinson was just draining his glass of tepid Liebfraumilch when he heard a voice behind him.

'You are Daniel Pinson and I claim my five pounds!'

Pinson snarled angrily to himself, but by the time he had turned round to face the speaker he was wearing an engaging smile. The man who had addressed him was rather older looking than he had expected from the voice. He was bald, neat, spectacled, cardiganed and carried a clipboard. A concession to the artistic had been made by his sporting of a brightly coloured cravat around his neck.

'I'm sorry?' said Pinson.

'You are Daniel Pinson, are you not?' It was a thin, pedantic, annoying voice. Pinson would have liked to have said no, but he could tell that he would not have been believed and even more annoyance would have resulted from a denial. He nodded.

'Ron Titlow, President and Principal Director of the Bidmouth Players,' said the man, extending his hand. Pinson shook it. Titlow's grip was cold, dry and surprisingly strong.

'So!' said Titlow, lowering his voice to a mock conspiratorial murmur. 'We are travelling incognito, are we?'

'You could say that.'

A Nightmare Sang

Titlow tapped his nose with a biro. 'Have no fear! Your secret is safe with me. Another glass of vino?'

'No thank you.'

Pinson saw that he would have to make himself agreeable to Titlow. He told him that he had come across the Bidmouth Players' production quite by accident. Titlow was surprised: hadn't he been informed by his agent or his publishers? The fact was that amateur productions showed up on Pinson's quarterly royalty statement from French's, the play publishers, and that was the first and last he knew or wished to know about them. Titlow seemed a little put out that Pinson had not been 'apprised', as he put it. (Titlow was head of the English Department at Bidmouth Comprehensive.)

'You do know this is the West of England Amateur Première of your play?' said Titlow.

Pinson put on his suitably impressed expression.

'Oh, yes. We pride ourselves on being rather ahead in terms of quality and innovation, you know. A little bit *avant garde*, as they say. Our production of *The Dance of Death* came second in the Amateur Dramatic Regional Finals last year.'

Pinson reinvigorated his features to adopt the same look as before. A bell rang to recall the audience to their seats. Pinson was not going to be able to escape.

'Now tell me honestly,' said Titlow. 'Be as frank as you like. Speaking as the expert here. In your professional opinion, what do you think of our little production?' Pinson hesitated. Another bell sounded. 'No, don't tell me now! Wait till you've seen the second half. Tell you what, we're having a little last-night, post-show celebration. Why don't you join us? Not a few bottles of the bubbly will be cracked, I can tell you. We'd really be honoured.'

'Well. . . .'

'That's marvellous. My little company will be absolutely thrilled.'

231

'Don't tell them now,' said Pinson. 'It might put them off.'

Titlow laughed, a curious falsetto giggle. 'You bet I won't. This is going to be our little surprise. Wait in the foyer after the show. I'll come and collect you.' The last bell rang. With that, Pinson re-entered the hall and Titlow disappeared into the lighting box.

The second half for Pinson was even more tedious than the first, with the exception of one moment. This involved the Abbé Guibourg. In the penultimate scene Guibourg, now in captivity, languishes in a cell in the prison of Vincennes. Because of his connection with the King's mistress he was not allowed to stand trial, but was condemned instead to perpetual solitary confinement. He has somehow acquired a bottle of wine and is singing a raucous song in his cell. It is one of those moments which playwrights create for which actors take most of the credit. The song is defiant, uproarious but at the same time utterly despairing. Done well it left an unforgettable impression on the audience.

Pinson had almost dozed off in the stifling heat of the hall when he heard the song, but something about it awakened him to full consciousness. It was as if a glass of iced water had been poured down his back. He stared at the stage where Guibourg was ranting out the song, waving his bottle in the air. Here was a man surviving in a state of living death pouring out his last maledictions upon a world he hated. Pinson realised that the actor on stage had achieved what perhaps only a non-professional can occasionally realise, a complete, unmediated identification with a character without the aid of technique or artifice. At that moment the man simply was Guibourg, the drunken, despairing Satanist, raving upon the lip of Hell. Pinson noted that the audience too were aware of it. They were watching the man on stage in an awed, alarmed silence, and, in the mortal stillness which followed the conclusion of the song, a young

A Nightmare Sang

woman got up from her seat and ran precipitately from the auditorium, her sobbing breaths audible to all.

But it was only a moment. When the dialogue was resumed the play went flat again. At the end, however, there was much gratifying applause. All the actors, with the exception of Alec Crowden who had played Guibourg, were beaming and basking in the public approval. Then Ron Titlow came on and took a bow. He smirked exultantly and winked at Pinson. When he calmed the audience to make his little speech Pinson was afraid that he might be mentioned, but he wasn't. Titlow was too full of himself to leave much credit for anyone else.

Pinson had been aware of Titlow's complacency during their conversation, but this address to the audience displayed another level of arrogance altogether. He spoke as if he and his actors were high priests and the audience their acolytes, privileged to breathe in the perfume of culture which the Players had wafted in their direction. Pinson thought that the audience took this condescension with remarkable tolerance; whether this was out of amusement or incomprehension he could not tell.

When they met again in the foyer, Pinson, who liked to push people who annoyed him to their extremes, complimented Titlow on his speech. Titlow who was obviously in one of those exalted states where praise seems commonplace said:

'I don't think these people fully realise quite what we do for them. And all for love. That's what "amateur" means, you know.'

'Thanks for not mentioning me in your speech.'

'Oh, I wouldn't spoil my little surprise on the boys and girls for anything.'

The back stage area in the Jubilee Hall had only two large communal dressing rooms, one for each sex. Titlow led him to the door of the women's dressing room where the bottles of Asti and sparkling Chardonnay were being popped and the well-wishers were gathered. Pinson could see that the female members of the cast, having removed their costumes but not their make-up, were gleaming in gaudy dressing gowns in front of the mirror lights. Titlow clapped his hands for silence to make an announcement.

'A little surprise for you, boys and girls. Allow me to present a special guest of honour who has come all the way down from London for the last night of our West of England Amateur Première.'

Titlow turned and winked at Pinson.

'Our author and my friend, Dan Pinson.'

A burst of delighted applause drowned any objections Pinson might have to being called 'Dan'—it was always either Daniel, or Danny to his intimates—or to the implication that he was here in an other than accidental capacity. He was immediately engulfed in unqualified approval and admiration, both of which, in small, controlled doses, can be very pleasant, even beneficial. Pinson could remember very little of the first twenty minutes in that dressing room. The heat and bright lights made him drink more sparkling Chardonnay than he should have; the adulation was equally intoxicating. He noticed how when the thin young woman who had played the Duchesse de Fontanges was talking excitedly to him, her husband (or boyfriend), an athletic, rugby-playing type, had his arm round her shoulder in a firm grip. Pinson's smile in his direction was greeted with stony vacancy.

Most of the time Pinson had Titlow at his side, steering the conversation, performing introductions. Then he was being guided slowly towards one corner of the dressing room where Jean Crowden, who had played Montespan, was holding court. When Titlow had manoeuvred Pinson to within speaking distance of Jean Crowden, he performed the introductions with the air of a man presenting one head of state to another.

'Now, Dan, I want you to meet our leading lady, Jean. I sometimes say that our Jean *is* the Bidmouth Players. Without her it simply would not exist? Isn't that right, Jean?'

A Nightmare Sang

'If you say so, Ron,' said Jean placidly. Pinson, who prided himself on a sensitivity to such things, thought he could detect a long history of antagonism and power struggle behind their badinage.

Jean was sitting in a wicker basket chair at an angle to her dressing room mirror which was festooned with cards. She wore a scarlet silk dressing gown decorated with Chinese dragons, the belt of which was tied tightly so that her ample curves showed. Her hair was bound up in a bright green silk scarf, and the stage make-up that she still wore was equally violent. No beauty perhaps; but there was something magnetic about those small dark eyes that glittered like shards of jet.

She was surrounded by a group of attendant admirers. For a moment or two she stared at Pinson, then she said:

'So you are the great author. You are naughty, Ron, not to tell us that the famous Daniel Pinson was in front. Oh, forgive me! Allow me to introduce you to some of my friends.' She indicated first a small, almost dwarfish old clergyman dressed in clerical black with a dog collar. 'This is Canon Doker. Retired Canon now. He's a great stalwart of the Players. He's the one who found our lovely costumes.'

Canon Doker nodded and smiled. Pinson was able to compliment him sincerely and asked him how he had managed to get hold of such magnificent and authentic garments. The Canon grinned and rubbed his bony little hands together.

'Oh, I have my methods. I have my methods!' he said.

Jean then introduced Pinson to others in her entourage, but she kept to the last the tall, bloated man who was standing behind her, the man who had played Guibourg.

'And this is my husband Alec,' she said. Alec extended his hand and Pinson shook something cold, slick and flabby, like a reptile's corpse. Close-to, the age difference between the husband and wife was even more evident: at a guess late sixties to mid-forties. A brief pause followed before Pinson steeled himself to the obligatory compliment.

'I was very impressed by the performance,' he said, making his remark as general as possible. It was a relief to find that no further assessment of the production was required of him. Jean's acolytes were anxious to offer praise which she accepted with languid pleasure while, from time to time, her eyes strayed towards Pinson. Whenever she did so, he looked away.

'So, Daniel,' she said eventually. 'How long are you going to be with us in Bidmouth?'

'I'm leaving the day after tomorrow,' he said.

Jean gave a little cry: 'But you can't! We must keep you a while longer. Where are you staying?' Pinson reluctantly told her. 'Oh, I know. Not bad as those sort of little places go. Now Daniel, leave this all to me. I'll fix you up with a proper place of your own where you can stay for at least another week. It'll hardly cost you a thing. I just *know* that you're struggling with a new play at the moment. Am I right?'

Pinson murmured something faintly affirmative.

'There, you see! I knew it. And Bidmouth is just the place where you can get a little inspiration in peace and quiet. Don't you agree everyone?'

Everyone agreed. On Jean's instructions Pinson was driven back to his bed and breakfast by Canon Doker in a car almost as small as he was. Doker told Pinson that he had been a Canon of Truro Cathedral, but had retired early, to 'devote myself to my interests'. Pinson did not know you could retire early from the Church, but he took little interest in the Canon's chatter because his long legs were aching from the cramped conditions of the car. The Canon was a great name dropper and seemed to know almost everyone there was to know in the theatrical world. He repeated several pieces of scabrous show-business gossip which Pinson had thought were known only to himself and a very few others.

A Nightmare Sang

Pinson hated being given lifts, especially when they were unnecessary, so he was relieved when the journey was over, but even when he was back in his own room at the bed and breakfast the unease remained. For a while it prohibited sleep, which, when it eventually came, was plagued by dreams of being driven in Canon Doker's car towards an uncertain and unwanted destination. With every mile the car became smaller, his legs and arms more constricted. Several times he burst out of his imprisonment into wakefulness, but when sleep returned, so did the dream.

Pinson's landlady was called Mrs Bread, a solid phlegmatic woman who rather resembled a loaf of the stuff. The next morning at breakfast she remarked, as she was bringing him the toast, that she had heard that he was at the Jubilee Hall last night. Pinson did not ask her how she knew, but it made him feel better about returning to London the next day. In response he told her that he was the author of the play that had been performed there. Mrs Bread shook her head, unimpressed.

'Those amateur dramatics people,' she said. 'I don't hold with all that.'

'Why not?' asked Pinson who found resolute philistinism intensely irritating.

'They're a click; that's what they are. A click.'

It took a few moments for Pinson to realise that she meant 'clique', by which time Mrs Bread had quitted the room in a marked manner. He lingered over his toast, musing on the nature of clicks and listening to the distant squeal of gulls. It was a pleasant morning; he might even get some writing done. Then the doorbell rang.

Pinson listened idly through the half-open door of the front parlour where he was breakfasting as Mrs Bread and another female with an oddly familiar voice appeared to be having a mild altercation. He recognised the soft but insistent tones in which women vie with each other for supremacy. Then the struggle was over and, followed by Mrs Bread, the winner entered the room. It was Jean Crowden in a lime green trouser suit.

Something about the moment—it may even have been the trouser suit—filled Pinson with alarm. In the background Mrs Bread was apologising for Jean's intrusion and, as she did so, Pinson felt a moment of decision pass from him. Dismissing Mrs Bread with a nod, he offered Jean a cup of tea. She shook her head and sat down.

'It's all arranged,' she said. 'We've found the perfect spot for you to do some writing. Spyhole Cottage. You'll just love it, I know. Very oldy-worldy.' Pinson opened his mouth. 'Now don't argue. The rent's going to be peanuts. It's owned by some old friends, Adela and Jim. You met them last night. Jim was the one with the withered arm, remember?' Pinson did not. 'Now I'm going to take you out and show you the sights of old Bidmouth. Then some of the gang are joining us for lunch at the Saracen's Head which is *the* place to eat round here. Then Jim and Adela'll show you Spyhole which you can move into tomorrow. How about that?'

By this time, Pinson told himself, the moment for resistance had long passed. Jean watched him intently while he finished his tea. He glanced over her head to the doorway in which Mrs Bread appeared for a second. She looked at him, shook her head, then disappeared.

Reluctantly at first, Pinson found himself enjoying his tour of Bidmouth in Jean's car, a comfortable, air-conditioned Mercedes. In her presence he felt free of restraint and obligation, even the obligation to like her. She told him all about Bidmouth's scandals and controversies, in many of which she and her coterie of friends—'the gang'—played the roles of heroic victims who finally triumphed over the forces of reaction and obscurantism. Pinson recognised an embryonic talent for fiction in her gift for mythologising events.

A Nightmare Sang

Having seen the sights of the town, mostly from the comfortable interior of the car, Jean said: 'There is one place I must show you before we go to lunch. It is rather special. The most wonderful views. You will love it.'

They drove out of Bidmouth and then along a coastal road that swooped and swung through the Devon countryside. The sky was clear but for a few high white clouds; the scenery was idyllic. Through gaps in the trees and dips in the fields Pinson caught flashes of sunlit sea. The dazzle of light and beauty put Pinson into a trance from which Jean suddenly aroused him.

She said: 'Of course, it's a marvellous play and all that, but you're quite wrong, you know.'

'What?'

'Your play about the Poisons Affair. You got my character, Madame de Montespan, the King's mistress, all wrong.'

'Ah. You think she was an innocent victim of rumour, then? All that stuff about black magic ceremonies was made up? Yes. Many historians think that.'

'Oh, no! She did it all right. What you got wrong was that she just made use of the magical ceremonies to keep the King in her bed. No. She was far deeper into all that stuff than you make out. The Abbé Guibourg was one of her people. She was Queen of the Witches.'

This was a novel theory which Pinson had never heard before, obviously culled from some trashy book on the occult.

'Oh, really?' he said, gently condescending. 'And how do you know that?'

'Canon Doker told me. He's an expert on that sort of thing. You know who you ought to write a play about next?'

'No,' said Pinson in what he hoped was a discouraging voice. If there was one thing he hated more than anything it was to be told by a non writer what he should write about.

'Joan of Arc,' said Jean who seemed oblivious to his tone.

'Done already, I believe.' Sarcasm was not disguised.

'I know. I know. But not properly. All that saint rubbish. She was actually a top witch, you know. Canon Doker told me all about it. I mean, her best friend was this bloke who was actually executed for black magic and all sorts. Jill, something or other.'

'Gilles de Rais. The original Bluebeard. Sorcerer and sodomite.'

'Exactly. There you are. She must have been a witch.'

'That is to assume guilt by association.'

'Who said anything about guilt?'

'You might just as well say that because Gilles de Rais was a friend of Joan's he must have been a saint like her.'

'Well, I think it's a fascinating idea. I've even thought of a title. *Joan the Witch*. Don't you think that's *the* most brilliant idea?'

At that moment Jean suddenly swerved off the road and onto a dirt track that wound towards the sea. Pinson noted that a white signpost at the beginning of the track had pointed the way to a place called DODMAN'S POINT. Having reached a flat open space over which a few sheep grazed Jean stopped the car and said:

'We'll walk from here.'

They got out of the Mercedes, which she had parked in the lee of a dry stone wall. Pinson followed Jean along a chalky little path towards a narrow grass-covered promontory. Its sides were steep granite cliffs which fell fifty or sixty feet into the sea. Screaming gulls wheeled about the cliffs and nested in their crevices.

'That is Dodman's Point, is it?' asked Pinson.

'Yes. Isn't it gorgeous?'

'Gorgeous' seemed the wrong word to Pinson: impressive or spectacular might have served better. Someone more mystically inclined might have chosen another adjective, like 'numinous'. About half way along the promontory, high above the sea, stood two upright granite menhirs, each about eight feet high, flat and roughly oval in shape, facing one another. Jean addressed his unspoken inquiry.

'They're called Dodman's Hands,' she said.

Pinson looked at them again and acknowledged that they did look curiously like two hands thrust up through the soil, as though they were about to come together in prayer or applause.

'When were they put there?' asked Pinson.

'Nobody knows, darling. Yonks ago.'

'Dodman. . . . Could that be a corruption of Dead Man?'

'Could be. There's some sort of legend about one of those old West Country saints. You know. Called St Egg or St Teeth or something stupid like that. Well, this saint fought a giant around here, and some people think the giant was a local god called Dod or Doddon, hence the name. Then when this saint had defeated the giant, the legend says he buried him on Dodman's Point, but the giant wasn't quite dead because he managed to thrust his hands up through the soil. At least, that's the story anyway. And there are all sorts of superstitions about the stones, like if a young girl sleeps between them she will dream of her true love. Or if you fuck between them you'll conceive a black haired male child.'

Pinson blinked at the unexpected use of the four letter word on such a pure, bright day. 'Then there are more sinister tales, like that there are times when the hands mysteriously come together and can crush anyone between them. Come on. Last one there's a sissy.'

And then this buxom provincial woman in her lime green trouser suit, her brassy jewellery and her white flat-heeled shoes took off down the chalky path towards the Hands. Pinson scrambled after her feeling quite ridiculous. Jean did not stop until she was on the Point very near the stones; then, when Pinson had caught up with her, she seized his wrist and dragged him between the Hands with a whoop. Once through the stones they stopped to recover their breath. Pinson looked at Jean astonished and she, seeing his expression, began to shriek with laughter.

'I've shocked you! I've shocked the great playwright!' she shouted triumphantly.

'You've horrified me,' said Pinson trying to sound amused.

༄

At the Saracen's Head, an over-decorated old pub which served pretentious bar-snacks with names like 'Thai Prawn Temptation', and for pudding, of course, 'Death by Chocolate', he and Jean met Jim and Adela Strange, the owners of Spyhole Cottage. Pinson recognised them as members of the 'gang' that surrounded Jean in her dressing room the night before. They were in their fifties, he gross, with an oversized, sensual head, she skeletally thin with a twitch. From the way she downed vodka martinis, probably an alcoholic, he speculated. They seemed to Pinson like figures out of a Medieval Morality: Sin and Death, he named them to himself. Jim's withered arm would not have been that conspicuous, had Jean not told Pinson about it. He found that his eyes were constantly being drawn to the offending limb, and this added to his unease.

After lunch Pinson was abandoned by Jean and placed in the hands of Jim and Adela who took him to see Spyhole Cottage. Before she went Jean had invited them all round to a barbecue at her house that evening. Pinson could not evade it because, ostensibly, it was being held in his honour. In his head Pinson heard his London friends all saying: 'what are you doing with these people?' Pinson did not know. He was not a weak person but he had an inclination at times to stand back from his own life and watch events take their course, as if they were happening to someone else. He would say it was what Keats called 'negative capability', a gift and a malaise. That was his excuse.

A Nightmare Sang

Spyhole was a whitewashed, converted fisherman's cottage on the outskirts of Bidmouth. Inside it was also whitewashed and decorated to the outermost limits of seaside picturesque. There were windows shaped like portholes, swags of netting weighted with green glass witch balls, framed prints of tea clippers, a clock set in a ship's wheel, and on sills and mantels various items of brass naval bric-a-brac, not to mention a flock of gulls in pottery and wood. Curtains and loose covers were a chintz pattern of pale pink anchors on a white ground. Pinson made suitable noises of wondering admiration.

'Marvellous, isn't it?' said Adela, 'Jean did all the interior design. She's so incredibly artistic. Normally this place would be let. People just love it, but we happen to have this fortnight free. Isn't that lucky?'

Pinson asked what the rent was to be, conscious that he was somehow being inveigled into staying two weeks. They quoted a sum which seemed to Pinson a little on the expensive side, but he made no objections, though he wondered again at his own weakness. It was, in its way, he supposed, a pretty place with lovely views. He told himself that this was just what he needed to begin writing again. They showed him the cottage in its entirety, inviting expressions of admiration at every room. The last one they showed him was the spare bedroom.

'We thought you could write in here.' said Adela. And who were 'we?' thought Pinson. 'There's a table at the window that you can use as a desk.'

There was indeed, and the view from the window was a splendid one of the Devon coastline. Unfortunately Pinson was one of those writers who prefer blank walls to distracting scenery when writing. Nevertheless, he dutifully admired the prospect, and in doing so was slightly shocked to find that he could see Dodman's Point in the distance. The Hands looked as if they were about to come together in applause: whether approving or ironic, he could not decide.

The Complete Symphonies of Adolf Hitler

When Pinson told Mrs Bread that he was moving into Spyhole Cottage she sniffed and said she hoped he was not going to pay a lot of rent for 'that place'. Pinson put it down to professional envy and drove to Jean's barbecue that evening with a light heart. Whenever Pinson allowed himself to let events take their course it was always in the superstitious belief that good fortune would follow. Sometimes it did.

Jean and Alec Crowden's house was a large white villa built around 1930 in a vaguely Spanish style. It was one of a row of similar houses in the most exclusive, though by no means the oldest, part of Bidmouth. The drive was already crowded with vehicles when Pinson arrived there. He hoped he was not going to be lionised. An instinctive snobbishness, of which he felt slightly ashamed, told him that it was one thing to be celebrated in an Islington drawing room, but another on the patio of a provincial Queen Bee.

As it happened, he was welcomed effusively by Jean but not, as he had feared, displayed like a trophy. Among the guests, he recognised most of the gang from the dressing room who said: 'Hello, Dan!' with friendly familiarity and then passed on. Someone handed him a glass of Asti Spumante, sweet and heady.

The main sitting room was decorated in a range of creams and pastel colours, what Pinson called 'tastefully tasteless'. Everything was new and spotless and showed the mark of Jean, the aspiring interior decorator. The only unconventional feature of the room was that on one of the side tables reposed a cage, painted white, containing straw, various ramps and wheels, and three white mice with fierce red eyes. Pinson had not put the Crowdens down as mouse fanciers. Sliding glass doors opened onto a patio where Jean's husband Alec was at the barbecue grilling burgers and sausages. He wore a bright red apron emblazoned with a comical representation of a chef and the

A Nightmare Sang

words: CHIEF COOK AND BOTTLE WASHER. This light-hearted legend was strikingly at odds with Alec's angry red face and morose expression. He looked as if he were wearing the apron as a kind of punishment, like the *sanbenito* of a repentant heretic. Pinson was so fascinated by this image that, until he was spoken to, he did not notice that Canon Doker had been standing by his side.

'And what are you doing in this *galère?*' said the Canon archly, indicating the guests.

Pinson shrugged his shoulders: 'I might ask you the same question.'

'Oh, I am conducting a little social experiment of my own,' he said. And, as if to illustrate this cryptic statement, Doker beckoned Pinson to follow him. He led him to the cage containing the three white mice. Their red eyes shone like rubies in firelight.

'I have always had a weakness for mice,' he said with an ambiguous smile that made Pinson wonder if it was their personalities or their flesh he valued. Giving Pinson a mischievous sidelong glance Doker took out a silver pill box from the pocket of his black silk vest. Having opened the lid, the Canon extracted a thin white disc, which looked to Pinson like a communion wafer, and pushed it between the bars of the cage. One of the mice seized the wafer avidly and began to devour it, then the other two fell on it and began competing savagely for the prize. Doker fed another through the bars with similar results.

'Are they what I think they are?' asked Pinson whose agnosticism could not extinguish shock at an apparent sacrilege.

Doker snapped shut the silver box and returned it to his waistcoat pocket. 'I consecrated them this morning,' he said casually. 'I think mice are far more deserving of the sacraments than some humans, don't you?' Pinson could find no answer to this, and none seemed to be called for.

'Is everyone here connected with the Bidmouth Players?' he asked.

'You could say that,' said Doker, for some reason laying his hand lightly on Pinson's shoulder. Just then, the thin girl who played the Duchess de Fontanges passed by. She gave Pinson a quick frightened smile. 'That's Helen Titlow.' said the Canon. 'She's married to our worthy director Ron Titlow, but estranged just at present and is now with Greg, the hearty whom you met in the dressing room the other night. I believe he's here tonight, but not poor Ron. Greg is the P.E. and Games Master at Bidmouth Comprehensive where Ron and Helen also teach. A complex and fascinating web of relationships, don't you think?'

Pinson thought it was rather banal, but he did not say so. Canon Doker appeared to relish his role as guide to the fauna of Bidmouth, and no doubt he flattered himself that he was providing a writer with useful 'copy'.

'Tell me about Jean and Alec,' said Pinson.

'Ah!' said Doker, rubbing his hands together, then lowering his voice. 'This strictly *entre nous,* you understand.'

'Of course!' He was beginning to be irritated by the Canon.

'Alec was one of the most distinguished eye surgeons in the country, you know. Oh, yes! Made a lot of money. Jean was his secretary or assistant or something. Well, there were some irregularities, or so they say, involving female patients. Drink also was involved. He was nearly struck off. As it was he was near retiring age, so he withdrew discreetly. Rumour hath it that he married Jean to purchase her silence. You must have noticed that she is not quite—how shall I put it delicately?—out of the top drawer? At least not in his social bracket.'

Pinson had not noticed. In fact from the little he had seen of Alec, he appeared to be utterly subservient to her. Doker chattered on about others present, betraying an indiscriminate fascination in their doings, unusual for a clergyman. It was a relief to

A Nightmare Sang

hear Jean shout 'Grub's up, folks!' and to have an excuse to move away from him.

Pinson ate burgers and sausages and chatted to various people who, Jean told him, were 'just dying to meet you'. Their eagerness had been overrated, but they seemed pleasant enough. Bland, brassy music started to emerge from the CD player in the sitting room. Pinson might have been at ease, if mildly bored, had he not had the sensation, from time to time, of being watched, not only by Jean and Canon Doker, but also by Greg, Helen Titlow's muscular boyfriend. Of course this could all have been Pinson's imagination.

When the pudding—a vast Pavlova—was served, Pinson took his portion to the far end of the garden. There was a little arbour where there was a bench on which he could sit and eat in peace. He was suffering from what he called 'social fatigue'; besides, the CD that was puncturing the night at that moment was entitled *The Amazing Sound of James Last*. Distance lent some enchantment to the view, and even to the sound. Pinson began to eat his Pavlova contentedly, feeling rather like a child devouring cake under the table at a family wedding. At least here he would not be spied on. Then he heard a rustling of leaves, and the next moment someone had sat down beside him on the bench in the arbour. It was Helen Titlow.

She brushed aside his genial welcome and said: 'Look, I've heard you've taken Spyhole for a fortnight.'

'News travels fast.'

'Yes. Well. I wouldn't. I'd get out of here. As soon as possible. I really would.'

'What the hell are you talking about?'

But Helen had got up and was looking around her, like some frightened woodland creature scenting danger on the wind. Then she had gone. An odd silence fell. Pinson noticed that the *Amazing Sound of James Last* had ceased. Presently another noise intruded, that of someone singing raucously and off-key.

A physical chill had invaded his body even before he had recognised that it was Alec singing, sounding exactly as he had that night on stage when he played the gaoled black magician Abbé Guibourg. Pinson felt that the horror of that noise could be diminished if he was able to see what was happening. He got up from his refuge and walked towards the house and the patio which in the gathering dark was now illumined by floodlights like a stage set.

A cruel sight met him. Alec, still wearing his comic apron, was lying on the flagstones by the barbecue, propped up on one elbow, his other arm brandishing a long handled fork, as he bellowed out his song. Pinson could just about identify it as an ancient Cliff Richard number called 'Devil Woman'. Jean was not there, but most of the guests were gathered round watching this spectacle. From a distance the scene looked like some grotesque parody of an eighteenth century history painting, such as 'The Death of Wolfe', with Alec Crowden as the dying general making his last oration on the field of battle, and the others as hangers-on grouped around in various attitudes ranging from concern to indifference. Some were even laughing.

Then the scene changed. Jean made an entrance through the patio doors carrying a heavily-weighted, red plastic bucket. The guests scattered to make room for her as, with a heave, she hurled the contents of the bucket, which was water, over the recumbent Alec. Some of the water hit the barbecue so that there was a great hiss and cloud of steam. Alec fell back without a cry and lay motionless on the flagstones, as the steam drifted over him like the fog of war. There was some nervous laughter, even a tentative round of applause. Jean looked round at the assembled guests with contempt.

'There!' she said. 'Satisfied? Now you can all bugger off!'

The party dispersed quickly without many words being exchanged. When Pinson came to say goodbye Jean said nothing

A Nightmare Sang

but squeezed his hand tightly, a gesture which seemed to suggest that he was absolved of any complicity in the proceedings.

Back in his digs Pinson seriously considered heeding Helen Titlow's advice, but he was too tired to move beyond consideration to resolution.

☙

Had it not been such a fine morning, he told himself, he might still have left Bidmouth for London and posted the keys to Spyhole Cottage back to Sin and Death, but they had already been given a cheque for a week's rent.

By ten o'clock Pinson was driving his car through Bidmouth on his way to the cottage. When he stopped at some traffic lights he thought he saw Helen Titlow crossing the road wheeling a baby buggy. He hooted cheerfully. She turned and saw him, then immediately turned away again. One side of her face had been marred by a fresh dark red bruise.

Spyhole Cottage welcomed him with a vase of freshly picked wildflowers from Sin and Death, and a bottle of champagne from Jean. Pinson spent some contented hours arranging the few books and possessions he had with him and setting up his laptop in the spare room. The mere sight of it gave him confidence and he indulged in the writer's daydream of uninterrupted hours filled with the gentle flow of flawless inspiration. He even sat down there and then to type a few words, but was distracted by the view through the window of Dodman's Point. Those two stones did look uncannily like a pair of hands thrusting out of the ground and seemed to presage the fearful resurrection of a giant. Perhaps he could make something of that. Being a writer who believes that art should never imitate life too slavishly he typed the words DEAD MAN'S HILL. Then for good measure he put the words in bold and underlined them.

The Complete Symphonies of Adolf Hitler

Having done so he looked again at the source of his inspiration. A human figure was standing by the stones. It was too far away to determine age or sex, but he could see that it was waving. The gesture was ambiguous—it could have been a warning or a greeting—but Pinson was quite irrationally certain that the figure was signalling to him. This lasted for only a few seconds; then the figure disappeared behind the stones and did not re-emerge. Its failure to reappear was not inexplicable as the landscape dipped and curved so much, but the whole experience was disquieting. Pinson decided to have an early lunch and then walk to Dodman's Point.

※

That afternoon he never reached the Point. The weather remained fine and he set off along the cliff path very cheerfully. The air and exercise was going to restore him, but he was so out of condition that he tired quickly. Besides, Dodman's Point was farther away than appearance had suggested, and was separated from him by a long inland creek. Still, it was a good enough walk as far as it went, and Pinson returned refreshed but pleasantly weary. As he came into the cottage he found himself humming a tune he could not quite place, irritatingly banal but somehow memorable. He noticed casually that the door of his bedroom was open, yet he was sure he had shut it on his way out. He went to the door and looked in.

On the bed, spread-eagled as on an altar of sacrifice, was the voluptuous naked body of Jean Crowden. Her bra had been draped over the bedpost with calculated erotic abandon.

'Hello, sailor,' she said.

Pinson was horrified and thrilled by her vulgarity. This was how Baudelaire must have felt with his filthy Parisian whores, he thought pretentiously.

A Nightmare Sang

It had been a long time since he had experienced a sexual encounter so utterly devoid of any emotion except lust. A part of his mind had remained quite detached. What am I doing? he kept saying to himself. The physical sensation that struck him most forcibly had been the coldness of her flesh. No doubt the feeling had been accentuated by the fact that he had come in hot and sweaty after a long walk, but there had been more to it than that, he thought. The way it had delayed the moment of climax had been oddly exciting.

Afterwards they had sat in the living room, he dressed, she wearing only a bath robe of his while they drank her champagne and talked as if nothing had happened. Despite being a prominent figure in the theatrical life of Bidmouth, Jean showed surprisingly little interest in the arts generally. Her talk was of the social world she inhabited, and Pinson soon realised how foolish he had been in supposing that to her amateur dramatics was anything more than a means of acquiring status. But she was a shrewd woman nonetheless, and could be entertainingly malicious. They did not talk about the incidents of the night before. Pinson was curious about her relationship with Alec but he sensed that a direct assault on the subject would be rebuffed. He decided to ask about Canon Doker instead, as it was he who had provided him with information about Alec and Jean.

'Ah! I thought you'd be intrigued by our Canon,' she said. Pinson hated assumptions being made about his likes and dislikes, but he let it pass. 'Teddy Doker is incredible. He knows everything. He's a sort of guru to us really.'

'And who is defined as us?'

'Us, darling. Surely you realise who "us" is?'

She let the bath robe fall open and splayed her legs so that a powerful scent of her sexuality was wafted across the room. It was a challenge.

Pinson said: 'You tell me.'

'You of all people should understand, darling. We call ourselves "The Gang", or "The Coven", but that's just a joke. Teddy teaches us, and he celebrates the Gnostic Mass. You know what the Gnostic Mass is, don't you, darling?'

'I know a little about Gnosticism, I suppose. It was a sort of heresy.'

'Yes, well that was theory, but this is practice. You thought all that stuff with Madame de Montespan and Guibourg and the rest is all history. Safely in the past. Typical writer. Oh, no it isn't, darling, it's alive and well and living in Bidmouth.'

'Good God!'

Pinson had not meant to betray shock but he did. Jean's reaction was to roar with laughter. She bounced in her chair, kicked up her legs and cackled. When she had subsided she said: 'Admit it, Dan, you're just eaten up with curiosity about us, aren't you?'

Pinson avoided her look. Jean said: 'I know you. You're going to put us all into your next play.'

'No I'm not,' said Pinson, 'because no-one would believe it for a moment.' Jean cackled with laughter again. Pinson could not be certain whether she thought this genuinely funny or was mocking the traditional response of writers in the face of intractable circumstance.

'These Gnostic Masses,' said Pinson. 'What precisely is the purpose that they serve?'

'Do you want to see one and find out?'

Pinson was irritated by the anticipation of his moves; so he tried to assume an air of casual indifference. 'That might be rather interesting,' he said.

'Right. You're on.'

A Nightmare Sang

During the next few days Pinson spent the mornings trying to write while, in the afternoons, Jean would come by for an episode of cold congress. Once he asked her where Alec thought she was going when she visited him, and she replied: 'Oh, he knows, darling.' Pinson looked at her hard but could not tell whether this was truth or bluff. She laughed at his feeble attempts at mind-reading.

On the fourth day after Pinson's move to the cottage Jean said: 'Are you up for it tonight?'

They were lying on the bed after a rather feverish bout. It was late afternoon. Pinson suddenly felt cold.

'What do you mean?' he said.

'You know what I mean, darling. The Gnostic Mass. It's on for tonight.'

'What is this Gnostic Mass?'

'There's only one way of finding out, darling. I'll pick you up at eleven.'

෩

'Where are we going?' said Pinson, as they got into the car.

'You'll see, darling.'

They drove to a part of Bidmouth that Pinson had never seen before—'the unfashionable end' said Jean laconically—and stopped in front of a large Classical-looking building in a state of disrepair. It was dark and drizzling, so that Pinson could see very little. They got out of the car, Jean flashing a torch to light the way.

As her torch played over the front of the building Pinson caught sight of a wooden board, cracked and blistered with neglect, which bore the words: EBENEZER METHODIST CHAPEL. Jean led Pinson round to one side of the chapel. The walls were covered with stucco, much of which had fallen away, leaving great raw patches of stonework like festering wounds;

weeds sprouted from every crevice. Pinson looked up at the windows, but saw no light coming from them.

'We sometimes rehearse here,' said Jean irrelevantly. The rain was beginning to come down more heavily. They descended some steps and stopped in front of a low door. Jean took out her car key and scratched on it three times. Almost immediately the door opened a crack and the narrow mean face of Death, Adela Strange, peered suspiciously out at them. She was holding an old oil lamp.

'Come on, Adela,' said Jean. 'Let us in! It's peeing down out here.'

'We're just about to start,' said Death querulously as she let them in. Pinson saw that she was wearing flip-flop sandals and a knee-length diaphanous gown through which her naked body, gnarled and emaciated, could plainly be seen.

'Dan and I will be watching from the gallery tonight,' said Jean.

'Well,' said Death, 'you'll have to find your own way up there. You can't borrow my lamp.'

'It's all right, Adela,' said Jean in a weary voice which implied she was used to such curmudgeonly behaviour. 'I've got a torch.' Death walked towards a thick damask curtain and disappeared behind it while Jean led the way up some dusty wooden stairs that creaked dangerously.

'Careful where you step,' said Jean. 'Some of the treads have gone.'

They emerged into a semicircular wooden gallery with long benches, some collapsed or broken, rising up on a series of graduated wooden platforms. Against the front wall of the chapel, behind the apex of the gallery, were the remains of a great organ whose cracked pipes mounted up to the ceiling like the towers of a ruined citadel.

Jean and Pinson sat themselves on a bench directly in front of the organ from which they could lean over the balcony and look

A Nightmare Sang

down into the body of the chapel. Before he could take in any visual impressions Pinson was struck by a wave of fetid heat that surged up from below, bloated with smells of bodies, washed and unwashed, of smoke, incense and burnt spices. The impact was so strong that he choked and recoiled. Jean giggled.

It took a few moments before Pinson could recover and look again. Long black drapes covered the windows allowing no light or sound to penetrate inwards or outwards. The great space was lit fitfully by a number of sanctuary lamps of gilt bronze and pink glass that hung from the ceiling on metal chains. Light also came from two large coal braziers onto which an elderly dwarf, dressed in the red cassock and white ruff of a choirboy, occasionally threw coals and handfuls of incense. The braziers flanked a great table draped in purple damask situated in the very centre of the chapel. Around it hung banners made of black cloth embroidered with pentacles, sigils, the goat of Mendes. In front of the altar was splayed a chaos of sofas, rugs and old mattresses on which lounged and sprawled an assortment of men and women, mostly middle aged to elderly. Pinson recognised members of the cast of his play, Sin, Death, Ron Titlow and others of 'the gang' that he had seen at the barbecue. They were either naked or scantily dressed in underwear or transparent negligees. Some drank from bottles. A long-haired bearded man in a pair of grey underpants whom Pinson had seen in the lighting box at the Jubilee Hall was injecting himself. Someone unseen was playing a long, skirling, dreary melody on some reed instrument.

'Come on! Come on!' said Jean, drumming her fingers on the balcony. 'I thought that bitch Adela said they were about to start.'

There was a sound like the banging of an old fashioned dinner gong. The piping ceased as did the murmur of conversation. In the silence a little tinkling bell was heard; then from the back of the church came the procession. It was led by a monstrous figure dressed, like the dwarf, as a choirboy with a curly blonde wig, swinging a censer. When he began chanting in a falsetto voice Pinson realised that it was Alec Crowden. He glanced at Jean but she was absorbed in the spectacle, inured to its strangeness.

The second figure was Canon Doker. His feet and legs were bare, but he wore a short lace cotta over which was a yellow chasuble embroidered with black pine cones. Pinson suspected he had nothing on beneath these two garments. He carried a huge silver chalice, with a domed cover whose finial was a silver Uraeus, the Egyptian cobra symbol, signifying supreme power.

The other two figures in the procession were perhaps even stranger. The first was a fit and muscular young man, naked but for a goat's mask covering his face. He carried an oblong box like a child's coffin and was leading on a chain a thin, naked young woman with a black blindfold around her eyes. Pinson believed this to be Helen Titlow whom he recognised from the still livid bruise on the side of her face. He deduced that the man in the goat's mask must be her boyfriend Greg, the games master at Bidmouth Comprehensive.

When the procession had reached the purple-draped altar table Helen was laid across it and the Canon began to intone words in Latin. As far as Pinson could tell they were the words of the Catholic Tridentine Mass. What made them hideous was the way he chanted them in a high, nasal voice and the way that the responses were yelled back by his two choirboys (Alec and the dwarf) who were kneeling, one each side of the altar.

He uttered the words of consecration as he held the chalice over Helen's naked body. Then he removed the chalice's domed cover which he placed carefully on Helen's belly. The opened cup was found to be full of white mice two or three of which escaped from it and ran across the altar into the congregation where amid screams and howls they were fought for and eaten by the worshippers.

A Nightmare Sang

As this was going on the two 'choirboys' were distributing chafing dishes laden with hot coals among the throng. On these were heaped crystals of incense so that the air became thick and poisonous with drugged smoke. Then Canon Doker gave a cry and the goat-headed man opened the coffin shaped box and drew out of it a great brindled snake which hissed and snapped at the worshippers, who roared their adulation and approval.

Doker stepped forward and, removing several white mice by their tails from the chalice, dropped them delicately into the serpent's jaws. This seemed to pacify the animal a little. Stretching his arms wide Doker intoned the words: 'Behold the Python and His Pythoness! Let their Union bring forth signs and wonders!'

At a signal from Doker Greg hurled the python onto the altar where it began to writhe and coil around the naked Helen. Convulsed with agonies, she began to scream. This was the signal for shouts and cries among the worshippers followed by frenzied couplings on the mattresses and couches provided for them. A great cloud of drugged smoke wafted across the scene and entered Pinson's lungs.

Pinson felt Jean undoing the zip of his trousers. There had been times during the proceedings when he had wanted to leave. He had been held only by the sheer inconvenience of having to find his way back to Spyhole in the rain, but now he was enthralled by a combination of the drugged fumes from the incense burners, the chanting, the fetid heat, Jean's sleazy attentions. In addition, he felt restrained by what he called a 'higher motive'.

He felt as if he had penetrated the sordid exterior, the sex and the blasphemy, which held so many captive to the cult. All this was only a means, perhaps a necessary means, of reaching another state. And he had reached it! He had entered a landscape in his own head, wind-bitten wild and cruel, but pure and breathlessly beautiful. The ceremony and the debauch had opened the door, that was all. He saw in this landscape all things as infinitely real: every blade of grass as heavy as a truck and as sharp as a razor, every breath of wind like a blow from a boxing glove. Rearing mountains tore open the sky, every crevice of their steep ascents visible from miles away. It was, above all, a land of freedom in which nothing was forbidden. Pinson no longer felt oppressed by the suffocating Sky God who had rained down moral injunctions upon him since childhood. The sky was open: no longer a vast blue vault, but roofless infinity. Everything was freely permitted, freely available, from a kiss on the lips to the slash of a knife, the lash of a whip. Death and life were one, love and hatred, pain and pleasure, all one: equally valuable, equally intense. Till now he had always thought of Crowley, with his sub-Swinburne verse and his music-hall humour, as a pathetic, posturing charlatan. Now he could see the point of his doctrines and the key to joy found in his motto: DO WHAT THOU WILT SHALL BE THE WHOLE OF THE LAW. It was not a command; it was an invitation.

Jean had brought him to a climax, but on one level he barely noticed it because the sexual spasm had been translated into another, deeper sensation. When she tried to speak to him he knocked her to the floor and kicked her into silence. His mystical experience had transported him beyond the trivial requirements of decency or kindness. He stood alone, erect, oblivious at last to shame.

He knew that everything he saw and felt was going on in his head, but that did not make it any less true. After all, every experience 'went on in the head', but now he knew that he could choose which one. He chose to look out on his wild landscape and, through its rearing mountains and shaggy forests which he was now viewing from a great height, as if he were a god, he saw the snake. It was a giant creature: its long tail was coiled in a valley and, when it paused to drink, it drained a river. It wound through the landscape and where it went the

A Nightmare Sang

power of its life caused cities and temples to spring up. Every scale on its body was a shining thought and a mirror of vision into which Pinson could see if he chose, and that vision would transport him to another world, and another, and yet another, because the snake was eternal, it circled the universe and devoured its own tail. At that moment Pinson had all knowledge and all power at his command.

He knew this was a supreme moment from which he could only descend, but the descent was slow and gentle. Gradually the little incidents and sensations of the 'real' world began to impinge upon him again. He saw Jean cringing at his feet, the bruises on her arms and face blackening as she stared up at him abjectly and without reproach. He smiled gently down upon her and helped her to her feet.

In the body of the chapel Canon Doker and his train had disappeared while the congregation was busy packing up to go home. Only the bearded man in the grey underpants who had injected himself was lying flat on his back, motionless. Perhaps he was dead: who knows? No-one paid him any attention.

Jean drove Pinson back to Spyhole Cottage in silence. When they reached Spyhole she stopped the car and said to him: 'You're one of us now. You will have to be initiated.'

Pinson nodded and got out of the car which instantly drove off. The sky was greying at the edges in preparation for dawn. The cold morning air was like a knife.

෨

Jean did not come to him for several days, and Pinson was quite alone. He did not mind this at all: thoughts and memories were far more engrossing companions. The experience of that night took a long time to fade. It lingered like a strong taste and he could from time to time relive its ecstasies to some extent. But he longed to recapture it whole and unadulterated. For that he supposed he would have to be 'initiated', whatever that meant.

He did not write anything; that might come later. For the moment, he was content simply to be and to wait. He went for long walks, each time intending to reach Dodman's Point, but he never did. On the fourth day after the Gnostic Mass in the Ebenezer Chapel he was out for a walk when he thought he saw a figure standing between the two stones on Dodman's Point. The figure waved to him as it had before, though whether the gesture was warning, threat or greeting he could not say. On his return Pinson found Jean lying naked on his bed. They spoke no word until they had finished coupling, a fierce affair in which each drew blood from the other.

'It's tonight,' she said as she climbed off him.

'The initiation?'

'Yes.'

'Where? Not that ghastly Ebenezer Chapel.'

'No. That's out of bounds now. They found someone dead in there. Hell of a stink.'

'Literally and metaphorically, I should imagine. Where then?'

'Dodman's Point. You will have to pass between the hands.'

'What if someone sees us?'

'They won't. No-one goes out to Dodman's at night. I'll pick you up at eleven.'

༄

It wanted a few minutes to midnight when they reached Dodman's Point. Pinson was relieved to find that the *galère* was not present, only Canon Doker and Greg. Greg dressed in a white track suit with the hood up carried a flaming lighted torch, Doker was in his usual black clerical garb except that he wore a purple silk stole embroidered with pentagrams surrounded by a snake devouring its own tail. When he saw them Pinson came to

A Nightmare Sang

his senses a little and was afraid. The wind was whipping around the stones and whispering as it did so. The sky was clear but for a few moonlit veils of cloud. Doker smiled and winked at him. In a voice that was meant to convey reassurance he said: 'We knew you were one of us.'

Jean said: 'It's only a short ceremony, but you'll need to take your clothes off.'

Pinson obeyed, telling himself that it was too late to change his mind. Naked, he was made to stand within two concentric circles painted in white on the grass. Various sigils and names had been painted in the circle, but Pinson could not make them out. Outside the circle Canon Doker sprinkled him with a pungent liquid from an aspergillum while intoning a Latin formula:

> Coniuro vos decem demones Oreoth, Pinem, Ocel, Tryboy, Noryoth, Belferith, Camoy, Astoroth, Sobronoy, Sismael, ut sicut in hoc circulo figurati, ita vere et efficaciter et existenter personam eius circuatis, et sensus eius taliter affligatis quod ignorans, demens, stultus et mente captus efficiatur . . .

The words were impressive and soothing; it was as if his mind had been made up for him. Pinson began to feel strong.

'Now, brother, you must pass between the hands,' said Canon Doker. In the torch light Pinson saw that Doker's face was set in a rictus of malign pleasure. Pinson stepped out of the circle towards the hands. Between them he could faintly see the grass extending towards the end of Dodman's Point and the sea fitfully shining under a slice of moon.

Then from beyond the hands he heard a heavy rasping breath and the shadow of a man came out from behind the stones to bar his way through them. Greg swung round his torch to show up the huge, blotched, swag-bellied, naked shape of Alec Crowden. Pinson thought he heard Jean's laugh behind him.

The Complete Symphonies of Adolf Hitler

'You must pass between the hands,' said Canon Doker.

Pinson advanced, thinking that, as in some Masonic ritual he had heard of, his adversary would retreat before him, but he did not. He stood his ground, like a sentinel between the stones. Pinson came on until Alec's great belly almost touched his. The thought of it filled him with nausea. He put out his hands and gave Alec a light push on the chest to thrust him back between the stones. The man's flesh was slick and icy, like a fish from the freezer. Alec roared and flung himself on him so that Pinson was thrown back by his weight and almost fell over. Alec threw his arms round Pinson in an attempt to squeeze the life out of him, his breathing stertorous and his open mouth spraying foul air and spittle. Alec was out of condition but he had the element of surprise, as it took some moments for Pinson to realise that he was fighting for his life. He called out for help, almost sure by now that it would not be forthcoming, so he summoned his strength and began to push Alec back between the stones. Alec tried to lift Pinson off his feet but failed in the attempt, toppled over and struck his head against the right Hand. Pinson falling on top of him plunged his fist into Alec's horribly yielding belly and winded him, while Alec tried to reach up and claw off his face. Pinson thrust Alec's arm aside and struck him on the point of the jaw. The back of his enemy's head struck the stone again and his body went limp. Pinson, barely knowing who he was or what he was doing, rose up from Alec's carcass and threw his hands in the air with a yell of triumph; then, seeing his way clear at last, he leaped over the body and ran between the Hands.

But when he reached the other side of the Hands, still shouting and exulting for a reason he never knew, something struck him on the back of the head and he fell unconscious.

When he came to he was lying on his bed in Spyhole Cottage. He was naked and, as consciousness slowly returned to his aching, anxious body, he became aware that another naked body was sharing the bed with him. But it was not Jean's body, it was the body of her husband Alec. The flesh was utterly cold; the man was dead.

It was not long after the full implications of this fact had been absorbed that he heard a car draw up outside the cottage. Through his thin bedroom curtains he saw the regular flash, flash of a blue light.

༄

At the police station he stuck to his story through many interrogations, but nobody believed him, not even the solicitor he had requested. The idea of the Bidmouth Players being a coven of Satanists was a ludicrous idea, and it became quite obvious that Pinson was unhinged when they heard him singing alone in his cell.

'She's just a Devil Woman . . .' he sang.

THE BABE OF THE ABYSS

I

One morning after breakfast, towards the end of the Trinity Term, I entered the Senior Common Room to be met by a familiar scene. Claverhouse and Wintle were standing by the window that overlooks the Fellow's Garden, as usual earnestly discussing recent world events, on this occasion Hitler's *démarche* in the Czech Sudetenland. Hoveton was sitting at a table, correcting the proofs of his latest book on Sumerian epigraphy; while young Simpson was, as always, hogging the best chair and reading the *Oxford Times*.

The Babe of The Abyss

'Says here,' said Simpson, a biochemist whose use of the English language is notoriously demotic, 'that a chap's died who was a fellow of this College.'

I was surprised, as I am the Dean and expect to be the first to know of such events. Thinking there must be some mistake, I asked the name of the 'chap'.

'It says here Ray. A Dr Simeon Ray. Never heard of him myself. What about you fellows?' Simpson by this time was looking round at the rest of us in some astonishment, for we were all staring at him in silence.

Finally Hoveton said: 'Good God! Panter Ray! It must be nearly twenty years.'

'How did he die?' I asked.

'Says here—' began Simpson. Then he handed me the newspaper, obviously disconcerted by the sudden change of atmosphere. 'Here, read it for yourself,' he said. 'By the way, why "Panter"?'

'A joke,' said Hoveton, 'merely a scholarly joke. You see, Dr Ray had a rather breathy, hurried way of speaking, so of course we called him Panter Ray, after the famous saying of Heraclitus.'

Simpson looked blank.

'Heraclitus, the Pre-Socratic Philosopher, whose great *dictum* was *Panta Rhei*, meaning "Everything is in Flux".' Hoveton turned to me and asked: 'How did the poor fellow die, Cordery?'

I gave them a précis of the *Oxford Times*'s rather formulaic prose on the subject. Unknown to us, Dr Ray had been living in Oxford for the last fifteen years, occupying a couple of rooms in a house on the Iffley Road. His landlady, accustomed to his reclusive habits, had not disturbed him until he was behind with the rent, by which time he had been dead for almost a week. His rooms had been bare of personal possessions, even books. The coroner's verdict on the cause of death was 'heart failure', but one curious fact was noted. Ray had died in bed, but he had covered the floor of his bedroom with salt. He had evidently done this immediately before getting into bed as a tin of 'Cerebos' salt was found on his bedside table and his foot marks were not to be found on the salted floor. It was not stated whether any foot marks other than his own had been discovered.

'So what happened to this Ray chap?' said Simpson. 'Why did he leave the College?'

'He left under a cloud,' said Hoveton abruptly as he returned with deliberation to his proofs.

I think that Simpson was just about to inquire into the nature of that cloud when the Senior Common Room Steward entered with a message from the Master. I was to see him immediately.

Lord Arlington's appointment to the Mastership of St Matthew's College has been political rather than academic. He had taken a good degree, and had been a tutor in economics for a brief while before leaving Oxford to become a Treasury official. Upon his elevation to the peerage he retired from the Treasury and condescended to become Master of his old College. He is no doubt an excellent Master in many ways, but I have never warmed to him, and always feel a certain anxiety when summoned to his presence. Even at the best of times, there is something chilly about his hospitality: Lord Arlington is a widower of long standing.

He met me in the library of the Lodgings with his familiar greeting: 'Ah, Dean!' Having waved me to a chair he walked to the window and stared abstractedly at the old mulberry tree in the garden. Tall, stooped and grey, he brings to mind one of those wading birds who spear fish in the shallows of wintry mountain lakes.

'You've heard about Ray, I suppose?'

'This very morning,' I said. Arlington sniffed, as though tardiness in receiving this information was an offence.

The Babe of The Abyss

'You will represent the College at his funeral,' he said. I nodded. 'There is a reason for your doing so,' he added.

'I do not require a reason,' I said. 'I would have done so anyway.' My intervention did not please Arlington, and his method of dealing with it was characteristic: he went on as if I had not spoken.

'I have received a communication from his solicitor today. Dr Ray has left his entire fortune to the College. A very considerable sum.'

'But I thought—'

'You no doubt thought,' he interrupted, 'that having died in rented accommodation and apparently reduced circumstances he was in fact destitute. This was not the case. Dr Ray possessed a considerable inherited fortune. He became prone towards the end of his life to a mental condition which made him irrationally fearful of dying penniless. The tragic irony was that he died as if he actually were in abject poverty.'

As he said this, I thought I detected a whisper of human sympathy in Arlington's manner. More brusquely he added: 'And we are the beneficiaries.'

There was a long pause while this fact was given its full entitlement of respect. Arlington's management of the College's finances has been greatly to our advantage since he is zealous in preserving and finding out new benefactions for St Matthew's. I could see, however, that something troubled him. He was still on his feet and was now pacing about restlessly.

Finally, he said: 'In addition to the money, he has also left us a property which he wishes to be used, as it was used in his lifetime, for the benefit of the undergraduates.'

At last I understood Arlington's unease: 'The Chalet?' I asked.

Arlington nodded. 'The Chalet. Alas, we cannot decline that benefaction. The will clearly stipulates that if we turn down the Chalet, we will forego the financial inheritance which I understand amounts to almost £70,000. That we cannot afford to do.

Dean, in a fortnight's time the summer vacation begins. I must ask you to go out then, on behalf of the College, to inspect the Chalet, deal with the local Notaire and so on, and then see what can be . . . what can be done.' For a man who is always precise in his language, these last words were remarkably vague. I would have liked to press him for more detailed instructions, but it was evident from the way he appeared to turn his attention back to the mulberry tree in the garden that the interview was at an end.

II

Perhaps this is the moment to explain a little about Panter Ray and the Chalet.

Simeon Ray was one of those old-fashioned, Edwardian bachelor dons, sound scholars, but not overanxious to prove themselves as men of learning. Ray's subject was Ancient History but his contribution to it, beyond his doctoral thesis on Pericles and an early article in the *Journal of Hellenic Studies* on the Ionian Revolt, in which he took a fairly conventional line, was negligible. He took his task to be the education of young gentlemen in the broadest sense and, being by birth and fortune a gentleman himself, he was a popular, easygoing sort of tutor. He had a way of, as we used to say, 'bringing men out', of putting the shy and the gauche at their ease. One could drop into his rooms of an evening and be sure of a glass of sherry and a friendly welcome. He was well liked. There were some who said he favoured the better looking and the more aristocratic young men, but I belonged to neither of those categories and never felt slighted as a consequence.

He owned a chalet, high in the mountains of the Haute Savoie to which, in the long summer vacations, he would invite groups of undergraduates on 'reading parties'. That is to say, the undergraduates would come with their books which during the morning they studied by themselves, either indoors or out on

The Babe of The Abyss

the lawn in front of the Chalet with its transcendent views of forest and mountain. In the afternoon they would go for long walks through idyllic Alpine landscapes. The food was plentiful but plain, the beds on the hard side, the only hot water available had to be boiled in kettle or copper; yet many remember their Chalet days as a little glimpse of Eden when it was bliss to be alive, and 'to be young was very heaven'. I went once, in the year 1920, the last year that Panter held one of his Chalet reading parties. It was as a result of certain events which occurred during this reading party that Panter was forced to leave the college in ignominy.

III

There is no such thing as a good funeral, but some are worse than others, and Panter's was one of the very worst. Because Panter had been a Catholic the service was held in an ugly, gaudy little Romish temple off the Iffley Road. Behind it was a squalid piece of scrub land which served as a burial ground, and there he was to be interred. Apart from myself, the undertakers and the priest, there was only one other person present at the service. He came in late and occupied a pew on the other side of the central aisle from me.

He was about my age, perhaps a little older, though the hair that fringed his bald cranium was still jet black. He was rather below average height and dressed in a well-tailored suit and an old-fashioned overcoat with an astrakhan collar. He had a potbelly which stuck out grotesquely, and a prominent lower lip, red and moist, which, together with his staring eyes, gave him an air of belligerence. I did not care to look at him long in case he noticed me. He seemed faintly familiar: I thought that I might have known him once years ago, but could not place him.

During the church service something happened which disquieted me. The priest, a young Irishman, had quite evidently never known the deceased, and though he conducted the service in a respectable manner there was, inevitably, a certain perfunctoriness about his recital. I remember, however, that in a few brief impromptu words for the departed soul, he bade us pray that 'our brother here departed's stay in Purgatory may not be of too long duration'.

At that moment I heard something like an explosion which echoed through the bare, unpopulated church. It came from the pot-bellied stranger. When I turned to look at him I saw that he was choking or sneezing into a large black-bordered handkerchief. I cannot be absolutely certain of this but I had the distinct impression that he was trying to suppress a fit of hysterical laughter.

I deliberately left the church last so that, during the internment in the graveyard, I could position myself as far away as possible from the stranger, and as near as decency would allow to the exit. Once the coffin had been put unto the grave, once words had been said over it, and holy water and earth had been sprinkled upon it, I turned away quickly, hoping to avoid any contact with him. Natural diffidence cannot entirely explain my deep antipathy to a meeting, but he was too quick for me. With a nimbleness and purpose that belied his unhealthy appearance, he managed to cut me off at the gate of the little cemetery. I could not now escape him without showing deliberate rudeness.

'Hello, Cordery,' he said. 'Representing the dear old College, are we?' It was the subtle, unemphatic tone of mockery in his voice which provoked a flash of recognition.

'Good God! Seddon! What are you doing here?' Foolish words, I know, but the sudden access of memory had robbed me of sense.

'Is there any reason why I shouldn't be here?' he said, fixing me with his hard, blue stare.

I could think of plenty, but, instead of citing them, I asked him how he had come to hear of Panter Ray's death. Seddon

The Babe of The Abyss

told me, enigmatically, that Panter's landlady had 'kept me informed'. I wanted to ask him why. I wanted to ask him many questions, but a stronger feeling prevailed over my curiosity. It was the need to get away from this man with the cold, staring eyes and the obscenely projecting lower lip, red and wet, like a secret organ of the body exposed by the surgeon's knife.

I sensed that he may have wanted me to invite him back to the College for some hospitality, and it was as much spite as revulsion that made me ignore the demands of courtesy. I shook hands—gloved, fortunately—with him, muttered something disingenuous about it being good to see him again after all these years, and left him there by the open grave.

IV

I came up to St Matthew's in the Michaelmas Term of 1919, directly from Uppingham, having avoided enlistment in the forces by a matter of months. Someone asked me recently whether I felt guilty that I had so narrowly missed serving in the Great War. I do not think that it is guilt I feel so much as a consciousness of having been denied an experience which, however terrible, would have made me a very different person. There is a curious sense of deprivation.

This feeling may have been accentuated by the prevailing atmosphere of post-War Oxford. About half the undergraduates had come, like me, straight from public school; the rest were older men who had been in the forces and were now either renewing or beginning their studies at the 'Varsity. St Matthew's had its quota of war veterans, among whom was Stanley Seddon, a man in his mid-twenties when he came up.

At the funeral Seddon looked like a savage caricature of his younger self, not that his appearance had ever been very prepossessing. However, with those eyes, surmounted by thick black eyebrows, the prominent lip, the general look of alert hostility, he could never have been called nondescript. I would not say that he was particularly unpopular, but no-one sought his company, and he made few efforts to recruit friends or participate in any particular social activity. Nevertheless, he made his mark at St Matthew's as the result of an incident which took place, as I remember, in the Hilary Term of 1920.

Oxford in those days was still looked on by some as a playground, a finishing school for the rich and privileged, but this attitude was generally held by those who, like me, had not been in the War. I, of course, had neither the money nor the inclination to waste my time on riotous living, but there were some—usually men from the 'better' public schools—who made a career out of drinking too much, breaking glass, painting the Founder's statue green and generally disturbing the peace. This activity did not bother me as I kept out of its way, but, in addition to troubling the authorities, it annoyed quite a few of the former servicemen who no doubt had had their fill of noise and chaos. These men also felt, with some justification I suppose, that the younger sparks were not giving them the respect that they deserved. It was in this climate that some of the war veterans decided to stage what they thought would be a dignified protest. They would go into Hall for dinner one evening wearing their old officer's uniforms. The idea, I imagine, was to impress the frivolous-minded with the sacrifice that they had made for them.

Seddon was no part of the demonstration, but he had got wind of it and he also appeared in hall in uniform: the uniform of an artillery sergeant. It turned out that, of the St Matthew's veterans who were undergraduates, he had been the only 'ranker'. There was no reason why he should not have been an officer—his father, a wealthy industrialist, had sent him to a good school—but whether he had refused a commission because of some principled objection, or had been denied it or, as was

The Babe of The Abyss

inevitably rumoured, had been reduced to the ranks, he did not say.

Neither did he reveal why he had made his particular demonstration: had he been protesting with the officers, or against them? My own conjecture was that he had done neither, but that he was simply asserting his individuality. If his intention had been to establish himself as a presence in our College, he certainly succeeded. All of us, I think, felt thereafter that here was a formidable personality who would 'stand no nonsense'. The very idea of throwing him into the college fountain, debagging, or subjecting him to any form of undergraduate ragging would have been seen as anathema, even by the rowing club after a Bump supper.

Occasionally I would meet Seddon of an evening in Panter Ray's rooms. I do not quite know how he came to them because Panter taught Ancient History and Seddon was a Modern Greats man. I expect it was Panter's kind heart which brought him there, because he was always on the lookout for the misfit and the lonely, anxious that they should not feel utterly displaced.

On these occasions Seddon was perfectly agreeable and did not push himself forward in any way. He was, nevertheless, a distinctive presence who gave his opinions, when asked, not tentatively, as most of us did, but with authority. His views were on the whole modernist and radical: he spoke with some approval of the Bolshevik Revolution, and it was from Seddon in Panter's rooms that I first heard the name of Sigmund Freud.

I doubt very much whether Panter agreed with or even understood much of what Seddon said, but he was one of those passive conservatives who tolerate the expression of any point of view, provided that blasphemy or obscenity is not involved. Panter was far from being a brilliant conversationalist, but he was adept at gently enabling others to talk. In his fifty-fifth year, he had boyish features, bright blue eyes and his sandy hair, still thick and curly, was just tinged with grey. Despite his rather youthful appearance it was hard for us to think of him as anything other than middle-aged, perhaps because he was so set in his habits. His way of speaking was old fashioned, part pedantic ('mobile vulgus' for 'mob'), part Edwardian upper class vernacular, many of his remarks being tagged by that archetypically 1890s expression 'dont'cher know'. Rumours of an adventurous youth in which he had shown literary promise and had been invited to take tea with Swinburne and Watts-Dunton at The Pines were dismissed as legend, but were later found to be true. Panter's charm and his great virtue lay in the fact that he accepted us as we were, and as equals.

That summer, the summer of 1920, I was invited by Panter to join the reading party at his Chalet in the Savoyard Alps. To arrive at this destination I spent a gruelling twenty-four hours or so travelling across France by train, standing mostly in third-class corridors, changing several times, until at last I arrived one fresh July morning at the little station of Saint Genièvre les Eaux in the foothills of Mont Blanc. I had sent a telegram ahead from Paris to say when I was to arrive so that the comforting figure of Panter in a linen jacket and a disgraceful pair of old grey flannels was waiting for me on the platform. Standing beside him was a tall, willowy and outstandingly good looking young man whom I recognised as Lord Felbrigg.

Even in those days some academic prowess was required to gain entry into Oxford, so how Lord Felbrigg managed to obtain a place at St Matthew's is something of a mystery. He had come from Eton with little to recommend him but his looks and his title (which was a courtesy title, he being the only son of the Marquess of Attleborough), but few resented him, because he was the most amiable and unassuming of beings. Panter had taken him up, some said because of his title, but I suspect because he was so helpless. At any rate, I felt as I saw them, standing side by side on the platform waiting for me, that they looked comfortable together. Panter was no fool, but there was

The Babe of The Abyss

something simple and childlike about him which responded to the same quality in Felbrigg.

Felbrigg had a motor car—a great rarity in those days—which he had bought in Paris and driven all the way to the Haute Savoie himself. It was an open-topped Bugatti, if I remember correctly, and in it we bumped along the sunny cobbled streets of Saint Genièvre, with its tall yellow houses whose every window box seems in my memory to have been bursting with scarlet geraniums. As we made our way to the little station of the 'Tramway de Mont Blanc', which was to take us up the mountain to the Chalet, we laughed, as children do, for no good reason but the excellent one of being alive.

The Chalet itself is situated four-and-a-half thousand feet up on the slopes of Mont Saint Genièvre, one of the foothills of the Mont Blanc massif to which it is joined by a neck of land called the Col du Prarion. It was at this Col that the Tramway de Mont Blanc deposited us, and from there that we took the short walk through pine woods to the Chalet des Pines which nestles in a clearing on the eastern slopes of Mont Saint Genièvre. It is a wooden structure on two floors, the upper one consisting of bedrooms, the ground floor being composed of a kitchen, a dining room and a large communal sitting room. The clearing in front of the Chalet is an oval shaped terrace of rough grass lawn which commands an uninterrupted view across a valley to mountains beyond.

Hoveton and three or four others were already there. It was the first week of Panter's reading party and others were due to arrive later. During that week we were cheerful, earnest, energetic, studious, frivolous and innocently happy. In the mornings we took deck chairs out onto the lawn to read our books. In that high, rare atmosphere even the hardest authors lost their density and became pellucid. Plato's dialogues sparkled like a drawing room comedy; the weighty paragraphs of Thucydides became as terse and gripping as an American thriller. In the afternoon we took strenuous walks up towards the snow line and beyond.

Our happiness was enhanced by the fact that Panter was in a mood that was sunny and benign even by his standards, and it did not escape our notice that this was due to the presence of Lord Felbrigg. It was not that they were constantly together, but that their acts and moods were always in accord. Their delight in each other's company was evident and sometimes comical because they were such an incongruous pair, the young lord and the old pedant. Yet they complemented one another: Felbrigg looked to Panter for security and wisdom, Panter to Felbrigg for youth and energy. Though mutually dependent, they wore their dependency lightly, as if it were a kind of joke. So we passed seven days in sunshine, study and dreamless sleep, and on the eighth day Seddon came.

I did not know that Seddon had been invited, but he had. Panter's kind heart had prevailed over his common sense. Seddon appeared suddenly in the Chalet shortly after seven as supper was being prepared and laid his heavy rucksack down with a bump in the middle of the sitting room. He had missed the last excursion of the Tramway and so had been compelled to make the uphill journey on foot, a good three hours of strenuous walking.

It is probably retrospective imagination which makes me believe that the atmosphere of the Chalet changed abruptly as soon as Seddon walked into it, but that night after supper unquestionably the mood darkened. We had gathered in the sitting room for the usual conversation before bed. Somehow the topic of the Great War was broached and Seddon, the only one of the party who had been a combatant, began to talk about it. For an hour, perhaps two, he told one story after another: stories of maimings, gassings, blindings, disfigurements, of men blown apart or buried alive in saps, or drowned in mud. The rest of us sat there, too stunned to interrupt, but longing for him

The Babe of The Abyss

to stop. Occasionally I glanced over at Panter, in the hope that he would call Seddon to order, but I saw from his glazed expression that he was as mesmerised as the rest of us. As the daylight faded outside, the only illumination came from an oil lamp on the table nearest to Seddon's chair. The occasion began to take on the atmosphere of a bizarre religious meeting in which all eyes were on the preacher as he ranted about human wickedness and the horrors of life and death. Seddon's war contained no heroism, no courageous comradely deeds, only degradation and suffering.

The recital was brought to a sudden end by a strange happening. Something was heard moving about above us, pattering along the wooden floorboards of the Chalet. Lord Felbrigg sprang from his seat and immediately ran upstairs to investigate. The rest of us stayed where we were in a state of shock. I looked across at Seddon. His eyes were fixed on the ceiling, apprehensive, perhaps troubled, but not, I thought, surprised. Presently Felbrigg came down, announcing that he had searched the place thoroughly, but there was nothing to be found. 'It must have been a rat, or something,' he said, unconvinced. 'Whatever it is, it's gone.'

'Time we were in bed,' said Panter rising, and we all obeyed gratefully.

It should have been a rat, it could only have been a rat, but it was not. In the first place the footfalls were too heavy; secondly they had the unmistakable rhythm of a biped, rather than a four-legged creature. Yet they were not quite human either. A flightless bird? No. They sounded most of all like the headlong, stuttering steps of a child that has just learned to walk.

The following morning was a fine one, so that some of our former cheerfulness was restored, but I noticed from the first a subtle alteration in the regime of the place. Before Seddon's arrival Panter had conducted the reading party with Lord Felbrigg as his lieutenant, allowing him on occasion to take command as leader of our afternoon expeditions into the mountains. Seddon was now a third factor in the partnership. He did not exactly usurp Lord Felbrigg's position: it was as if he stood behind Panter and Felbrigg, directing them both.

Felbrigg was aware of this shift in the social balance, and did not like it. He took a strong dislike to Seddon, but was unable to express it clearly. The nearest he came to an analysis was when he said to me once that he thought that Seddon was 'the sort of chap who pulls the wings off flies'.

Panter was also uneasy about the situation and seemed equally incapable of doing anything about it. I often saw him engaged in long intense conversations with Seddon. The rest of us, not in Felbrigg's presence, would speculate on the nature of their discussions. I only heard what was said once, and that was only a fragment.

One afternoon, a few days after Seddon's arrival, we had decided not to go on a walk as a party, but to split up into singles and pairs for our constitutionals. This had not happened before and was a sign of the dissolution which Seddon's arrival had caused. I had gone off by myself to explore the wooded slopes of Mont Saint Genièvre, had lost myself a couple of times and was returning to the Chalet rather later than I would have wished. It was a hot day and the sun had filled the forest with a heavy, pine-scented air. I was scrambling down a slope towards a path when I heard the voice of two walkers coming along it, Seddon and Panter. I squatted down behind a bush to listen. At first I could not hear what they were saying, but I could tell that Seddon was doing most of the talking and that what he said was sharply authoritative. Then, as they came close to where I was hidden, I managed to make out a few sentences. Seddon spoke first.

'You must stop hiding from yourself, Panter. Look your desires in the face. Act upon them if necessary.'

The Babe of The Abyss

'Oh, I say, but look here, Seddon, I'm quite happy as I am, dont'cher know.'

'What's happiness got to do with it? It's being alive that matters.'

Then they passed ahead of where I was concealed, so that they had their backs to me and I could no longer hear them. This was how I realised, before all the others, that whatever else Seddon intended, he did not mean to alienate Lord Felbrigg from Panter's affections: quite the reverse, in fact.

I could, I suppose, explain in detail how the situation at the Chalet became daily more intense, more fraught with unspoken emotions, but I have no stomach for it. I can only say that with each day Seddon's influence grew, even as it became less and less obviously manifested. As for the strange noise, it was heard a few more times, always on the upper floor while one or other of us was on the ground floor, but we never heard it again as a group.

About a week after I had overheard the conversation between Panter and Seddon there came a day which changed everything. The morning passed as usual, then, in the afternoon, most people dispersed as usual for their walk. I remained behind because I had a slight stomach upset. I noticed that the last pair to leave the Chalet were Panter and Lord Felbrigg. They seemed deep in conversation, Felbrigg laughing a good deal, in a forced, nervous way which was unlike him.

I sat in a deck chair on the lawn idly flicking through a Tauchnitz edition of *À Rebours* that I had unexpectedly found in one of the sitting room's crammed bookshelves. I felt reluctant to go indoors in case I heard those footsteps again. None of us had speculated on their origin, perhaps for fear of coming to irrational conclusions. When I did venture inside, to change my book for something less demanding, I heard no footsteps from the upper floor, but I thought I heard a laugh. That was even more troubling because it seemed to be the laugh of a two-year-old child, with the peculiar gurgling catch in the throat characteristic of that age. And yet it had a power, a purpose and a malice which were quite beyond any child I have ever known, or would like to know. I dismissed it, though, as an auditory hallucination brought on by my slight illness, picked up a battered copy of Rider Haggard's *She*, and went out onto the lawn again.

I had been reading for about two hours when I saw Lord Felbrigg walking rapidly down the path towards the Chalet. His face was very red and rigid. Ignoring my greeting, he stamped into the Chalet. I heard him thumping upstairs and banging a door. I abandoned my reading and waited in ignorant apprehension for the next event.

Five minutes later Hoveton and Demple-Smith (a pallid undergraduate, now, I believe, the Suffragan Bishop of Tonbridge) came down the path, swinging their alpenstocks, deep in conversation.

Hoveton came up to me and said: 'I say, Cordery, have you seen Felbrigg?' I told them what I had witnessed. 'It's all very odd,' said Hoveton. (I saw Demple-Smith frowning deeply, as if to reinforce his companion's words.) 'We saw Panter and Felbrigg from a distance about half an hour ago. They were by a stream in the woods. Very pleasant sort of spot.' I nodded impatiently. 'They were sort of struggling together, then Felbrigg broke away. You won't believe this, but it looked as though Panter was—well—sort of attacking Felbrigg.'

'Assaulting,' said Demple-Smith, with a semantic subtlety that I had thought beyond him. I knew then that the all-male Eden of the Chalet des Pines had been desecrated.

When Panter appeared not long after, he was in a distracted state. Hoveton and Demple-Smith had gone into the Chalet while I remained on the lawn. Panter wandered about it, looking wildly around him, approaching the Chalet occasionally, then retreating, never entering it. He took a handkerchief out of his pocket and began to chew one corner, a habit of his when in deep thought. Finally he approached me and asked where Felbrigg was, so I told him, but Panter continued to dither. I went into the Chalet, leaving him to pace the lawn alone.

That evening seethed with unspoken anguish. Hoveton and I busied ourselves with cooking the supper in the kitchen, while others murmured in the sitting room. We heard Panter come into the Chalet and go upstairs. There were some bangings on doors, then the anguished voices of Felbrigg and Panter could be heard. The words were indistinct, but the intonations conveyed a clear meaning. Panter was pleading, begging for forgiveness which Felbrigg, hurt and indignant, was savagely denying him. As we listened Seddon strolled into the kitchen, his manner calm, apparently indifferent to the scene that was being played above our heads.

'What have you done?' I said to him.

Seddon stared back at me, unmoved, unoffended but defiant. He shrugged his shoulders, turned and walked out of the kitchen.

I really cannot remember how we lived out the rest of that evening. I woke late the following morning to be informed that Felbrigg had already gone down the mountain into Saint Geniévre to 'post a letter'. He returned for lunch, which passed off stiffly but without incident. Felbrigg was not himself: his face was rigid, expressionless, his manner chilly and disdainful. Panter remained polite but subdued; only Hoveton attempted to lighten the occasion, if not very successfully, with a long anecdote about a hoax played on the Seely Professor of Homeric Archaeology. Like most academic hoaxes it was excessively complex and utterly devoid of humour. There was no discussion about what walks we would take, but as soon as the ghastly meal was over Felbrigg announced that he was going 'up to the glacier', took an alpenstock out of the bamboo umbrella stand and strode out of the Chalet. It was a bright, cloudless day, as I remember.

The Complete Symphonies of Adolf Hitler

We knew where he was going. Beyond the Col du Prarion, which joined our lesser mountain to the Mont Blanc massif, there is a steep climb through pine woods until the path reaches the snow line at which point it winds upwards along a ridge on one side of which can be seen the glacier, crawling its wrinkled way down the mountainside. I remember how disappointed I was when I first saw the glacier close to. The word 'glacier' had always evoked for me an idea of exquisite, icy purity, but what I saw had the colour and appearance of badly made porridge, clotted and riven with deep fissures. At its dripping margins it looked like a vast, dirty green sponge. Once seen, it no longer attracted me.

That afternoon, however, I was drawn back to the glacier. I knew that Felbrigg needed company, even though he might spurn it, so, some ten minutes after he had left the Chalet, I set out to find him.

I had just come out of the woods and was approaching the snow line when I thought I saw him. He was walking along the ridge that borders the glacier about four hundred yards in front of me. He was moving quickly, but occasionally he would stop and look about him furtively, like a man pursued. This behaviour convinced me that I must reach him and talk to him. Though I risked frightening him off I decided to call to him, but, just then, I thought I heard a cough behind me. It was not an adult cough, but the kind of cough I remember my younger sister making when she had croup as a baby. I turned around and peered into the pine wood behind me, but saw nothing. When I turned my eyes again to the ridge Felbrigg had gone. He could only have taken one of the numerous little tracks that wound down from the ridge towards the glacier. I hesitated again, then started violently because I had felt a hand on my shoulder. It was Seddon. I told him what I had seen and of my anxieties, with rather more frankness than I would have done

The Babe of The Abyss

had I not been surprised. He merely nodded impassively and suggested that we go to look for Felbrigg on the glacier.

So we climbed down onto that leprous field of icy vomit and wandered over its cracked surface calling occasionally for Felbrigg. The only answer we received was a distant echo from the mountains which hung over us. Eventually I persuaded myself that Felbrigg had not been on the glacier at all, but had taken some different path, yet when we returned to the Chalet Felbrigg was not there. He did not return for supper. Anxiety mounted until we all decided collectively to set out for the glacier with electric torches to search for him. Two hours later Felbrigg's body was found lying at the bottom of a crevasse. The conclusion reached by the authorities when they arrived on the scene was that he could not have fallen into it by accident, but must have jumped. As he was last seen walking alone, any suggestion that he had been pushed was discounted.

The reading party dispersed and Felbrigg's body was taken to England where, at his funeral, I heard that Panter would not be returning to St Matthew's the following term. When Felbrigg went into St Genièvre on the morning of his death he had sent a letter to his father, the Marquess of Attleborough. That letter contained accusations which Lord Attleborough relayed to the authorities at St Matthew's, stating that, provided Dr Simeon Ray left St Matthew's at once, never to return in any capacity, no scandal would be made, no court proceedings instituted. St Matthew's College did not call the Marquess's bluff.

I never saw Panter Ray again, and, to my shame, I never even thought of trying to make contact.

V

At the end of that Trinity Term of 1938 Arlington insisted that I go at once to the Haute Savoie to look into the matter of the Chalet. This was unfortunate as I had already made arrangements to go down to Frinton with my wife, Margery, my two children and their nanny for our annual holiday. I told Margery that I would only be away for the first week. She said, with perhaps a touch of sarcasm, that she supposed that Lord Arlington's wish was my command, then added, quite inconsequentially, that my hair was beginning to go decidedly grey.

Before I left for the French Alps I paid a call on Mrs Ramshaw, Panter's landlady, a woman of limited intellect and somewhat incoherent speech. From her I tried to obtain an impression of Panter's last days. She had very little to say, which did not, of course, prevent her from saying it at inordinate length. He 'kept himself to himself' apparently, went out little. She had no idea how he managed to feed and water himself, as she did not cater for him. She admitted that she had, for a small consideration, reported on Panter to Mr Seddon. Seddon had paid odd, infrequent visits, the last of which had been only three days before Panter's death and on that occasion he 'had brought something with him for Dr Ray'. Precisely what this thing was Mrs Ramshaw was either unable or unwilling to specify.

I asked her about the salt on Panter's bedroom floor and received for my pains a torrent of complaint about the appalling inconsiderateness of spreading condiments all over her nice linoleum. And why had he done it? She could not possibly say.

Then she added: 'You know, Mr Cordery, there was footprints all over that salt when I come in to find him passed on. Not his. They was too small. They was like the feet of a little kiddie. But I didn't see no kiddie. I won't have 'em in the house.'

I asked if I might see the rooms, and, for a small inducement, she agreed. As we toiled upstairs I heard more bitter complaints about how, since the death of Dr Ray, she had been unable to rent his rooms. When we arrived on the top floor I saw two bare chambers of unredeemed drabness and melancholy. Mrs Ramshaw presented me with a leather suitcase which contained, she

The Babe of The Abyss

said, all of Panter's worldly goods. I looked through it, but the contents were only old clothes, so I told Mrs Ramshaw to dispose of them as she thought fit. Only one possession of Panter's remained in his sitting room. It was on his mantelpiece and Mrs Ramshaw said she had not touched it because 'you don't know where it's gone and been'.

The object in question looked at first like a curiously shaped stone with a worn smooth surface, some three inches high and two inches across at its widest. Closer examination showed that it was crudely carved into a squat, roughly human shape. I guessed that it must be very ancient from its patina, and from its resemblance to those bulbous female figurines that had lately been excavated from various European Stone Age sites and have, inevitably, been categorised as 'fertility goddesses'. But this statuette (if one could dignify it with such a term) was of indeterminate sex, and resembled rather a bloated child than a full-grown adult. I put it in my pocket, resolved to show it to Hoveton, our college's tame archaeologist, and perhaps present it to the Ashmolean or the Pitt-Rivers.

'That's right,' said Mrs Ramshaw impertinently. 'You keep it, dear. I won't say nuthink.'

VI

Upon my arrival in Saint Genièvre I booked in to the Auberge du Mont Blanc and at once set about making an appointment to see the Notaire, M. Belgence. When I saw him the following morning I presented him with papers establishing Panter's death and the college's title to the Chalet. M. Belgence, a round, genial, pompous little man, expressed himself satisfied with them but remarked that he was surprised to hear of the owner's death. Only a few months before, he said, 'Monsieur le Propriétaire' had paid a visit. It was now my turn to be surprised. I asked what this 'Monsieur le Propriétaire' looked like. M. Belgence replied that he had seen him himself: *'un homme aux cheveux foncés avec un regard agressif'*. I kept my council, for 'a man with dark hair and an aggressive look' was certainly not Panter. M. Belgence said that though it would take some time for the transfer of the property to be formalised I had his full permission to inspect the Chalet des Pines at my convenience. It was a somewhat empty gesture of liberality, since the Chalet was not kept locked. Remoteness and the fact that it contained nothing of value guaranteed its safety.

My interview with the Notaire ended at midday and I decided that, after lunch at the Auberge, I would take the Tramway up to the Chalet to inspect it there and then. I have to admit that I rather lingered over lunch. I do not often take my meals alone so that perhaps I drank more wine than I usually do, with the result that when I found myself taking the old Tramway up the mountain it was almost four in the afternoon. The sun was shining, and though I noted a thick cluster of dark grey clouds massing behind the distant mountains I paid very little heed to them.

In nearly twenty years almost nothing had changed. The walk from the Col du Prarion to the Chalet was perhaps rather longer than I expected, but there was the Chalet des Pines, nestling in the woods, with its rough grass lawn in front of it, exactly as I remembered. I lifted the latch on the front door and went in.

Nothing had changed inside. Immediately I was aware of the familiar scent of pine and old books, a sweet scent which might have been redolent of innocence, had it not been for Felbrigg's death. As it was, it smelt to me like corruption.

The place was in a surprisingly good state of repair, and there was very little dust. This I attributed to the high Alpine atmosphere, though I had some thoughts about the mysterious dark-haired visitor. The rooms were as I remembered them; the thin mattresses rolled up on the narrow wooden beds, even the linen in the armoire looked as if it could be used. Above all, I was

The Babe of The Abyss

pleasantly surprised to find that the roof was not leaking and there was no damp anywhere. Yet, I could not help feeling oppressed by the place; though this may have been because of my memories, or the fact that while I had been in the Chalet the sky had darkened over the mountain. Clouds the colour of lead were now swagged over the Chalet. There was a flash and a rumble as rain began to fall. I found a candle in the kitchen and lit it from a box of matches that I had prudently brought with me. I would have liked to have left and taken the Tramway down the mountain into Saint Genièvre but the rain was now heavy. Scintillating screens of falling water obscured everything outside the window and battered the roof, blocking out all other sounds. I suddenly felt tired, so I sat down in one of the wicker armchairs. Despite its rather Spartan upholstery I fell asleep almost at once.

When I awoke it was dark outside and my candle was guttering. I fetched another from the kitchen, lit it and looked at my watch. It was past six and I had missed the last train down the mountain. It was still raining. Having no torch, I did not feel like a three-hour tramp down a dark, wet mountainside, with all the attendant risks of losing myself or my footing, so I decided to bed down for the night in Panter's old room and take the first train down from the Col the following morning.

There was nothing to eat of course, but fortunately I had lunched well—rather too well as it turned out—but there were some old logs and kindling in the log basket. With these I made a fire in the cast iron stove that stood in the centre of the sitting room. The fire would also warm Panter's old room since the stove pipe passed through it on its way to the roof. To ignite the kindling in the grate I sacrificed some pages from a Tauchnitz edition of *Marius the Epicurean*. It had never been a favourite of mine, but I remember that it had been one of the few books about which Panter, who rarely expressed an opinion about anything, had shown enthusiasm. I speculated whether, like

Wilde, the young Panter had been to its author's lectures at Oxford.

Once the fire was established and I had dampened it down a little, I decided on an early night. The rain was still pattering away and it was utterly black outside. I riddled the stove with a poker, then, on an instinct, I took the poker up to bed with me.

With pillows and blankets from the armoire I managed to make myself comfortable on Panter's bed. It was warm and the gentle fall of rain had a soothing effect. Nothing barred sleep except the slight unease that prevented me from extinguishing my candle which I put on my bedside table next to the poker.

Sleep, of a thick and troubled kind, came eventually. It must have lasted seven hours or so because it was past one o'clock when I woke again, yet I was woken not by noise, but by silence. The rain had stopped, there was no wind, and I was engulfed in the utter isolation of the mountain. Though my candle had expired long ago my room was lit from the window by a full moon in the clear night sky.

I cannot now remember how long I lay listening to the silence, but I think it was no more than a few minutes before small sounds began to intrude. They were the usual little creaks and ticks that you hear in any building made entirely of wood. Indeed, I was surprised that I had not heard them before, but perhaps the joists and boards had paused before addressing themselves to the task of drying out after the rain. I imagined the Chalet as being like a great dog, shaking its body and scratching itself to be rid of the wet.

Then came another sound, very faint to begin with, like the patter of running feet. I thought at first it might be a recurrence of rain, but the noise was localised: it appeared to come from the passage outside my door. The noise would recede, then return, and each time it returned, it would come closer to my door which was at one end of the Chalet's long upper corridor. I could make it out clearly now, and it was a sound I had heard

The Babe of The Abyss

before. It was the stamping, stuttering step of a child who has just learned to walk, a triumphant slapping of little bare feet on bare boards.

The thumping came nearer and seemed to fill the house. If it was a child it was a giant, a monster child weighing as much as a fully grown man. Then it thumped against the door of my room. In my stupid terror I closed my eyes, willing it to go away.

When I opened them again I saw in the moonlight a face staring at me directly from the end of my bed. Good God, that face! It was a bloated grey face which should by rights have been old, but it was not, it was that of a child, almost a baby, but too big for any child. I could not really tell if it was looking at me because its eyes were black. Its mouth was open and that revealed not the usual pink inner parts of the mouth, the incipient teeth, but a gulf of infinite and infernal blackness. I shouted at the thing. I told it to go to Hell. I said mad things to it, but it continued to gape. I wanted to throw something, beat it with the poker, but I had no strength. Then the face leaned back, let out a great gurgling yell, and appeared to fall away from the end of the bed. At any rate it disappeared, and at the same moment I heard a thump as something heavy fell onto the floorboards.

Released, I leapt out of bed grasping the poker, but the room was empty. It was utterly empty, so I looked in the armoire, but that had nothing in it but sheets and blankets; then I fetched another candle from the kitchen and roamed the house but found nothing. I knew that the creature had disappeared, yet I could not rest.

I have no idea how long this went on but I remember the relief I felt when, standing by a window in the corridor of the upper floor, I saw a slight greying in the sky where the mountains across the valley rose up to meet it. I thought that this was the beginning of the end of my ordeal until I heard something move downstairs. It was a sustained creak, and it sounded like a body sitting down in one of the sitting room's wicker armchairs.

I did not fear what I had heard as my sense of fear had been numbed. Poker in one hand, lighted candle in the other, I descended the stairs.

What I saw shocked me, not because it was unexpected, but because my mind had so accurately predicted it. Sitting in the armchair by the stove, and facing me as I came down, was Stanley Seddon.

'Hello, Cordery,' he said.

'What are you doing here?' I asked. 'You do know that you are trespassing. This Chalet now belongs to the college. Panter left it to us.'

'He had no right to! It's mine!' said Seddon, almost shouting. Those aggressive eyes were now liquid with rage; the lower lip thrust itself out even further, quivering. 'He gave it to me.'

'When?'

Seddon took a moment to recover some composure before replying: 'That's none of your business.'

'Why did he give it to you??'

'Because I treated him.'

'You are a doctor?'

'I am a psychiatrist.'

'A trick cyclist, eh?'

'Yes, I thought you might be the sort of person to employ that puerile term of abuse.'

I apologised diplomatically and sat down. It would have been quite useless to be angry with him; besides, I had to find out what I could. I asked him what brought him here.

'I thought I'd drop by. I have been at Cap d'Antibes attending to the King's sexual problems.'

I said: 'Don't try to shock me with that nonsense, Seddon. I know perfectly well that the King is not at Cap d'Antibes; he is at Sandringham.' Seddon laughed.

The Babe of The Abyss

'I am talking about *the* King, Cordery. The true king, Edward VIII. He may be returning to his rightful place on the throne of England sooner than you think.'

I merely nodded. Seddon was a curious creature: at one moment self-contained and authoritative, the next full of rage, almost a madman. He told me quite steadily that he was the owner of the Chalet, because he had a document signed by Panter himself before witnesses, which transferred the ownership of the Chalet to him. I asked to see it, but he said we would be hearing from his solicitors.

On an impulse I said: 'I'm not sure we'd want to keep this place anyway.'

He asked why not. I thought he seemed disappointed by this capitulation. I gave him a brief account of what I had heard and seen in the night. He nodded several times and asked me to describe my vision in greater detail. Reluctantly I complied. He nodded again. 'You have seen the Babe of the Abyss,' he said.

I merely raised my eyebrows in enquiry. He leaned back in his chair and for a while there was silence. I think both of us were expecting to hear those footsteps above our heads but none came.

'It was the Summer of '16 just before the big July offensive on the Somme,' he said. 'There were four of us, Maddern, Tommy Johnson, Peters and I, all of us subalterns in the Somerset Light Infantry. Yes, I was an officer then. For a short while, before we went up to the line again, our battalion was billeted at a place called Maulincourt. They put us subalterns in a place that called itself the Château de Maulincourt. It sounds grand, but actually it was a terrible old place, little better than a ruin: damp, great holes in the roof, bats everywhere. The Maulincourt family had abandoned it years before, having fallen on hard times, and I heard that the last Baron de Maulincourt was living in a hovel somewhere in the village. Well, thanks to some sort of administrative lash-up among the brass hats at HQ, we found ourselves stuck in this hole for over a week with no orders, and virtually nothing to do. It was a dump, as I say, but we found that there was one room in the Château which was almost habitable and it was the library, so that was where we passed most of our time. There was an ancient piano on which Tommy Johnson tried to beat out some tune or other. The others drank or played cards, but I explored the books which were still on the shelves and looked as if they hadn't been touched for generations. Most of them dated from the eighteenth century or before and were in French, or some other foreign language, and many were so riddled with damp and mildew that they were quite useless. But I noticed that there was one locked glass-fronted case that looked as if it contained some comparatively undamaged volumes. In war everyone is a vandal, you know, so I thought nothing of smashing the case open with an iron bar.

'The books inside were in a remarkable state of preservation, all things considered. They were mostly very old, vellum bound, and some were in manuscript. There was one in particular which attracted my attention because it was handwritten on parchment and contained a number of diagrams, also hand drawn. I noticed that various hands had contributed to it, and that the scribes had signed and dated their entries, the first of them being a Joffroi de Maulincourt in—would you believe it?—the year 1343.

'It looked like an old family recipe book, which in a curious way it was. It turned out to be a Grimoire, a book of spells. The last entry was dated 1866, which meant there must have been quite a long tradition of sorcery in the family.

'I don't know whether you know anything about this sort of thing, Cordery. You probably don't; you've led a sheltered life, but take it from me, most occult writing makes no sense at all, or at any rate takes half a lifetime to decipher. That was the case with nearly all of this stuff which anyway, up to the late seventeenth century, was written in the most appalling Latin. But there were some pages written during the late 1770s by one

The Babe of The Abyss

Etienne Leroyer de Maulincourt which were exquisitely lucid and legible. They were penned in a beautiful eighteenth century copperplate, not crabbed, but flowing and elegant, the sepia ink barely faded. It detailed several ceremonies with clarity and even wit: for instance, Etienne had headed his section of the book *Moyen Court de la Magie Luciferienne,* no doubt with a mocking nod towards the famous Christian prayer manual known as *Le Moyen Court*. I suspected that a sly pun on his own family name was also intended.

'For my own amusement I began to transcribe and translate some of Etienne's formulae, at which point my chums began to take an interest. Dear God, we must have been bored out of our silly heads, but one night when we had had too much cognac, a barrel of which we had liberated from a local *estaminet,* we decided to give one of old Etienne's spells a try.

'It was a ceremony for summoning a demon called Nybbas. Nybbas is often called "the Babe of the Abyss" because he usually manifests himself in the form of a child about two years old, though somewhat larger than life size. I don't mean that he really exists in the way that this chair exists, but he is an archetype of the collective unconscious. Read any Jung? No, I thought not. He represents the primacy of what some call evil. He asserts that evil is not somehow the corruption of innocence, but is itself, in its way, innocent. He stands for what theologians call "original sin", the state into which we are all born. Psychologically he symbolizes a great and unacknowledged truth, that we spring from the womb wicked, or rather, untrammelled by any notion of either good or evil. We are all the children of hellfire and we hide the fact from ourselves at our peril.

'Well, we performed the little ritual in the library one night, and you will be disappointed to hear that nothing much happened except that the whole place became filled with a thick, disgusting smoke that made mustard gas seem like Attar of Roses by comparison. It seemed like a total failure.

'Then, the next day, as it happens, our orders came to go up to the line. It was July, and, in the Somme push that followed, Maddern, Tommy Johnson and Peters all bought it. Only I was left, and I soon discovered that that night had left its legacy.'

'In what way?' I asked.

'I don't want to go into it. You wouldn't understand anyhow. But I will say this. I don't regret it. Never in a million years because the Babe has given me my life's work. I had already begun to read Freud and Jung; now my experiences told me of the necessity to awake and acknowledge the demon within us. If we do not admit to its presence we become its prey. I do not want to talk about Panter. I warned him, but he was fool enough to allow himself to become a victim.

'Everything is in a state of flux. It must be. For there to be Peace, there must be Chaos; for there to be Chaos, there must be Peace. We are entering the age of Chaos and Chaos will purge the world. It is not so much wrong to suppress it as useless. . . .'

He went on and on like this, talking interminable rubbish. Already the sun was beginning to rise and I knew from the voices within me that unless I did something about it I would become a victim too. So I did what I was told because I still had the poker in my hand.

As I beat his head into a pulp, I could distinctly hear above the confusion the obscene, gurgling laughter of a child.

When I had washed the blood out of the wooden floor of the Chalet, I dragged the body outside to the edge of the lawn and buried him in a shallow grave. It was dawn and, as the sun rose, it shone aslant the rough grass, turning its green to gold, and its heavy burden of dew into a crown of diamonds.

VII

Three days later I was sitting next to my wife Margery at the entrance to our beach hut in Frinton, watching my seven-year-old daughter Helen and three-year-old son Maxim running in and out of the sea. Maxim stamped triumphantly at the thin lace border of foamy water on the polished sand. One of his stampings sent up a splash of brine into Helen's face so that she screamed. Maxim laughed and was duly scolded by Nanny Benton who was supervising their activities at the water's edge.

'Charles!' said Margery suddenly. I turned to look at her. The Frinton weather had been kind for once and had brought out the freckles on her sweet, ordinary face.

'Yes, my dear?'

'What were you looking at?'

'Helen and Maxim, of course! What else?'

'Well, if I may say so, you were looking at your offspring in a most peculiar way.' It was the closest thing to reproach that I have ever heard in her voice.

I could not explain to her that, though I was looking at them, I was seeing other things. I saw the splash and spray not of water, but of blood; and in the distance I heard the tramp and slap of tiny, angry marching feet.

BLOODY BILL

I

That afternoon the season of mists reigned over Timbralls, Dutchman's Farm and Agar's Plough, Eton playing fields which had once long ago been the fertile domain of Thames Valley farmers. Who Agar had been and who the Dutchman I never knew, but their names still ring in my memory, evoking uneasy nostalgia. It was November. The air had a damp chill in it, and the breath of the cheering spectators on the touchline augmented the fog. Everything, the thick thud of the football, the hoarse cries of the players, even the referee's whistle, seemed muffled

Bloody Bill

and dim. Mist had sucked colour from the shirts of the players and the mud-churned green of the pitch.

It was the quarter finals, as I remember, of the inter-house championships. On our house notice board a paper had been pinned up which gave details of the time, location and team for that day's match. Below this the house captain had written in capitals the words: ALL MUST WATCH AND CHEER. It was an injunction which someone of my lowly status in the house could not afford to disobey. I disliked games, but if there was one thing I disliked even more than games, it was being made to watch them.

A group of us, roughly contemporaries, who resented being forced to turn out for this dreary event, were huddled together on the touchline, occasionally stamping up and down on the ground to warm our feet, trying to keep ourselves entertained by making ribald remarks. Eventually our lack of enthusiasm was noted by Hellmore-Henderson, a boy in a junior position of authority in the house with a taste for power and a dull, earnest streak. He strode along the touchline towards us.

'Take a brace, you spastics!' he shouted. 'Cheer! That's what you're here for. Don't you want us to win?' It was obvious that he was going to stay with us and make our lives a misery. I searched for something to distract him and amuse us.

Further along the touchline stood our house master Mr Naughton (usually known by his initials R.F.N or as 'My Tutor') shouting lustily and accompanied by his wife (always known bizarrely as 'Mrs My Tutor') who was smiling in her dutiful, bemused way. Some distance from them, and still further from us, an elderly man in a heavy overcoat was standing alone. He was bareheaded and staring at the game intently, his head thrust forward, his heavy jaw jutting out in an aggressive way. It was difficult to tell at that distance and in the mist, but I judged him to be in his seventies.

The Complete Symphonies of Adolf Hitler

What struck me immediately about him was his size. He was broad, heavily built and must have been over six feet six in height. The mist and the distance only enhanced the impression that this was a giant of a man. I was intrigued.

'Who's that chap over there?' I asked Hellmore-Henderson.
'That's Bloody Bill,' he replied, as if I ought to have known.
'Who's Bloody Bill?'
'He was a beak here once.' ('Beak' is the Etonian for master.)
'Why was he called Bloody Bill?'
'Because he was Bloody Bill, that's why. Now, come on, stop shirking and cheer.' Presently Hellmore-Henderson got bored with trying to instil 'keenness' (that popular Etonian virtue) into us and moved off to torment others.

'So that's Bloody Bill,' murmured Johnny Scott, one of our group, when Hellmore-Henderson had left.

'You know about him!' I said, passionately curious, almost in spite of myself. It turned out that Scott's father had been at Eton before the war and had told him something of Bloody Bill, who had been a legend. His real name was William Hexham, a beak whose formidable athletic and academic prowess had made everyone believe at the start of his career that he was destined for great things, even the headmastership. He gave every appearance of having been built in the mould of the legendary giants of public school education, like Arnold of Rugby and Thring of Uppingham. When he became a house master, his boys carried away many of the available prizes, both on the playing field and in the classroom, but then rumours began to spread about his harshness, and his use of the cane, excessive even for the interwar years in which he flourished. He acquired the sobriquet 'Bloody Bill', and the name stuck. He eventually had to give up his house 'because,' according to Scott, 'he once nearly killed a boy,' but he had still been retained by the school as a teacher.

'My God,' I said. 'Why the hell wasn't he sacked?'

Bloody Bill

Scott looked rather shocked. 'Oh no. Bloody Bill was a brilliant rowing coach,' he said, 'and anyway he was an Old Etonian.'

Not myself having a father who had been at Eton, I was unimpressed. The man was clearly a monster, but this only enhanced my curiosity. Just after half time I sauntered away from my group and towards Bloody Bill, trying to make my movements appear aimless.

He seemed barely to have moved from the position in which I had first seen him. Closer to, the strangeness, the sheer formidableness of the man, was enhanced rather than diminished. His face had a monumental quality as if it had been carved out of a mountainside. Like a Greek statue the nose ran straight from the brow without any indentation at the top; the heavy chin jutted out truculently. His pose was slightly hunched and his hands were thrust deep into his pockets.

His hair was white and still fairly abundant, with that fine, slightly woolly quality which made one suspect that it had once been curly and blonde. His face was grey, which enhanced his resemblance to an archaic stone statue of a god or hero, unrelieved by colour, except for the remarkable eyes. If it is possible for a pale colour to be intense, I would say that they were an intense pale blue, the colour of a cloudless winter sky.

As Bloody Bill continued to watch the game with extraordinary concentration, I saw that his jaw was working up and down, as if he were chewing or muttering to himself. The steam of his breath came out in great heavy puffs to unite with the chill vapour that surrounded him.

Suddenly he turned and looked at me. It was a look that spoke, and I shall never forget it. It was not so much that it expressed menace, or malevolence, though those elements were undoubtedly present; more significantly, it was a look which said: 'If you know what is good for you, keep away.' It warned. I withdrew to a safer distance.

The Complete Symphonies of Adolf Hitler

Presently I saw R.F.N, my house master, walk up to him. They exchanged a few words, then glanced in my direction. This made me nervous, so for the rest of the match I devoted myself conscientiously to cheering on my house side which lost that day.

The image of Bloody Bill, the ruined giant in the fog, stayed with me, especially as I began to notice him around Eton. If I had not known who he was, had I not been somehow sensitised to his presence, I might have missed him. As it was, I often saw him, usually in the playing fields, at a distance, alone, motionless and watching some game or activity; and when I noticed him I was frequently invaded by the sense that he had also noticed me. This feeling threatened to develop into a complex, so that whenever I had to go out to a game in the afternoon I would keep my eyes averted from places where I expected to see him. I was fully conscious of my irrationality, but the idea would not leave me, so that it became a kind of personal superstition, like not walking under ladders, or avoiding the colour green.

II

It was about that time that I began to develop a friendship with a boy from another house called Tristram Ronaldson. We had discovered a shared interest in Egyptology and Tristram, though like me only in his second year, had plans to found an Egyptological society. He had the misfortune to be the son of a famous man, the great explorer and naturalist, Sir Jasper Ronaldson. Most people I knew had read his famous book *A Stroll in the Arctic*. Then there was *Ambling in the Himalayas, Amazon Excursions*, and others. I had read them myself, and enjoyed them, even if I found that air of phlegmatic nonchalance in the face of appalling danger a little artificial at times. And though the concept of racism did not figure largely in my moral consciousness I was slightly bothered by the tone of amused condescension he evinced towards 'the natives'. Nevertheless he was a considerable figure whose war exploits had been legendary.

Perhaps, in being very different from most other boys I knew, Tristram was deliberately making a bid to establish an identity beyond his father's shadow, but there was more to him than that. Tristram had a naturally individual approach to life.

I remember it was in my second Summer Half, as terms were called at Eton, that I first visited him at his house. The decor of his room immediately marked him out as an original. The walls were not adorned with the usual team photographs and posters of The Beatles, Raquel Welch in a fur bikini, or a youthful Marlon Brando sitting morosely astride a motorcycle. There was a row of severely framed lithographic prints by David Roberts of Egypt, and numerous photographs framed in *passe partout*, probably taken by Tristram himself, of Egyptian deities and *objets d'art*. On his 'burry' (the Etonian for desk) was a skull. The lid of his ottoman was up and Tristram himself was engaged in throwing a dagger at it. The ottoman was situated just below the window which was open. It looked out onto a narrow pedestrian thoroughfare called Judy's Passage.

'Suppose you miss and the knife goes sailing through the window and kills someone in Judy's Passage,' I said.

'I'd rather risk that than break a window,' said Tristram. 'I've already broken two this half and my Tutor is getting pee'd off. Here's the book you wanted to borrow.'

He tossed me the volume in question, D.P. Simpson's *Funerary Rites of Ancient Egypt*.

'I'm fed up with this. Shall we go for a walk? You can sock me a Brown Cow at Rowlands afterwards.'

I soon discovered that Tristram had inherited at least some of his father's intrepid genes, as his idea of a walk was to explore areas of Eton which were out of bounds. This afternoon, brilliantly sunny and breezy, he had set his heart on Luxmoore's

The Complete Symphonies of Adolf Hitler

Garden, a slender eyot, attached to the Eton side of the Thames by a wooden Chinese bridge. This sequestered spot was allowed only to the most senior boys, but Tristram was determined to visit it. I was marginally more afraid of being thought a coward by Tristram than being caught so I went along with him.

Luckily, everyone else seemed to be out on the river that afternoon or playing cricket so we had the place to ourselves. With its shady walks, exotic vegetation, and little emerald lawns, the place seemed to us like a secret paradise, all the more delicious for being forbidden.

In the heart of the garden is an oval lawn at one apex of which stands a bronze bust of Luxmoore himself and below it a bench. We were approaching this, shielded by a screen of trees, when I stopped and restrained Tristram. I could see that someone was sitting on the bench, a large man, who, despite the mildness of the weather, wore a heavy overcoat.

'Let's get out of here,' I said. Tristram consented to withdraw a little into the undergrowth.

'Who was that?' he asked.

'Bloody Bill. He's—'

'God! Bloody Bill! I know who Bloody Bill is. He was my pa's Tutor.'

'Let's get out of here.'

'No. Wait!' Tristram seemed strangely excited. 'I want to have a word with him.'

'Good Grief! Why?'

'Because my pa says he's the only person he's ever been afraid of.'

That seemed to me a poor reason for approaching Bloody Bill, but I knew I could do nothing to stop him. So I remained concealed in the undergrowth while Tristram walked towards the old man sitting on the bench. Though I moved as close as I could to them without allowing myself to be seen, I could still

Bloody Bill

not hear clearly what they said to each other. The only words I caught were Tristram's first. He said: 'Are you Bloody Bill?'

As the old man looked up I saw those pale sapphire eyes blaze with anger, but Tristram stood his ground. They talked for about five minutes, Bloody Bill seated, Tristram standing in front of him, and it seemed an age to me. Eventually Tristram extended his hand which Bloody Bill took and shook reluctantly; then Tristram turned and walked away from the old man.

We left Luxmoore's Garden in silence, and I could tell that Tristram was full of repressed excitement. I asked him what they had talked about, but all he would say was: 'He remembered my pa.' Even when I socked him a Brown Cow (a glass of coca cola with vanilla ice cream in it) in Rowlands he still refused to give me any further details.

Nothing more of significance happened that half. Tristram and I remained friends but our efforts to set up an Egyptological society did not progress. In the summer holidays I read that Tristram's father had died suddenly of a heart attack in the Sudan. When we returned for the Michaelmas Half I wondered how he would be, but he seemed much the same as ever, though perhaps a little more withdrawn. I heard rumours that he had an air pistol in his room, but I never saw it myself.

November came again and I remember that one afternoon I was going for a run. It was my preferred form of exercise, not because I liked it but because it was a solitary pursuit requiring no skill, in which one was not being perpetually urged to demonstrate keenness. It had been prescribed by the authorities that this run should be to a place called Easy Bridge by a path which took one through an unattractive landscape of flat, featureless grassland, a kind of steppe, that bordered the Thames. Windsor Castle loomed in the far distance on the opposite bank; nearer at hand the way led past gas works and under railway arches. That day the chilling mists had come up from the river so thickly that I could barely see my way in front of me. I felt unusually isolated. Other runners, out to perform the same dull task as myself, either overtaking me, or coming in the opposite direction from the goal of Easy Bridge, would suddenly appear out of the thick white vapour and with almost equal suddenness disappear, pounding and puffing like steam engines, seeming about as human.

As I was approaching Easy Bridge the mist began to clear slightly so that I found I could now see about a hundred or so yards in front of me. Ahead of me on the track, and barely visible, two people were walking in the same direction as myself, their backs to me. Poor runner that I was, I was overtaking them rapidly and was almost upon them before I realised who they were. A huge bareheaded, white haired old man in a thick black overcoat was walking beside a slim, dark, curly-haired boy in school dress. It was Bloody Bill and Tristram. I stopped running, not wanting to overtake them and risk being recognised. The sight of them together filled me with perplexity and fear. It was bad enough that they should be together, but the horror of it was, they were holding hands.

Even now I cannot fully explain to myself the revulsion I felt. Let me state quite clearly that I did not believe then, nor do I now, that anything like a physical intimacy existed between them. No, what shocked me, I think, was simply the sheer strangeness, the unlikelihood of it all: that this monstrous old man should hold hands with anyone, let alone a fourteen-year-old boy, and that the boy should consent to be held. It sickened me then and, sad to say, it still does.

I cannot exactly remember what I did then, but I know that I turned aside and ran back the way I had come. That day I offended my small, conscientious, unadventurous spirit by ticking a box against my name on the house notice board to declare that I had reached Easy Bridge when I had not.

Bloody Bill

The following Sunday Bloody Bill came to lunch at my house, joining R.F.N. and the senior boys on the top table. From my lowly vantage point I kept my eye on him throughout the meal, and I think that once he noticed my doing so. He did not appear to say much, but I noticed that he ate and drank voraciously. Later that day I found myself in a position to ask one of those who had lunched at the top table, a boy called Dennis, about the occasion.

'It was rather unexciting, I'm afraid,' said Dennis. 'No famous flogging anecdotes. The one thing that seems to interest Bloody Bill is rowing, so of course Straker, being in the Eight and our resident rowing hero, got his full attention. I can't say I envied him being subjected to those famous X-ray eyes. Straker of course thinks that Bloody Bill was after his body. Typical Straker vanity. I can't really see why My Tutor wanted to have him to lunch. Mrs My Tutor says it's because he feels sorry for Bloody Bill, but I can't say that's the impression I got. My Tutor was terribly nervy and jumpy with the old bugger.'

'Perhaps Bloody Bill knows some frightful secret in My Tutor's past and is blackmailing him,' I suggested light-heartedly.

'You keep your ideas to yourself, please,' said Dennis, suddenly recollecting his seniority.

About a week later I returned from a run to Easy Bridge to find my room occupied by three boys from my house, Ker, Bullard and Pemberton-Pigott. These three were only a year ahead of me but they were good games players and had set themselves up as arbiters of all that was right and proper in the house. You were either with them or you were an outsider, as a result of which they exerted a kind of unofficial jurisdiction over the manners and morals of anyone junior to them. From the way they were seated on my furniture, I could tell that I was about to be the victim of a tribunal, probably on the subject of my lack of 'keenness' at games.

'What's this about?' I said with an attempt at defiance. The answer I received was quite unexpected.

'We saw your friend Ronaldson having a queer-up with Bloody Bill,' said Bullard.

'What!'

'Yes. They were holding hands on Sheep's Bridge.'

'Holding hands is not having a queer-up,' I countered.

'Are you the expert on queer-ups then?' said Ker who had a kind of subtlety that his beefy appearance belied.

'Bloody Bill is an old man.'

'That's what makes it even more disgusting. God! A queer-up with an old man! Ugh! So you approve of queer-ups so long as it's with old men, do you? God! What kind of a perv are you?'

This was clearly going to be one of those arguments you could never win, so I grabbed a towel and left my own room, to much jeering and laughter from the tribunal. By the time I had returned from a shower, Ker, Bullard and Pemberton-Pigott had gone, but their suspicion and disapproval remained behind like a miasma.

I decided to see Tristram at once. I knew how rumours could spread in the school, and how easy it was to be tarnished with guilt by association. My motives were cowardly and dishonourable, but I told myself that I was going to warn Tristram to curtail his association with Bloody Bill for his own good.

I found him in his room. He was engaged in rolling a pair of dice and writing down the result of each throw in a notebook. I cannot recall what I said to him exactly, I suspect that it was feeble, but he listened patiently as he continued to throw his dice. There was a silence when I had finished, then Tristram said, with apparent inconsequentiality:

'My pa was afraid of him, but I'm not.'

By now I was ashamed of what I had said so I asked him:

'Was your father beaten up by him, then?'

Bloody Bill

'Oh yes, but it wasn't just that. Apparently the reason why Bloody Bill was such a holy terror was that he always seemed to know exactly what you were up to. People actually began to think he had some sort of psychic power. Of course that was all bollocks. My father started to get suspicious when he found that his copy of *The Picture of Dorian Gray*, which naturally he kept hidden, was missing—a signed limited edition on handmade paper too! Would be worth a bomb today. Bloody Bill was a terrible prude about that sort of thing, you see. Anyway, pa began to suspect that Bloody Bill was poking about in chaps' rooms when they were out. So he used to fix hairs across the lid of his burry to see if Bloody Bill had been prying. The hairs were often broken but of course there was nothing he could prove. Would you like to have tea with him by the way?'

'What! Bloody Bill?'

'Of course. He lives a couple of miles away in a little house in Dorney Wick. We could bicycle out there next half holiday. He's promised to help us out with the Egyptological society.'

My astonishment had not robbed me of all sense. I knew that Tristram had issued a challenge and that if I refused to take it up he would despise me and I would lose his friendship altogether. Reluctantly I agreed to accompany him, but I had no heart for the adventure.

The following Thursday, I went to My Tutor and obtained permission to visit Dorney Wick by bicycle. When I told him where we were going R.F.N. scrutinised me wordlessly for a while, putting his head only a few inches from mine, a habit of his which I found disconcerting rather than alarming as the proximity of his face was due more to acute myopia than a desire to intimidate. Finally he simply nodded and dismissed me.

It was raining when Tristram and I set out, a slight drizzle only, but enough to lower my spirits and expectations still further. Dorney Wick, a few miles from Eton, is a dull, desultory hamlet that trails along a winding road in the flat meadows of the Thames Valley. The houses were all of brick the colour of dried blood and built at the turn of the last century. Bloody Bill's house was an isolated detached villa with narrow Gothic windows. It reminded me of an elaborate Victorian mausoleum. There was a short gravel drive up to a front door which had a wooden gabled porch painted dark green. The little front garden was dominated by laurels and other shiny-leaved shrubs which glistened and dripped with the recently abated rain.

Tristram hauled on a bell pull in the porch and I heard a faint clanking from the bowels of the house. Presently the door was opened by a small, bony old woman in an overall whom I took to be Bloody Bill's housekeeper but later discovered was his wife. Without a word she showed us into the front parlour where Bloody Bill was seated upright in a tall wing chair facing the door.

I had the impression that he had been awaiting our arrival for some time, like a cat at a mouse hole. Tristram began to be very voluble and cheerful, a little more than was quite natural, presenting me to Bloody Bill with elaborate and jocular formality. Bloody Bill made no move but nodded and said: 'Ah, yes. I have heard a great deal about you,' words that have always made me feel uneasy.

It was as if Tristram were putting the old man on display for my benefit. He rallied Bloody Bill and eventually persuaded him to show me the many curiosities he had in the room. Besides shelves full of books, mostly Oxford Classical Texts and the occasional Loeb, there were several glass-fronted cabinets full of meticulously arranged objects. Bloody Bill was an eclectic rather than a monomaniacal collector. There were trays of bird's eggs, impaled butterflies and the bleached skulls of small mammals and reptiles; there were a dozen or so late Imperial Roman coins embedded in dark blue velvet; there was a case of fossils and coprolites. Bloody Bill had something to say on all of these items, but he seemed chiefly interested in interrogating us, gauging the

Bloody Bill

extent of our ignorance and commenting upon it with a kind of sour humour. Tristram showed a very creditable range of knowledge; I was a dunce by comparison.

Presently I noticed that Tristram was becoming restless. Finally he burst out with the words: 'Come on, sir. Show us your Egyptian stuff. You promised you would, sir, last time I was here.' I saw a look of pure rage pass across Bloody Bill's face. He stood for a few moments motionless staring at Tristram, evidently trying to intimidate him, but he did not succeed. For some reason unknown to me Tristram's will prevailed. Bloody Bill moved towards a black lacquer cabinet which stood against one wall, then opened it with a key from his watch chain. Within the cabinet were two deep shelves lined with pale yellow velvet.

On the lower shelf were four Canopic jars in which, according to the customs of Ancient Egypt, after embalming, the viscera of the deceased were placed, their tops made in the shape of the heads of the four sons of Horus. Bloody Bill had the complete set, one each for the liver, intestines, stomach and lungs. These were impressive enough, but it was the two items on the top shelf which attracted our greatest admiration.

The first was a black bronze statuette, no more than eight inches high, of the jackal-headed god Anubis. He was standing, the left foot extended stiffly in front of the right, in the conventional marching pose. Yet there was something about the set of the god's bestial head which was thrust unusually far forward, that gave the statue a disturbing, aggressive dynamism.

'Anubis, the psychopomp,' said Bloody Bill. Then, turning to us, he said. 'Do you know what that means?'

'Conductor of souls to the land of the dead,' said Tristram as if irritated to be asked such a simple question.

Bloody Bill nodded and took down the second object with great tenderness. It was an ancient terracotta model of a boat, almost a foot long with flakes of paint still clinging to its surface.

It was a marvellous object and must have been, like his other Egyptian curios, perhaps as much as three thousand years old. Prow and stern were fashioned in the form of the cow-headed Hathor, guardian of cemeteries. The boat was populated with about twenty figures in all: in the prow eight of them were in the posture of rowers though their oars were missing. Under a canopy in the centre of the boat three or four persons of indeterminate sex reclined and appeared to be playing some kind of board game. In the stern in front of the steersman a half-human creature knelt with arms raised aloft, making a supplicating gesture.

'Presented to me by the Boat Club when I retired as their coach,' said Bloody Bill. 'It was very generous of them, but I doubt if they knew what they were giving me. Do you?'

'It's a Neshmet boat, of course,' said Tristram almost contemptuously.

'It is a Neshmet boat, as you say. A boat in which the souls of the dead are conducted to the infernal regions. Perhaps Boats did know the significance and were wishing me a speedy journey to the nether world. If that is the case they have been sorely disappointed. It is over twenty years since I was presented with it. Now then, shall we have a dish of tea and play a hand or two of cards?'

Swiftly and delicately Bloody Bill picked up the Neshmet boat, restored it to its place on the shelf and locked the cabinet. We would have liked to stare at it for longer, but he had decided that the entertainment was over.

At that moment, as if responding to a secret signal, Mrs Hexham entered the room with three cups of tea on a tray and a plate of uninteresting looking biscuits. She deposited them on a card table and left without a word. With a little grunt of annoyance Bloody Bill moved the tea to another table, set the card table between us three and took out two packs of cards from

Bloody Bill

one of its drawers. As he was shuffling these he asked me how much money I had on me.

I owned up to seven-and-sixpence. He nodded to Tristram who went to a japanned tin box which stood on the bureau. In it were piles of silver threepenny pieces which had long since ceased to be legal tender. Reluctantly I handed over my seven-and-sixpence and received in return the appropriate number of these makeshift gambling counters. Tristram was made to cash in a ten shilling note with almost as much reluctance.

I cannot now remember the names of the card games we played—Bezique? Gin Rummy? Canasta? Piquet? Vingt-et-un?—I know we played several, but they are just names to me now. What remains with me is the manner in which Bloody Bill played: greedily, with a skill and speed that utterly defeated me. He played only to win, and he did. By the end of an hour or so my seven-and-six, which I could barely afford to lose, was all gone. Tristram lost too but not as quickly or as comprehensively as I had. Bloody Bill looked at me in triumph, then sidelong at Tristram.

'I am afraid that our friend has been soundly thrashed,' he said. 'What say we give him five shillings on account in return for an I.O.U?'

Tristram looked embarrassed. I was silent.

'Don't you want your revenge?' he asked me mockingly, as if the possibility of my obtaining it was too remote to be anything other than laughable. I shook my head and muttered something about being late for Absence, the roll-call that was held at the end of a half-holiday. Tristram rose too, also eager to go, and Bloody Bill grudgingly released us.

'You must come back soon and have your revenge,' he said. They were the last words he spoke to me. With those devouring blue eyes fixed on me I was conscious of a terrible hunger in the man, a hunger for battle and the chance of crushing an adversary, even if the end result was humiliation.

Outside in the corridor we met Mrs Hexham and thanked her perfunctorily for the tea. She moved not a muscle, said not a word. Tristram and I bicycled back through the gathering dusk to our respective Houses swiftly and in silence.

III

I did see Bloody Bill once more, at least I think I did, but I cannot be absolutely certain. One afternoon a couple of weeks after our visit, I was returning exhausted from a junior inter-house match on Agar's Plough. Nobody, least of all myself, had wanted me to be in the team but the sickness and injury of better players had necessitated it. There had been some hope expressed, I believe, that I might rise to the occasion and show 'keenness', but I had not, and that small part of me which still yearned for conformity and acceptance was dejected.

I was walking along the path towards Sheep's Bridge. To my left, behind a belt of trees, the Thames ran softly through the mist and it was there that I thought I saw Tristram with Bloody Bill, standing side by side, he bareheaded, as usual, and in his heavy overcoat, Tristram in school dress, black tail-coat and pin-stripe trousers, like an old fashioned undertaker. They had their backs to me and were watching the river, still and intent. It was absurd, of course, but something in the way they were standing made me think that they were both about to jump in. There was a poised look about them. I thought for a moment of going over to join them, but only for a moment. So I went on my way, and when I got to Sheep's Bridge, I turned to see if they were still there, but they had gone.

The following evening R.F.N. came to see me in my room. He was a solemn-looking man who habitually wore an expression of complex disapproval, so that when something serious had happened a considerable effort was required to make this show on his already troubled features. This evening his brow was

Bloody Bill

furrowed to an even greater extent than usual. He fidgeted with one of my books before addressing me via the mirror.

'Er . . . I believe you are friendly with erm . . . Ronaldson from R.D.F.W.?'

I said I was. He said that Tristram had disappeared from his House the previous day and had not been seen since. A search was being instituted and the police had been informed. If I knew anything of his whereabouts—at this point, R.F.N. turned to me and, as was his habit, thrust his face unpleasantly close to mine—I was to tell him at once. So I told him that I had seen him the previous afternoon near Sheep's Bridge 'with Bl—, erm, I mean, with Mr Hexham.'

R.F.N.'s reaction astonished me. He became both extremely indignant and very nervous at the same time. He picked up the book he had been fiddling with before and might have torn it apart if it had not slipped out of his hand and fallen into the waste-paper bin.

'No. No! Impossible! That's ridiculous. He can't have been. You're lying to me. You're not telling the truth. You're mistaken. No. No indeed . . .'

I tried to ask what made him so certain I was mistaken, but he abruptly left the room. The following day I discovered a possible reason for My Tutor's disquiet. On the afternoon that I claimed to have seen him by the river Bloody Bill had been on his deathbed in Slough General Hospital.

This naturally made me very worried for Tristram, but a few days later he turned up at his house, somewhat dishevelled, but otherwise apparently unharmed. I do not know the full details, but I gathered he told the authorities that he had had some kind of blackout and could not remember where he had been. The recent death of his father and other family circumstances having been taken into account, his story was accepted, though I believe he was taken to see a psychiatrist.

The Complete Symphonies of Adolf Hitler

I visited him in his house about a week later, not long before the end of the Michaelmas Term. He was pale, restless and barely seemed to know who I was. I mentioned our project of an Egyptological society, but he showed very little interest. His room was untidy and I noticed that the familiar skull on the top of his burry had been joined by two other objects. There was no mistaking them: somehow he had managed to become the possessor of the bronze figurine of Anubis and the Neshmet boat. When I commented upon them, Tristram became extremely agitated and almost pushed me out of his room. He did not return to Eton after the Christmas holidays.

IV

I did not see Tristram for another seven years, and when I did it was quite by accident. It was in the summer of my last year at university and I had decided to take a day off revising for my exams in order to go to the Fourth of June at Eton. This is the great day of Eton festivities when there are picnics and speeches and promenades and cricket matches. In the evening there is a great procession of boats off Fellow's Eyot, by Luxmoore's Garden. As each boat passes the spectator stands, the crews, composed of senior boys dressed in antique naval uniforms, stand up in the boats with their oars, doff their boaters and shake the flowers with which they have been bedecked into the water. All this is accompanied by cheering from the watching crowd, applause and the sweet sounds of a silver band playing the Eton Boating Song. It is a charming spectacle for those who are not disposed to be alarmed by its elitist implications.

I was standing rather dreamily watching all this and thinking that it was really about time I returned to Oxford when I saw Tristram. He was standing a few feet away from me with his arm round a girl in a long floral-print Laura Ashley dress. He wore one of those fur-lined Afghan coats that were fashionable

Bloody Bill

at the time, despite the fact that it was a very warm evening, and his black curly hair rested on his shoulders. His face was very pale, but otherwise he seemed in fairly good shape. The girlfriend looked uncannily like him, with the same round, white face, the same mid-length black curly hair. When I went up and greeted him, he appeared to be pleased to see me.

We exchanged news. Tristram was living on a commune in Wiltshire. He told me that he was 'going to be a writer' and had already published a volume of verse. He insisted on taking my address so that he could send me a copy. I asked him if this was the first time he had been back to Eton.

'Oh, no,' he said. 'I've come back many times.'

The girl gave him a look that was both troubled and protective. He in turn hugged and kissed her reassuringly on the cheek. I had the impression that theirs was a relationship based more on mutual dependence than on passion. Soon after this we bade farewell and allowed ourselves to be separated by the crowd.

A few days later a signed copy of Tristram's book of verse arrived for me in the post. It was called, rather pretentiously I thought, *Signs and Sigils*, and the cover was decorated with ankhs, hieroglyphs, alchemical symbols and the like. The contents were no better and no worse than many another produced by an aspiring young writer barely out of adolescence, though much of it was horribly obscure. The only poem which struck me in any way was the last one, and that was really only because of the title, 'To W.N.H.'. W.N.H. of course stood for William Neil Hexham, or Bloody Bill.

To W.N.H.

The shadow of white on white,
The shadow of black on black:
We crossed the river at night;
You stayed, but I came back.

The Complete Symphonies of Adolf Hitler

> I saw what I should not see;
> I heard what I should not hear;
> A life was returned to me,
> But never the loss of fear.
>
> You stand by the river at night;
> You stay until I come back:
> A shadow of white on white,
> A shadow of black on black.

I do not know what this means, and I hope I never will. One year later a newspaper paragraph informed me that Jasper Ronaldson's son, Tristram, had died alone in London from a drug overdose. The jury returned an open verdict. I have never had much time for talk about 'wasted lives'—after all, a life is a life, and who are we to judge whether it has been wasted or not?—but in my selfish way I do still regret the loss to me of that vital, original mind.

All this was over forty years ago now. It is November again and the mists have descended into the little Oxfordshire valley where I live, alone since my wife died two years ago. There is a stream running along the bottom of my garden and yesterday evening as I took my walk down to it I thought I could make out through the cold white haze two figures standing in the trees on the opposite bank. A big old man, bare-headed in a heavy overcoat was holding hands with a thin adolescent boy. The boy appeared to be naked and covered in blood, his left leg thrust forward in a stiff marching pose, but my eyesight is very poor these days and I cannot be sure. The boy raised a stick-like arm and seemed to wave or beckon to me.

I have yet to see their faces.

A CHRISTMAS CARD

In the late winter afternoon the sky had faded to a rose-tinted, duck-egg blue. Beneath it a thick mantle of snow covered roofs and the ways through the city. The ancient houses on either side of the narrow street leaned inwards towards each other as if huddling together for warmth, golden light glowing from behind their mullioned windows. In the street a boy in ragged clothes was attempting to sweep the snow from a doorway. Passing by on the other side, his back to the viewer, was a tall, elderly man with a stick, a shovel hat and a long brown overcoat which came down almost to his feet.

The Complete Symphonies of Adolf Hitler

It was in many ways a scene typical of those found on Christmas cards of the late Victorian period, at a guess mid-1870s. The colours, produced by a superior chromolithographic process, were surprisingly fresh and the card had evidently not been used. The white border, deckled and heavily stamped to look like lace, was crisp and intact.

Hugh Rider found it lying in a transparent plastic pocket on a stall at the Woodstock Antiques Fair. The little round sticker attached to the pocket had £50 written on it in blue biro. That was rather more than Rider wanted to pay, but the card was in superb condition, and he had never seen that particular image before. He screwed himself up to ask the stall holder what was his 'best price'—a phrase he loathed—but he was anticipated.

'You're "trade", aren't you?' said the man behind the stall, as if he had been reading Rider's thoughts. 'You can have it for £20.'

Rider looked up and saw the stall holder for the first time, a small, thin, bespectacled man in his late sixties. He was looking straight at him and smiling.

'That's very generous,' Rider said, breaking the cardinal rule of the antique dealer, which is never to suggest that anyone is doing you a favour. He took a £20 note out of his wallet and handed it to the man before he could change his mind.

'You obviously admire it,' said the man, as if this were a reason to lower his price rather than raise it.

'It is unusual,' said Rider guardedly.

'It is unique,' said the man, handing him the item. 'Take my card,' he said, pointing to a little pile of business cards on the front of the stall. Rider took one and read the name, Anthony Salvin.

Rider felt he would have liked to have had further conversation with Mr Salvin, but by the time he had put the card in the inside pocket of his overcoat he found to his annoyance that the man was already occupied with another customer, a lady who was interested in some early nineteenth century engravings of Morchester. While he was talking to her Salvin briefly turned back to Rider and gave him a nod, friendly but dismissive. Rider walked away in search of other prizes, but that day—a week before Christmas, as it happens—he found none.

A difficult man was Rider: clever, sharp, sardonic, with a round self-indulgent looking face which seemed at odds with his occasionally abrasive manner. He was someone who persistently misunderstood the effect he had on other people: when he thought he was being humorous, to the rest of the world he appeared rude; when he imagined himself to be honest and straightforward, he seemed harsh, even cruel to everyone else. Having given others, quite free of charge, the benefit of his unrivalled knowledge of Victorian prints and ephemera, he would be surprised when his generosity did not receive the gratitude it deserved because he had no idea how patronising he sounded.

As he grew older, a vein of bitterness was added to this gaucherie. It began in his fortieth year when his wife left him and returned to America, taking with her half the value of the antiques business they had built up, along with their daughter, Stephanie. The reason for her departure was no more sinister than that she could no longer bear to live with him. Carla had been a very social person—a 'social climber' Rider had sometimes called her to her face—and she found her husband persistently embarrassing in company. Without fail, he would strike the wrong note: either he talked too much, or he remained aloof and silent; in louche company he would be censorious, with the staid he would suddenly launch into a scabrous anecdote from which no amount of disapproving looks or kicks under the table could deflect him. When Carla reproached him afterwards Rider would at first be penitent if a little baffled; then, when she pursued her theme a little too vigorously, his pride would suddenly assert itself. Why, he asked, did she do nothing but criticise him the whole time? When the parting of the ways came both felt that they were the injured party, but Rider felt the more injured because he was losing the one being for whom he felt and expressed unqualified love, their daughter, Stephanie, then nine years old.

That parting had occurred five years ago. Every year since then at Christmas a letter had arrived containing a photograph of Stephanie looking a little older, a little more beautiful, a little more interesting, a little more achingly remote. This year even that bittersweet experience would be denied him. Stephanie had died in October as the result of a road accident, a stupid 'American' road accident, Rider had called it.

He went to the funeral in Los Angeles and hated everything about it. It had seemed to him utterly artificial, from the impossibly green lawns of the vast 'Garden of Rest' in which his daughter had been interred to the mawkish little poem that one of Stephanie's school friends had read out at the grave side. Carla and he had barely spoken a word to each other. Their mutual sorrow had not met, so Rider took a plane back to England the day after the funeral with nothing but anger in him.

As he drove back from Woodstock, Rider wondered vaguely what he would do with his find. He knew several collectors of Victorian Christmas cards who would pay a hundred or so for it; in addition, he could probably interest a company who made fine reproductions of early Christmas cards and to whom he acted as consultant. Under other circumstances these prospects would have interested, even excited him, but just at the moment his life was a heap of ashes. A fortnight before he had decided that there was no point in continuing to live.

It was a wet night: rain drops sparkled on his windscreen, lit by the headlights of oncoming traffic. They shone for a moment before being rudely shoved aside by the arm of the windscreen wiper. More than once Rider felt the urge to drive into the lights that surged towards him out of the darkness, but the impulse was only momentary. Rider was going to commit suicide with the least amount of trouble to anyone else. The idea of taking others with him offended his sense of pride. He did not want to be thought utterly heartless in his grief. On the other hand, had someone driven into him, or stabbed him in some act of road rage, he would have blessed them—assuming that he could—from beyond the grave.

Rider had always called himself an atheist, because he despised the milksop term 'agnostic'. He was convinced that nothing stirred after death, but his refusal to entertain any notion of spirit was actuated as much by revenge against the way he thought life had treated him as by hard rationality. Given these convictions, however, he found it difficult to understand why he hesitated so long in the face of suicide, but he did. The idea of ceasing to be filled him with a horror which reason could never quite extinguish, and the irrationality of this fear annoyed him.

Nevertheless, over the previous weeks he had investigated various sites on the Internet devoted to suicide and acquired the relevant information and pills for the task. He had taken some pride in the way he had made his preparations so stoically and methodically, but still he hesitated. Then that night, as he was driving back to his Camden Town flat from Woodstock, he came to the decision that he must act at once.

It was really that Victorian Christmas Card which clinched his decision, he told himself. If he could no longer derive satisfaction from the acquisition of such a bargain, then he was without an occupation: the last remaining thread that bound him to life had snapped.

It was a long drive back. In the rain and the dark Rider drove cautiously, and he smiled at the irony of that. He passed several cars, no doubt driven by people far happier than he, which had skidded off the road. By the time he reached Camden Town it was after ten o'clock.

The Complete Symphonies of Adolf Hitler

Though he was very hungry, Rider decided to waste no time on a meal which might in any case blunt his resolve. Briskly, trying hard to think as little as possible about what he was doing, he fetched the pills and the bottle of whisky from the kitchen cupboard where he had hidden them and brought them into the sitting room.

Next to his favourite armchair, he placed a small table on which he put drink, pills and a tumbler. He then put a disk of Mozart's clarinet quintet into his CD player which he set to repeat endlessly the exquisitely serene *Larghetto* movement, after which, on an impulse, he took the Victorian Christmas card out of his pocket and put it on the table with the pills and whisky.

He removed it from its cellophane pocket and stood it upright on the table so that this might be the last image he saw. For a moment he admired it once again, wondering whether its previous owner had any more like it. Then he remembered that he had the man's business card in his wallet. Without pausing to reflect he took the card out and examined it.

ANTHONY SALVIN
Antique Prints, Ephemera,
Clocks & Watches, Objects of Virtu

Underneath was a telephone number which he had already underlined in pen to remind himself to ring the man. It had been the briefest of acquaintances, but somehow he had rather liked him. Then Rider remembered that there was no need for all this. He would not be ringing anyone ever again.

He dropped the business card on the table and took a last look round the room. Curiously, at the very moment when all had been decided, he was full of hesitation. Odd things worried him. Before oblivion took hold of him would he tire of that endlessly repeated Mozart movement, beautiful as it was? He

A Christmas Card

had put the electric fire on: would he get too hot as he waited? He went round the room tidying and straightening pictures, anxious to leave behind the impression that his act of self-destruction had not been in any way impulsive, but had been calm, Ancient Roman in its deliberation.

It was only when he had finished his task that he permitted himself to reflect on its absurdity. What he was about to do would destroy not only himself but everything else. As far as he was concerned, he was turning the whole world black. What others would think should be of no concern to him. In death there would be no others. He sat down in the armchair that was ready for him.

In the end he took the pills and the whisky for much the same reasons that A.J.P. Taylor said the Great War had begun, because the arrangements had been made, the timetables had been altered and the machinery of death had been meticulously prepared. He no longer felt that overwhelming sense of futility and grief which had seemed so like fear it was frightening, but he knew it would return if he went back on his resolve. He felt serene. The Mozart was doing its work, so too was the Victorian Christmas card which gave him an unexpected—almost unwelcome—stab of aesthetic happiness when he looked at it. Nevertheless he swallowed the pills and carefully drained two large tumblers of whisky, not enough to make him sick, but sufficient to interact lethally with the pills. Having done this he could at last sit back and allow events to take their course.

Rider tried to take a dispassionate interest in what was happening to him. There was, after a few minutes, a sensation, not altogether pleasant, of sinking. It was as if he was being drawn down into an abyss by soft black furry paws which fumbled at the edges of his thoughts but did not extinguish them. He told himself that this was only temporary and that very soon there would be nothing. It was frustrating though. His body was wrapped in paralytic sleep, but his consciousness remained stubbornly awake. The Mozart quintet began to stretch and distort; the clarinet no longer soothed, it wailed and wept. Was this the CD player or his brain? He looked again at the Christmas card. The sentimental Victorian colours throbbed and pulsated; the two figures in the scene almost moved. Rider shut his eyes and longed for the nothingness to come.

He was standing in the snow-draped street wearing a shovel hat and an overcoat that went down to his ankles. He was leaning on a stick. Across the narrow street a boy in rags swept snow from a doorway. The cold penetrated even his coarse garments and the heavy boots that he wore on his feet.

Rider did not like this at all. He concluded that the pills had induced in him a curiously vivid hallucinatory state in which he had become a figure in the Christmas card which he had bought. It was absurd. Rider would have none of it. Far better to think himself back into his comfortable armchair in his Camden Town flat, so he shut his eyes and tried to do so. The next moment he was lying on his back in the snow feeling colder and more uncomfortable than before. As he struggled to his feet he became aware of a sound, a rapid succession of shrill cries. It took him a moment to realise that what he was hearing was laughter. He looked around him and saw that it was the ragged boy, leaning on his broom and cackling at him. Rider studied the face of the boy which was hollow-eyed and pale, for all its human features, curiously lacking in humanity. Then he studied himself, or what he could see of himself: long legs—longer than his had been—but somewhat unsteady and sagging at the knees. His hands, encased in mittens, were not his hands but bony and shrivelled, the long fingers curled and arthritic. As he turned he caught sight of a reflection in a darkened window.

A Christmas Card

There was a long slow moment before he was forced to acknowledge that the figure that he saw in the window was that of the body he was occupying, himself. The face was ancient, late sixties at least. A pair of fierce eyes stared angrily out from under bushy white eyebrows. He had a great hook of a nose and long grey hair framed a mean and narrow face. Was he bald beneath that shovel hat? Rider did not want to know.

To the accompaniment of the urchin's harsh laughter he turned round and round in the snow, mad with bewildered fright. There was no escape. He had drugged himself out of his own reasonable body and into that of an ancient Dickensian grotesque. He would have screamed aloud if it had not been for the mockery of the boy.

Rider now had to stop to confront the reality of the impossible. He was in the snowy street of an old town. He was an ancient, ugly man. At least, for the time being he was, until death in its complete darkness robbed him of all illusion.

He bent down to pick up the stick which he had dropped in his fall. When he held it once more he felt steadier. He started to walk across the snow towards the boy who had now ceased laughing and was staring at him with something approaching abject terror. Rider stopped.

'I won't harm you, boy,' he said. 'What's your name?' His voice was cracked and peevish.

'Tim, sir!' said the boy. 'Tim Button.'

Tim Button indeed! This was absurd. Anger was beginning to take over from astonishment.

'What town is this, boy?' he asked.

'What, sir! Don't you know what city you're in? Morchester is the city, sir in the county of Loamshire.' The boy had a faint rural accent.

'Yes. Yes, of course. I wonder if you could tell me—'

But just at this moment the door whose step the boy had been brushing was opened by a tall, brutal looking woman in a brown floor-length overall. She seized the boy by an ear and dragged him indoors, then addressed Rider.

'You! Old Man! Haven't you got anything better to do than keep idle young varmints from their work? Be off with you before I fetch you a box on the ear.' And with that she slammed the door behind her.

Rider stood in the snow alone. Faint sounds of city life reached him, voices, the rattle of wooden wheels, sounds innocent of nothing except modernity. He had hoped to hear the strains of the Mozart he had put on—that would at least have reassured him he was in a dream—but though he strained to hear, there was not a trace of it. The air was beginning to darken and turn from cold to icy. Every physical sensation was present to him, piercing rapier-like through to the centre of the old lean body which he inhabited.

He began to shuffle along, in no particular direction, just for the sake of moving. The streets were not busy. Occasionally he saw in the distance the odd individual, no more than a shadow in the gathering gloom, hurrying along. Their movements seemed furtive, perhaps even fearful, as if they were anxious to get to their houses before night fell. There were no street lamps and what illumination there was came from the windows of the houses, some of which now had their curtains drawn. Soon, Rider conjectured, when the last curtain had been drawn, there would be complete darkness, and then death? He began to feel that of all things, he must avoid that utter darkness.

Rider now kept close to the houses as he walked the snowbound street. Perhaps there would be an inn that was open. (He felt there would be an inn, as the place had the picturesque intensity of a Dickensian world.) The buildings were mostly Jacobean in structure, half timbered, with mullioned casements, often sagging and uneven, leaning drunkenly against their neighbours for support. There were some more regular and classical eighteenth-century buildings but they were set back from the

A Christmas Card

street and their windows, mostly shuttered, yielded few chinks of light. Snow had begun to fall, a windless gentle descent of flakes from an opaque sky that darkened by the minute.

Turning one of the strange, irrational corners in the city maze, Rider was relieved to see a light shining from a ground floor window that bulged onto the street. He went up and pressed his face to the glass.

Within he saw a parlour lit by many candelabra and warmed by a fire in the grate. Yes, he had somehow strayed into a mid-nineteenth-century world, for there was a bright, busy overcrowded air to the scene he saw, and the women wore ringlets, and the men tightly fitting Nankeen trousers and embroidered waistcoats. There were about a dozen of them, an extended family with velveteened and ruffled children. On the table a bowl of punch—Smoking Bishop perhaps?—was being attended to by a bald, rubicund gentleman who laughed as he dispensed the steaming liquid into cups. Rider could not hear what was being said but he saw jollity and heard laughter.

A boy, about seven at a guess, in plum-coloured velvet knickerbockers, was chasing a little golden-ringletted girl of about five around the room. In the general merriment they were ignored, but Rider's attention was drawn towards them. The boy had a pale, hollow-eyed clever face and his chasing of the girl had an air of deliberation to it which Rider did not quite like. The girl, pink, bright-eyed, seemed oblivious of any malignity. She was running for the sheer joy of running.

Rider saw that, in his pursuit, the boy picked up a lighted candle from a table still unnoticed by the adults whose merriment was augmented by one of the young women sitting down at the piano and beginning to play and sing. The boy by now had cornered the little girl, who was beginning to show signs of fear. He put the lighted candle right up to her face, then, quite deliberately, set fire to the little girl's dress. The adults, by this time fully occupied in singing along with the pianist, were oblivious. Rider tapped frantically on the window pane. The adults stopped singing and turned towards the window. One of the women screamed, seeing Rider gesticulating wildly as he tried to draw attention to the little girl whose dress was now ablaze. The rubicund man, who had been dispensing punch, came sternly to the window, waved Rider away and drew the curtains. He never knew what happened next, the sounds that emanated from within were so confused.

By this time it was almost completely dark in the street, so Rider felt his way along. Presently he saw a few chinks of light and heard raucous laughter. The laughter was not of a pleasant kind, but it was a human sound and it did indicate that there was an open door somewhere. He moved towards the faint traces of light, crossing the street, now calf deep in snow. He could just discern a low, unevenly shaped building, in the centre of which a scratch of light could be seen under a door. Above the doorway hung something which creaked slightly as it swung, an inn sign perhaps.

Rider approached the door and opened it. Three wooden steps, supported on one side by a rickety balustrade, led down into a wooden chamber lit by a few dim lanterns. At the far end of the room was a bar. Huddles of men sat on settles and at tables, supping from pewter tankards. One or two looked up sullenly as Rider entered, then went back to their beer. Rider stood at the bottom of the steps, wondering what he should do next. He felt in his pockets for money but found nothing. Behind the bar the landlord—or so Rider assumed—gave him a brief appraising glance before returning to his task of polishing glasses. Rider, whose senses felt unnaturally sharp and exposed, became aware that someone else was looking at him, fixedly.

In a dim corner sat a big man on his own, with a pewter mug on the table in front of him. He had a large red face that looked intelligent enough, in a mean sort of way. His small, wary eyes met Rider's and then flinched from them. Rider walked towards

A Christmas Card

the man who sat still, made immobile by what looked like fear. This encouraged Rider who sat down opposite the man.

'You seem to know me,' said Rider. 'Who are you?'

'I do know you; and you should know me,' said the man in a whisper. 'I'm Joey Gadby.'

'And who am I?' said Rider, trying to put an amused tone into the croak of his voice but failing dreadfully.

'By rights you should be a dead man, Izzy, for that's what they told me you were.'

'Oh, and what was it they told you, Gadby? And who are you to call me Izzy?'

'All right then, Mr Skeggs,' said Gadby, lowering his voice still further. 'They told me that the law was on your track at last. Someone talked after Mobbs was found dead. Mobbs's girl, they said. They said they followed you to your crib at the old Smokehouse and got you trapped there. But you was always smart, Mr Skeggs. You was always one step ahead and they wasn't going to trap you alive. They said that when the peelers broke in to the attic, they found you swinging from a beam by a rope and you were dead as mutton. But they lied.'

'They lied,' said Rider dumbly repeating his words. 'Here, give us a sup of that drink of yours. I'm half parched.'

Gadby slid the tankard across the table to Rider, never taking his eyes off him for a moment. Rider put the tankard to his lips and drank. The next moment he was clutching his throat in agony. He felt a burning sensation in it. A greasy scarf had been knotted around his neck. Rider tore at it and wrenched it off, but the pain was no better. It was worse. Gadby was staring at him in horror.

'Gawd strike me,' he said. 'You did top yourself. I can see the marks. The rope!'

By this time every man in the room was staring at Rider, whose pain was so great he barely noticed the stir he was causing.

The Complete Symphonies of Adolf Hitler

'As I live and breathe, Ezekiel Skeggs, you're a dead man!'

At that moment Rider passionately wanted to say something which would explode the whole grotesque situation. He thought of several things to say, none of them particularly pithy: 'Oh, don't be so ridiculous!' 'This is absurd!' 'I don't believe a word of this pathetic melodrama!' He would have said them, but none of them could come out, his throat was in such agony.

He saw all the men in the inn moving towards him, fearful but united in hostility. From behind the bar the landlord emerged, less afraid than the others, his hand round the neck of a squat black bottle. Rider took advantage of the few moments of grace left to him and hurled himself up the steps into the snowy street.

He did not count on anyone following him, but he ran nonetheless. The pain in his throat was still great, and the sheer exhaustion of pounding along the street through the snow distracted him from the tearing burn in his throat. Any moment now, I am going to faint and fall at last into oblivion, he told himself. This is what his old brain told him, but some other part of him told him that it would not be so. So what was happening to him? Were these the streets of Hell?

Rider stopped. He wanted to weep; he wanted to scream; but he knew the pain that would come from doing so and he checked himself. Here he was, trapped, neither alive nor dead, neither asleep nor—surely!—fully awake. If there had been misery before it was nothing to this moment. Could there be anything in the universe worse than this? What God other than a monster could inflict such timeless cruelty?

The next sound he heard, of all improbable sounds, was the chiming of a clock. He counted the chimes, silvery, melodious even: one, two, three, four . . . eleven! Was it really that late? But, more importantly, where had the sound come from? He looked about him for some sign of where the sound came from. Then he heard another clock, also chiming eleven, a high-pitched

A Christmas Card

ping; then another, then another, some clanking, some ringing high, some deep and sonorous, almost like a church clock. He listened hard to the cacophony, cupping his ears to get a better sense of their location.

By this time the sky had cleared a little and a moon behind ragged clouds was giving a dim and fitful light to the street. A little old building that jutted its upper floors into the street seemed to be the source of the chiming. Against the tattered moonlight Rider could just see a thin thread of smoke emerging from one of its chimneys, so there must be occupation.

Physical sensation continued to oppress him. He was utterly exhausted from his running and he still felt the raw burn marks of the rope at his throat. He had long since stopped trying to make sense of his situation; was he Rider, or Skeggs, or both? Despair drowned all answers. His one object was to reach the house of the clocks; not because he hoped for any relief there, but because it was a place to go.

Beneath the sign of a dial which indicated not only hours of the day but phases of the moon was a small narrow doorway. Upon the door there was an iron knocker in the shape of a hand, long-fingered and sinewy but strong. He could just make out an inscription in brass letters on the door.

KNOCK AND IT SHALL BE OPENED

Rider knocked and heard a penetrating reverberation from within. They could not fail to hear. A long silence ensued and Rider was just about to knock again when the door opened.

He could not see who had let him in at first because whoever had done so stood behind the door and let him pass into a narrow passage lit by a single candle in a sconce.

Before Rider could turn round the door was shut behind him, and there stood a small, thin, bespectacled man in his late sixties who seemed faintly familiar. The man carried a little oil lamp which he held above his head, as if in deference to Rider's height.

'Who are you?' asked Rider.

'I am the clockmaker. Come through,' said the man, walking past him towards a door at the end of the passage.

The room they entered was unexpectedly large, as high as at least two floors of the house, and filled with clocks and their multitudinous clanks, whirrings and tickings. A great brass chandelier, hanging from a high beam, illuminated the vast horological landscape: grandfather clocks, lantern clocks, carriage clocks, water clocks, wooden clocks, delicate porcelain clocks with ormolu mountings, and on benches there were heaps of pocket watches of all shapes and sizes in gold and silver and pinchbeck, hunters, half hunters, repeaters: their heartless hearts noisily beating, all busily pursuing their relentless, soulless lives.

Rider spoke no word while the clockmaker went to a bench and began to scrabble in a pile of pocket watches. Having found what he wanted, a rather large and clumsy fob watch made of gunmetal, he came over and presented it to Rider.

'For you,' said the clockmaker, placing it in his hand.

Rider stared at the watch which was the oddest he had ever seen. It was an ordinary white enamelled dial with the hours indicated by Roman numerals in black, but there were only two numerals, eleven and twelve, with the quarters drawn between them. The rest of the face of the watch was blank. And there were only two hands, a second hand, and an hour hand which stood roughly half way between the eleven and the twelve.

'What sort of a watch is this?' asked Rider, his heart suddenly beginning to pump rather hard. The clockmaker smiled.

'It is yours,' he said. 'You do not need another watch. This is all the time you have left.'

'There is time left?'

'Come with me.'

A Christmas Card

The clockmaker led the way out of the room of the ticking clocks, snatching as he did so from behind the door a long black cloak with a hood and putting it on.

The next moment they were outside in the snowy street, the clockmaker leading the way without looking back. Though he was shorter than Rider and took tiny bustling steps, he moved so briskly that it was hard to keep up with him. Once, when Rider had begun to lag behind, the clockmaker said without turning round:

'Hurry up! Can't you see from your watch? There's hardly any time left.' And indeed, when Rider did glance at the watch, he saw that the hour hand had moved on to a quarter to twelve.

By this time, the sky had cleared and a full moon lighted their way. The clockmaker led Rider on through the city until they came to a church on a hill, surrounded by a low wall. Within the wall and surrounding the church was a graveyard full of tombs and gravestones on which the snow glittered in the moonlight.

But the clockmaker did not lead Rider into the graveyard. Increasing his pace, he skirted the low wall until he came to a piece of rough ground, to one side of the church, just outside the boundaries of the wall. This was, apparently their destination, a tract of scrub land, no more than a quarter of an acre in area, uneven, bumpy, punctuated by a number of oblong mounds overgrown with grass and weeds. The clockmaker stopped in front of a hole which had been dug in the ground, beside which was heaped a fresh pile of earth. He beckoned to Rider who reluctantly joined him at the hole.

'Why have you brought me here?' asked Rider.

'This is where they bury those who cannot be interred in consecrated ground.'

'Suicides, you mean?'

The man remained silent. Rider heard the ticking of his watch. He looked at it and saw that now only the hour of twelve midnight was showing and it wanted only two minutes to that time.

'Is that my grave?' he asked.

'Look into it.'

Rider stared at the grave, which seemed to him less like a hole in the ground than a doorway into another infinity, a sea where black wrestled with deeper black. Movements and sounds stirred in it. There were entities there which had a kind of life, parting, colliding, coming together again, endlessly restless without purpose. As Rider looked into the abyss he began to sway. He heard his watch ticking. At that moment he knew that he did not want to fall into the hole. Barely capable of controlling the rest of his body he tossed his head back from the great gulf. He felt himself caught by the clockmaker's arms and held up, barely alive, as he almost drowned in a sea of nausea. The pain would have gone had he fallen forward through the hole, but he submitted to the agony of life.

The next moment Rider was in a hospital bed being violently sick.

※

In the flat above Rider's lived a man called Henry Bevis, a podgy eternal bachelor with a private income and no job. He was by way of being a collector and occasionally bought things off him. Though Rider did not care for Bevis particularly—he thought, for no very good reason, that Bevis might have paedophile tendencies—the two got on after a fashion. Bevis tolerated Rider's tendency to lecture and they could occasionally be seen dining together, at Bevis's expense, in a local Indian restaurant.

Bevis was morbidly curious about Rider in a way that only someone with too little to occupy his mind can be, so that when he returned at about midnight from a session at a gambling club and saw Rider's flat door ajar, he had to go in. He justified his

A Christmas Card

inquisitiveness by the fact that he heard music playing—Mozart, was it?—and that this was unusual for Rider at any time of the night, let alone at that hour. On entering Rider's living room he found that his friend had fallen out of an armchair and was lying on the floor. Bevis, who was far from stupid, drew some rapid conclusions from the whisky and the empty pill bottles on the table and at once phoned for an ambulance.

Two days later Rider was sitting up in his hospital bed with Bevis sitting opposite him, stolidly eating his way through the grapes he had brought for his friend. The two were staring at each other in mute astonishment. Bevis was quite as baffled by his new role as saviour as Rider was to be alive and to be quite pleased to be so. Rider didn't want to thank Bevis because that would place him under an obligation to the man, and heaven knew what that might lead to. All the same, he felt he should commend him.

'You acted very promptly, I must say,' said Rider.

Bevis put another grape into his soft little mouth and continued to stare at his friend.

'It was all a terrible accident really,' said Rider. 'I was just . . .' He didn't finish the sentence, not out of embarrassment, but because he had no idea what he could say to explain.

Bevis said: 'I've arranged for you to go and stay somewhere when you get out of here.'

'What? That's impossible. I can't possibly afford—'

'Oh, no. You don't have to pay. It's with a friend.'

'What friend?' Rider was suspicious. He had no friends to speak of, and none that he knew who would be prepared to have him to stay.

'Anthony Salvin,' said Bevis.

'Who?'

Bevis explained that at the hospital the staff had asked Bevis to get in touch with 'next of kin' as there had been a distinct probability that Rider would not survive. Bevis had found nothing of use apart from a business card with a telephone number on it. The card had been that of Anthony Salvin.

'He seemed to know all about you,' said Bevis. 'He knew the strain you'd been under, and he's asked you to stay with him in his little cottage over Christmas. It's in the Peak District.'

So that seemed to be it. The following Friday, which was, of all good days in the year, Christmas Eve, Rider took a train to Derby, not knowing why, but content, for once, to be ruled by others. Salvin was waiting for him in the station concourse. Rider recognised him at once as the man who had sold him the card. There was nothing at all remarkable about him to look at, though, except a kind of stillness. Salvin took Rider's bag and led the way to the station car park.

It was raining outside, and the streets glistened under the streetlights. Rider was reminded of an Atkinson Grimshaw painting. A group of Carol singers in what they fondly imagined to be period costume, one of them holding a gaudy approximation to a Victorian lantern on a stick, were singing 'Hark! The Herald Angels Sing!' Another of their party, a bald, rubicund old gentleman rattled a tin in aid of charity. Salvin and Rider put money in the tin and hurried to the car.

It was a twenty minute drive out of Derby, and most of it was taken in a perfectly companionable silence. Salvin was obviously not one of those people who thought that speech was necessary, even under the unusual social conditions in which they found themselves. Eventually Rider decided he must say something.

'This is very generous of you,' he said. 'How long do I stay with you?'

'As long as you like, but I would suggest a couple of days. At least till after Boxing Day.'

'And you'll be here?'

'And I'll be here.'

'And I can talk to you?'

'Yes. Or be silent. Whichever you prefer.'

A Christmas Card

'I don't understand. Who are you? What are you?'

'Well, I used to deal in antiques, rather like you. I still do the occasional trade fair. Nowadays what I mostly do is pray for suicides.'

Rider should have asked him more there and then, but the reply astonished him so much that he was silent until they got to Salvin's cottage. Later on, asking him seemed irrelevant.

It was very dark when they arrived, so Rider could tell very little about Salvin's cottage, or its surroundings, except that it was a compact, whitewashed building and, it would appear, very remote.

The interior was warm and unpretentious, surprisingly uncluttered for an antique dealer's retreat. They ate supper together without talking much and drank some wine which Rider had brought as a gift. The little conversation they had was on neutral topics, such as their common profession. Salvin appeared to know quite as much about Rider's specialism as he did himself.

There were no televisions or radios in Salvin's cottage—somehow Rider had not expected there to be—but there were books, and many of them, crammed into shelves. After supper Salvin invited Rider to borrow one, and take it with his candle up to bed. Rider obeyed, choosing a volume from a set, almost at random.

His little room was small, simple and warm. The bed, made with crisp old fashioned sheets—no duvet—faced the drawn gingham curtains of a small window. There was a chest of drawers, a bedside table, a bentwood chair, a washbasin and no more. Rider undressed, put on a night-shirt and got into bed. He found that his candle provided a perfectly adequate light by which to read.

Rider opened his book at random. It was one he had not read since childhood but he knew it well. He turned to the last chapter—or Stave Five, as it called itself, for some unknown reason. Almost before he had set eyes on the first words, he began to weep, as he remembered that final chapter had always made him weep long ago. In the end he closed the book and dedicated himself to the shedding of tears, but what the tears were for? Nostalgia? Grief? Relief? Gratitude? He could never say. Then, at some point, he fell asleep.

The next morning when he awoke in the little bedroom he noticed that the curtains had been opened and that the room was full of light. He saw from his bed that the sky was a pale, cloudless blue, but from the luminous white glare projected onto the ceiling he suspected something else. He went to the window and saw that his guess had been correct. Across a rolling pattern of fields and copses, with barely another house in view, snow, fallen in the night, robed the landscape, unstained as yet by wheel or footprint. The outcrops of trees and hedges shone gold in the sun.

Standing at the window, Rider began to sense hope of a kind that is not thrilling to describe or feel. It was like the small hope of a diver who, having touched slime at the floor of a dark sea, knows that he must rise; and that inevitable issue is a kind of promise, but a grey kind.

He remembered that in his overnight bag was the card he had bought from Salvin. After Christmas he would send it to Carla.

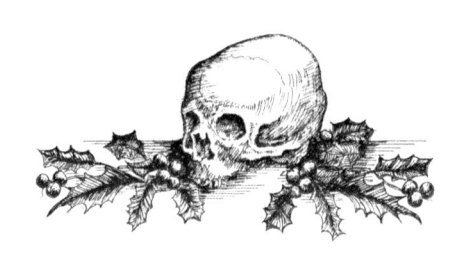